"If you're a sucker for plucky women who rise to the occasion, this is for you."
—USA Today

"Wax's trendy premise makes for a surprisingly poignant and enjoyable story about friendship."
—Booklist

"In the style of Karen Joy Fowler's *The Jane Austen Book Club*...The book engrosses its reader in the drama of these women's love lives and emotional struggles."
—Deseret News

continued . . .

"Wax does a wonderful job of carrying new readers into the story and all the many characters she juggles so well . . . The plot raises both questions and deep emotions to keep readers racing to the end to find out what happens."

—*RT Book Reviews*

"[A] very talented writer who knows how to craft a great story with complex characters [and] a great plot, and plug in just enough steamy romance to satisfy everyone. Finely done!"

—*The Best Reviews*

"Wax puts on display what most would expect when this many women live and work together in the same environment: laughs, tears, anger, occasional cattiness, and every emotion in between."

—*Fresh Fiction*

TEN BEACH ROAD

"Showcases three women who rise above their shattered realities with grace, determination, and a little elbow grease."

—*Publishers Weekly*

"A lovely story that recognizes the power of the female spirit, while being fun, emotional, and a little romantic."

—*Fresh Fiction*

"A near perfect summertime read . . . Beautiful setting and lovable characters . . . Full of: laughter, heartache, secrets, loyalty, and courage."

—*Night Owl Reviews*

"Funny, heartbreaking, romantic, and so much more . . . This story about recovery and restoration on so many levels is just delightful!"

—*The Best Reviews*

"Wax keeps the plot twists coming . . . Great escape reading, perfect for the beach."

—*Library Journal*

WHILE WE WERE WATCHING
DOWNTON ABBEY

·WENDY WAX·

BERKLEY BOOKS, NEW YORK

THE BERKLEY PUBLISHING GROUP
Published by the Penguin Group
Penguin Group (USA) LLC
375 Hudson Street, New York, New York 10014

USA • Canada • UK • Ireland • Australia • New Zealand • India • South Africa • China

penguin.com

A Penguin Random House Company

WHILE WE WERE WATCHING *DOWNTON ABBEY*

A Jove Book / published by arrangement with the author

Jove Books are published by The Berkley Publishing Group.
JOVE® is a registered trademark of Penguin Group (USA) LLC.
The "J" design is a trademark of Penguin Group (USA) LLC.

For information, address: The Berkley Publishing Group,
a division of Penguin Group (USA) LLC,
375 Hudson Street, New York, New York 10014.

ISBN: 978-0-515-15469-6

PUBLISHING HISTORY
Berkley trade paperback edition / April 2013
Jove mass-market edition / January 2014

PRINTED IN THE UNITED STATES OF AMERICA

10 9 8 7 6 5 4 3 2 1

Cover photograph by Cultura / Frank van Delft / Getty Images.
Cover design by Rita Frangie.
Text design by Kristin del Rosario.

To Julian Fellowes
with admiration and thanks for creating Downton Abbey
and the delicious characters who inhabit it.

ACKNOWLEDGMENTS

As always, thanks are owed to Karen White and Susan Crandall, critique partners extraordinaire. I'm grateful for your honest feedback, your encouragement, and the loan of brainpower when my own seems in short supply.

Thanks also to Susan Shapiro, whose home tour helped me imagine the Alexander; Barry Eva, author of *Across the Pond*; and Facebook friend Diana Bowie, for insights and tidbits that contributed to the creation of expat Edward Parker.

And a thank-you to Alicia Culp, Mimi Davenport, LeaAnn Larsen, Erin Galloway, Wendy McCurdy, Stephanie Rostan, and Rebecca, Logan, and Callan Ritchie for lending me their names. Some of you supported charities or won the opportunity to see your name in this book. Others simply couldn't escape. I thank all of you for the loan. I did my best this time not to turn any of you into villains.

And finally, my gratitude to Leslie Gelbman for coming up with the kernel of the idea that became Samantha, Claire, Brooke, and Edward.

CHAPTER ONE

A S A CHILD SAMANTHA JACKSON DAVIS LOVED fairy tales as much as the next girl. She just hadn't expected to end up in one.

Every morning when her eyes fluttered open and every night before she closed them to go to sleep, Samantha marveled at her good fortune. In a Disney version of the airline passenger held up in security just long enough to miss the plane that goes down, or the driver who runs back for a forgotten cell phone and barely avoids a deadly ten-car pileup, Samantha averted disaster in the once-upon-a-time way: she married the prince.

Over the past twenty-five years Samantha had sometimes wished she'd spent a little more time and energy considering alternatives. But when your world comes crashing down around you at the age of twenty-one, deep thinking and soul-searching are rarely your first response.

There was plenty of precedent for prince-marrying in the fairy-tale world. Sleeping Beauty had not ignored the prince's kiss in favor of a few more years of shut-eye. Cinderella never considered refusing to try on the glass slipper. And Snow White didn't bat an eyelash at moving in with those seven little men.

It wasn't as if Samantha had gone out searching for a man to rescue her and her siblings when their world fell apart. She hadn't feigned a poisoned apple–induced sleep or gotten herself locked in a tower with only her hair as a means of escape. She hadn't attempted to hide how desperate her situation was. But the fact remained that when the handsome prince (in the form of an old family friend who had even older family money) rode up on his white horse (which had been cleverly disguised as a Mercedes convertible), she had not turned down the ride.

The fact that she hadn't loved the prince at the time he carried her over the threshold of their starter castle was something she tried not to think about. She'd been trying not to think about it pretty much every day for the last twenty-five years.

SAMANTHA SMILED SLEEPILY THAT EARLY SEPTEMBER morning when her husband's lips brushed her forehead before he left for the office, but she didn't get up. Instead she lay in bed watching beams of sunlight dance across the wooden floors of the master bedroom, breathing in the scent of freshly brewed coffee that wafted from the kitchen, and listening to the muted sound of traffic twelve floors below on Peachtree Street as she pushed aside all traces of regret and guilt and renewed her vow to make Jonathan Davis happy, his life smooth, and his confidence in his choice of her unshaken.

This, of course, required a great deal of organization and focus, many hours of volunteer work, and now that she was on the downhill slide toward fifty, ever greater amounts of "maintenance." Today's efforts would begin with an hour of targeted torture courtesy of her trainer Michael and would be followed by laser, nail, and hair appointments. Since it was Wednesday, her morning maintenance and afternoon committee meetings would be punctuated by a much-dreaded-but-never-complained-about weekly lunch with her mother-in-law. Which would last exactly one hour but would feel more like three.

Samantha padded into the kitchen of their current "castle," which took up the entire top floor of the Alexander, a beautifully renovated Beaux Arts and Renaissance Revival–styled apartment building in the center of Midtown Atlanta.

When it opened in 1913, the Alexander, with its hot and cold running water, steam heat, elevators, and electric lights, had been billed as one of the South's most luxurious apartments. Like much of mid- and downtown Atlanta it had fallen on hard times but had been "saved" in the eighties when a bottom-fishing developer bought it, converted it to condos, and began the first of an ongoing round of renovations.

A little over ten years ago Samantha and her prince spent a year turning the high-ceilinged, light-filled, and architecturally detailed twelfth-floor units into a four-bedroom, five-bath, amenity-filled home with three-hundred-sixty-degree views and north- and south-facing terraces.

For Samantha its most prized feature was its location in the midst of trendy shops, galleries, and restaurants as well as its comfortable, but not offensive, distance from Bellewood, Jonathan's ancestral home in Buckhead, one of Atlanta's toniest and oldest suburbs, where both of them had grown up and where his often-outspoken mother still reigned.

The doorbell rang. As Samantha went to answer it she pushed thoughts of Cynthia Davis aside and gave herself a silent but spirited pep talk. She'd married into Atlanta royalty. Her prince was attractive and generous. A difficult mother-in-law and a life built around pleasing others was a small price to pay for the fairy-tale life she led. As Sheryl Crow so aptly put it, the secret wasn't having what you wanted but wanting what you got.

*   *   *

SHORTLY AFTER THE MORNING'S TRAINING SESSION
ended Samantha rode a mahogany-paneled elevator down to
the Alexander's marbled lobby. The gurgle of the atrium
fountain muffled the click of her heels on the polished surface
as she took in the surprisingly contemporary high-backed
banquette that encircled the deliciously carved fountain.
Conversation groups of club chairs and sofas, separated by
large potted palms, softened the elegant space. A burled
walnut security desk, manned twenty-four-seven, sat just
inside the entrance. The concierge desk sat in the opposite
corner and commanded a view of the lobby as well as the
short hall that accessed the parking garage and the elevators.

"Good morning, madam." Edward Parker's British accent
was clipped, his suit perfectly tailored, his starched shirt
crisp. His manner was deferential but friendly. A relatively
recent addition to the Alexander, the concierge was tall and
dark with rugged good looks that seemed at odds with his
dignified air. "Shall I have your car brought around?"

"Thank you." She was of course capable of simply going
into the Alexander's parking garage to retrieve her own car,
but the last time she'd insisted on doing this Edward had
looked genuinely disappointed, and the minutes saved would
come in handy if she ran behind or hit traffic between
appointments or on the way to lunch with her mother-in-law.
Punctuality was a virtue that Cynthia Davis prized; tardiness
a vice to be stamped out at all cost.

"Very good," he said, his brown eyes warm, his white-
toothed smile decidedly un-British. When he lost some of
the stiff upper lip that seemed welded to his accent and his
occupation, there was a rakish George Clooney–ness about
him. Although Parker was in his early fifties, Samantha's
younger sister Meredith had pronounced him both "hot" and
"dishy."

Samantha arrived at the Piedmont Driving Club—where

the Davises had belonged since its inception as a gentleman's club in the late 1880s—ten minutes before noon, buffed, coifed, and polished. Though she was early her mother-in-law was already seated at a favored table with her back to the window, the better to keep an eye on the room's comings and goings. Samantha smiled and leaned down to kiss her mother-in-law's rouged cheek. Cynthia Davis might be seventy-five, but she was still formidable. Like her son and the husband she'd already outlived for a decade, she could drive a golf ball straight down a fairway and had a tennis backhand that was almost as sharp as her tongue. Born into one of Atlanta's oldest and most revered families and married into another, she remained a snob at heart; one who liked to remind anyone who would listen that "you can't make a silk purse out of a sow's ear" and the vaguer but more ominous "breeding will out." Samantha had heard these summations applied to everything from a disappointing fund-raiser to the scandal that had ensued when Samantha's father, Davis & Davis's managing partner, had dipped into client trust accounts, almost ruining the firm that had been in the Davis family since shortly after the Civil War. He'd been under investigation when his car had run off the road just a few miles from home, killing both him and Samantha's mother instantly.

Cynthia Davis had been horrified when her only son chose to marry the daughter of onetime friends who had disgraced themselves publicly before dying spectacularly. Samantha's failure to produce a grandchild had made her even less desirable in her mother-in-law's eyes.

Samantha had barely settled into her seat when Cynthia leveled her steeliest look at her and asked, "What do you intend to do about Hunter and Meredith?"

"Do?" Samantha ordered a glass of Chardonnay. Hearing her brother and sister's names on her mother-in-law's lips made her regret she could have only one glass. As she considered possible replies, she made a mental note not to schedule anything after their weekly lunch in the future so that she could drink as much as the meal required.

"I don't believe either of them are employed at the moment, are they?" Cynthia asked, as if there might be some doubt. For Cynthia Davis idleness was an even greater personality defect than lack of income.

"Not exactly, no."

"Then perhaps we need to put our heads together to come up with something for them to do." This was not a question. "After all, Hunter's last venture did show some . . . promise." Cynthia was referring to her brother's recent attempt to launch a chain of soul food/sushi restaurants in the Midwest, which had ended badly. Hunter could make a better first impression than almost anyone she knew and could sell almost anything while in the first flush of enthusiasm. Unfortunately, follow-through was not his forte.

Samantha smiled and nodded as if Cynthia's comment had been meant as a compliment, and perhaps it had been. Her mother-in-law did not approve of Hunter Jackson, or the money Jonathan spent on Hunter's upkeep, but she was not immune to Hunter's charm.

The basket of corn bread and rolls that neither of them would touch arrived. A group of women stopped by the table to pay their respects on their way out.

"Don't you think it's time we find Meredith an opportunity here in Atlanta where she can make use of her degree? She did spend quite a lot of time in school acquiring it." Cynthia had been furious when she'd realized the size of the tuition Jonathan had paid for Samantha's younger sister to receive a master's degree in Historic Preservation from the College of Charleston. But while Jonathan loved his mother and preferred her happy—or at least satisfied—he didn't ask her input on his decisions or bow to her wishes unless they happened to coincide with his.

"I don't imagine the Atlanta Preservation Board has heard about her little contretemps in Charleston yet. Maybe I could put a word in." This was so Cynthia—first the slap down, then the oddly magnanimous gesture. Samantha allowed herself another measured sip of wine. At least Cynthia hadn't brought up her sister's taste in men.

"And that last boy she brought to the Labor Day party at the club?" Cynthia shook her head sadly. "Really, dear. Meredith is quite presentable when she tries. I'd think she might aim a little higher."

Samantha swallowed slowly, bracing for the "bless her heart" that Cynthia all too often tacked on to the end of Meredith's name; the final condemnation of her sister and the job Samantha had done raising her. A job for which she'd been unprepared and which had led her to marry the first prince who had galloped to her aid.

Chapter Two

CLAIRE WALKER HAD BARELY PLACED ONE dyed-to-match silk pump on the church aisle when she realized she was making a big mistake. Unable to find the courage to call off the ceremony, she'd walked as slowly as she could down the aisle to Daniel Walker's side. When she got there she smiled and said "I do" even though she didn't.

That was nineteen years ago, and to this day she could still remember the lightning bolt of revelation, the bitter taste of the words she couldn't speak, and her fear that she might gag on them as she struggled to swallow them. For a crazed moment she'd imagined them bubbling up and spewing all over the minister, Daniel, and the two-thousand-dollar dress that her mother, who had eloped with Claire's father and deeply regretted not having a church wedding, had insisted on buying her.

She still wasn't sure how she made it through the ceremony and reception, but by the time the limo arrived to whisk them to the airport, she could hardly refuse to go on the island honeymoon that Daniel's parents had given them.

Nor could she maintain the fiction of a weeklong headache, which was how she'd come home from Belize pregnant with Hailey.

She'd tried to convince herself that love and respect weren't absolute requirements for a successful marriage, but three years later, holding her two-year-old daughter in her arms, she'd done what she should have done that day at church; she apologized for the screwup and with equal parts fear, regret, and relief sundered what should have never been joined together.

Sixteen years of single parenthood on a shoestring had followed.

Today her life had changed again. Tonight she stood on the small balcony of the Midtown Atlanta condo she'd spent the Labor Day weekend moving into, trying to come to terms with that change.

She took an exploratory breath of the night air. It was thick with humidity, redolent with the aroma of marinara from a nearby Italian restaurant, car exhaust, and possibility. Bits of music arrived on the warm breeze, carried from one of the bars over on Crescent Avenue. Below on Peachtree, horns sounded. A siren blared. Voices rose from the sidewalk where despite the late hour a steady stream of people walked alone, in pairs, in groups; all of them going somewhere to do something.

Here, dark and quiet were not synonymous.

"You are so not in suburbia anymore," she whispered on another breath of night air. Here, people were living the kind of life that she'd barely allowed herself to imagine. A frisson of excitement ran through her and she leaned farther out over the railing, not wanting to miss a thing. She'd have to be very careful not to accidentally click her heels together three times and end up back where she'd come from.

Her cell phone rang and she hurried inside. As she hunted for the instrument, a part of her brain reveled in the fresh-paint smell of her new home, the sparkle of the tall windows

that overlooked Peachtree, the gleam of the polished wood
floor.

She stepped around the new gray flannel sofa and area rug
from West Elm, scanned the Crate and Barrel dining room
table that would double as her office, and checked the nightstand next to the brand-new never-before-slept-on-by-anyone
queen bed, which she'd tucked into a corner behind a tri-fold
screen.

Sidestepping half-opened boxes, she searched the stand
on which her new flat-screen TV perched and the bookcases
that bracketed the Murphy bed that would be her daughter
Hailey's, when she came home from college. *College.*

Claire exhaled heavily. Breathed in shakily. Out with the
old life. In with the new.

She found the phone hidden behind a box on the kitchen
counter—a lovely dappled granite that she'd fallen in love
with the first time she'd entered the studio apartment—and
managed to answer it before it went to voicemail.

"Hi, Mom." Her daughter's voice was achingly familiar
and surprisingly grown-up after only two weeks in Chicago
at Northwestern University.

Claire reached for a framed photo that lay on the counter
and was intended for the nightstand. It was from Hailey's
high school graduation and showed the two of them with
their arms slung around one another's shoulder staring happily into the camera. They were both of average height and
had the same even features and wide smiles above pointed,
some might say determined, chins. Their heads were bent
together in a tangle of hair—Hailey's long and smooth, the
blond tinged with honey overtones, Claire's a shade that
resembled dishwater and which she kept cut in short, low-
maintenance layers.

Claire listened to the hum of happiness that infused Hailey's voice. It made her happy just to hear it. It also made her
aware of just how alone she was.

No. Claire silently rejected the word and all its synonyms.

She refused to be lonely. No new beginning was without its bumps.

"How was the move?" Hailey asked.

"Good," Claire replied. When you'd sold or given away 95 percent of your former life and arranged to have most of your new life delivered, moving wasn't particularly onerous. She'd been able to fit the few things she couldn't part with in her SUV.

"Have you met any of your neighbors?" Hailey asked. She had helped her search for a rental unit before she'd left for Chicago, tramping in and out of every unit in the geographical area Claire had outlined on her map. They'd made the choice together over cardboard containers of pad Thai and panang chicken, just as they'd made so many other decisions over their years of dynamic duo–dom.

"Not really. The concierge has been helpful and the other residents seem nice enough." There seemed to be a diverse group of owners and tenants, which was part of what had attracted her to the building. And while Claire hadn't seen anyone who looked like they were counting their pennies quite as carefully as she was, no one had turned up a nose or been unfriendly.

"Edward Parker is way hot," Hailey said, turning the conversation back to the concierge. "That British accent is fabulous." She giggled. "I could probably be okay with him for a stepdad." She said this as if it were only a matter of time before she had one; just as she had since she turned five and began trying to picture pretty much every man they ran into—including her soccer coach, the mailman, and her favorite elementary school janitor—as potential husband material for her mother.

"I've talked to him exactly twice for about five minutes each time," Claire pointed out.

"But he's cute, right?" Hailey said.

"So are puppies, but I don't have the time or energy to housebreak one." Even Claire had to smile as she pictured leading the elegant Englishman to a pile of newspaper or out to a strip of green between buildings and ordering him to "piddle." "I'm not here to get married, I'm here to write," Claire reminded her daughter. Somehow in the years filled with work and single parenting that added up to too much stress and too little sleep, Claire had managed to write two historical romance novels and see them published. Writing *Highland Kiss* and *Highland Hellion* had been her great escape from the often overwhelming responsibilities of her real life; a chance to live in another time and place and to experience the kind of romantic love and devotion that people like her could only dream about; the kind of love that led to happily-ever-after.

"You're there to have a life, too," Hailey added.

"I already have a life."

"No, you had Grandmom and Grandpop to take care of all those years before they died. And you've had me and everything you had to do to take care of me," Hailey corrected. "That's not a life. Now it's your turn to just take care of you." There was a brief pause. "Or find someone else who will."

"I'm going to ignore just how chauvinistic that statement was to say that raising you has been a privilege and an honor. And I'm still here to take care of you when you need it," Claire said.

"I'd rather you write your breakout bestseller and find some hot men to go out with," Hailey replied. "And FYI, I don't think those things are mutually exclusive."

"God," Claire said, feigning displeasure. "How did you turn into such a relentless optimist?"

"I learned it from the same woman I learned everything else from," Hailey said quietly. "You deserve the best, Mom. I hope you're going to go for it."

A silence fell, reminding Claire just how far away her daughter was and how completely their lives had changed. She'd sold their home, bought what she needed to start fresh, and had exactly enough money left over to pay the rent on this condo for one year. That meant she had three hundred and sixty-five days to plot and write a new and hopefully bestselling novel.

"One thing at a time," she said, falling back on the adage turned mantra that she'd used to get over each new hurdle. To put one foot in front of the other. To take care of increasingly infirm parents and raise her daughter alone. To keep going no matter how tired she was or how short of cash.

Claire plugged in her earbuds and tucked her cell phone in the pocket of her jeans. "Tell me about your classes while I make up the bed," she said as she located the box marked *sheets* and ripped off the packing tape. "Did you finish that paper for Sociology?"

Hailey chattered happily while Claire smoothed on the bottom and top sheets, slipped pillowcases over the pillows, and arranged the comforter, turning one corner down invitingly. The bed might be new, but the sheets were well worn and familiar.

Moving into the bathroom, she laid out a towel and stacked the others in the linen closet, then arranged her toiletries on the bathroom counter. She'd do just what she had to tonight and tackle the rest in the morning. As they talked, Claire focused on Hailey's voice and her obvious happiness and knew that Hailey was hearing the same in hers. Both of them were poised to add a new and exciting chapter to their lives.

Hailey yawned midsentence and Claire glanced at the closest clock. It was getting late.

"I think it's time for both of us to turn in," she said when Hailey yawned a second time.

"Okay." The word was followed by another yawn. "G'night, Mom. I'll text you tomorrow."

"Night-night, sweetheart," she said automatically as she had so many times over the years. And then despite the fact that her daughter was eighteen and too grown-up and too far away to be tucked in, she finished with the same nonsensical cliché she'd uttered when the bedtime story was over and the lamp turned off. "Sleep tight. Don't let the bedbugs bite."

The line disconnected and Claire stood alone in the center of the cluttered condo. *Hers, all hers.* A thrill of anticipation coursed through her. How in the world would she ever calm down enough to fall asleep?

"Don't be a goon," she said aloud as she plugged in the Snoopy night-light that had always glowed in a corner of Hailey's room and which Claire had not been able to throw away. "You wanted a new life and you've got one."

Now all she had to do was hurry up and go to sleep so that she could wake up tomorrow morning and start making the most of it.

CLAIRE GAVE HERSELF TWO FULL DAYS TO UNPACK, hang her artwork and photos, and organize the kitchen. She slept fitfully both nights, thrown off by each unfamiliar noise that reached her from within the building and the streets below. Each time she woke she had to remind herself where she was. Then she would look around the apartment and consciously think the word "home," but as excited as she was to be here, her brain was not fooled. Home was the house on Juniper Lane with the fenced backyard and the cul-de-sac out front that filled with kids each evening after dinner.

In between bouts of unpacking she explored the Alexander, trying to make it familiar and vowing to use the fitness room, the pool, and the clubroom with its big-screen TV, kitchen, and bar, which was available for entertaining. Even though she didn't know enough people in this part of town to fill her tiny bathroom.

Late on the second afternoon she stood in the center of her new home and pronounced it "done." Her laptop and a yellow pad of character notes and ideas sat on the dining room table/desk right next to the brocade-covered journal that Hailey had given her to record her new life.

Other than her brief conversations with Hailey, a food-and-drink order on a quick stroll up Peachtree, and a deep Dumpster discussion with Edward Parker, she hadn't really communicated with anyone. She cleared her throat just to make sure her vocal cords still worked.

"Okay," she said aloud just to confirm that everything was operational, "you're going to walk to Piedmont Park and find a nice shady spot where you can prime your pump by writing in your journal." Eager to get outside, she put on her sneakers, tucked the journal and a pen into her cross-body bag, and left the condo. In the lobby, she strode purposefully with her chin up and her eyes on the front door; a woman on a mission. Which may have been why she didn't see whatever it was that got tangled in her feet. Or understand how she ended up on the hard marble floor with something small and heavy on top of her and an unfamiliar woman's voice yelling in the distance.

CHAPTER THREE

BROOKE MACKENZIE CLOSED HER MOUTH abruptly. It was too late for yelling anyway. Not that yelling at either of her daughters or the dog ever actually worked.

A blond woman lay splayed on her back on the lobby floor. Brooke's five-year-old daughter Ava lay facedown on top of her, chubby arms and legs spread out like a starfish. Darcy's leash was wrapped around one of the woman's legs. Brooke's older daughter Natalie was kneeling next to the woman and had already extended one grubby hand toward the woman's closed eyelids as if she intended to pry them open.

"Don't touch!" Brooke hissed, unable to infuse her voice with the calm but steely mother tones that *Parenting in Small Doses* promised would stop a child in his or her tracks—not that she'd seen any proof that these techniques worked. Or been able to parent in any dose smaller than constant since Zachary walked out on them. "Get up and step away from the lady."

Neither of her daughters moved.

Brooke drew a deep breath, tucked her hair behind her ears—a move that did nothing to keep it from frizzing out from her head like a bright red Brillo pad—and said, "Now!"

Worried at the woman's lack of movement, she reached down and grasped Natalie's wrist just before her sticky fingers made contact with the woman's eyelid, and pulled the seven-year-old away.

The woman opened her eyes and blinked up into Ava's round, freckled face, which hovered mere inches above hers, but she didn't move. It was unclear whether this was a result of shock or injury.

"Are you all right?" Brooke reached down, put a hand on each side of her youngest daughter's waist, and lifted her straight up off the woman's chest as gingerly as one might extract a pickup stick from the top of a jumbled pile. For a moment she held her suspended in the air, Ava's arms and legs extended, as if she'd dived out of a plane and hadn't yet yanked her parachute cord.

"I think so," the blonde said as Brooke set Ava down on her feet and hurriedly untangled Darcy's leash.

Sighing in relief, Brooke stretched out a hand to help her. Their eyes met and Brooke was further relieved to see that the woman appeared dazed, but not angry.

"I'm so sorry," Brooke said. "They were racing each other for the elevator—it's mortal combat to see who gets to push the button no matter how many times we're in and out each day." She pulled gently until the woman was on her feet. "Are you sure you're okay?"

Brooke braced for a snide comment about unruly children and/or Brooke's ineptitude as a parent. There were no other kids anywhere near Natalie and Ava's ages in the building; something that had apparently not occurred to Zachary, her now-ex-husband, before he'd chosen the Alexander and moved them into it. Only to abandon them there.

Even normal exuberance, which her children rarely dialed down to, was often met with frowns and disapproval.

"I've told them so many times not to run on the sidewalk or in the lobby, but I don't seem to be getting through."

"Don't worry about it. It was an accident." The woman put her hand out, not for assistance but in greeting. "I'm Claire Walker. I just moved into a unit on the eighth floor a couple days ago."

"We're on the ninth floor," Natalie said. "We're on the next floor right on top of you."

"Nine-oh-four." Ava said this proudly. Much of her first month in kindergarten had been spent memorizing her address and phone number.

"I'm Brooke Mackenzie," Brooke said, relieved. "This is Natalie." She placed a hand on her eldest's bright red hair and then on her youngest's. "And Ava." Brooke smiled apologetically. "And this . . ." She tightened her grasp on the leash attached to their dachshund. "This is Darcy, the disobedient wonder dog."

"It's nice to meet you." Claire Walker looked and sounded sincere, though Brooke knew here in the South that what was said wasn't always what was meant. "And don't worry about the collision. I have a daughter of my own. She's in college now, but she had lots of extra energy when she was little." She smiled. "I used to expend a lot of my own trying to get rid of hers."

"The only time these two are quiet is when they're asleep." Brooke was about to apologize again when Edward Parker walked up to them, calm and unperturbed. The concierge's formal elegance was a perfect match for the building's magnificence. He belonged there in ways Brooke knew she never could or would. But he didn't frown at her in disapproval or attempt to reprimand the girls. Beneath the polished efficiency she sensed warmth and a belief in fair play. If he disapproved of her, her children, or her sad little cliché of a life, he never let on.

"Is everyone okay?" he asked, reaching down to scratch behind Darcy's ear.

The dog's tail wagged with happiness. She raised her long nose and looked up at him adoringly. So did Natalie and Ava.

"Mr. Mackenzie left this off for you a little earlier." He handed Brooke a sealed envelope, with her name on it in her ex-husband's tight, angular writing. Her own smile fled, but her daughters, ever hopeful, assumed this was a good thing.

"Daddy was here!!" Natalie's happy voice cut right through her. Both girls looked around the lobby expectantly as if their father might be hiding behind one of the potted palms or a section of the banquette, waiting to surprise them. As far as Brooke was concerned, none of Zachary Mackenzie's surprises had been remotely pleasant. Since he barely showed up to spend time with the girls when he was supposed to, she doubted the envelope contained a hint or clue in a first-ever game of lobby hide-and-seek. If she were lucky, it might be the monthly maintenance check that he always seemed so reluctant to turn over.

"Thanks." Brooke's hand tightened reflexively on the leash. "Let's go, girls." This time she didn't have to work on the commanding tone because she needed to get upstairs to see what the envelope held. Experience had taught her that bad news—and Lord knew there'd been a ton of it over the last year—was better received and digested in private. She nodded to Claire Walker. "It was nice meeting you."

There was the click of high heels on the marble floor and Brooke looked over Claire Walker's shoulder to see the woman she'd mentally labeled "rich bitch" headed toward them. Or as it turned out, toward the concierge.

Brooke had seen her coming and going, sometimes with a tall, good-looking blond man she assumed was her husband. She knew little more than her name and that they lived on the top floor—the entire top floor—and were always beautifully dressed and in the process of sweeping off to somewhere undoubtedly wonderful. Zachary had told her stray bits and pieces about the Davises as he'd gleaned them and had been convinced that living near and rubbing elbows with people like them would help build his medical practice in Atlanta. A woman like Samantha Davis could bring him a boatload of influential patients.

Brooke glanced down at her lumpy pear-shaped body, practically feeling her thighs and stomach straining against the "miracle" fabric that was supposed to make her look ten pounds lighter. Maybe she'd been wrong to turn down Zachary's offer of a tummy tuck and boob lift after she'd finished nursing Ava, but Brooke had resisted what her husband had referred to as those "small enhancements."

Her friends and family believed free corrective procedures were simply one of the perks of being married to a plastic surgeon. Her divorce attorney had insisted that putting Zachary through medical school and supporting them while he completed his residency and built his first practice in Boston had earned her the right to free plastic surgery for life. But Brooke was even less interested in being "fixed" after the divorce than she had been while she and Zach had been married. What she wanted was to be loved regardless of the elasticity of her skin or the shape of her breasts.

Brooke's vision blurred and she willed the tears away. She was not going to cry in the middle of the lobby in front of her children and these strangers. No way in hell.

Samantha Davis gave Brooke, the girls, and Claire a small smile; it wasn't an unfriendly one, but her attention was focused on Edward Parker.

"Excuse me." The concierge inclined his head to them then walked toward the woman.

"Who's that?" Claire Walker asked. Like Ava and Natalie, she seemed unable to take her eyes off the other woman's beautiful face. And hair. And clothes.

"Samantha Davis," Brooke said keeping her voice low. "Although I always think of her as Lady Samantha." Brooke blushed at the fanciful description.

"Royalty, huh?" Claire asked.

"In Atlanta terms, yes. Her husband is from some old

southern family. He's the managing partner of an important Atlanta law firm. You know, one of those white shoe kind of firms that's been around since before the Civil War."

"What does she do?"

"Do?" Brooke had expended a good bit of envy on but not a lot of thought about Samantha Davis. "Whatever women like that do, I guess. Lunch at a club. Afternoons at a spa? Charity balls and fund-raisers." She shrugged. "We've never done more than nod or say hello." She smiled ruefully at Claire, ashamed of the note of envy in her voice. "Sorry. That was cattier than I meant it to be. I really don't know her at all. But I'm very grateful that it was you and not her that my children mowed down."

"Gee, thanks," Claire Walker said, her tone dry.

"Oh. I didn't mean . . ." Brooke felt her cheeks flush. That's what happened when she wasn't careful. Once at a plastic surgery conference at which Zachary was the guest speaker, he had accused her of only opening her mouth in order to change feet. "Really, I shouldn't have . . ."

"Don't worry about it," Claire said. "I know exactly what you mean. That kind of perfection can be hard to stand too close to."

Darcy tugged on the leash. Her tail wagged madly. Her doggie eyes were fixed on Samantha Davis and Edward Parker, but Brooke held on tight. The last thing Brooke needed was for Darcy to throw herself at the immaculate pair.

"Let's go!" Natalie said.

"Mommy!" Ava whined, tugging on her hand. "I need to go to the potty."

"Okay." Brooke looked at Claire Walker. "I'm not the most organized mother in the world, but I know better than to ignore a potty request. We'll see you around—but hopefully not quite so up close and personal."

"Yes," Claire said. "I hope we do. I'm headed for Piedmont Park to blow off a little steam of my own."

"We go there a lot in the afternoons after school if you ever want to join us." She winced, realizing that Claire Walker probably had better things to do than hang out with her and her daughters. "I mean . . ."

"No. That would be great. Thanks." Claire sounded like she meant it. "Are you in the building directory?"

"Yes." Brooke smiled as Claire headed for the door, relieved that the other woman hadn't blown her off. Even if she never called they could smile and say hello and pretend that one day they'd get together.

Ava tugged on Brooke's hand, and with a potty-induced sense of urgency, Brooke herded the children and Darcy toward the elevator. As they passed, she tried not to stare at Samantha Davis just as she fought the certainty that if she looked like Lady Samantha or had a tenth of her confidence and poise, Zachary would not have bailed out on her, their life, and their children.

CHAPTER FOUR

EDWARD PARKER KNEW THINGS ABOUT PEOPLE that he sometimes wished he didn't. Within the first week of landing the concierge contract at the Alexander, he knew that Mr. Lombard in 310 had a girlfriend and often didn't actually leave town on business as he told his wife, but holed up instead in the Vinings condo where the younger, blonder woman had been installed.

Late one Saturday night he discovered that Mr. Morrisey, the prominent investment banker in 212, occasionally went out at night dressed in his wife's clothing—and that when he did he looked much better in them than she did.

He'd had to hide his surprise one afternoon in his second month when he'd found out that the elderly Mimi Davenport, whose family had donated a wing to the children's hospital and to Saint Joseph's, had been caught fleeing from a store security guard, who informed him that Mrs. Davenport was on a store "watch list" because she liked to pinch things that she could have easily bought.

No matter how weird the revelation, Edward never lost sight of the fact that one of a concierge's most valuable assets was discretion; a trait his grandfather, who'd been "in service" at Montclaire Castle in Nottinghamshire just as his father before him had been, had begun to teach Edward somewhere around his tenth birthday.

Edward reached for his cup of tea, taken at four each afternoon and allowed to go slightly tepid just the way he liked it, and looked around his small office tucked away in a corner of the Alexander's lobby. He'd hung his black blazer on a hanger on the back of his office door in much the same way that his grandfather had removed and hung his jacket when he went "below stairs" at Montclaire. But Edward had hung his own diploma from the Cornell School of Hotel Administration next to it.

He'd begun to fully understand—and practice discretion—when he landed at a Hilton property in Maui as an assistant manager—a glorious posting from which he'd sent two years' worth of sun-filled postcards home to the Hungry Fox, the family pub in Newark-on-Trent, upon which Edward estimated some fifty to sixty inches of rain fell annually. It was in the Aloha State that he'd handled his first celebrity peccadillo and learned the art of misdirection and the value of resisting bribes. The lessons—and postcards—continued in big-city hotels in San Francisco, New York, and Miami Beach.

There'd been smaller postings, too; a fancy dude ranch in Montana where he'd fallen in love with the sweeping vistas of the American West and bought a pair of snakeskin cowboy boots that he owned to this day. A charming B and B in the historic heart of Charleston where he'd reveled in the beautifully restored buildings and come to terms with the pairing of shrimp and grits, and enjoyed the languid blend of heat, humidity, and manners.

The Hungry Fox would go to his older brother, Bertie, much as the title and country estates his forebears had served in had gone to oldest sons. But that was all right with Edward, who had pulled plenty of pints behind the Fox's scarred wood bar but could never imagine staying there; not even to keep the woman he'd loved.

Bertie continued the tradition of mounting Edward's postcards, which now papered an entire wall of the bar.

The last seven years' worth had been sent from Atlanta, making the Fox's patrons among the lucky few in England to know exactly what the Fox Theatre, a restored Egyptian-themed 1920s movie house, looked like. He'd sent postcards of other Atlanta landmarks—like what was left of the apartment Miss Mitchell had written *Gone With the Wind* in; Stone Mountain, Atlanta's answer to Mount Rushmore with its three-acre mountaintop carving of three Confederate heroes of the Civil War; CNN Center; Turner Field; the World of Coca Cola.

Six months ago he'd sent not a postcard but a sales piece he'd had printed after his newly formed personal concierge company, Private Butler, had been selected by the Alexander's condo board. It was a wide shot of the Alexander's Beaux Arts façade, shot from across Peachtree. In one corner of the brochure was the Private Butler logo—the company name wrapped around a photo of Edward's grandfather, William Parker, in the Montclaire livery he and his twin brother had worn so proudly.

Edward took a final sip of his tea, checked the time, and removed his jacket from its hook. He wanted to do a tour of the fitness room and clubroom/theater. Then he'd take another look at the adjacent pool deck to see what it would need in the way of winterizing.

He smoothed his collar, slipped his silenced cell phone into his jacket pocket, and added a stop at the security desk and an assessment of the valet's uniform to his mental to-do list. He had always taken pride in a job well done, but it had taken the heavy-footed approach of his fiftieth birthday to make him look at building something for himself. Private

Butler was a company that he could shape and build; one whose seeds had been sown in his forebears' years "in service."

Edward had every intention of making them proud.

IT WAS LATE AFTERNOON AND SAMANTHA STOOD IN her gourmet kitchen staring into the pan of what was meant to be saltimbocca alla Romana, but which looked like a rolled-up lump of shoe leather—and not the expensive Manolo Blahnik kind.

Damn.

For a few moments she debated whether the veal could be saved. Doctored. Buried in some kind of sauce, preferably bottled, that would disguise its leathery qualities. She went to the pantry and walked inside to peruse the shelves, but unsurprisingly, nothing called out to her.

Her attempts at family dinners had been more laughable than edible when she and Jonathan had first gotten married, but she had kept at it, ignoring the fact that he'd taken Meredith and Hunter out on "errands" after many of those meals and returned smelling like McDonald's fries or Burger King onion rings.

Then he'd started bringing home takeout a couple of nights a week. But Samantha remained determined to feed her cobbled-together family and she took the series of cooking lessons Jonathan gave her as a joke on their first anniversary very seriously. Just as she did the cooking schools in Tuscany, Provence, and the South Carolina Lowcountry, where she'd failed to master everything from deveining shrimp to whipping egg whites.

With a sigh, Samantha stepped out of the pantry and closed the door behind her. It would take more than a can or jar to save the shriveled, congealing lump now burnt to the roasting pan. Conceding defeat, she pulled her cell phone out of her purse and speed dialed the chef at one of Jonathan's favorite Italian restaurants.

"Giancarlo?" she asked when she heard his voice. "This is an SOS call. What's the special today?"

"What would you like the special to be, *cara?*" he asked as he always did.

"Well, I was aiming for saltimbocca alla Romana. I'm still thinking veal, but Jonathan will be home by seven and I'd like to have everything, um, in the oven warming before he gets here."

"Yes, of course." She could hear the smile in his voice. "How many are you serving?"

"There are four of us, but Jonathan and Hunter can eat enough for two. And it would be good to have leftovers."

"Perfect. Let me see what I can whip together, hmm? How about a mozzarella and tomato—an insalata Caprese—to start? And perhaps chocolate chip cannoli or tiramisu for dessert."

"Tiramisu." She hesitated for a second. "I'll tell them I stopped to pick up dessert, but can you make sure the rest is . . ."

"Not too perfect."

"Right." She began to relax. "You know that I'm in love with you, right?"

"The feeling is most mutual, *signora*. The only thing is I have no one available for delivery and a large party due in when we open."

"No problem," she said, quickly eyeing the clock and planning it out in her mind. "I'll have someone there at six thirty if that's all right with you."

"Certainly," he replied. "Tell them to come to the back door. And send your cookware as we did last time."

"Grazie."

"Per niente," he said gallantly. "It is my great pleasure."

With a far less harried smile, Samantha pressed speed dial for the concierge. Edward Parker had a wonderful British accent, but the man was a veritable sphinx.

"Edward?" she said when he picked up. "Do you have time to take care of something for me?"

*   *   *

SAMANTHA'S YOUNGER SISTER MEREDITH WAS THE
first to arrive that night for dinner. At thirty-six, the years
of partying and serial dating had begun to take their toll.
She was athletic with a swimmer's shoulders, a strong,
straight body, and wavy dark hair that frizzed around a
square-jawed face that didn't make the most of its individual
parts. Her temperament was mercurial—one minute sweet
and confiding, the next prickly and confrontational. Worse,
she was often jealous of what she saw as Samantha's cushy
life and Hunter's blinding beauty and effortless magnetism;
traits he'd inherited from their father and which he wielded
with abandon.

After dropping her purse on the counter, Meredith walked
directly to the drinks cart where the alcohol and mixers
awaited. Samantha had opened a bottle of red wine earlier
and left an unopened Chardonnay chilling in ice. "Can I pour
you something?" Meredith asked.

"No. I've got a glass, thanks." Samantha set out the Caprese salads that Giancarlo had drizzled with a special bal-
samic vinaigrette. A loaf of crusty Italian bread waited in
the warming oven. The veal was in an oven-to-table pan from
which she could fill their plates. At the moment, all felt right
with the world.

"I haven't seen you for almost a week," Samantha said.
"What's going on?" Meredith lived in a Buckhead condo that
Jonathan had bought for her. Hunter preferred Midtown and
lived just a few blocks away from the Alexander in a unit
that had once belonged to Jonathan's law firm.

"I heard from Fredi Fainstein." Meredith named a friend
from college. "She's working up in New York now, and she
invited me to come visit."

"For how long?" Samantha was careful not to mention
Cynthia's intention to refer her to the Atlanta Preservation

Board in case it didn't work out, but she didn't want to see Meredith miss out on the opportunity.

Meredith shrugged her shoulders, which looked even broader in the striped boatneck sweater she wore. It was an unfortunate choice, but Samantha had learned long ago to never comment on any article of Meredith's clothing, unless it was to tell her how wonderful she looked. "What difference does it make? It's not like I'm employed at the moment."

Samantha hated how blasé she sounded about her lack of employment, as if there were nothing wrong with being idle and letting Jonathan continue to foot her bills. "It won't be too expensive. I can stay at Fredi's place. And if you loan me some of your frequent-flyer miles," she said as if she might one day return them, "the trip will hardly cost anything at all."

"It's New York City," Samantha replied. "*Breathing* is expensive there."

Meredith's mouth tightened. "You live in the lap of luxury and Jonathan has more money than God," she said. "What difference does it make if I go to a few restaurants and shows and pick up a few clothes?"

There were footsteps in the foyer. "Did Meredith just refer to me as God?" Jonathan asked as he entered the living room. He leaned down to kiss Samantha and accept the drink she'd mixed for him, then gave Meredith a brotherly hug. When Meredith was little he used to ruffle her hair and treat her like his own sister, something he'd said he was glad to have, given his only-child status and the amount of attention his mother had always trained on him. For a time he'd called her Merry, but the nickname had been more about wishful thinking than reality and it hadn't survived the turbulent teenage years when Meredith had been anything but.

"Not exactly." She shot Meredith a disapproving look.

"Not exactly what?" Hunter had come in so quietly that his voice surprised her. It was as rich and smooth as his appearance and was a potent tool or weapon, depending on his mood. He was just shy of six feet with a lean runner's body, a chiseled face, the Jackson green eyes, and an almost feline grace. He also had glossy black hair that fell onto his forehead and long, thick eyelashes that both of his sisters envied.

"Nothing," Samantha said. "I hope everybody's hungry."

Jonathan looked at her over his highball glass. From the day they'd married she'd made sure that no matter what she'd done that day, she was dressed and made-up when he got home from the office and had a Tanqueray and tonic waiting for him when he walked through the door. When her siblings had gotten old enough to notice, they'd given her a good bit of grief about being stuck in the fifties, but she had seen it as a token of her appreciation for all he did for them.

"What's for dinner?" Jonathan asked.

"Veal." Although Samantha hid the evidence that others had cooked, she was always careful not to come out and actually claim that she'd cooked it. "In fact, we're having saltimbocca alla Romana."

"Bless you," Jonathan said. "I was hoping we'd have Italian tonight."

"Shocker," Meredith said. "You'd eat an Italian shoe if someone put marinara sauce on it."

"I think you have," Hunter added sotto voce. "Hell, I think we all have."

Samantha was very glad she wasn't going to have to serve the leathery lump she'd created. Her brother and sister would have never let her live it down. Jonathan would have asked for a second helping and managed to somehow chew and swallow it. She'd never been sure if this was due to his kind streak or his optimism. Unlike her brother and sister, he still clung to the belief that one day the cooking lessons would kick in and her inner Julia Child would emerge.

Meredith chattered on about New York during dinner as

if it had already been decided that she would go. Then she said that Fredi had offered to introduce her to a contact at the Frick Museum who might be a good job contact. Even Samantha might have fallen for it if Meredith hadn't given her a "take that" look when Jonathan turned away.

In the kitchen, Samantha dished up the tiramisu and told herself it might not be a bad idea for Meredith to get out of town for a bit. She'd just have to make sure that Meredith did, in fact, renew contacts and look into the possibilities in New York while she was there. If Cynthia came through with an interview at the Preservation Board, she'd insist that Meredith fly home immediately.

Dessert had been cleared away and after-dinner brandy poured when Hunter asked Jonathan if he knew anyone in nanotechnology.

Her brother's tone was so casual that it stopped the brandy snifter midway to Samantha's lips. She knew that tone and recognized it for what it was. Hunter was many things; meticulous, crafty, even predatory. Casual wasn't even on the list.

She watched her husband's face as Hunter told him about the great investment opportunity he had if only he could put his hands on the half million dollars he needed. He presented it with the same level of conviction with which he'd presented the green energy company out of Kansas, the oil exploration in North Dakota, and the soul food/sushi restaurant franchise that the prospectus had claimed would catch on in the Midwest and then spread "like wildfire" across the United States.

Her husband had been financing Hunter's investment schemes since shortly after their wedding, when he'd underwritten the nine-year-old Hunter's plan to create and corner a secondary market for *Star Wars* action figures. Over the years, Hunter's investment schemes had grown bigger and riskier while Jonathan's losses grew larger.

She thought it would actually be cheaper and less stressful if Jonathan simply deposited a certain amount per month as he did for Meredith, rather than allowing the fiction that Hunter was an entrepreneur on the verge of the big score, to continue. It frightened her how much like their father he seemed; how easily he burned through money and people. How careless he was.

She'd warned her brother after the last debacle, when some of Hunter's investors had threatened lawsuits and Jonathan and his firm had been embarrassed by the association, that she'd cut him off herself before she'd allow Jonathan's name to be sullied.

She prayed regularly that her warning would suffice and told herself that a Hunter engaged, however briefly or expensively, was better than a Hunter with too much time on his hands.

She saw the flare of triumph in Hunter's eyes when Jonathan said he'd look over the materials and think about it. And she knew with a sinking heart that what that really meant was yes.

CHAPTER FIVE

THE SKY WAS DARK AND THREATENING BY THE time Brooke returned to the Alexander that Tuesday morning. She'd taken Darcy in the car to drop Natalie and Ava off at school and after parking the Volvo wagon, she hustled the dog outside to her favorite tree behind the parking garage.

Normally Darcy took her time, holding out until the last possible moment to prolong the time outside. But Darcy wasn't a big fan of "wet" and did her "business" in record time. She didn't even whimper in protest when Brooke packaged the doggie doo-doo in a clear plastic bag, dropped it in the Dumpster, and speed walked them back into the building, making it seconds before the rain began to fall. Brooke wished she could package up and throw away the refuse of her life as quickly and efficiently, but the wounds Zachary had inflicted would not heal or disappear.

On the way upstairs Brooke considered her reflection in the shiny brass of the elevator. She'd spent a good twenty minutes before she woke the girls that morning trying to club her humidity-charged hair into submission and applying enough makeup to disguise the night spent tossing, turning, and trying to resist the leftover pizza in the refrigerator.

When Zach had first insisted that they enroll the girls in the ridiculously expensive private school, she'd flinched each time the tuition check was written.

"It's a no-brainer," he'd said dismissively when she objected to paying the equivalent of a year of college for a year of prekindergarten. "Look around you. These women care what they look like. And they have the money to pay for improvements." He'd looked at her as he'd said the last, long past bothering to hide his displeasure in the way she looked and the fact that she didn't seem to care that she was not a good advertisement for his skill with a knife.

On the girls' first day of school, she'd discovered that frayed capris and a faded Boston Red Sox T-shirt were not going to cut it in the Woodward Academy carpool line. But while she'd learned to make the time to dress more appropriately in the mornings, she'd continued to refuse to let him tweak or alter her. By then her imperfections were the only thing in their marriage that she still recognized.

Now that she and Zachary were divorced, the school fees and expenses were the only checks that Zach wrote without begging or prodding. He religiously attended the PTA meetings and parent events not because he wanted to participate in his children's lives but because Woodward Academy was the perfect place to mine for patients.

Back in the condo, Brooke contemplated the breakfast dishes in the sink, the bulging bag of garbage that needed to be taken to the chute, and the pile of unopened bills that Zachary was supposed to pay, but didn't. *To hell with it,* she thought as she pulled the pizza box from the refrigerator.

Darcy wagged her tail hopefully. "Sorry, girl." Brooke ate the last piece of pizza cold out of the box while she wandered around the condo. It was a beautiful, spacious three-bedroom unit, with wood floors, lots of windows, and high ceilings. Zach, flush with money for the first time in their married life and certain more was coming, had insisted on hiring a designer. As a result their home was long on style and short on warmth. For a few minutes she eyed the shiny surfaces and sharp angles and imagined how she might make the space cozier if and when she got the funds to do so.

In the girls' rooms, she picked up stray clothes and toys, then spent longer than she needed to arranging Ava's stuffed animals on her bed.

When she'd finished everything she was willing to do, it was barely nine a.m. The rainy morning stretched out in front of her long and empty. It was odd to have so much time on her hands after all the frantic years of working to support them while Zach finished college and then medical school. His residency had been the final hurdle, zapping her formidable reserves as she juggled two babies, two jobs, and a husband who was half asleep on the occasions when he was actually present. Like a long-distance runner in an important marathon she'd wheezed on, putting one foot in front of the other, her eyes and her will focused on the finish line.

She stood motionless in front of the window staring out over the rain-splattered street wondering why it had never occurred to her that fulfilling Zachary's dreams would end hers.

"That's enough." She said it out loud just to be sure it got through. "Find something to do." She couldn't imagine going back down to the garage and leaving in the car. Where would she go anyway? They'd moved to Atlanta a year and a half ago and the first six months had been spent settling in; the second had been spent consumed by the divorce Zach had demanded. There'd been no time or energy to make friends or create a life that didn't revolve around Zach or the girls. Now she had all the time in the world and no one to spend it with.

"You're going to leave the condo now." She could go down and sit in the lobby and pretend she was waiting for . . . something. Maybe there'd even be someone down there to talk to. Or she could take the newspaper to the coffee shop next door. Except now that she'd had the leftovers from the girls' breakfast and the overrated piece of pizza, she didn't need to sit somewhere that served eggs, hash browns, and cheese grits.

She considered the building's other possibilities. It was too wet for the pool deck on the eighth floor, where she sometimes took the girls to run around and blow off steam. The clubroom that overlooked the pool was only open for specific activities, but the fitness center was right across from it. She'd seen the equipment when they'd first toured the building, sworn to use it, and had never gone back.

Exercise would be positive. If she did enough of it, maybe some of those endorphins she'd read about and never actually experienced would kick in and make her feel better. She looked down. She *was* wearing expensive workout clothes.

Before she talked herself out of it, she gathered her keys and headed for the door. Thirty minutes. The Realtor had told them that the equipment was state of the art and extremely user-friendly. So simple, she'd claimed, that even a child could program it. She'd get on a treadmill or an elliptical machine, put it on low speed, and exercise for thirty minutes. She could do anything for thirty minutes, right?

SAMANTHA LAY IN BED LISTENING TO THE STEADY patter of rain falling on the balcony outside her bedroom. She should've been in the middle of her morning workout right now, but Michael had called thirty minutes before he was due, his voice so nasal from a cold that it took awhile to decipher who it was. Before he'd hung up, he'd made her promise that she'd do the workout on her own or at least do cardio. Instead she'd lain here for almost an hour listening to the rain and contemplating what it might feel like to do that for the rest of the morning. Maybe she'd even download a book and lie here reading it just for the pure pleasure of it.

She smiled as she imagined her mother-in-law's shock and horror at such slothful thinking. Then she pictured her husband boarding the seven a.m. flight for Los Angeles, working all day, taking clients out for dinner. Her smile dimmed. Jonathan could have easily afforded to work half as hard as he did or not at all, but he was no dilettante. Vacations were carefully planned and scheduled; even weekends or holidays at the lake house were fit in around his client's needs; a work ethic far more reassuring than her father's all-consuming passion for money and position and her brother's schemes and plans, few of which involved any actual work at all.

Her "job" as his wife did not include lying around in bed reading regardless of the weather or the health of her personal trainer.

Dutifully rallied, she threw off the covers and put on the workout clothes she left folded on the chaise longue near her side of the bed. Then she washed her face, brushed her teeth, and pulled her hair up off her face. A quick glass of orange juice and she was on her way down to the eighth-floor fitness room, which was always empty.

She spotted the chubby red-haired woman through the plate-glass wall as she rounded the corner. Biting back a groan, Samantha entered the glassed and mirrored space and moved toward the vacant elliptical machine next to the one the other woman occupied.

The big-screen TV on the wall in front of the machines wasn't on. Samantha cut her eyes to the other woman whose head was bent over the control board. Samantha couldn't tell if she was studying the digital readout or praying. Her feet were in the footpads, her legs frozen as if in midstep. Her workout clothes looked both new and expensive, but they stretched across her rear and back a little more tightly than they should. She'd seen her in the building before—the last time in the lobby with a dog and two little girls.

"Do you mind if I turn on the TV?" Samantha asked.

The woman shook her head, but she didn't look up. "No." Her voice caught on the word.

Samantha put on the TV and skimmed through the channels finally settling on the *Today* show. Telling herself she didn't know this woman and shouldn't pry, she got on the elliptical and began to answer the questions that flashed on the digital screen. She committed to forty minutes, plus the automatic five-minute cooldown. But then came the annoying weight query. Did the machine really need to know how much she weighed? Irritated she punched in her weight—or at least a close approximation. Then it asked for her age.

"Good grief!" She spent a long moment picturing the skinny little geek who'd come up with the mathematical equations that required such personal information. If she could have figured out how, she would have told the machine to go screw itself, but there didn't seem to be a place to input that.

Would it make a significant difference if she put in forty-six, which she'd only recently said good-bye to? She'd just decided that a year couldn't possibly make a significant difference in the number of calories burned, when she heard what sounded like a sob from the next machine.

Samantha got her legs moving in that odd walking/climbing motion then turned toward the red-haired woman. "Are you all right?"

"I can't figure out how to make it start." The woman's voice was heavy with choked-back tears.

"Are you sure you want to?" Samantha asked gently.

The woman looked up and met Samantha's eyes. Her whole face looked tight from the effort of holding in the tears that shimmered in her eyes. "No. But as you can see I clearly need to."

Samantha kept her legs moving. "Whether you work out is definitely not my business," Samantha said carefully. "I mean, I'm not the Jehovah's Witness of exercise or anything. I'm not even sure *I* want to be here."

"Sorry." The woman averted her eyes. "It's probably better if I go so that you can exercise in peace." She aimed her gaze somewhere over Samantha's left shoulder as she spoke. "I just thought it might make me feel better. You know, if I could dredge up a few endorphins or something." There was another half sob. A look of horror spread over the woman's broad freckled face. "Oh, God. I'm sorry. I can't believe I'm crying in front of someone like you."

Samantha blinked.

"Oh, shit. That's not what I meant to say."

Samantha braced, hoping the woman wasn't going to keep at it until she said whatever other insulting thing she'd actually meant. She hadn't even done five minutes yet and she didn't see how she could just leave the woman here alone when she was so upset. She'd never read of a suicide by elliptical, but that didn't mean there'd never been one.

"Don't worry about it," she said as casually as she could, turning her gaze to the television. Pedaling, she tried to focus on the screen, but the feminine hygiene commercials were no match for the crying woman still standing immobile on the next machine.

"People like you are one of the main reasons people like me don't exercise," the woman said.

"I beg your pardon?" Samantha said.

"Oh, God. I didn't mean to say that, either."

Samantha had no idea how to respond so she just kept moving. She completed five minutes before she snuck another look at the woman who was focused on the control panel. Mercifully, she had stopped crying. She was short, probably no more than five-four, and looked to be somewhere in her midthirties. Her face wasn't bad. Or it wouldn't have been if she'd done something to camouflage the freckles. An eyebrow shaping and the right makeup would have been a good start. Briefly Samantha considered offering her the name of her favorite aesthetician, but it seemed clear that the last thing this woman needed today was anything that resembled criticism.

The other woman blew a heavy red curl off her damp forehead. She seemed to be sweating kind of heavily given her lack of movement.

"I'm . . ." the woman began. "I'm really sorry." She looked up and met Samantha's eyes. "But the thing is. I'm not having a good day."

No shit, Samantha thought.

"But I've made it this far." The woman hesitated. "If you could, um, just tell me how to start this thing, I'll do what I came here to do and I . . . I promise I'll leave you alone."

"Sure." Samantha couldn't tear her eyes from the redhead's face. Even her freckles looked sad and anxious. "Hit 'reset' and start moving your feet."

The woman did as she was instructed. Carefully, Samantha talked her through each step, the woman only balking when it came time to put in her weight.

"I know," Samantha said. "Sadistic, isn't it?"

"I guess lying would defeat the whole purpose?"

Samantha nodded. "But at least the age thing won't be a negative for you. Not all of us can say the same."

What might have been a smile flickered over the woman's lips. "So I gather I'm supposed to put in my real age and not how old I feel right now?"

At Samantha's nod, the redhead said, "It's just as well. The numbers probably don't go up to a hundred anyway."

Surprised and glad that the woman had managed to make something approximating a joke, she said, "My name's Samantha Davis, by the way."

The redhead began to puff from exertion. "Brooke Mackenzie," she said. Beads of perspiration already dotted her forehead.

"Nice to meet you." Samantha nodded and turned her attention to the television.

They pedaled in silence for a while. Samantha kept her eyes on the television, but she couldn't quite tune out the woman beside her.

A movement through the plate-glass window caught Samantha's eye and she spotted Edward Parker in the hall. She watched him post something on the elegant notice board he'd installed outside the clubroom. He looked up, saw them, and waved.

Brooke Mackenzie gave a little moan of distress when the concierge pulled open the fitness room door, but her legs kept moving.

"Ladies." The concierge stopped between them and flashed a smile that dimpled his right cheek. "You both look remarkably industrious. It's nice to see the facilities in use."

Brooke smiled but didn't speak. A glob of sweat ran down the side of her face and dropped near his well-shod feet.

Not at all bothered, the concierge set down the cards he was carrying, retrieved two fresh towels from a cupboard and bottled waters from the small refrigerator. "We keep towels and water stocked twenty-four-seven. If there's anything else you'd like to see in here, please let me know."

"Thank you." Brooke swiped at her face and hung the towel around her shoulders.

"Yes, thanks." Samantha twisted the cap off her water and took a long drink. "What have you got there?" Samantha nodded to the cream-colored cards in Edward Parker's hand.

"It's an invitation to a screening," he replied. "Email blasts seem terribly . . . impersonal, so I'm posting invitations in all the common areas and putting them in resident mailboxes."

"Oh?" Samantha asked as Brooke Mackenzie continued to pedal beside her.

"We're going to be watching the first two seasons of *Downton Abbey* as a buildup to the start of season three in January."

"Ah," Samantha said. She'd overheard people talking about the British television series but had never seen it. "Isn't that set in an English castle or something?"

"Yes. Highclere Castle in the countryside west of London serves as the fictional Downton Abbey." He gave them one of his dazzling smiles. "I thought it would be fun to have a weekly get-together for anyone interested. We're going to watch the very first episode on the big screen in the clubroom this Sunday evening at eight.

"Interesting." Samantha definitely didn't see herself heading to the clubroom every Sunday night to watch a stuffy British drama with strangers, but there was no need to come out and say so.

"Have you seen it, Mrs. Mackenzie?" the concierge asked, drawing the other woman into the conversation.

"I've seen a few episodes," she said, and Samantha could tell she was trying her hardest not to huff or puff. Not sweating was no longer an option. "But not in order." She fell silent for a moment. "It was beautifully done, though."

He considered them both. "I'd like to create more of a sense of community in the building. The series is a huge hit all over the U.S. and the rest of the world, really, which would make us very . . . current." His voice turned conspiratorial. "And, frankly, I'm up for a bit of home."

He set an invitation on the small shelf of each of their elliptical control panels. "I hope you'll come give it a go if you're around this Sunday evening." He turned and pinned an invitation up on the fitness room bulletin board. "There'll be popcorn and wine to start. And maybe some English-themed nibbles and drinks."

Samantha smiled noncommittally. She was glad to see Parker taking the initiative and relieved that Brooke Mackenzie seemed at least a little less ready to throw herself under a bus. It was amazing what a good-looking man with a devastatingly sincere smile and a gorgeous accent could accomplish.

"Thanks," Brooke said, actually raising her chin and meeting the concierge's eyes. "It sounds like . . . fun." The word came out sounding odd, as if it were unfamiliar on her lips. "I'll have to see what the girls have scheduled."

"Wonderful," the concierge said with a final smile. "I'll cross my fingers and hope to see both of you on Sunday."

Samantha and Brooke watched him go without comment. With a final huff the younger woman stopped pedaling and levered herself off the machine. Brooke's skin shimmered with perspiration, her red hair hung limp around her freckled face, but there was a look in her eyes that Samantha recognized as satisfaction. "Can I get you another water or anything?"

"No, thanks. I'm good," Samantha replied.

Brooke wiped down the elliptical, then took a long drink of water. "Well, I appreciate you getting me started."

"No problem," Samantha replied. "I was glad to help."

The redhead looked at her for a few moments, then nodded. Finally she turned and walked toward the door.

"I hope your day gets better," Samantha called after her.

"Thanks," the younger woman said, reaching for the doorknob. "I only fudged a little bit and the machine says I burned three hundred calories, so things are already looking up." She smiled a lopsided smile. "But then I guess they couldn't have gotten much worse."

CHAPTER SIX

BOOK CLUB IN THE NORTHERN ATLANTA SUBDIVI-
sion of River Run began that Thursday night as it
always did—with shrieks and hugs of greeting, the pouring
of wine, and a growing roar of conversation. The book, E. L.
James's *Fifty Shades of Grey*, would get its fifteen to twenty
minutes of discussion later—possibly more given the titil-
lation factor—but only once their husbands, ex-husbands,
mothers, absent neighbors, and their children had been thoroughly dissected.

Attendance varied between ten and fifteen depending on
schedules and the chosen book. Most of the members would
readily admit that as much as they liked to read they were
mostly here for the company. For many it was the only activity in a given month that belonged solely to them. For Claire,
who had moved into the neighborhood newly divorced and
with a two-year-old, a job, and already aging parents, the
River Run Book Club—and the women in it—had been a
lifeline. The meeting had always been a two- to three-minute
walk, depending on who was hosting. Tonight, one week

after her move into Midtown, it had taken her over an hour in traffic to get there.

Dropping her purse in a corner, Claire hugged her way to Amanda White's kitchen, where opened wine bottles and snacks covered the granite-topped island and conversation flowed almost as quickly as the alcohol was poured. This was the first meeting after the summer hiatus and there was a lot of catching up to do.

"I wish you all could have seen Shelley Gordon's face when she told me that Bradley didn't get into the University of Georgia." Lisa Breckenridge snorted as she reached for a wineglass. "After four years of hearing how many Advanced Placement classes he took, how high his test scores were, and how many schools were begging him to apply, it's kind of hard to fathom."

"I know!" Marilyn Bender stepped up to give Claire a hug, then reached for a bowl of mixed nuts. "I ran into her at Kendra's lacrosse game and she was going on about how happy he was at Georgia Southern after all and that he might not even want to transfer to Georgia later." She rolled her eyes.

There were titters of amusement as Claire joined a group ogling the sponge and marzipan cake that had been shaped into a four-poster bed with a bare-chested, pant unzipped version of billionaire Christian Grey leaning against it. Black lace panties and a short brown whip hung from the dining room chandelier. Invitations had been short suggestive emails and the signature drink was the Greyhound—a combination of vodka and grapefruit juice. Whether it was chick lit or S and M the River Run Book Club dearly loved a book that lent itself to a theme.

"I know you didn't get that cake at Kroger!" Marilyn said.

"You're right about that," Amanda crowed. "I ordered it online and it arrived in a plain brown wrapper."

"Welcome back to the hinterlands!" Woman after woman hugged Claire and proclaimed how wonderful it was of her to come all this way—as if she'd moved thousands of miles from them instead of in town.

"It's exactly twenty-three-point-four miles," Claire said the fourth time someone commended her on her fortitude. "If it's not rush hour, it's only thirty-five to forty minutes."

"But it's always rush hour nowadays," Amanda said. "I swear you have to be crazy to get on a highway anywhere in the metropolitan area between seven a.m. and seven p.m."

"Isn't it weird to go from a three-bedroom Colonial to a studio apartment?" someone asked.

"Do you really walk to the grocery store?" Lisa asked as if she'd claimed she'd walked on the moon.

"I have. But driving is allowed," Claire teased. "The Publix near me has a parking lot and everything."

"But what do you do if it rains?"

"I'm guessing she gets wet or opens up her umbrella," Amanda deadpanned. "Kind of like we do out here in the 'hood."

There was laughter, but Claire knew that in a place as dependent on the automobile as the Atlanta suburbs completing tasks on foot really was an alien concept. As they plied her with questions they looked at her warily as if the desire to throw off a life and start a new one might be contagious.

"How's Hailey liking it up in Chicago?" Diana Grayson asked.

Claire launched into a story Hailey had told her about getting lost on the El and the group laughed, though she could tell from their expressions that they didn't understand why her daughter had chosen to go to college in the Midwest any more than they understood why Claire had shed life as they knew it for a tiny condo in the middle of the city.

The laughter and conversation flowed around her but didn't quite touch her. She wasn't sure how she could possibly feel so far removed from the life she'd lived for so long so quickly, but the long-awaited neighborhood clubhouse remodel, an email war about the landscaping for the front of the neighborhood, even home values already felt like ancient history. Another glass of wine or a Greyhound might have helped, but she was afraid of drinking too much, because when she left she wouldn't be cutting through the Graysons' yard and down two houses, she'd be driving two interstates to get back to the Alexander.

"Your eyes are completely glazed over," Kerry Morgan said with a laugh. "It's too tacky of us to bore you with the same old neighborhood shit, when you've already shaken the red clay of River Run off those adorable new ballet flats you've got on. Let's go grab those empty seats over there and you can tell us all about your new place." Kerry picked up one of the opened bottles and led Claire and Hannah Simpson to an overstuffed sofa. "I think Hailey told Savannah that your building isn't far from the Fox Theatre?"

"It's about six blocks north," Claire replied. "I walked down there just the other day and had a coffee at the Georgian Terrace." She named a landmark hotel across from the theater.

"Are you just having the best time?" Hannah asked. "I admire you so much for starting fresh this way. I swear I'd never have the nerve to just pick up and move myself into a whole new life."

"I know," Kerry added. "I keep picturing you all dressed up like an adult all the time. Picking up lattes at the corner cafe. Eating in restaurants that don't ask if you want fries with that, whenever you feel like it."

Wendy Madden came over and joined them, dropping onto a kitchen chair that had been placed next to the sofa. She was a recent divorcée whose husband had finally admitted to a long-standing affair with their daughter's tennis coach. "I'm so jealous. Are there cute men in your building? Do you meet people in the streets? Do you go to the clubs?"

"My goodness, let the woman breathe," Hannah said.

Claire smiled in gratitude. The answer to all of Wendy's questions was no—at least so far. She'd been in her new home for a week and except for when she'd been mowed down in the lobby and said hello to the security guy at the building entrance or thank you to the girl at the Starbucks counter, she'd barely looked another human being in the eye.

She looked at the wine bottle with real longing and tried not to stare when the others tilted their goblets up to drain their glasses. It sucked being the only completely sober person in the room, and although everyone who chimed in on their conversation professed envy of her new life, it was clear that none of them would ever actually consider trading their life for hers.

"So how's the new book coming?" Elsa, who had lived two doors away from the time Claire and Hailey moved into the neighborhood, asked. "It must be incredible to have all that time just to write."

Claire smiled. "I've been unpacking and getting settled all week," she said. "I'm taking the weekend to get my head in the right place and then I intend to get down to work first thing Monday morning." She hadn't even had time to review her notes or look at the character sketches she'd roughed out after the contract had been signed. She felt an odd little stutter in her stomach, which she assumed was anticipation.

Still, she was almost relieved when Amanda clapped her hands together like the kindergarten teacher she was and ordered everyone to find a seat so that they could discuss the book. It was nine fifteen. The meeting would end somewhere around ten p.m.

It wasn't until Claire had started writing and trying to be published that she'd paid attention to how much more time was spent drinking and talking than discussing the book. It had taken her two and a half years to research and write her first historical romance and another year after that to find an agent to represent it. *Highland Kiss* had come out to strong reviews and modest sales a year and a half after that. The River Run Book Club had thrown a great launch party to celebrate and each and every member of the club had bought at least one copy. But the meeting at which they were to discuss it had been no different than all the others; lots of fun followed by a discussion of her book, her process, and her inspiration that lasted for exactly 20.5 minutes.

Claire's watch read ten fifteen when they began to carry glasses and plates into the kitchen.

"Maybe we could have a meeting down at my place one month," Claire said once she'd located her purse.

"That would be so cool!" Amanda said.

"You can show us around," Elsa added.

"Maybe we could go to a book event at the Margaret Mitchell House—it's only a few blocks away—and then come back to my place for dessert or something," Claire offered.

There was a lot of excitement and chatter over the idea until someone pulled out her phone to calculate the mileage.

"We could draw straws for who would be the designated driver," Wendy said.

"Drivers, you mean," said Amanda. "If we all went, we'd need more than one vehicle."

They looked at each other calculating their odds of not only having to stay sober but drive home in the dark on unfamiliar roads.

"I'll send you all a link to the Margaret Mitchell website and we can put something on the calendar," Claire said as if she thought this might actually happen.

"That sounds perfect." Amanda gave her a hug and handed her a plastic-wrapped slice of cake. "Drive carefully."

"I will."

There were more hugs and some halfhearted promises to come into town for lunch or shopping. She said good-bye and couldn't help noticing that others who had said they were leaving hung back in twos or threes to talk about the next day's carpool or some event at the middle or high school— just as Claire once would have done. She walked out to her car alone.

All was quiet in River Run. On a whim she turned left

instead of right and drove slowly past their old house; the one she'd worked so hard to hold on to. There were lights on in the back family room and in the master bedroom upstairs. Out on the grass a tricycle lay on its side. A plastic orange-and-yellow coupe sat "parked" at the top of the driveway, its door hanging open. It was so strange to think of others living in *their* house.

She felt like a disembodied spirit with one foot in the old life and one in the new but belonging in neither. She picked up her cell phone and called Hailey, who had anchored her life for so long. Even if she'd stayed here, without her daughter to revolve around, her life would have been permanently altered. She would have still felt the emptiness that yawned at her center.

The call went to voicemail and Claire pressed the phone tight to her ear the better to hear her daughter's voice. "Hi, sweetie," she said after the tone. "I'm just on my way . . . home . . . from book club." She hesitated. "Everybody asked about you. And it was great to see them. But weird, too, you know?"

She drove south on Alpharetta Highway and took the Northridge ramp onto Highway 400 South. "I'll be in the car for the next thirty minutes or so if you want to call back. Or we can talk tomorrow." She swallowed around a ridiculously large lump that rose in her throat. "I love you. And I miss you."

Merging onto the highway, she was surprised as she always was by the amount of traffic that whizzed by. She wondered where all these people were going and had the horrible feeling that every single one of them was going home to someone. Everyone but her.

Quietly, she disconnected and set the cell phone in the empty cup holder. Carefully, she arranged both of her hands on the wheel and clasped it tightly, trying to hold on to some small part of herself—and her life—that still looked familiar.

CHAPTER SEVEN

BROOKE WAS HALF OUT OF HER CHURCH CLOTHES
Sunday when the doorbell rang. She was trying to yank
the zipper of her dress back up when a key sounded in the
lock. The girls' shrieks of joy and the happy yips that Darcy
began to emit explained the lack of a call from the security
desk. Although Zachary no longer lived here, he had decided
the fact that he paid the mortgage entitled him to keep and
use his key. She didn't like the idea that he could simply "pop
in" any time he felt like it, but since his interest in the three
of them hovered around zero this rarely happened. The key
had become one more thing that wasn't worth fighting for.

Unable to get the zipper back up or her one remaining
shoe off, she limped out to the foyer with her arms clasped
across her middle to keep her dress from falling down. He,
of course, looked attractively windblown, which meant he'd
come over in his new BMW convertible, and casually elegant
in khakis and a polo she didn't recognize, which probably
meant his socialite girlfriend was now dressing him. Natalie,
whose Sunday-school dress bore evidence of every crayon and

snack she had touched that morning, had her arms around her father's hips and her head buried in his stomach. Ava, who had managed to shed her Sunday dress and everything else except her underpants and one frilly sock, had had to settle for clasping her chubby arms around his thigh. Darcy rubbed her sausage body against his pant leg like a cat. Her long dachshund nose sniffed the air around him happily, despite the fact that Zachary had never wanted, fed, or cared for her.

The excitement on their faces made Brooke want to cry. So did the irritation on his.

"You didn't answer my text." He looked her up and down dismissively.

"We were in church," she replied quietly and she hoped, with more dignity than her half-dressed state might indicate. "I had my phone off."

"I guess you didn't check messages on the house phone when you got home, either." His words were clipped.

"We just walked in a minute ago," she said, although the truth was she probably wouldn't have checked since there was so rarely a reason to. "What do you want?"

"I came to pick up the girls." Given how little time he'd been spending with them, Brooke was not the only one who started in surprise at this. "If you can pack them each a small bag and their school uniform, we, I mean, I can drop them off in the morning."

There were more shrieks of joy, but the girls didn't let go. Which just went to show that while they both might have gotten her short, chunky build, red hair, and freckles, they had grasped certain truths about Zachary that she had not; namely that their father was someone they would have to make noise to attract and then cling tightly to hold on to.

He started to move toward the living room with the girls still attached, which produced a straight-legged, clunky, Frankenstein-monster sort of gait. The girls giggled as if he were playing the game he used to where he pretended to not even know they were there as he moved from room to room, but Brooke could feel the desperation in how tightly they'd locked their arms around him and the hysterical note of their laughter. She hurried after him, praying—as she hadn't been able to find the energy to do in church—that he wouldn't hurt their feelings or disappoint them yet again.

"So what made you decide on today?" Brooke asked as she pried first Natalie and then Ava off of him. Last weekend, which had been his scheduled weekend, he'd called barely ten minutes before she was supposed to have them waiting down in the lobby, to say that he wouldn't be able to make it; something that had happened so many times in the last six months that she was more surprised when he showed up than when he didn't.

Zachary hesitated and she could practically see his brain ducking and dodging, considering and rejecting possible answers. Which meant he feared the truth might prevent him from getting what he wanted.

"Go pack your bags, munchkins," he said, spearing the girls with a false smile that matched the jolly tone. As if he actually expected a five- and seven-year-old to pack an overnight case with everything they might need without assistance.

"Yes," Brooke added. "Go get started and I'll be there in a minute to help you finish up."

They raced to their rooms without further prompting, which was something that she'd often dreamed of but which was almost frightening when it actually happened.

"What's going on?" she asked when the children were out of earshot. Her arms were growing tired from holding up her dress, but she couldn't bring herself to ask him for so simple a thing as a zip up.

He shrugged. "Sarah has her son for the weekend, so . . ." He shrugged again. Sarah Grant was a wealthy socialite who had started as a patient and become his best advertisement. Sometime before, during, or after the round of procedures that had perfected her facial features and enhanced many of her body parts, Zachary had started sleeping with her. Now Sarah was, as Zachary had told Brooke more than once, everything Brooke refused to be.

"So if you're going to have one child cramping your style, you might as well have three?" Brooke asked.

The flush spreading across his face told her she'd hit the mark. Brooke didn't know Sarah well, and she hoped to keep it that way. She didn't feel at all good about the fact that the only reason her children were going to see their father was because his girlfriend was parenting.

"I hope you're not planning to complain," Zachary said. "You're always wanting me to take them."

Her mouth dropped open at the unfairness of the accusation; after all they'd been through, he only ever saw her in the worst possible light. "I want you to take them when you're supposed to because you're their father and they miss you," she said. "Not because your girlfriend has her son so you might as well have your kids there, too."

She stared up into the hard planes and angles of his face and into the emerald-colored eyes that had once glowed with enthusiasm for their life together. All they held now was the cold sharpness of his disdain for her; she who had stood and delivered in adversity and crumpled like a wadded-up piece of paper in the face of success.

"Can you hurry them along? Sarah and Trent are waiting in the car downstairs." He took her by the shoulders, spun her around in much the same way you might move a sack of potatoes out of the way, and zipped up the back of her dress. "We're taking them to Piedmont Park, so no dresses or Sunday-school shoes. I want them dressed appropriately."

Brooke's head jerked up at his tone. She couldn't remember when he'd begun to talk to her in that hurtful condescending way. But years of writing off his shortcomings to the stress of medical school and the demands of his residency and then to avoid confrontations in front of the kids had allowed him to treat her like a doormat. She heard the girls calling her. With difficulty she swallowed back the retort that had sprung to her lips and hurried toward their bedrooms to help them pack.

AFTER A LEISURELY MORNING DAWDLING OVER COF-fee and the *New York Times*, Claire spent Sunday afternoon rambling around the fifty-plus-acre Piedmont Park. She and Hailey had driven in from the suburbs for different festivals and events at the park over the years, but she'd never had the time or opportunity to explore it in earnest until now. It was an easy walk from the Alexander and throughout the week, she'd varied her route each time she went, entering the grounds from a different access point and covering a different quadrant. Today the breeze was warm, still tinged with summer and laden with humidity. The grass was green and lush from summer rain and the leaves had not yet begun to turn. As Claire walked and watched the families cavort, she pushed her brain toward the book she would start on in earnest tomorrow, but it resisted, preferring to skitter and float like the summer scents of jasmine and sunscreen that floated on the breeze.

Her cell phone rang and she pulled it out of her pocket to answer it. "Hey, stranger," she said, keeping her tone light. "Where have you been?" Hailey had sent the occasional text between classes or late at night, but it had been days since she'd heard her daughter's voice—or any voice at all.

"I've been swamped," Hailey said. "I'm not sure what made me think that taking an intensive writing class in my first semester was a good idea. And I got the part-time job in the library and had to go to orientation there twice this week." Hailey had been awarded a good deal of scholarship money, but had insisted on working to help supplement her living expenses—her contribution to what she called Claire's "grand year of writing."

"You know you don't have to . . ." Claire began.

"Yes, I do, and I don't want to talk about it again," her daughter replied. "You've done enough. It's my turn to step up for a while."

Claire swallowed the automatic protest, not wanting to diminish Hailey's pleasure in her contribution. "Okay. So tell me what's going on there. I need some detail so I can picture what you're doing."

Claire walked and listened with pleasure as Hailey chattered on, describing her roommate's borderline compulsive cleaning routines, her professors' various quirks, and even the sharp spicy scent of the head librarian's perfume, with an evocative economy of words that the writer in Claire envied. She kept the phone to her ear, enjoying the sound of Hailey's voice, treasuring the connection.

"Where are you now?" Hailey asked.

"I've just left the park and I'm back on Piedmont walking west toward Peachtree."

"Are you going home?" Both of them paused at the word.

"Yes." When she reached the Alexander she put her key in the lock and stepped inside. The security guard nodded and smiled. "I'm in the lobby and headed for the elevator," she said in the tone of a travelogue host. "Oh, and what is that I hear?" As she passed the fountain, she took the phone from her ear and held it out for a moment so that Hailey could hear the splash and spill of water.

"Is that the fountain?"

"Ding, ding, ding," Claire said. "You got that one right."

She kept up the travelogue as she stepped onto the elevator.

"I'm on the eighth floor now, nearing my front door." She jiggled the key in the lock so that Hailey could hear it. The door creaked slightly as it opened.

"Phew." She slammed the door and threw the dead bolt. "Thank God I made it in one piece."

Hailey laughed. "So what do you have going on the rest of the day?"

"Oh, a little of this and a little of that," Claire said evasively. Both of them had dreamed for so long about Claire's new life that she didn't want to spoil their vision with anything that even sounded like a complaint. "I picked up the Sunday *New York Times* and you know I can spend a full day on the crossword puzzle alone."

"You'd be better off going out to a movie or to dinner with a friend," Hailey said.

Claire did not want to point out the obvious—if she wanted to see any of her existing friends she was going to have to drive out to them. "I had emails from Susie and Karen." She mentioned her online critique partners. One of them was at her vacation home in Florida, the other in Indiana. Typically they brainstormed by phone and critiqued online. Once a year they met up at a writers' conference. Every other year they rented a mountain cabin where they wrote all day and drank wine, brainstormed, and watched movies each night.

"Emails and phone calls aren't the same as having someone there to do things with," Hailey pointed out.

"That's true," Claire conceded.

"I think this would be the perfect time to give online dating a try," Hailey said, not for the first time. "You should post a profile and get started."

Claire bit back a groan. "Oh, Hailey. There's no way I'm doing that." She wasn't even sure what she'd do with a man at this point. "I really need to focus on my book. And it's not like I've never dated."

"Mom, you've had what—three or four dates in the last fifteen years? You haven't been out with a man in this century!"

"I'm sure it's like riding a bicycle . . ." Claire began.

"I hate to break it to you, Mom, but dating is *not* like

riding a bicycle. Things have changed. One out of three people meet significant others now online."

"Really?" Claire said, her tone dry. "And here I thought I could just mosey on into a bar, drink too much, pick up someone, and live happily ever after."

"Isn't that how you met Dad?"

There was a silence.

"There are some really great sites, Mom. I could set up your profile for you if you want."

"No, Hailey," she said as clearly as she could. "I appreciate you wanting to help, but no."

"Well, then you at least have to try to make some friends there. Maybe you could join some sort of organization. Or do volunteer work. I bet there are some people in the building you'd like."

"I appreciate your concern, Hailey, but I don't need you to orchestrate my social life or find friends for me."

"Yes, you do."

"I've only been here a week," Claire protested. "And I don't have any problem with my own company."

Hailey gave her a teenaged version of "humpf." "Have you seen anyone in the building who looks interesting?"

"I met someone just the other day." She thought about the red-haired woman with the children and the dog that had plowed her down. She'd recognized the harried look in the woman's eyes. Claire had worn one very like it for most of Hailey's toddler and elementary school years.

"Maybe you should go to some activity or something." There was the sound of fingers clattering on a keyboard. "I'm on the building's website." More clattering. "Hey, the concierge has posted a calendar for residents. He's going to be previewing the first two seasons of *Downton Abbey*, Mom. There are a ton of people here on campus who are in love with the series. It's kind of an Edwardian England soap opera with really great clothes and cool accents that was filmed in a real castle."

Claire vaguely remembered seeing an invitation in her mailbox, but did she really want to go watch a television show with a group of strangers when she had her very own brand-new flat-screen TV right here? "I don't need to go to a formal screening. If I want to see the series I can get it from Netflix or download it. Or, I don't know, my fabulous daughter could give me the DVD for Christmas."

"Mom," Hailey said as if talking to a child. "The point isn't that you have to see the series, although it sounds totally up your alley—I mean, you do write historical fiction. The point is it's an opportunity to meet people you might like. I'm sure it'll be mostly women. How bad could it be to spend an hour once a week with a group of women from your building?

"What was it you used to tell me practically every day of my life?" Hailey asked pointedly.

A smile tugged at Claire's lips. "That you have to put yourself in the right place. That things don't just happen without effort," Claire said as she had so many times during Hailey's angst-filled teenage years. They had been words to live by, but she hadn't imagined having them turned on her.

"You need new friends," her daughter said. "This is exactly the kind of situation where you might make some."

"Honestly, Hailey. This is ridiculous. I don't need you managing my life."

"Just trying to return the favor," Hailey replied crisply. "I say you go tonight and make an effort to meet people or . . ."

"Or what?" Claire asked.

"Or I'm going to post your profile to every dating site I can think of."

"That's blackmail," Claire observed.

"Kind of."

"There's no 'kind of' about it," Claire protested. "When did you get so bossy?"

"Well, my mother taught me that sometimes you do have to lead the horse to water and make him drink."

"I'm not a horse."

"No," Hailey conceded. "But you are kind of acting like a horse's ass about this."

"I am not. I just . . ."

"I know." Hailey's voice turned softer. "I know it's not all that easy to start over. Especially at your age."

"I'm not that old," Claire protested.

"I get it, Mom. But that doesn't mean I'm going to let you off the hook," Hailey said with finality.

"Hailey. I . . ."

"Gotta run, Mom. But I'll expect a report about the screening tomorrow."

"I . . ."

"And no Cliffs Notes or Internet watching. I want to hear who was there, what the concierge had to say, and whether he served anything 'British' like the description says. Maybe you'll have tea and crumpets."

"Hailey!"

"I'm not kidding, Mom," the steamroller formerly known as Hailey Walker said. "I'll call Edward Parker myself and ask if you were there if I have to."

Claire couldn't decide whether to laugh or cry. She began a last sputtered protest, but Hailey cut her off.

"It's *Downton Abbey* screenings on Sunday nights," Hailey said. "Or Internet dating. The choice is yours."

CHAPTER EIGHT

S AMANTHA DIDN'T EXACTLY TRY TO OUTRUN
Edward Parker on her way from the parking garage to
the elevators that Sunday evening. But she might have moved
a little more quickly than necessary when she saw him crossing the lobby in her direction and realized where he was
headed.

She'd had the most amazing weekend. With Jonathan
unexpectedly delayed out on the West Coast, her mother-
in-law laid up with a head cold, Meredith in New York, and
Hunter up at the lake house with friends, Samantha had had
the entire weekend to herself; something that had happened less than a handful of times in the last twenty-six
years.

Feeling a bit like a soldier who surprises himself by going
AWOL, she'd blown off all kinds of things before she'd even
realized she intended to. Yesterday she'd skipped a symphony
guild committee luncheon in order to have lunch at the Var-
sity instead. There, she'd pulled up to the curb of the seventy-
five-year-old institution near the Georgia Tech campus, let

a carhop deliver her chili cheese slaw dog, frozen orange shake, and fried peach pie, and devoured every bite.

Last night she'd dodged a formal fund-raiser in order to stay in and watch a *House Hunters* and *House Hunters International* marathon on HGTV. Today instead of stopping by Bellewood to check on her mother-in-law's health, Samantha had spent a delicious afternoon at IKEA where she'd covered every inch of every floor of the massive showroom, studying each inexpensive accessory and stick of space-saving furniture with the same fascination she'd once displayed at the Museum of Modern Art, the pyramids at Giza, and the impressionist wing at the Louvre.

She'd dawdled happily for hours, confident she wouldn't run into anyone she knew, hemming and hawing over a $9.99 desk lamp and a $2.00 mouse pad shaped like a stiletto. Famished from all the delectable dithering, she stopped in the cafeteria where she bought and consumed a huge helping of Swedish meatballs and mashed potatoes buried in cream sauce.

When Jonathan got home tomorrow, their "schedule" and the parameters of their life would snap back into place. But for these last remaining hours she really, really wanted to do more—or was that less—of the same.

"Mrs. Davis?" She'd made it to the elevators and pushed the call button when the concierge's voice sounded somewhere behind her.

She liked Edward Parker and was genuinely glad that he had been awarded the concierge contract. She was also wholeheartedly in favor of his ideas for enhancing the sense of community in the building. But she was having far too fabulous a weekend flouting her obligations to give in to one now. She didn't turn around.

The elevator arrived and the door opened with a ding. Samantha stepped on.

"Can you hold the elevator?" Parker's voice had drawn closer.

Samantha moved a finger toward the "door close" button. Hesitated. Aimed it toward the "door open" button. Pulled it back. She'd already begun imagining lying around the condo in her oldest, most comfortable pajamas, idly flipping through channels while consuming a final high-calorie-artery-hardening meal—maybe even a Double Coronary Bypass Burger from the Vortex down the street.

Still struggling with her conscience, Samantha pushed a button but wasn't completely sure which one. The doors began to close.

A white-cuffed black-sleeved arm inserted itself between the closing elevator doors. They sprang open and Edward Parker stepped inside. "I was a bit afraid that my arm would go up with you and the rest of me would stay here on the first floor."

"I'm so sorry," she began. "I couldn't seem to get to the 'door open' button in time. Are you all right?"

"Yes, I could see there was quite a struggle going on." His words came out in an amused lilt that matched the knowing look in his eyes.

"Sorry," she said, trying not to look guilty. "Which floor do you want?"

"Why, eight, of course," he replied. "Here, allow me." He reached forward and pressed the button. "I do hope you're planning to attend the screening."

She feigned surprise. "Is that tonight?" she asked with a regretful shake of her head. "Oh." She shook it again for good measure. "I'm so sorry. I completely forgot." Not quite able to meet his eye, she glanced down at her watch. It was seven forty-five. "I don't see how I could possibly change and be there by eight." The elevator began its ascent. "Maybe next week."

He flashed her a knowing smile and she sighed. For someone who professed to have forgotten a scheduled event, she was embarrassingly aware of the details. "We're going to socialize a bit before we get started. You can take all the time you need to change, though I think it will be quite casual."

"Oh, I don't know . . ."

"And since I'm the emcee and the projectionist I can make sure we don't begin until you come down." He smiled at her, un-fooled and unfazed by her excuses. His brown eyes remained warm and slightly amused. A dimple creased his cheek.

They reached the eighth floor and the doors slid open. He pushed the twelfth-floor button for her since she'd completely forgotten to, then kept his finger on the "door open" button; a move that was, of course, far less complicated than she'd tried to make it appear.

"Really," he said. "I don't want to be a nuisance about this, but I think your presence would give the activity an important stamp of approval."

There were voices in the hall. A good-sized gathering of women milled around the clubroom door.

"It looks like you've already got a good turnout," she said, relieved. Surely it wouldn't matter whether she was there or not as long as there was a crowd.

"Yes," the concierge said, pleased. "But I'm looking for a cross section of residents and as I said I think it's a good idea to have a board member participate." He smiled the warmly elegant smile, then shot her a wink. "I'll save you a seat and have wine and popcorn waiting."

The man was smooth. And persistent. But at least he was gentleman enough to keep the triumph out of his eyes.

"I'll see you in twenty minutes." She conceded as gracefully as she could. "I prefer red wine. And I'll be expecting extra butter on my popcorn when I get there."

"As you wish, madam," he said with a small bow and a large smile. The elevator doors slid smoothly shut.

PLEASED WITH THE TURNOUT, EDWARD CONTEM-plated the dozen-plus women who'd come for the screening and took a moment to match up faces with names. He greeted Sadie Hopewell, a sixtyish widow who'd moved to Atlanta to be near her children, and her neighbor Myra Mackelbaum, whose husband had invented some sort of elastic band, and introduced them to the white-haired, and apparently light-fingered, Mimi Davenport.

There was Anna Bacall, a no-nonsense RN who worked the overnight shift at Emory Hospital talking to Melinda Greene and her longtime partner Diana Smith, both of whom taught comparative literature at Georgia State and Georgia Tech respectively.

The twentysomething Ritchie twins, nice-looking girls who'd recently graduated from Savannah College of Art and Design and moved back in with their parents while they looked for jobs, had come with their mother, Rebecca. Thanking them all for coming, he drew Claire Walker, who'd moved into a studio unit and was reported to be a writer, closer to the bar and into conversation with the women in front of and behind her.

In keeping with the *Downton Abbey* theme, he'd dressed two of his staff as servants of the period and brought them up to serve food and drinks. James Hicks wore livery copied from Edward's grandfather's actual uniform, and smiled and bowed formally as he poured and offered wine behind the bar. Isabella Morales, an aspiring actress, was dressed as a ladies' maid and seemed to be having a "go" at a British accent as she passed out bags of popcorn and offered appetizer-sized mincemeat pies.

He was surprised, but glad, to see that Brooke Mackenzie had come. She sat on the edge of one of the sofas clutching the arm as if for support. He knew her husband had left her soon after he'd moved the family into the building and he'd seen the uncertain desperation in her face as she'd ridden out the divorce that had quickly followed. He suspected the tears in the fitness room were but a drop in the bucket she'd shed. He carried a bottle of wine over. "I'm so pleased you could join us. May I refill your glass?"

"Oh, I don't know if I should," she said immediately, shaking her head.

"That's one of the advantages of coming to an event in the building," he said. "You don't have to worry about drinking and driving, do you? What do you say? May I?" He laid on the accent a bit. In his experience some people found it oddly reassuring.

She smiled and held up her glass.

"There you are," he said as he poured. "I'll ask Isabella to bring you a spot of popcorn, too. Do you mind saving the seat next to you? Another resident asked me to reserve her a space as well."

"Sure." Her face brightened and a faint blush spread across her cheeks, blending the relief map of freckles into a becoming pink. Her hazel eyes were quite nice when she wasn't casting them down.

At the bar he instructed Isabella to give Samantha Davis wine and popcorn when she arrived and then escort her down to the seat next to Brooke Mackenzie.

"Aye, I will, cap'n," she said with real Cockney fervor. "Ye can be sure o' that."

"Not bad," he said. "You might want to aim for the accent of someone bent on improving herself and rising professionally by imitating her mistress's accent. Rather than emulating a pirate in a Walt Disney film."

"Right, cap'n."

He raised an eyebrow, careful not to laugh.

"I mean, yes, milord." She curtsied.

"Better," he said. "You do have an ear, Isabella. You just have to be careful what you're listening to."

She nodded. "Yes, sir."

"Better still," Edward said. "You'll see what I mean when the program airs. Pay careful attention to Joanne Froggatt, who plays Anna. She's nailed the part of a person in her station perfectly."

Shortly after eight he invited everyone to find a seat and

made sure no one sat off alone. Once everyone was settled, all eyes turned to him expectantly. The room fell silent.

"Thank you so much for coming tonight," he said. "I believe I've met all of you since taking on the Alexander six months ago. I love this building and am very happy to be serving as your concierge. I hope that you'll let me know if there's anything I, or the rest of the building staff, can do to make things more comfortable. My firm, Private Butler, also works with individual clients, so if anyone should need more than the building provides, please let me know."

The door opened and Samantha Davis stepped into the room. He nodded to Isabella and she did as he'd asked, though in what sort of accent he didn't know. Brooke Mackenzie's eyes went wide with apprehension as Samantha was shown to the seat next to her. Hoping that he hadn't erred in placing them together, Edward gave them both a nod and a smile, then resumed his introduction.

"I suggested screening *Downton Abbey*, which airs here on PBS in the winter after showing first in England, because it's all the rage—I believe it's showing in some one hundred countries. I also chose it because I feel a special affinity for the production. As some of you may have noticed, I'm British." He paused for the laughter. "Shocking, I know.

"*Downton Abbey* is a beautifully done Edwardian drama. Like the earlier *Upstairs Downstairs* series of the 1970s, it chronicles the life of an important English estate both above and below stairs.

"The thing is, a number of generations of my family were 'in service.' In fact, both my grandfather and great-grandfather were valets to the Earls of Montclaire in Nottinghamshire, which is very near where my family still lives. My great-uncle Mason was a footman.

"As those of you who've seen my résumé know, after a long career in hotel management, I wanted a more personal experience more closely based on what my ancestors had done. I became a concierge—which a lot of my colleagues saw as a step backward—and now I'm applying many of the things my forebears learned and passed on regarding enhancing the quality of life for others."

He watched their faces and saw their interest. It was time to let the program speak for itself.

"My father owns and runs a pub, so I also know the importance of a generous 'pour.' Who else would like their drinks topped off or more popcorn before we begin?"

There were murmurs and glasses raised. It was clear most of the crowd had come intending to enjoy themselves. "Good," he said. "I'll pour while Isabella refills popcorn."

He picked up a bottle each of red and white, then began to move about the room. He kept an eye on Samantha Davis and Brooke Mackenzie as he made sure everyone was comfortable and settled in. The two had nodded to each other when the latecomer had been seated, but they looked horribly stiff. Almost, he thought, as if someone had run a broomstick up their backsides. If they didn't watch out, someone, possibly him, might accuse them of being closet Brits.

KEEPING HER BACK STRAIGHT, BROOKE LEANED away from Samantha Davis and into the arm of the sofa. She did this carefully so as not to appear rude and in order to avoid jouncing the other woman's arm as she drained the glass of red wine. Brooke had only come tonight because the apartment had felt so empty without the girls. She'd needed to be somewhere else for at least a little while; somewhere with people who wouldn't see her as Zachary did. But this woman in her designer clothes and expensive hair, who could show up late and be led to a front-row seat, had seen her at her absolute worst.

"Do you have enough room?" Brooke asked tentatively.

"Yes," Samantha said. "Thanks." Setting her glass on the cocktail table, Samantha settled the bag of popcorn on her lap and reached inside it, scooped up a buttery handful, and began to eat with relish. "Mmmm. I haven't had real buttered popcorn in ages. Not even out of a microwave." She munched contentedly, occasionally pausing to lick the butter from her fingers.

Brooke, who could gain two pounds just driving by a fast-food restaurant, felt a burst of envy. It figured that someone like Samantha Davis, who'd clearly been born under a lucky star and spent the rest of her life basking in its glow, could eat whatever she wanted to whenever she felt like it.

The silence spooled out between them. Maybe Samantha Davis didn't even recognize her. Or if she did maybe she saw no reason to acknowledge Brooke or what had passed between them. Brooke was just beginning to relax when Samantha leaned closer, glanced over her shoulder as if to make sure they wouldn't be overheard, and asked, "Are you feeling better?"

"Oh. Yes," Brooke said surprised and embarrassed. "Thank you."

There was a silence, which Brooke felt compelled to fill. "I don't think I've burned many calories since the other day in the fitness room. But I haven't cried, either."

"That's a definite step in the right direction then," Samantha replied.

Brooke glanced at the other woman's face, trying to judge her sincerity. Experience had taught her just how easily a certain type of southern woman could charm you even while they were laughing at you inside.

Brooke waited for Samantha to pull away and signal the end of their conversation. Instead she said, "I've heard the first program starts with the sinking of the *Titanic*. I don't think I can take watching people freeze to death. This isn't a tearjerker, is it?"

"God, I hope not," Brooke said. "Although I may not be the right person to ask since apparently even exercise equipment can make me cry."

There was a small, but encouraging, hiccup of laughter from a pair of lips she didn't think even Zachary would try to improve on.

"I haven't seen the opening episodes," Brooke replied. "And what I have seen was out of order. But it was really well done."

"All right, ladies," Edward Parker said, holding white and red wine bottles aloft. "Last call for alcohol until after the program. Who's ready for more?"

"I'll have another glass!" A gray-haired woman off to the side yelled.

"Me, too!" said the woman next to her.

There were some cackles of laughter. A happy sort of hum filled the room.

Brooke realized as she watched their concierge in action that she'd been expecting some sort of prim and proper evening—but Edward Parker clearly knew how to handle a crowd of women. She felt her body begin to loosen slightly— no doubt a result of the two and a half glasses of wine she'd drunk. Which was two and a half more than usual. She'd learned how dangerous it was to deal with Zachary if her senses were the least bit dulled; if she weren't careful she and the girls would be living out on the street in a cardboard box from one of his pieces of fancy equipment.

"I don't know, Mrs. Mackelbaum," the concierge said to a gray-haired woman who hooted at him. "I may have to cut you and Mrs. Hopewell off."

There was laughter.

"Don't forget I practically grew up in a pub. I know how to handle the likes of you!" the concierge teased.

The mood in the room grew more buoyant with laughter and expectation. With a nod from Edward Parker the lights dimmed. "All right, ladies. Sit back, relax, and enjoy. You are now about to enter the luscious and thrilling world of *Downton Abbey.*"

He aimed the remote at the hundred-plus-inch screen.

Brooke leaned forward in her seat as the television flickered to life and the PBS logo filled the screen. Laura Linney welcomed them to Masterpiece Classic.

Brooke barely breathed as she watched a finger tap out a message on a Teletype. A train whistle sounded. The train cut through the countryside while an unknown man stared out the window. Scenery swept by. Music played lightly. The hum of the telegraph wires that ran along the track could be heard, an urgent clacking. The message arrived at a British telegraph office, but it was too early to deliver it.

The music swelled and a magnificent castle loomed large, framed in blue sky and green grass. Brooke leaned toward the screen to better breathe in the stunning opening visuals as the servants began their day and the fateful telegram arrived. Beside her Samantha Davis went still as Robert, the Seventh Earl of Grantham and his rich American wife awoke to discover what the sinking of the *Titanic* would mean to all of the inhabitants of *Downton Abbey*.

CHAPTER NINE

THERE WAS SILENCE AS THE PROGRAM ENDED with Matthew Crawley receiving the fateful message from Lord Grantham. The silence continued as the music swelled and the closing credits began. Then someone, Samantha wasn't sure who, began to applaud. Brooke who hadn't seemed to move so much as a muscle during the program joined in. There were whistles and one "woo-hoo!"

"Wow," Brooke said.

"Yeah," Samantha agreed. It was odd to be so transported, inserted so cleanly into such a different time and place.

People stood, but no one made a move for the door.

"Just as I feared," Edward said. "You absolutely hated it."

There was laughter and conversation. An angular woman with shaggy blond hair walked over to Brooke and Samantha.

"This is Claire Walker," Brooke said. "Claire, Samantha Davis. Claire and I met the day my dog and my daughters mowed her down in the lobby."

Samantha shook Claire's hand. "Yes, I think I witnessed the tail end of that encounter."

Brooke smiled apologetically. "I seem to have a special talent for memorable introductions," she said. Samantha was glad Brooke didn't elaborate about their first encounter in the fitness room. It still made her uncomfortable.

"So what did you think of *Downton Abbey*?" Claire asked.

"It was fun. It reminds me a little bit of *Dallas* and *Dynasty* only with fancier accents, better breeding, and no shoulder pads," Samantha said. "Well, except on the men."

"It's a soap opera all right," Claire agreed. "But it's so well done and offers such a great glimpse into the time period and the life of the nobility that it feels far more enlightening."

"The clothes and the house are unbelievable." Brooke sighed.

"They are spectacular," Claire said. "But I'm not sure you're allowed to call it a house."

Edward clapped his hands to get everyone's attention, with no discernible effect.

"We'll have to ask Edward," Samantha said. "I suspect he'll know."

"Ladies, before we do anything else, I'd like to get a photo of our very first *Downton Abbey* gathering."

The chatter continued as Edward directed them. "That's right, move in a bit there. Good. Um, Mrs. Mackelbaum, can you . . . yes that's just right." He gestured and coaxed until they were in something that resembled an intentional grouping. "Okay now, let's put Isabella on one end and James on the other so we can see their uniforms and get a bit of atmosphere going. That's good. Squeeze in a bit, Mrs. Davis. That's right. That's Mrs. Hopewell next to you. Say hello, will you? I don't *think* she bites. You don't, do you, Mrs. Hopewell?"

The concierge lowered the camera. "Actually, maybe we should just sound off with our names in case there's anyone who hasn't met everyone and all that."

"Egad!" Isabella said. "Ees a bit of a tyrant, ee is!" She looked expectantly at Edward.

"That was a bit ED, I'm afraid," Edward said.

"Erectile dysfunction?" one of the Ritchie girls asked in surprise.

Edward winced as if in pain but couldn't quite hide his smile. "That's what comes of so many Viagra commercials on the air. No, love. The ED I was referring to was Eliza Doolittle. *Before* Professor Higgins turned her into a lady."

"Ahh," Isabella replied quite cheekily. "Then I guess I should be telling you to 'move your bloomin' arse!' "

"Only if you don't want to work here anymore." Edward laughed. "In my experience it's almost never a good idea to call your employer an 'arse.' "

There was laughter. Samantha could tell she wasn't the only one surprised by the wicked sense of humor that dwelt inside the proper Edward Parker.

"Okay, ladies, sound off. Just give us your name and a brief bit about yourself. We'll start in the back corner and work our way forward."

"Anna Bacall, RN. I live on the sixth floor."

"Melinda Greene," a petite brunette next to her said. "I teach Comparative Lit but I have a minor in drama and"— her voice rose in the clipped upper-class accent that the above-stairs actors in *Downton Abbey* had used—"I agree with Eliza that Edward Pah-ker is *quite* the tyrant."

There was more laughter as they introduced themselves. Samantha was surprised by the diversity of ages and backgrounds and by what a good time everyone seemed to be having. She kept her own intro brief—just her name and how much she loved the Alexander, et cetera, et cetera. Beside her Brooke tensed when it was her turn. She cleared her throat. Swallowed. "Brooke." The younger woman cleared her throat again, blinked rapidly. "Brooke Mackenzie." Her face turned bright red. "I'm a, um, stay-at-home mom. Of, um, two girls." Her mouth closed and didn't reopen.

"I'm Claire Walker. Writer and recent empty-nester—my daughter's a freshman at Northwestern," Claire said, filling the awkward silence. "I just moved here from OTP." That was

Atlanta slang for outside the perimeter—or outside of Highway 285, which encircled Atlanta. To those who lived and worked inside the perimeter, OTP was synonymous with in the middle of nowhere. "I've got the year to adjust to living ITP and to write a third novel. I'm not sure which is more alien: my location or the opportunity to write full-time."

"All right, ladies," Edward said when the introductions had been completed. "Look right into the lens now. That's it, big smiles. Right-o. Now, how about one more?" He smiled and clicked away. "Very good."

Samantha had no idea how many photos had been shot when the concierge put down his camera. "I brought what we call biscuits at home. What you would call cookies," Edward said. "Isabella will be pouring tea. James has coffee for anyone who doesn't want to go too English as yet."

"Trying to sober us up before we go home, Edward?" Mrs. Davenport asked.

"You've caught me out, Mrs. D. I don't want any of you rowdies joyriding in the elevators or running up and down corridors ringing doorbells." He gave them a mock stern look and then led them to the large dining room table where he led them in a discussion of the first episode.

"How can Lord Grantham not fight the entail?" one of the Ritchie twins asked. "Why should Cora have to give up her money?"

A spirited debate ensued with Edward explaining the law at that time and the way Grantham would have been raised—more as a caretaker of Downton Abbey and its lands—who would preserve it for the next lord rather than an outright owner.

"Well, I think that sucks," the other Ritchie twin said. Samantha really couldn't tell them apart. Even their voices were identical.

"Yes," the twins' mother added. "It's hard to imagine an American agreeing to anything like that. But I just love Elizabeth McGovern."

"Other favorite characters?" Edward prompted.

"The duke was creepy. I couldn't figure out why he wanted to go into the servant's quarters," Diana Smith, Melinda Greene's friend said, with a flip of her long blond hair over one shoulder.

"O'Brien and Thomas are such schemers. But they're delicious," Myra Mackelbaum said.

"Well, I felt sorry for poor Bates," Sadie Hopewell said. "I can't believe they kicked his one good leg out from under him."

"I can't stop thinking about how completely the servants' lives revolve around the family upstairs." Brooke's voice dropped so low that she might have been talking to herself. "I guess things haven't changed all that much. Some people have lives while others only exist to make those people's lives better."

Samantha kept her eyes carefully averted so that Brooke Mackenzie wouldn't know she'd overheard. But the younger woman's observation struck a chord. She found herself hoping that Brooke Mackenzie would find a way to pick up the reins of her life and steer it in a more positive direction.

They sipped tea and coffee and nibbled on the cookies. Samantha looked around the group, surprised at how comfortable it all was. No one seemed to expect anything of anyone: no donations, no hours committed, no introductions to other potential donors.

"We'll meet next week at the same time," Edward said as Isabella and James began to clear cups and plates. "I expect to see you all here. And if you know anyone who'd like to join us, I can make the first program available so that they'll be up to speed. But no cheating by watching in advance. Believe me, I'll know."

Melinda, the lit teacher/drama minor, mimed fear at his threat. There was laughter.

"All right," Edward said. "Before we call it a night, I'm interested in hearing who has a favorite line?"

"Matthew Crawley when his mother asks whatever does

Lord Grantham want—'He wants to change our lives!' "
Claire said.

"Lord Grantham," Melinda Greene added. "When he said,
'His Grace is graceless!' And at the end, 'If the duke doesn't
like it, he can lump it!' "

Sadie Hopewell said, "The duke to Thomas right before
he burns the incriminating love letters, 'One swallow doesn't
make a summer!' "

"Yes," Samantha surprised herself by saying. "You have
to love a show that imparts such important words to live by."

CLAIRE AWOKE MONDAY MORNING TO THE DING OF
an incoming text from Hailey. It was one word long. *Well??*

Claire smiled and stretched. She'd slept deeply and
dreamed happily, lost in Edwardian England and the stone-
hewn halls of Downton Abbey. *Went and watched,* she texted
back. *Not bad,* she added not wanting Hailey to know just
how much she'd enjoyed herself. How nice it had been to be
with other people after a full week of solitude. How much
fun Edward Parker had made the evening, how skilled he
was at making people comfortable and a part of things. There
was no point in encouraging Hailey's dictatorial tendencies.

Proof? came the reply.

Prepared, Claire sent the group photo that Edward had
taken at the end of the evening. She couldn't help smiling at
the shot of all of them bracketed by the costumed footman
and upstairs maid, who'd kept grinning and saying "Blimey!"
and "What's up, guhv'nor?" much to the concierge's distress.

Claire smiled again at the memory. All of them had loved
the program. Although it had taken awhile to get the hang
of the characters' accents, especially those of the below-stairs
staff, the script and acting were first-rate.

Brooke Mackenzie had been the only resident that she'd
recognized when she arrived, but Edward Parker had made sure
that everyone was introduced. The group had been friendly and

inclusive—even Samantha Davis, who was a bit intimidating and whom Brooke had referred to as the "rich bitch" that day in the lobby—had joined in the fun. Claire had left the screening feeling a little less alone. While she didn't intend to tell Hailey, she'd already put Sunday nights at eight on her calendar. It wasn't as if there was no room on her dance card.

Turning on her shiny new Keurig single-serve coffee-maker, Claire popped into the bathroom to wash her face and brush her teeth. Leaving on her pajamas because she was now officially a full-time writer who could work any way she saw fit, she creamed and sugared her coffee and carried it and her journal out onto the balcony where she sipped, scrawled her impressions of *Downton Abbey*, and watched the morning traffic on Peachtree.

Two cups of coffee and a granola bar later, she went inside, stashed the journal in her nightstand drawer, and sat down at her dining room table/desk. As her laptop booted up she positioned her chair so that she could see out the French doors and the front windows. For years she'd written by the light of a small desk lamp in the early morning hours before getting Hailey up for school, during her lunch hour in the windowless break room at Teledyne Communications, and anywhere else she could grab a stray fifteen or twenty minutes. Now that she was going to do this full-time, she intended to write under the most optimal circumstances. Which meant a view out one or more windows, maximum light—both natural and artificial—and absolute quiet.

Ahhhh. Satisfied, she cracked her knuckles, stretched her fingers, and arranged her right hand on her mouse.

"You've got mail."

Without conscious thought, she clicked on email and found two new messages waiting; one from each of her critique partners. Karen's included a photo of her sitting on her vacation house deck, the beach visible over her shoulder. The text read: *What are you doing here? Get to work!*

The second was from Susie, now the proud grandmother

of a four-month-old. *Rocking her gorgeousness. Isn't she beautiful?* A photo of this was inserted next to the words. *No more email! Get to work!*

Claire laughed and shot back snotty replies. Not quite ready to turn off the Internet—she might need to do research—she turned off the audio notification and pulled up her notes for her new novel; a third romance set in the Scottish Highlands shortly before the Battle of Culloden. Her editor had been excited about Claire's idea of picking up several years after the conclusion of her second novel, *Highland Hellion*, which had ended with the announcement of an arranged alliance between the youngest of three Douglas brothers and the high-spirited daughter of a neighboring laird. The proposal had gone in under the title *Highland Mismatch*, which her editor had rejected as "more appealing to wrestling fans than romance readers," and so her working title had been simplified to a more generic *Highland 3*.

Her agent believed it could be "the book" that put her on some of the bestseller lists and had managed to negotiate a slightly better contract, which she insisted would be even better next book. Assuming her writing continued to develop. And her earlier books continued to sell.

Hmmm. Claire clicked on to her Amazon Author Central account to look at her BookScan sales numbers, which supposedly reflected 70 percent of all sales. Then wished she hadn't.

Since she was already there, she clicked on both of her previous books to check Amazon sales and reviews. *Crap.* Her sales were stagnant here, too. Worse, some reader who didn't like the name of one of her characters because she reminded her of someone she'd hated in elementary school, had given her a one-star review.

Forget it, she scolded herself. *Get to work. Just focus on your characters and what happens to each of them.*

Her gaze strayed to the refrigerator. At home—she stopped midword reminding herself that *this* was home now. Okay. Back in the house in River Run she would have had to walk downstairs to reach the kitchen. Here—in her *new* home—she could practically reach out and touch the refrigerator from her "desk." She studied her diffused features in its stainless-steel door and tried not to think about the slice of cherry cheesecake inside it.

Fighting off the spike of hunger the thought produced, she reread her notes and made herself think about why her heroine was opposed to this marriage despite the secret attraction she felt to Rory Douglas. Had she been raised like a favored son and was therefore afraid of losing all chance of independence through marriage? Or maybe her mother and her sister had died in childbirth and she feared a similar fate?

This last made her think about Hailey away at college. The journals they'd given each other and what her daughter might have written so far in hers. The look on Hailey's face when Claire had insisted on discussing STDs and birth control.

She forced her gaze back to the screen, but her brain was slow to follow. Plotting was definitely not her strong suit. Maybe she should call Karen or Susie? Or email them to see if they could do a conference call one day this week.

She was back checking email before she realized it. Once she was there, she began to type an email to her critique partners laying out some of the possible scenarios.

"No!" she said aloud even as she got up and walked over to the window so that she could see the traffic moving on Peachtree. "You don't need your critique partners for this. You have a brain. Why don't you try using it before you run to them?"

Leaning into the window, she spotted the big orange CB2 sign a few blocks north. If she took a break she could walk through the store, maybe pick up another desk lamp. This one was definitely not bright enough. She went back to the table and peered at the bulb. It was only a 45-watter.

Except what would she be taking a break *from*?

Back in the chair she reread her notes, added a few

thoughts, then stared out the front window at the bright blue sky.

Maybe Rory was the one who objected to the marriage. Because he thought he wanted a more biddable wife? She groaned aloud and turned her head away so she wouldn't have to look at the big question marks she'd just typed across the screen. A bird sang happily out on the balcony railing. Squinting, she tried to determine what kind it might be. She was still trying to figure this out when it flew away.

Her mind, which appeared to be as reluctant to settle down as the unidentified bird, flitted to last night's screening and the lush beauty of *Downton Abbey*.

Her fingers moved on the keyboard and she was back on Amazon. Big bad Amazon, who was ruining publishing, putting bookstores out of business, and deflating the price of books in general. Not to mention making readers believe that an ebook should cost half as much as a printed book just because it didn't have paper.

Her mental rant didn't prevent her from typing the words "Downton Abbey" into the search box. A book titled *The World of Downton Abbey* popped up. It appeared to be written by Jessica Fellowes, niece of series creator, Julian Fellowes. The hardcover, which had received sixty-seven customer reviews and averaged four and a half stars, had lots of cool photos and background on the series, the time period, and the real stately home, Highclere Castle, where the series was filmed. As she clicked around, Amazon informed her that customers who bought *The World of Downton Abbey* also bought *Lady Almina and the Real Downton Abbey: The Lost Legacy of Highclere Castle*, which was written by the current Countess of Carnarvon about an Edwardian-era Countess of Carnarvon.

Claire's fingers, which once again seemed to be functioning independently of her brain, added them to her cart. Which was when Amazon pointed out that many of the customers who'd bought both of these items also bought the series on DVD.

She could order them right now and watch both previous seasons whenever she wanted. In case she had to miss a Sunday night. Or just couldn't wait a whole week. It would be a treat to watch whenever she felt like it. In fact, she could probably download episodes from iTunes and not even have to wait for the mail. She clicked over to see, and sure enough, there they were.

But it felt like cheating. As if she were reading the last page of a book first instead of reading it in the way that the author intended; something that members of her book club had admitted to doing.

Claire shuddered. *No.*

The Amazon confirmation appeared in her inbox midshudder.

After her mini online-shopping frenzy, she tried to refocus her attention on the new book, but the characters and their motivations continued to elude her. For about thirty minutes she free-typed imagined backstory for both main characters and attempted to decide in whose point of view the book should start. But without her critique partners to bounce ideas off, her brain circled in a nonproductive loop. There was a reason brainstorming was a group activity. Doing it alone was sort of like cheerleading without a game or a crowd—you could shout really loud and jump up and down, but it didn't accomplish much.

At noon she made and gobbled down a PB and J sandwich with a glass of milk, promising herself the cheesecake for that night's dessert. *If* she completed at least the main characters' sketches and committed to those characters' backstories and motivations, she'd allow herself to eat the cheesecake. Yes, that was better. The cheesecake would be her reward.

At two thirty she admitted temporary defeat. Tucking the journal into her bag, she left her apartment with no clear destination in mind. Which was not at all surprising since her mind hadn't been clear about much of anything but *Downton Abbey* for most of the day.

It's all right, she told herself as she walked north on Peachtree where she cruised the aisles of CB2 before making her way toward Piedmont Park. Today might not have been the jackknife off the high dive and into the book that she'd anticipated. But surely now that she was a full-time writer there was nothing wrong with wading in slowly. When you had three-hundred-fifty-plus days of writing time left you didn't have to maximize every available moment of every possible day, right?

She picked up her pace as she entered the park. But even as she sought to reassure herself, one of her critique partner's favorite sayings echoed in her mind: "Writing time is like closet space. The more you have, the less efficiently you use it."

That night, the character sketches unfinished, she ate the cheesecake anyway. Because she could. And because as Scarlett O'Hara so famously pointed out, tomorrow was another day.

DUE TO THE IMPORTANCE OF THE CLIENT BEING wooed, Samantha had arranged an intimate catered dinner served in their dining room instead of at a restaurant or even one of the exclusive clubs to which Jonathan belonged. She would have preferred not to entertain on a Wednesday, which was jammed with committee meetings stacked around the weekly lunch with her mother-in-law, but it was the only night both the coveted client and his wife were in town and free. By the time Samantha got home late that afternoon, fresh flowers had been delivered and the caterer and his staff had begun to set up in the kitchen. She'd just finished dressing when she heard Jonathan arrive. "Be right out," she called as she hurriedly opened the bedroom safe to pull out her jewelry. She was fastening the clasp on her bracelet and holding the pearl necklace Jonathan had given her for their last anniversary as she hurried into the living room. "Do you mind?"

She turned and lifted the hair off her neck. The pearls

were cool and solid against her skin as he hooked the clasp then turned her to face him.

"Ready?" Jonathan asked her when the front desk buzzed up to announce their guests' arrival.

"As I'll ever be." Samantha smoothed a hand down the side of her black cocktail dress.

"How was lunch?" he asked.

"Fine." She dropped her eyes to double-check the drinks cart. She tried to be honest with Jonathan, but she was also careful not to criticize his mother—that was Jonathan's prerogative. She lied only to keep the peace or avoid giving offense. But those lies were small and white.

"I hope you're not letting her push you around . . ."

She'd been no match for her mother-in-law when she was twenty-one and had lost tons of skirmishes and a good number of battles. The only reason Cynthia hadn't won the war she'd waged to dislodge the unsuitable and unwanted daughter-in-law was that Samantha couldn't even consider defeat because she wasn't fighting for creature comforts for herself as her mother-in-law had believed, but for a life and some version of family for her sister and brother.

"Who, me?" Samantha teased looking up into her husband's blue eyes, which could be harsh and commanding like Cynthia's but which could also be far kinder and gentler. His blond hair was sun streaked from the long summer days out at the lake house and the hours on the golf course. His nose was long and aristocratic. A flare of the finely wrought nostrils served as an early warning sign of displeasure. Right now at the end of summer a light smattering of freckles banded the bridge of his nose. She liked the look; it made him so much more approachable. "Not a chance. Well, maybe just enough to keep her happy."

His eyes darkened as he looked down her décolleté. "Maybe the elevator will get caught between floors. Or they'll decide that they'd rather go back to their hotel and have sex than have dinner with us."

She laughed nervously. Despite twenty-five years of sleeping with this man she was still surprised by the visceral reaction his desire caused in her. But then he was the first and only man she'd ever actually had sex with and she supposed it had become a Pavlovian response. "I thought you said they were in their seventies."

"And your point is?" he asked.

The doorbell rang.

As it turned out seventy was apparently not too old at all.

Victoria and Andrew Martin were tall, lean midwesterners with a plainspoken manner and a shared sense of humor. Andrew had made a fortune in newspapers and radio stations and been smart enough to sell his most profitable holdings at the peak, before the new technologies began to supplant the old.

"Have to make way for the new," he said with a smile as they drank cocktails and nibbled on passed hors d'oeuvres. "But I must admit I'm very relieved that I can just enjoy all the new without having to compete with it."

"Andrew's always had impeccable timing," his wife said in an amused, but loving, tone. "He was smart enough to swoop in and convince me to marry him right before he went to Vietnam."

"You have to know when to swoop," Andrew said. "Been married fifty-one years now. When you know something's right you can't waste time dillydallying." Andrew Martin looked at Jonathan. "It seems like you knew the right woman when you met her, too. How long have you two been married?"

"Twenty-five years," Jonathan said.

Samantha shifted uncomfortably in her seat. She suspected their courting and resulting marriage would be a severe disappointment to the Martins, who never seemed to move too far from each other. Even now they were holding hands on the sofa.

"Not everyone's lucky enough to fall in love for a lifetime at such a young age," Victoria said.

"No." Samantha smiled but was careful not to look at Jonathan. "Not everyone's that lucky."

"Well, I know it's an old-fashioned notion." He addressed himself to Samantha. "But I like doing business with people who understand long-term commitments and partnerships. I've been with my old lawyer almost as long as I've been with Vicky." He said his wife's name as if she were still a young girl he couldn't believe his good fortune in snaring. "But the old coot up and died on me. Wasn't all that impressed with his son; the boy's had way too much handed to him. A friend of mine here in Atlanta told me about your husband." He smiled. "I'm glad we found a time for the four of us to get together. I trust Vicky's people instincts. After all, she had the smarts to pick me, right?" He laughed heartily. Vicky rolled her eyes. Samantha wasn't sure she'd ever seen someone in their seventies do that. She tried to picture her mother-in-law doing it and failed miserably.

"Yep. Still can't believe she said yes," Andrew said. "Why, the first time I told her I loved her I was shaking in my boots so hard I was afraid she'd hear my knees knocking. I wasn't absolutely sure that she felt the same way about me."

Jonathan laughed. She watched his face as he shared a story about shaking in his boots the first time he had to argue a case in court and neatly changed the subject. He didn't look at all like what he was: a man who had married someone out of pity and gentlemanliness and without any talk of love at all.

It wasn't that the word had never been used in the ensuing twenty-five years, but it was a word that they used with extreme caution in public and on important birthdates and holidays. Or conversely with no caution; as in right before, during, or after an orgasm, which Samantha suspected shouldn't count at all.

The meal was one of the more pleasant business dinners Samantha could remember. They lingered over coffee and dessert, talking easily. When brandy was poured she found herself remembering how the men at Downton Abbey withdrew from the ladies to go enjoy their brandy and cigars. She could just imagine Victoria Martin's eye roll if anyone in the room were to suggest such a thing.

It was nearly eleven when the door closed behind the Martins.

"I think that went pretty well." The arm Jonathan had slipped around Samantha's waist tightened.

"Yes," she agreed.

He turned her so that he could slip both arms around her waist and draw her closer. His face lowered to hers. "You look great in that dress," he said softly. "But I happen to know you look even better without it."

She felt a tingle go up her spine as he pulled her up against him and reached his hands down to cup her buttocks.

There was the clatter of pots and pans. Voices rose from the kitchen.

"I need to go check on the caterer," she said. "It sounds as if they've packed up. I'm sure he must be ready to go."

He leaned down and brushed his lips across her ear. "To be continued then," he said, sending a shiver over her bare skin. "If you're up for it."

As if she'd ever refuse the prince who'd scaled the tower, slayed the twin dragons of debt and despair, and carried Samantha and her loved ones to safety. Or ever even wanted to.

She sighed when he pressed a kiss to the nape of her neck before straightening.

"I'll be looking forward to it."

CHAPTER TEN

BROOKE HELD A CHILD'S HAND IN EACH OF HERS and Darcy's leash looped around her wrist as they raced toward the Alexander. Everyone but Darcy, who would have clung to each bush and tree if she'd had hands and who had dawdled outside shamelessly, was in dire need of a bathroom.

"Hurry, Mommy!" Natalie cried as they speed walked down Peachtree.

"We're almost there. Hold on!" Brooke moved faster, slightly afraid that Ava's feet were no longer touching the sidewalk. One last tug had Darcy breaking into a trot. Brooke ignored the startled looks of passersby. There were plenty of dogs being walked in Midtown. Young children were more of a rarity, which was something she'd tried to point out to Zachary when he'd fallen in love with the Alexander. "Look! There's Daddy!"

Brooke looked up, surprised. Zachary lounged next to the BMW, which he'd somehow managed to park directly in front of the building. His hair was windblown and his face was sun-kissed. He looked as if he'd just stepped off a golf course, which he probably had.

As she watched, Sarah Grant came out of the building. She hesitated for a moment under the awning, her face ashen. There was a large wet spot on the shirt of her golf ensemble— as if she'd tried to blot or remove a stain. When she spotted Brooke and the girls she moved quickly to Zachary's side. Together Zach and his girlfriend looked like On the Links Barbie and Ken.

She wondered when Zachary had started playing golf on weekdays. As soon as he'd moved out and no longer had to be home for dinner or pretend he was paying attention to his family?

With the smallest of nods to Sarah, Brooke let go of Natalie's hand long enough to thrust Darcy's leash at Zach. "Potty emergency. We'll be right back."

In the lobby they rushed past the security desk and sped toward the restrooms. "We gotted back just in time." Ava looked up at her seriously while Brooke helped her wash her hands. "I almost had a acc'dent."

"I know," Brooke said. "Me, too." She remembered triangulating the distance to the nearest bathroom when they'd been potty training and didn't miss the mental exercise, but she appreciated the lobby restroom almost as much as the beautiful water feature.

"Mommies don't pee in their pants," Natalie chided.

"Well, we try not to," Brooke said. "But everybody has an accident now and then. Nobody's perfect." Unless you were Zach Mackenzie, she thought. Or one of his patients.

She took a minute to finger comb both girls' heavy red hair, which was just as useless as trying to wrest control of her own. Once upon a time Zachary had thought the springy waves of red hair were exotic, but over the years it, like her, had become something that needed to be controlled. "Let's go get your bag at the concierge desk. I'll pick you up tomorrow after school for ballet class. Okay?"

At the desk the young Isabella pulled out their overnight bag and handed it to Brooke. "'Ow's it goin' then, m'lady?" she asked Brooke with an unservantlike grin. "I'm workin' on me accent in case I gets to 'elp out on Sunday night again."

"Yes, very . . . good," Brooke said. The young woman's earnestness made laughing out of the question.

"I asked the guhv'nor if I should wear the maid's costume more regular-like to get into me character, but he said no."

"Really?" Brooke smiled. She could only imagine the other residents' surprise if Isabella began to show for her shift dressed like an English house servant of a hundred years ago.

There was a "woof" and the sound of footsteps approaching. Zachary accepted a hug from each of the girls, but his gaze was fixed on Brooke. "I wanted to let you know that I'm going to start taking the girls on Sunday nights." He was not asking.

"But you're supposed to have them every other weekend for the whole weekend."

"Sundays are better for me," he said.

And Sarah, Brooke thought even as she swallowed the words. She did not want to argue with him in front of Natalie and Ava. Taking them every Sunday was better than *not* taking them for two whole weekends a month. The main thing was that the girls spent time with their father.

"Fine," she said. "Did you bring the maintenance check?" It was as always embarrassingly overdue.

"I figured you'd already paid it and I'd reimburse you later."

"I can't, Zachary." Her account had exactly three hundred dollars in it, not even enough for an emergency should it arrive. The only payments that happened regularly and on time were those that went through the court. Everything else depended on Zachary's conscience, which seemed to have shriveled to the size of a pea. "I don't have enough money to 'front' what you owe."

"The condo *is* expensive to keep up, Brooke." He said this as if this might be news to her.

"That didn't seem to be a problem when you decided on this building. Or when you were living here."

"I wasn't running two establishments," he replied.

This of course was not her problem, or shouldn't be. "That was your choice, not mine," she said, as she had so many times before. She cast an eye down at the girls to try to gauge how intently they might be listening. "And there's really nothing to discuss." Her hand tightened on the leash. She did not want to have this conversation in front of the girls, had vowed she wouldn't drag them into the middle of the discord between her and Zachary, but she couldn't bear to let him twist everything this way. "I had two and three jobs at a time while I was putting you through medical school. Remember? That was one of the reasons the judge thought it was your turn now." Brooke's attorney had warned her that male judges were sometimes biased toward the husband in divorce proceedings. Judge Walton had been decisive and fair, but over the last six months, she'd learned that what you were awarded and what actually arrived each month were often different things.

"The settlement stipulates that the girls will continue to live in the home they know. The home you insisted they live in." Her jaw was tight, her teeth clenched in an effort to stay calm.

"I know you never really wanted to live here, Brooke," he said in a conciliatory tone that surprised her. "But I do. And so does Sarah." He threw this last comment out as if it were incidental and not, as she was now beginning to realize, the whole reason they were having this conversation. "If I took over the condo, the girls would still have their own rooms."

Brooke flushed with anger. This was going too far, even for Zachary.

"No," she said clearly, and she hoped, calmly. The blood rushing to her head made it hard to tell for sure. "I'm not giving up the condo so that Natalie and Ava can come sleep in their rooms on those rare occasions when they actually get to visit you."

"But you can't really afford to stay in it, can you?" he asked again.

"I can if you do what you're morally, ethically, and legally obligated to do," she replied through still-clenched teeth. Her head began to throb. She still couldn't believe that after all the years as the family breadwinner, when she had treated every penny she'd earned as "theirs" that Zachary now held on to every penny he was supposed to give her as if it were his last.

"I'd give you current fair market value for it," Zach said. "Then you could buy a little house somewhere like you always said you wanted."

She looked at this man whom she had once loved beyond all reason. And who had turned out to have the moral fiber of a gnat.

"I can't believe you would even suggest this," she said. "The real estate market here is nowhere near a recovery, as you've pointed out on endless occasions. Our unit is worth half of what it was when we bought it. And even if I wanted to sell, I'd never sell it to you and that Barbie doll you created. Never." She would burn down the whole building before she let Sarah Grant live in their condo with Zachary. Better yet she'd go out and get a job to pay for maintenance fees and all the other things that Zachary used in order to manipulate her.

The click of heels on marble reminded her that they were in the middle of the lobby. She looked at her children's faces and knew that although they might not have followed all that had been said, she shouldn't have allowed them to overhear it.

"Oh, 'ello, Mrs. Davis, mum." Isabella's voice reached them from the other side of the lobby.

Brooke turned at Isabella's greeting and saw Samantha Davis smile pleasantly at the girl as she breezed by the concierge desk. Brooke and Samantha's eyes met and Brooke offered the closest thing to a polite smile she could muster, fully expecting the woman to offer a regal nod as she passed.

Instead Samantha Davis walked over to them. "Hello, Brooke," she said pleasantly. "How are you?"

"Um, fine. Thanks. How about you?"

"Good."

There was an awkward silence. Beside her, Brooke could feel Zachary waiting to be introduced or at least noticed, but Samantha Davis had already turned her attention to the girls. She leaned down and put out a hand to Natalie. "I'm Samantha, what's your name?"

"Natalie." The seven-year-old's chubby hand slipped into Samantha's as she'd been taught.

"Well, it's very nice to meet you," Samantha replied, shaking her hand. "Your mommy and I watched a movie together the other night." Brooke was relieved there was no mention of their first meeting in the fitness room; something she was still trying to erase from her memory banks.

"I'm Ava." Never one to be overlooked, Ava extended her hand toward Samantha Davis.

"Do you have any little girls for us to play with?"

The look that passed over Samantha Davis's face was gone in an instant. "I'm afraid not. But I have a sister just like you do. Well, she's a good thirty years or so older than you are now." She turned to Natalie. "Big sisters need to look out for their little sisters."

"Uh-huh." Natalie nodded. "Except for when they're being 'noxious."

"Ah, but that's when they need looking after the most," Samantha said.

Natalie looked skeptical.

"You sound like you have some experience with that," Brooke said, still unsure why Samantha Davis hadn't departed as soon as she'd displayed her good manners.

"I do," Samantha replied.

Zachary inserted himself into the silence that followed. "Hello." He gave Samantha the big white-toothed smile that he reserved for the wealthiest and most influential clients.

Like Sarah Grant. He stuck out his hand. "*Doctor* Zachary Mackenzie."

Samantha placed her hand in his and allowed him to shake it. "Is this your husband?" she asked Brooke.

"Oh, no!" Zachary said before Brooke could speak. He used the dismissive tone that now seemed attached to even a mention of Brooke. "Well, not anymore." His relief at not having to claim her was excruciatingly obvious. "We're divorced."

"Oh." The brunette's expression turned cool. Any hint of the warmth she'd shown Brooke and the girls disappeared. "Samantha Davis." She retrieved her hand and turned back to Brooke.

Shocked surprise at the slight flashed across Zachary's face; the sight warmed the cockles of Brooke's heart.

"Are you going to the screening Sunday night?" Brooke asked Samantha.

"I'm not sure. But I have to say I really loved the first program."

"Me, too," Brooke replied.

"I thought they did a good job with the whole *Titanic* thing," Samantha said.

"Yes." Brooke had no idea what else there was to say. She'd cried in front of this woman and sat through an hour television show with her. Other than that she didn't see that they had much of anything in common. But she absolutely loved the way Samantha had cut Zach out of the conversation.

"Well, I'm afraid I really have to be going." Continuing to ignore Zachary, Samantha gave Brooke a quick hug and said good-bye to the girls. All of them watched her leave.

"Good God, that's Jonathan Davis's wife. How in the world do you know *her*?" Zachary asked.

Brooke shrugged, embarrassed by the way he'd fawned over Samantha while managing to distance himself from her. "We've run into each other a few times in the building."

"It figures that you'd start meeting the right people *now*," he said. "Maybe you could tell her a little bit about my practice." He reached in his pocket and pulled out a small stack of business cards. "She could help me tap into a whole new level of clientele."

She stared at her former husband, appalled. If she hadn't been willing to be surgically altered to advertise for him while they were married, why on earth would she want to shill for him now? Was it possible he hadn't registered how completely Samantha Davis had dismissed him? "I barely know her, Zach."

"She hugged you." It was clear he still couldn't believe it. "She knows you well enough to hug you." He shook his head baffled.

"I'm sure she was just being polite," Brooke said. But Samantha had only been polite to Brooke and the girls. Not to Zachary. This made her smile.

Natalie reached out and tugged on her father's hand. "C'mon, Daddy. I'm hungry."

"Me, too!" Ava added.

Darcy woofed.

"You better get going." Brooke leaned down to kiss the girls. "Have fun. I'll see you two tomorrow."

Brooke watched them go, then wrapped the leash handle more tightly around her hand. "What do you say, Darcy? I bet you're hungry, too. Let's go up and have dinner." As she walked the dog to the elevator she realized that she felt far less bruised than she usually did after an encounter with her ex-husband. She'd nipped his condo takeover idea in the bud—at least she hoped she had. And then she'd gotten to watch Samantha Davis put him in his place. What a pleasant change to have someone on her "side." Someone who seemed able to see Zachary for what he was. And didn't seem to only see Brooke for what she was not.

With a small but satisfied smile, Brooke deposited the stack of *Doctor* Zachary Mackenzie's business cards in the trash can and stepped into the waiting elevator.

* * *

"PRIVATE BUTLER." EDWARD PARKER ANSWERED HIS
phone and leaned back in his chair. A few seconds later he
propped his feet up on the desk, ankles crossed. He wasn't
due at the Alexander until later in the afternoon. Mornings
spent at his home office were decidedly less formal. "This is
Edward. How may I help you?"

The man's voice was deep, but his tone was tentative. "I
have to put on a birthday party and I'm . . . well, I'm, I think
I need some help."

Edward smiled. For so many men doing for others was
surprisingly intimidating. "Do you need help with the planning, the guest list, or the implementation?"

"Yes."

"All right then." Once Edward might have said that they
weren't really party planners, but the company tagline was
"Making your life more civilized, whatever it takes." He'd
discovered that what it took varied almost as much as each
person's definition of what was civilized.

Edward pulled a yellow pad in front of him and uncapped
his pen. "What can you tell me about the person for whom
you're planning the event? Do you have a theme and location
in mind?"

"She's turning six," the potential client said. "It's her
birthday. I'm thinking the backyard?" The question in his
voice made it seem that all of these things were up for nego-
tiation.

"I see." This was Edward's best fall-back-and-regroup line.
He'd learned it when he was a young trainee. It was used
primarily in situations where he didn't yet see at all.

"My wife used to handle all of this. But we're . . ." There
was a long pause in which Edward silently filled in the word
"divorced." But the man said, "I'm . . . she's . . . she died."

"Oh, I'm so sorry," Edward said, meaning it. He could
actually hear the pain in the man's voice.

"Yes. Thanks." Another pause and then, "So can you organize it?"

"I'm sure one of our staff can handle this for you, Mr. . . ."

"Dalton. Bruce Dalton."

"Let me take down a few particulars, Mr. Dalton, and then I'll schedule an appointment for a meeting between you and the staff member I assign. He or she will work on an hourly rate plus cost of materials and so on." He began to search through available freelancers and part-time staff in his mind. This wasn't their usual kind of request. But then he made a growing living out of unusual requests.

"Good. Fine. Whatever it takes," Bruce Dalton said. There was another pause. "The thing is I kind of suck at this sort of thing. And my daughter's been through a lot and I, well, I really don't want to disappoint her."

"I understand," Edward said. "We all have different strengths and weaknesses."

"Right. But it's one thing to suck at, say, your short game on the golf course. Or maybe power point presentations aren't your specialty. But it's a whole other thing to suck at making your motherless child happy."

"Yes, I can certainly understand that," Edward said, already considering and rejecting people he might assign to the project.

"I don't mind spending money," Dalton said. "But I don't want this to be too slick, you know? I want something that feels like a real mother might do for her six-year-old daughter." He hesitated. "Do kids still play things like pin the tail on the donkey? Or drop clothespins into milk bottles?"

"I haven't actually seen a milk bottle in many years, Mr. Dalton." He wrote down two names and scratched them out. They'd been born too long after wooden clothespins and delivered milk to even know what he was talking about.

"But you know what I mean," Bruce Dalton pressed.

"Yes," Edward said. "I believe I do."

CHAPTER ELEVEN

❧❧❧

T HE PHONE LINE TO ENGLAND WAS SO CLEAR
that Edward imagined he could hear the ducks quacking in the pond that separated his great-uncle Mason's cottage from the Hungry Fox.

"So how's it going, my boy?" Mason asked. "How'd the video go?"

"It actually went even better than I expected," Edward replied. "Of course, I had to coerce people into coming. I may have dragged one or two by the scruff of the neck. But we had a good dozen and I've had several residents ask to view the first program so that they could join in on Sunday."

"Well done. You know, if you'd like to skip right ahead and give them the big payoff, the third season's showing here right now. I could fill you in on each episode or send you a bootlegged copy. One of your nephews could probably do something through the Internet or some such."

"There's no way I'm going to spoil the buildup or the anticipation, here," Edward said. "And I must say I'm shocked and horrified that any Parker would even consider such a thing," he teased.

"So you're claiming you're not even tempted to see Shirley MacLaine take on Maggie Smith?"

"Not even a little bit," Edward replied, though this was not completely true.

"Well, if you change your mind all you have to do is let me know," his great-uncle said.

Edward smiled. It would serve the old man right if he said yes. His great-uncle wasn't exactly a techno whiz. In fact, he considered email similar to a phone call and could never quite understand why when he managed to send one, Edward didn't pick up and answer.

"And how's the business?" Mason asked.

"Good," Edward replied. "Actually better than I expected there, too."

"Well, then it seems to me you need to be raising up your expectations so you won't be so surprised." His uncle gave a small bark of laughter. "I knew you'd make a go of it. Even if you did put my dear departed brother on the logo instead of me."

"You were twins," Edward pointed out as he always did. Mason and Edward's grandfather, William, had never lived or worked more than a stone's throw away from each other. The loss of his twin had been a heavy one. "It could be you. I've told you, you can tell people it's you."

"But it isn't," Mason said.

"Right," Edward agreed as he always did. "So as I was saying, Private Butler is doing well. In fact, so well that the freelancers I've trained and trust are getting spread a bit thin." He thought about the call from Bruce Dalton. "Plus I've been getting requests that are a little more challenging than the usual." He told his great-uncle about the birthday party his new client was looking for. He couldn't really see the more staid members of his staff loosening up enough to handle a child's birthday party with or without clothespins. And he wasn't sure he wanted to send Isabella Morales and her unwieldy British accent into a crush of five- and six-year-olds.

"All the better for proving your mettle and resourcefulness, Edward. Remember discretion . . . persistence . . . valor. These will always win the day."

"Yes." Edward agreed, though he wasn't sure how these attributes were going to find him the right person to handle a panicked widower with a nostalgic bent. "They're definitely words to live by."

"Of course, they are," Mason said. "But at the moment it seems to me we might need to add another word or two into the mix. I'm thinking creativity and originality would serve you well."

"Oh?" Edward smiled at the ring of certainty in his great-uncle's voice. Mason had always been the ebullient and enthusiastic twin; William had been quieter and steadier, the ballast that stabilized his brother's quick-sailing ship.

"There's a saying in your adopted country that I quite like and that I think sums the situation up nicely," Mason concluded. "I think the time has come, Edward, for you to begin to 'think outside the box.'"

FOR CLAIRE, WHO'D BEEN PRETENDING TO BE PRO-ductive for much of the morning, the ring of her doorbell felt like a reprieve from the governor. She was so grateful for the interruption—honestly she would have greeted Attila the Hun with a kiss to each cheek—that she practically skipped to the front door. Without the slightest peep through the peephole, she threw the door open. James, the part-timer who'd been dressed as a footman at the *Downton Abbey* screening, stood on her doorstep, a package in his hands.

"Mr. Parker told me to bring this right up because, well, it's from Amazon and you're a writer and everything." He looked down at his shiny shoes for a moment. "He thought it might be important. You know for your research or something."

"Thank you." She took the proffered package. "I've been waiting for this," Claire said though a truer statement would have been "I've been waiting for anything that would allow me to stop pretending I'm working."

"Thank you so much," she said to James.

"A pleasure, ma'am." He tipped his hat and turned.

She stood in the doorway watching him walk back toward the elevator. Now that she'd gotten up, it would take a whip and chair to get her back to her desk, where she'd be forced to confront her lack of progress. She still couldn't understand how she could have been writing full-time for almost two weeks now and have so little to show for it. Oh, she had scribbled notes and stray character thoughts and ideas, but the elements of the book she was supposed to write kept swirling, none of them grabbing hold. It was like walking into a department store packed with too much fabulous clothing; it was possible a lot of it might look good on you. If only you could figure out what to try on.

James gave her a little wave before he stepped onto the elevator. Claire forced herself back inside where she set the unopened package on the kitchen counter—far enough away not to rip it open as she wanted to—but in her line of sight so that it could serve as motivation. When she was finished working she'd let herself open it and maybe read a few pages of one of the *Downton Abbey* books over lunch. But how would she know when she was finished when she couldn't seem to get started?

Panic welled inside her. She beat it back by wrapping her fingers around the mouse. Before she could stop herself she was clicking onto Facebook where she posted an update about how excited she was to be starting a new novel.

Liar.

Then she did the same on Twitter after retweeting about

another writer's new release. Her publisher wanted her to use social media to connect with readers, so this was working, right?

Liar, liar, pants on fire.

Quick forays to Amazon and BN.com to check her numbers followed. An email from her editor's assistant asking for a new bio arrived—she saw it the moment it appeared in her new mail folder even without the usual ding—and she spent fifteen minutes writing one and then twenty more tweaking and tightening it. She waited ten more minutes before sending it because she didn't want to look as if she were just sitting here, staring at the screen, with the time to jump on any query or request the moment it came in.

Scrolling down, Claire saw that chapters had arrived from Susie and Karen. Which meant both of them were actually writing and producing.

With a groan she got up and went out on the balcony and stared out over the railing. It was warm, but the heat and humidity had cut back a notch. A slight breeze stirred the branches of a nearby tree. Banners advertising a new exhibit at the nearby High Museum fluttered.

Maybe she should take a walk. Or maybe she should go ahead and check out the exhibit and then go out for lunch. Any or all of these things might jump-start her brain, get her juices flowing. It was called "filling the well." Writers talked about this all the time. She'd read lots of articles that pointed out how important it was for creative people to have experiences, to live life fully. Maybe her well was just empty and needed refilling? Were there dipsticks for measuring this? If she showed up at the museum, would someone say, "Sorry, ma'am, but you're down a quart?" Or, "Good thing you came in when you did. Your well is dangerously low. Hang on just a minute and we'll fill it up."

Except that she'd barely had a minute to breathe or put food in her mouth, let alone refill her well for years and had managed to write just fine. "This is not about your well," she said aloud. But the words faded into the breeze and disappeared.

"Fine." Not even aware she'd made a decision, Claire went inside, washed her face, and brushed on mascara and lipstick. Sneakers laced, she closed the laptop, straightened her notes and then, like an alcoholic giving in to the bottle or a dieter reaching for the hidden candy bar, she ripped open the Amazon box. Inhaling the delicious new-book smell, she ran a hand over the glossy hardcover copy of *The World of Downton Abbey* and the smaller paperback *Lady Almina and the Real Downton Abbey*. Slipping the paperback into her cross-body bag, she left the condo and walked to the elevator. Her sigh of relief was covered by the ding of its arrival.

In the coffee shop next door, Claire spotted Brooke Mackenzie at a small table near the window. The redhead had a newspaper folded in front of her and a pen in her hand. Claire was debating whether to greet Brooke or walk to the counter when the younger woman raised her head and spotted her. A shy smile tugged tenuously at her lips. Unable to ignore anything that seemed to require that much effort, Claire walked over to her.

"Would you like to join me?" Brooke asked, the smile wavering on her lips.

"Sure, thanks." Claire sat down and removed her bag. When the waitress appeared Claire ordered a Diet Coke. "What are you reading?" Claire nodded to the newspaper.

"The want ads," Brooke said.

"Ahhh." Claire didn't want to pry, but the redhead didn't look or sound at all happy about the idea. "Are you looking for anything in particular?"

"Not really." Brooke set the pencil down. "Something that I can do part-time around the girls' school and after-school schedules. You know, something flexible."

Claire's drink arrived and she took a long sip. "I know what you mean. I worked multiple jobs while Hailey was growing up, depending on what we needed. My ex paid child support, mostly, but we were married such a short time and all that I didn't ask for alimony."

"Really?" Brooke asked.

"Well, I was the one who wanted out, so I felt like I couldn't ask for too much, you know?" Claire said. "How about you?"

"I wasn't the one who wanted out, if that's what you mean. And it's not like I never worked. I put my husband—or rather my ex-husband—through medical school. And setting up his practice."

"Wow." Claire could see the anger and hurt that clouded Brooke's eyes.

"Yeah," Brooke said. "But we were up in Boston and my parents and sister were there, so I had child care covered. Here it's just me. And Zach when he remembers or feels like it." She took a deep breath like she was trying to calm herself down. Claire remembered all too well how that kind of anxiety felt.

"I know how hard it is to do it alone," Claire said. "I was an office manager at a communications firm for a lot of years, but I took a lot of extra small jobs to supplement. I even delivered pizzas for a while." This had ended when she'd seen the discomfort on the faces of Hailey's friends' mothers on the occasions when she'd arrived at their doors with their pepperoni pizzas and wings. Every Christmas season she'd worked as many evening and weekend hours as she could get. "I sleepwalked through a lot of those years. But Hailey and I always had each other. I'm not sure who raised whom."

"Is it true you're a writer?" Brooke asked.

"Well, I did manage to write and publish two novels," Claire said. "But I didn't do it particularly quickly."

"I think it's a miracle you did it at all," Brooke said. "Single mother or not. Are you still writing?"

"Yes." Or she would be soon. "In fact, this is supposed to be my year of writing full-time."

"That's so cool," Brooke said. "Am I allowed to ask what you're working on?"

"You are," Claire said, almost embarrassed by how much more enjoyable it felt to talk about the book than try to write it. "I write historical romance—both of my books were set in seventeenth-century Scotland and so is my new one. It's about a hero and heroine whose parents have pledged them to each other but who realize they don't want to get married."

She watched Brooke Mackenzie's eyes for a reaction to the story pitch/blurb and was gratified and relieved to see her hazel eyes light with interest.

"That sounds cool," Brooke said. She leaned forward. "Why don't they want to get married?"

If Claire knew the answer to that question, she would be up in her condo right now typing her heart out. It took all she had not to ask Brooke what *she* thought should keep them apart. Claire shifted uneasily in her seat. "Well, I'm still trying to nail down the story details," she said, as if this were not a problem.

Brooke watched her for a long moment as if waiting for more, but Claire had nothing else to offer.

"So was Hailey's father involved in her life?" Brooke finally asked. "I mean, if you don't mind my asking?"

"He was. In his way." Claire knew this was a nonanswer, but Daniel Walker's approach to parenting and responsibility were even harder to explain than her writing or lack thereof.

Brooke twirled the pen on the paper but made no move to pick it up. "Zachary only takes the girls when his girlfriend has her son. He's so far removed from the man he was when I married him I hardly know who I'm talking to anymore."

"People change," Claire said. "And not always for the better."

"That's for sure," Brooke replied. "But it really, really sucks."

"I know." Claire looked at the redhead, who'd let go of the pen and was now fingering a long red curl uncertainly. "Look," Claire said surprising both of them. "I know your girls don't really know me, but if you need help—well, I'm in the building and I'm sure I could do in a pinch."

Brooke's eyes glistened and Claire was afraid the woman was going to cry. "Thanks. I really appreciate it."

"No problem," Claire said, fiddling with her straw as a silence fell between them.

Brooke finished her coffee. "Will you be at the screening Sunday night?" she asked.

"I think so," Claire said. "My daughter's trying to manage my life from school in Chicago. She threatened me with dire consequences if I don't attend."

"How dire?"

"She threatened to post my profile to all the online dating sites. I'm just a mouse click away from the new version of the blind date."

Brooke laughed. It changed her face completely.

"I'm not planning to let her know how much I enjoyed the screening. I probably would have gone back even without the threats." Claire finished off her Diet Coke. "To tell you the truth, I can't wait to see what happens when the Crawleys show up at Downton Abbey. How about you?"

"It looks like Zach will be taking the girls on Sunday nights, so I'm in." Brooke leaned forward. "Do you think Samantha will be there?"

"I don't know. She seemed kind of into it, but I'm guessing she has a pretty packed social life already."

By unspoken agreement they paid their checks and prepared to leave. "I feel kind of bad for calling her a rich bitch," Brooke said. "I mean she is rich, at least according to my ex-husband who seems to know these things, but she's a lot nicer than I expected."

"Yeah," Claire said though she was still reserving judgment. "I guess she didn't seem quite as hoity-toity as she looks."

Out on the sidewalk they said good-bye and headed their separate ways. As she walked north on Peachtree, Claire chewed over the fact that Brooke Mackenzie's life was far more complicated than she'd suspected. Which meant there was every chance that there was also more to Samantha Davis than expensive clothes, a posh southern accent, and a wealthy husband.

CHAPTER TWELVE

AH, MR. AND MRS. DAVIS," EDWARD PARKER SAID
with a nod of his head. "How are you this fine Sunday
afternoon?"

Samantha and Jonathan had just returned from eighteen
holes of golf and had only an hour or so before they were to
report to Bellewood for Cynthia's semi-regular weekly Sunday supper.

"Good, Edward." Jonathan smiled easily at the concierge.
"Anytime I'm three strokes or more under par is a good
afternoon."

Samantha considered her husband. Even after all these
years she couldn't understand how he'd turned out so polished but with none of his parents' superciliousness. He
expected and received white-glove treatment in almost every
aspect of his life, and therefore never seemed to have to
demand it.

"And you, Mrs. Davis?" Edward asked. "Did the greens
roll your way?"

"Oh, I squeak by."

"She underrates herself," Jonathan said. "Her short game is very impressive."

Samantha held back a laugh. She played golf because her husband asked her to. And she'd managed to achieve a level of competency that allowed her to avoid embarrassment. When he was in town, Jonathan played in a regular Saturday morning foursome. On Sundays the two of them often did brunch at the club followed by a round of golf together. Samantha played in the occasional charity tournament or when a client wanted to bring his wife along. It could be amusing to play when they traveled. But Samantha could not remember ever waking up in the morning eager to go play golf.

"And will you be able to join us for our *Downton Abbey* screening this evening?" Edward asked Samantha.

"Oh, I don't think so, Edward," Samantha replied. "I only came last week because Jonathan was out of town." And because the concierge had refused to let her off the hook.

"What's *Downton Abbey*?" Jonathan asked.

"It's a television series," she said. "From Britain. Edward has started screenings of the first two seasons in anticipation of season three here in the States in January."

"Oh?" Jonathan asked.

"Yes, it's set in this fabulous castle in the English countryside. It's a very elaborately done soap opera with enough history thrown in to make you feel virtuous," Samantha said, surprised at the enthusiasm she heard in her voice.

"There was quite a nice turnout for the first episode," Edward said.

"It was fun," Samantha conceded. "We had an upstairs maid and a footman serving wine and snacks. And biscuits for dessert."

"What you would call cookies," Edward explained to Jonathan.

"It does sound like fun. You should go," Jonathan said to her.

"Oh, no, I don't see how. I mean we're expected at your mother's." The only cloud on the Sunday horizon. "You know how she looks forward to seeing you. I mean, us."

"I imagine something could be arranged," Jonathan said, his lips quirking. "Unless of course you'd *rather* go to Bellewood?"

Samantha schooled her features. "I didn't say that. I mean I don't . . ." Her voice trailed off. If Jonathan had been her savior, his mother had been her penance. "I mean I know I'm expected," she said. Like death, taxes, and Wednesday lunches, Sunday supper at Bellewood was something that rolled inexorably around.

"Yes, well. If you're able to work it out, I know we'd all like for you to join us, Mrs. Davis," Edward said. "I was very glad to have a board member present last week and would love for that to continue." He nodded and smiled pleasantly. "If you'll excuse me?" With a nod, the concierge headed toward the security desk.

Samantha and Jonathan walked to the elevator. When they were inside he said, "You know, I've been trying to think of a way to give Mother a little more of my time. Maybe we should change things up a little. Representing the condo board is a valid commitment, which I'm sure she'd understand. Besides you already see her for lunch every week." He fixed his gaze on hers. "How do you think she'd feel about spending Sunday evenings just with me? Just until the screenings are over?" he asked as they exited the elevator.

"Seriously?" Cynthia Davis would probably be turning cartwheels at the thought. If it wouldn't have shocked Jonathan to the core, Samantha might have done a few down the newly re-carpeted hall herself even at the idea of being excused from the formal Sunday meal in the dining room that was far too large for the three of them.

"I'm sure she'd love some time alone with you," Samantha said carefully. Cynthia would have the best of all possible worlds—her son to herself and a legitimate excuse to criticize her daughter-in-law. "But I wouldn't want her to think that I'm avoiding her." She waited while he put a key in the lock and pushed the front door open.

"I'll take care of it," Jonathan said, following her into the condo, through the kitchen, and back into the bedroom. "I'll tell her it was my idea and I had to talk you into it."

She looked at her husband in admiration. "You can be so Machiavellian."

"I've got some skills. But I try not to use them for evil." He shucked off his golf clothes and reached into the two-person shower to turn on the water. Her eyes strayed to his wide shoulders, then skimmed down to his trim hips and muscled thighs. He turned and caught her looking. His blue eyes darkened.

"Here, let me help you." His sure fingers unbuttoned her golf shirt, then moved to the waistband of her shorts. A moment later she was down to her bra and panties. "There. Much better." He unhooked her bra and cupped a breast, skimming the pad of his thumb across her nipple.

Samantha shivered as he removed the rest of her clothing. Sunlight penetrated the clerestory windows and streaked across their naked bodies. "It's the middle of the afternoon," she said, feeling deliciously wicked.

"I know." His lips passed over her bare shoulder on their way to the nape of her neck.

"You'll be late for supper," she protested as he brought his lips down on hers and pulled her tight against him.

"She'll forgive me," he murmured against her lips. "And it's not like I can go there without showering first."

She didn't understand how he turned her on so easily; a look, a touch—sometimes that was all it took. Was it his knowledge of her body that gave him this power? Or was she simply conditioned to respond to him? She didn't know. At the moment she didn't care.

"Come on." His voice turned husky as he took her hand and led her into the shower. Steamy heat enveloped them.

Water sluiced down their bodies, turning them slick and wet. "Come here." He pulled her up against him. "I'll scrub your back if you scrub mine."

BROOKE COULD HARDLY BELIEVE HOW MUCH SHE was looking forward to that night's screening of *Downton Abbey*. For the first time since Zachary had moved out, she had something she wanted to do and people she wanted to do it with.

She made a salad for dinner, picked up the girls' rooms, then adjourned to the large walk-in closet where she contemplated the sparsely filled space. Her clothes were few and chosen for serviceability; things that didn't wrinkle or require too much thought or maintenance. Zachary had been the clotheshorse and she'd had no problem with him taking up more than half of the considerable closet space. He'd believed that clothes could, in fact, make the man. And said repeatedly that you only got one chance to make a first impression. Which was, after all, what plastic surgery was all about.

She frowned as she noticed not just how few things there were but how beige those things seemed. Once she'd loved bright colors accented with bold blacks and whites. Somewhere along the way she'd begun to gravitate toward what she'd at first called earth tones, but which actually turned out to be various shades of beige and brown. The boldest thing in her closet was a brown-and-beige striped shirtwaist. She put it on, trying not to look at the way the fabric strained across the bust and waist. In the bathroom she applied more makeup than she'd worn in the last month to no discernible effect—she could still see every freckle that dappled her face. "Oh, stop," she said to herself. "No one's going to be looking at you anyway. You're going to go, watch the program, and leave." But she hoped Claire Walker would be there so she'd have someone to sit with.

Not wanting to be the first to arrive, she watched the

clock and waited until exactly eight o'clock before taking the elevator to the clubroom. Hand on knob, she drew a deep breath and squared her shoulders. "There's nothing to be afraid of," she reminded herself. "You live here just like everyone else. All you have to do is smile, eat some popcorn, have a drink, and watch *Downton Abbey*." Despite the pep talk, she suspected that if Callan and Logan Ritchie and their mother, Rebecca, hadn't come up behind her and swept her inside with them, she might have turned and fled.

Edward Parker stood just inside near the bar and food table. The popcorn machine was frantically popping and the smell of fresh buttered popcorn reached her nose. Bags stood at the ready. Appetizers she didn't recognize had been laid out on the table.

"Welcome, Mrs. Mackenzie. I'm so glad you could make it."

Brooke smiled at the concierge. "I'm glad to be here. What is that Isabella is dishing up?"

"Angels on horseback—those are oysters wrapped in bacon. We also have miniature Cornish pasties—a pastry shell filled with meat, potato, and onion along with a bit of rutabaga. In their full size they're a meal all wrapped in one. James is serving shandies tonight—a mixture of lager and lemonade that I think you'll enjoy. I hope you'll give everything a try."

"Absolutely." Ignoring the feel of the too-tight dress that encased her, she stepped up to the table.

"'Ello, Miz Mackenzie, 'ows ya 'angin'?" Isabella asked brightly as she handed Brooke a plate of hors d' oeuvres.

Edward winced, but his smile didn't waver. "A shandy for Mrs. Mackenzie, please, James."

James, apparently content with a nonspeaking role, gave her a friendly nod and began to pour. When Brooke looked up from her glass she noticed that the concierge was studying her intently. He turned when the door opened. Sadie Hopewell and her neighbor Myra Mackelbaum arrived. Mimi

Davenport stepped in right behind them. Diamonds sparkled
on her fingers and at her throat.

"Ah, ladies, welcome." Edward reintroduced Brooke. "You
look lovely tonight, Mrs. Davenport. Very sparkly."

"Why, thank you, Edward," the woman drawled. "But
I've told you to call me Mimi," the petite woman said with
a coquettish smile at the concierge. She offered Brooke a
smile. "Very nice to see you again," the woman said in a blur
of long vowels and consonants.

"We'll get started in about ten minutes," Edward said to
both of them. "So do try the food and drink."

The professors Melinda and Diana arrived as did the
nurse, Anna. As he had with the others, Edward greeted each
new arrival, escorted them to the food and drink, and reintroduced everyone, initiating conversation. The noise level
began to rise. Brooke had finished the appetizers and her
shandy was almost gone. She was weighing the advisability
of having another when Claire Walker arrived. Brooke felt
her shoulders relax as the woman walked toward her.

"I thought you'd decided not to come," Brooke said.

"And end up plastered over every dating site known to
man?" Claire laughed. "No, there's just something about
living so close that makes me think there's no rush. I'm just
down the hall, so I figured I had plenty of time. What are
you drinking?"

"It's a shandy." Brooke held up her empty glass. "It's a
combination of lager and lemonade."

"Really?" Claire wrinkled her nose. "I'm not a big beer
drinker."

"Me, neither, but it's pretty good," Brooke said. "Light
and tart. I could hardly taste the beer."

"Sounds . . . interesting."

They walked to the bar together. James served them with
his sweet smile and nod. Raising their glasses in salute, they
drank.

"Ummm, that is good," Claire said.

"Yeah, you don't want to miss the Cornish pasties or the angels on horseback, either."

Claire smiled. "This just gets better and better." Her glass empty, she held it out to James for a refill. Without asking she took Brooke's glass and set it in front of him then accepted a plate of hors d'oeuvres from Isabella.

"'Ave to pace yourself, mum," Isabella said with a curtsy. "The drink packs a bigger wollop than ye might think."

Brooke laughed. "Thanks for the warning, but it looks like we're both having another one."

"Damn straight." Claire raised her glass and clinked it against Brooke's. "Let the mingling begin."

Edward left them to their own devices, only stepping in to facilitate a conversation or to draw someone on the fringes into the group.

The decibel level was nearing a dull roar when he stepped up in front of the big-screen TV. "Ladies," he shouted with a smile. "We're about to get started. The bar will remain open, but there's no intermission planned, so you might want to take care of refills now."

Still chattering, women began to make their way to sofas and chairs. Samantha Davis entered, her face aglow, her hair artfully blown-dry, her form-fitting T-shirt tucked into skinny jeans that rode low on her slim hips. She looked so perfect— so not in need of Zachary's services—that some of Brooke's sense of well-being fled. Out of the corner of her eye, Brooke watched her accept the concierge's effusive greeting and a drink from James. Instead of hot appetizers, she took a bag of popcorn from Isabella and began to scan the crowd. When she spotted Brooke and Claire, she smiled and headed their way.

"Hi," she said, stopping in front of them. "How are ya'll doing?"

"Good," Brooke said.

"Better," Claire said raising her glass in silent toast.

Samantha took a first tip of her drink. "Wow. I see what you mean."

Claire smiled. "If I hadn't seen James mix this, I would have sworn there was no alcohol in it." She took another long sip. "I don't know why I haven't had one of these before. It's pure genius."

"Genius," Samantha agreed, also taking a sip. "Where are we sitting?"

Brooke looked at her in surprise as Claire nodded toward the front of the room. "It looks like 'our' sofa is free," she said, leading the way.

Without discussion they sank into the sofa. Brooke sat in the far corner and tried not to look as if she were hiding in it. Samantha settled in the center with a contented sigh. Crossing one long leg over the other, she took a delicate sip of her drink then set it on the cocktail table. Claire plopped down in the other corner, careful not to spill a drop of her drink. Brooke snuck a peek at Samantha from beneath her lashes, then flushed in embarrassment when she thought about Samantha witnessing Zachary's put-downs and the way he'd tried to fawn all over her.

"I wasn't sure you'd be back," Brooke said tentatively.

"Me, neither." A funny look passed over Samantha Davis's face. "But I'm glad to be here. How about you?" She studied Brooke carefully. Was she searching for a warning sign of tears to come?

"Yes, I'm glad to be here," Brooke said. "Ava and Natalie are with Zachary. He's decided that he prefers Sunday nights to full weekends."

Samantha considered her. "That's good though, right? That they're with him and you can come here?"

"Yes," Brooke said, realizing that this was true. "It's almost weird to have an activity of my own. I've kind of forgotten what that feels like."

"I know what you mean," Samantha said.

Certain the other woman had to be joking, Brooke studied her more closely, but saw no hint of humor in the earnest green eyes.

Claire raised her glass. "Let's hear it for somewhere to go and something to do." She took a long pull on her drink. Brooke and Samantha joined her.

"Now then, ladies," Edward Parker said, clapping his hands to snag their attention. "We have plenty of seats so please go ahead and claim one. Drink and snacks are headed around." Isabella, serving plate in hand, performed a curtsy. James bowed, holding the beer and lemonade aloft. They began to circulate.

The chatter died down as Edward spread his arms wide. "It's a pleasure to have you all here tonight for episode two of *Downton Abbey*. Please let your friends and neighbors know that they're welcome and that I can loan them the episodes missed if they want to be caught up when they arrive." He gave them a stern look. "And no peeking ahead. No secret screenings. Remember, we're in this together."

There were murmurs and laughter. Beside her, Claire held her glass out for another refill, then drank eagerly. Brooke felt a kind of rosy glow surround her. Or maybe it was rising from the shandies within her? She took another sip and decided it didn't matter where the feeling had originated as long as it continued.

She felt a tingle of anticipation as the lights went down and the room fell silent. Claire and Samantha leaned forward, their eyes fixed on the screen. The opening strains of music began. Downton Abbey appeared on the screen, solid and massive against the blue English sky. And Brooke was sucked into another world. One in which a middle-class lawyer meets the privileged world he must reluctantly join, a privileged young woman rebels against duty and expectation, and a less privileged woman dreams of something better.

*   *   *

WHEN THE EPISODE ENDED, THEY APPLAUDED ALL
the way through the closing credits.

"Now then, ladies," Edward Parker said as the credits
came to a close. "We have trifle for 'afters.' Which you may
have with tea or another shandy."

Only two people opted for tea. James poured fresh drinks
for the rest of them while Isabella passed out small bowls of
trifle. Claire swayed slightly but remained propped upright
in the corner of the sofa. Brooke had lost count of how many
shandies the woman had had.

"I'm curious about your favorite characters this week,"
Edward said. "Anyone?"

"I like Bates and Anna," Callan said.

"And I wish Daisy would pay attention to poor William
instead of Thomas," her twin added.

"Maggie Smith still rocks!" Anna, the nurse from Emory,
offered. "She's so droll."

"Any favorite lines?" Edward asked, egging them on.

"When Lady Mary says to Matthew, 'Oh, I wouldn't want
to push in,' after she hears him talking about how he knows
the Granthams are going to try to push one of the daughters
on him," Mimi Davenport said. "Especially after we see how
taken he is with her."

"I like the dowager countess's line—'what is a weekend'?"
Samantha said. "It's such a telling remark."

There were more shouted lines and laughter. They chatted
animatedly amongst themselves, no one seeming in any hurry
to leave even though it was close to eleven p.m. on a Sunday
night.

"I wish we could have a *Downton Abbey* marathon," Brooke
said to Samantha. "Just sit down and watch one episode after
another."

"I don't think I could drink that many shandies," Claire
said, her words starting to slur a bit. Brooke had the impres-

sion that the only thing keeping her upright was the corner of the sofa back.

"I don't think the drinking part is mandatory," Samantha said. "Besides, sometimes it's better to spread out the good things. You know. So you have something to look forward to."

Brooke looked at Samantha Davis in surprise. Surely the woman's life was a string of good things, each one better than the next.

"Well, I wouldn't suggest the marathon to Edward," Claire said. "You might be put on a DA watch. He's got a plan and I don't think he wants us to devee-date." She rolled her eyes. "I mean dee-vee-ate." She looked inordinately pleased when she got it right.

Slowly people rose and began to say their good-byes.

"I'm walking you home," Brooke said to Claire.

"Me, too," Samantha said.

"Home is only six doors down the hall," Claire said with what sounded like surprise.

"I know but the way you're swaying, I'm afraid you'll get on the elevator and end up somewhere else," Brooke said.

"Like the bottom of the pool," Samantha said.

Claire perked up. "Swimming would feel good right now."

"I rest my case," Brooke said.

"You're definitely in no condition to be anywhere near a body of water." Samantha smiled.

Edward came up behind them. "Is everything all right, ladies?"

Yes," Samantha said hooking her arm through Claire's. "It's been a great evening. And I see our numbers are growing."

The concierge nodded, pleased. Then he turned his attention to Brooke, looking at her in the same assessing way he had earlier. "I wonder if you might be available to come talk with me sometime this week?"

Brooke's good mood began to evaporate. She couldn't imagine what the concierge would want to talk to her about.

Was it the maintenance fees? Had there been a complaint about Darcy or the girls? "Is there something wrong?" she asked.

"No, not at all," he said quickly. "I just think it's too late to cover the topic I wanted to broach."

"Oh, no," Claire said. "Did he say there were roaches? I hate roaches. I spray the shit out of them—make them sleep with the fishes." She said this in a fair imitation of Marlon Brando in the *Godfather*.

"That was 'broach,'" Edward said drily. "And I promise you it's nothing negative."

"Well," Claire said. "Thanks for . . ." Apparently unable to find the right words, she raised her arms to encompass the room. "It was fun."

"Yes, it was really great," Brooke agreed, but she felt his eyes on her as she followed Samantha's lead and hooked her arm through Claire's other elbow.

Claire swayed slightly on her feet. Because they were connected Brooke and Samantha swayed along like passengers on a wave-tossed deck.

Carefully, Brooke and Samantha walked Claire down the carpeted hallway. At Claire's door they waited while Claire fumbled with the key. The second time it landed on the floor, Samantha bent down to pick it up. "May I?" At Claire's nod, Samantha inserted the key smartly in the lock, then pushed open the door.

"Hey, thass good." Claire's voice indicated her admiration

"Now you go inside and lock the door behind you." Brooke said this slowly and carefully as if speaking to one of her children.

Claire stood and stared into her condo as if she'd never seen it before. Brooke and Samantha looked at each other.

"Okay," Samantha said. "I guess we'll escort you in."

"'Kay." Claire stood and waited patiently, but she didn't move.

"Turn sideways," Brooke said. "If we're going to stay

linked together like this we're not going to fit through the doorway head-on."

"'S right. Too wide." Claire nodded sagely, not moving. "No offense."

Samantha snorted. "None taken. Hold on." Keeping her arm linked through Claire's, she realigned herself so that she was facing the doorjamb. Brooke did the same pulling Claire around with her. Samantha led a sideways sashay into Claire's condo. "There." They walked her to her bedroom alcove. "This is a great unit," Brooke said, looking around.

"Yes, really functional. And very cute," Samantha agreed. They lowered Claire onto the edge of her bed and pulled off her shoes. "Do you have any aspirin?"

Claire stared blankly at both of them. Then she yawned.

"Check the bathroom medicine cabinet," Brooke suggested. She tucked Claire's shoes halfway under the bed so Claire wouldn't trip over them if she got up during the night. A picture of Claire and a girl in cap and gown stood on the nightstand. "Is that your daughter?"

"Hailey." Claire nodded in confirmation. Her eyelids fluttered shut.

"Hold on." Samantha returned with a bottle of aspirin. In the kitchen she filled a cup with water from the refrigerator door dispenser. "Take these first," she said, opening the bottle. "You'll thank me in the morning." They waited while Claire slitted her eyes open and complied. "Thirsty."

"I bet." Brooke took the cup from her and set it on the nightstand. "Okay, we're going to go so you can sleep. Why don't you just come lock the door behind us and . . ."

Claire fell backward onto the bed. Her feet remained on the floor.

"No." Brooke grabbed one limp arm and hauled her up. "We leave. You lock the door. Then you sleep."

Brooke let go of Claire's arm and she fell backward again. "What now?" she asked Samantha as Claire's breathing evened out.

"I don't know. I haven't dealt with anything like this since college," Samantha admitted. "I guess we tuck her in, lock the door, and slip the key under the door when we leave?"

"Good plan," Brooke said. She'd done little partying herself in college. And once she'd dropped out to put Zachary through she'd been far too tired for drinking or much of anything that didn't revolve around him.

Together they tucked Claire under the covers. Samantha refilled the glass of water and made sure it was within reach.

It was a short ride to the ninth floor. After saying good night to Samantha, Brooke stepped off the elevator and headed down the silent hall. All the way to her door and as she let herself in to her even more silent condo, she tried to imagine why Edward Parker had been looking at her in that X-ray sort of way of his. What he might have seen. And what in the world he could possibly want to talk to her about.

Chapter Thirteen

ERNEST HEMINGWAY AND HIS PRODIGIOUS ALCO-
hol consumption notwithstanding, Claire had never
found alcohol a particularly helpful part of the writing process. She couldn't imagine how running in front of a herd of
pissed-off bulls would contribute to anyone's word count,
either. But then she—and most female writers she knew—
had never had a Paris, or any other kind of wife, to take care
of them and keep the rest of the world at bay while they
wrote.

She woke late Monday morning groggy and with a throb-
bing headache that seemed way out of proportion to beers
laced with lemonade.

"Aarggh," she said, though this was a word better typed
than spoken. Burying her face in her pillow in an attempt
to block out the sunshine, she willed herself back to sleep
but it was a halfhearted effort. Finally she flipped onto her
back, opened her eyes, and squinted up at the ceiling, hoping
to find something there that would motivate her to get up.
What she saw was a fresh coat of white paint and a circus of

dust motes performing in the spill of sunlight that streamed through the windows.

"Shit." This word was equally satisfying in printed and spoken form and she repeated it with relish. Her head lolled to the side and her eyes fell on her "desk" where her computer, and the book she was supposed to write on it, awaited. She closed her eyes and lolled the other way.

Slowly she replayed the night before in her head. Edward Parker's warm smile. Bits and pieces of the *Downton Abbey* episode. Brooke and Samantha walking her back to her apartment. Squeezing sideways through the front door.

She groaned in embarrassment. Opening her eyes she contemplated the ceiling once again and tried to pull up Rory and—-oh, God, she couldn't even envision her heroine well enough to give her a name—but her characters were twisted up with the inhabitants of *Downton Abbey* and the women who'd watched it with her. All of whom were far more fleshed out than her own paper-thin characters.

A tight fist of panic formed in her chest. *It's okay. You have a whole year to do this. What difference does one day make?*

But that's what she'd been telling herself for two weeks now and she had virtually nothing to show for it. Her eyes went back to the table and her laptop. In her former life, in those stolen minutes and hours, she would have already completed her character sketches and begun the first chapters. And she most definitely would have known her heroine's name.

In the bathroom she washed her face and brushed her teeth. "You better get it together, girl," she said to the ravage-faced woman in the mirror. "If you intend to write twenty pages a day like Nora Roberts does, you're going to have to get started. Now. Today." Nora hadn't written the number of books she had or built a career that had spawned a legion of avid fans the newspapers referred to as "Noraholics" by avoiding her computer as if it carried the plague.

What would Nora do if her head throbbed and her stomach rumbled its emptiness like Claire's was right now? Claire had no doubt Nora would sit down and produce those twenty pages anyway. And she'd make sure they were good ones.

Claire shucked off her wrinkled clothes and started the shower. A text dinged in from Hailey; just the word *Well?* accompanied by a smiley face. Claire flushed with embarrassment, glad her daughter wasn't here to see her ravaged face and lack of will.

"You are going to figure this out today. No more avoiding, shirking, or panicking," she told herself as she washed her hair, shaved her legs, and exfoliated her face. "No more excuses. No more bullshit."

Resolute, she towel dried her hair, pulled on her sloppiest, hole-iest, most comfortable writing clothes and headed for her dining table/desk.

There was no shame in taking time to settle in and acclimate. Today was the day that she'd officially start. And if she faltered she would pick herself back up by thinking WWND—what would Nora do?

She detoured into the kitchen to make a cup of coffee and stared out the window as she drank it. Today was most definitely the day. She'd definitely get started. She would.

Just as soon as she replied to Hailey's text. And ate some toast to settle her stomach. And right after she got all that had happened down in her journal so she didn't forget.

BROOKE MACKENZIE'S FACE BORE THE LOOK OF A child who'd been summoned to see the headmaster as she stepped into Edward Parker's office later that week.

"Good morning, Mrs. Mackenzie," Edward said as he rose and came around his desk eager to put her at ease. Given the things that he knew were going on in her life, he imagined she could use every ounce of kindness and consideration she could get. "Thank you so much for coming."

She watched him carefully, a line of worry creasing her

forehead, her nice hazel eyes wary. "I've been wondering what you might want to talk to me about," she said. "If it's Darcy or the girls, I can try to . . ."

"No, no, it's nothing like that," he hastened to reassure her. "I think they're quite a breath of fresh air to tell you the truth. The Alexander is a beautiful and very regal building, but we wouldn't want it to get too stuffy now, would we?"

"No?"

"No." He said this as emphatically as he could without frightening her. Although "casual" was not his "go-to" demeanor, he leaned back against the edge of his desk and motioned her to the chair across from it. "Please have a seat, won't you?"

He waited for her to be seated though he wasn't certain that perching that gingerly on the edge of a chair qualified.

"I've actually asked you here to discuss something quite unrelated to the building. The truth of the matter is I have a favor to ask of you."

Surprise suffused her face, turning it almost as bright as her hair. "I'm not sure I understand what I could do for you," she said quietly.

"I've made quite a muddle of this, haven't I?" He offered his most winning smile. "I think you've heard me mention my company, Private Butler?"

She nodded warily.

"Well, in addition to the Alexander I've been providing concierge services to private clients as well."

She nodded again. Her body remained rigid.

"The thing is," he said, "business is growing quite rapidly. But on occasion I get a request that is quite beyond my usual sphere. Or that of the people in my employ."

"And you have something in *my* sphere?"

"I think so. Or rather, I hope so."

She waited, her eyes locked with his. He could read the doubt in them.

"You see I've had a request for a child's birthday party.

More specifically a six-year-old girl's birthday party. With, um, all the pertinent trimmings."

"Seriously?" It was clear that whatever she'd been anticipating, this was not it.

"Yes," he replied. "And since you have daughters right around that age I assumed you'd know what would need to be done."

She continued to study him, waiting for more. If nothing else, he had her attention.

"You'd be earning close to five hundred dollars for the planning and implementation. Plus the client will pay all the out-of-pocket expenses."

He saw the glimmer of interest that lit her eyes, but wasn't sure whether money alone would be enough to tempt her out of her comfort zone. "The father is a fairly recent widower and he wants to have his daughter's party at home in the old-fashioned way. With"—he looked down at his notes— "pin the tail on the donkey and clothespins dropped in milk bottles."

She cocked her head to one side. "I'm not sure they make those kinds of clothespins or milk bottles anymore."

"Yes, well, I imagine some sort of improvising—or negotiating—may prove necessary. But he felt very strongly about the party feeling . . . homemade. And he's given us carte blanche to make it feel that way."

She looked at him. "Did someone tell you I needed a job?" she asked quietly.

"No," he replied, though he had sensed from the day he'd met him that Zachary Mackenzie was not one to treat others as well as he treated himself. He'd had to call on every ounce of training he possessed not to blanch when the man had come in to look at available units for himself and his girlfriend.

"I'm the one in need, Mrs. Mackenzie. I didn't want to turn the gentleman down, but I promise you he doesn't want me showing up to plan and implement this party. It's very important to him." He hesitated. "And to his motherless daughter." He did not look heavenward or cross himself when he said this, but he hoped he'd be forgiven for making so free with the Daltons' tragedy. "Is this something you would know how to do?"

"I've given parties at home for both the girls. But they were simple, inexpensive things. Nothing special."

"Well, that's exactly what he's looking for. And I'm sure he'd be perfectly happy with whatever you suggest."

"But I . . . I don't know this man or his daughter. And I'm not really good at . . ."

"Before you refuse, would you at least meet with him to discuss it?" he asked.

"Oh, I don't know." Her eyes had clouded with uncertainty, but he thought he saw a glimmer of something else there, too.

"You'd be making a real difference to a little girl who's lost her mother." He imagined the lightning bolt he so richly deserved, but forged ahead. "The birthday girl's name is Marissa Dalton." He pulled a notepad over and wrote Bruce Dalton's name, address, and phone number on it. He scribbled *Marissa* beneath it and ripped the page from the pad.

"You know, I'm really not sure . . ." Brooke Mackenzie was shaking her head, preparing to retreat.

"Just promise me you'll call him and set up a meeting to discuss the party with him," Edward cut in smoothly. "After that meeting, if you feel it's not something you want to do, I'll let him know we won't be able to help him."

"I guess I could do that," she said, though she didn't look happy about it.

"Splendid." He stood and she did the same. He'd learned long ago that once you got what you wanted it was best to conclude the conversation before the other party could change his or her mind. "Here's his information. Just tell him you're part of Private Butler and that I asked you to call."

"All right." She held the notepaper by one corner as if it

were a telegram from outer space, but she didn't hand it back. "I'll call him today. And I'll let you know what I think after I meet with him." She hesitated. "But I'm really not certain that I have the skills necessary to represent your company in this kind of a professional capacity."

He studied her closely and thought how misleading an exterior could be; how small a part of a person it really revealed. Brooke Mackenzie wasn't beautiful. She didn't have a veneer of sophistication, did not possess so much as a hint of swagger. Her eyes were clouded with self-doubt. But buried deep inside there was bedrock, he was sure of this. "If you'll forgive me for saying so, I think you underestimate yourself, Mrs. Mackenzie."

She looked at him oddly, clearly not understanding what he meant.

"I'm certain you can handle this," he said gently. "After all, it's not everyone who could handle having her ex-husband and his girlfriend move into her building with such aplomb. You have an amazing amount of self-possession. I'm sure a child's birthday party is nothing in comparison."

"What did you say?" Brooke Mackenzie's voice didn't rise above a whisper. But that whisper was fraught with the same horror he now saw reflected in her eyes.

Good Lord. Edward felt a great deal of horror himself at what was apparently a complete and utter lack of discretion on his part.

She blinked rapidly. He could feel the effort she was expending not to cry.

"I'm so sorry," he said, wishing there was something, anything, he might say that would erase his horrible, inexcusable mistake from both of their memories. "I assumed you already knew that Mr. Mackenzie had purchased the three-bedroom on the tenth floor. He and Ms. Grant are scheduled to move into it in two weeks' time."

CHAPTER FOURTEEN

"ARE YOU SURE?"

"Absolutely." Samantha eyed her husband, who was already dressed for their Sunday round of golf. "I do have a bit of a headache and a round of golf *and* Sunday dinner with you is going to make Cynthia feel like it's her birthday, Mother's Day, and Christmas all rolled into one."

"I hate to leave you all afternoon when I'm flying out to Boston right after dinner."

"It's okay," Samantha said. "It'll be my gift to your mother for arranging an interview for Meredith at the Atlanta Preservation Board. But if you tell her I begged you to stay home and you insisted on asking her to play instead, she'll enjoy it even more." She had no doubt that this many hours alone with her son would send Cynthia into the genteel version of hog heaven.

"All right. But I'm tempted to tell her the truth so you get at least a little credit." He leaned down to kiss her.

"Up to you," Samantha said as he turned to go. "But why hollow out her sense of victory?"

After Jonathan left Samantha downed two more Advil and reached for her cell phone. The headache had begun as a small throb behind the eyes the day before when Jonathan had handed her a copy of her American Express bill. He'd said only, "When exactly are you expecting Meredith back?" but his eyes had been carefully blank and the tick in his cheek pronounced.

Samantha had already been trying to reach Meredith for almost twenty-four hours at that point. Her interview at the Preservation Board was set for Tuesday and Samantha had booked a flight home from New York for her on Monday, but was not at all positive Meredith would be on that flight since she hadn't yet spoken to her.

Now, with renewed determination—and desperation—she found Fredi Fainstein's cell phone number and called it, holding her breath as it rang.

"'Lo?"

"Fredi?"

"Yes?"

"This is Samantha Davis. Meredith's sister."

"Oh."

There was a silence. As if a hand were covering the mouthpiece.

"Fredi," Samantha said. "Please put her on the phone now." She imitated the tone she'd heard Jonathan use when he would brook no argument.

There was what sounded like a scuffle and then Meredith was on the line.

"What's the big emergency?" Meredith asked, her tone belligerent. The clatter of cutlery and laughter-laced conversation sounded in the background.

"If you'd responded to any of my emails, phone messages, or texts you'd know that Cynthia has arranged an interview at the Atlanta Preservation Board first thing Tuesday morning."

Silence.

"We pay for your phone and Internet primarily so that we have the ability to communicate with you. And yet you don't respond." Samantha realized she sounded as sullen as Meredith. No, not sullen. She was well and truly pissed.

"I've been busy."

"Yes, I realized that when I saw my AmEx bill," Samantha said.

"But I don't want to come back now," Meredith whined. "Fredi's been introducing me to absolutely everybody. I met Mary-Kate and Ashley Olsen at a party last week. And I sat at a table right next to Ashton Kutcher's table at this adorable little restaurant in SoHo. Our knees were practically touching."

"And this would help you find a job how?" Samantha asked.

There was a brief pause. "The Frick thing didn't pan out. But I did meet someone who knows someone at Sotheby's. I think I might be able to turn that into . . . something."

"Meredith. Today is Sunday. The interview is Tuesday. I've booked a flight for you out of LaGuardia at ten a.m. tomorrow."

Meredith remained silent.

"The job's not yours yet. You have to actually show up and impress them." She backed off a notch. If she made Meredith too angry, there'd be no talking to her. "As you are perfectly capable of doing when you want to."

"But I can't come back now. Not when I'm starting to make inroads here." There was a pause as Meredith regrouped.

It was Samantha's turn to remain silent.

"It's not fair. It's easy there for you married to Jonathan and everything. But I like it up here where things are actually happening. And . . . I met someone, Samantha. I need to stay here and see where it leads."

Samantha knew exactly where it would lead if in fact it were even true. She'd heard the same thing far too many times to hold out any real hope that Meredith would ever be attracted to or settle for the kind of man she really needed. Or a life that didn't revolve solely around herself.

And whose fault was that? she asked herself. Herself did not answer. "I'm sorry," Samantha said determined not to be swayed. "But Cynthia's called in quite a few favors on your behalf. You will be at that interview and you will be charming and professional. Once you have a job and the money to take yourself back to New York for a visit, you'll go. Or you can invite him down here. We'd all be glad to meet him."

Samantha could feel the waves of resentment behind Meredith's silence. "I'll be at the airport to pick you up. If you're not there, your credit cards will be canceled and your bank account closed." And then because she couldn't stay on the phone another minute, she said, "Have a nice day," and hung up.

Barely thirty seconds later her phone rang. She drew a shaky breath of relief. She'd been afraid Meredith wouldn't come to her senses. Meredith had never mastered the art of apologizing. Samantha would meet her halfway.

"Meredith, I'm sorry. I know you didn't mean—"

"Sorry," Hunter's voice cut in. "Wrong sibling."

"Oh." Samantha hurried to regroup. "What's going on?" She hadn't seen Hunter in more than a week. "Is everything all right?"

"Of course," he said heartily. Too heartily. "I was just wondering if I could come by and speak to you tonight."

Samantha's antennae quivered. "About what?"

"Can't a guy just stop by to see his sister without an ulterior motive?"

It was possible that some brothers did this. Hunter wasn't one of them. Hunter Jackson was a weigher of options, a contemplator of angles.

"Of course," she said. "I've got a screening in the building tonight. And I'm picking Meredith up at the airport around twelve thirty tomorrow, but other than that I'm pretty open.

"Tomorrow could be too late," he said curtly. Which

pretty much eliminated the possibility that this bore any resemblance to a casual drop-in. "I'm getting ready to board a flight back from DC and I need to stop off at my apartment when I get in," he said. "Can't you just go to whatever you're doing after we talk?"

Samantha's jaw clenched. As always, he expected her to drop whatever she was doing simply because he wanted or needed something. But she'd been looking forward to the *Downton Abbey* screening and it was clear that whatever he wanted to talk about was not going to put a smile on her face. Still agitated from her argument with Meredith, she wasn't inclined to humor him.

"I'm going to be in the clubroom on the eighth floor," she said, making up her mind. Maybe if she spoke to him in a public place it wouldn't be as bad as she was starting to fear it would be. "It's right across from the fitness room on the way to the pool. Just come in and get me."

"Okay." His agreement was grudging. She could tell he was surprised that she would put her own plans before his needs. Once again she had to ask herself whose fault was that? Once again her "self" didn't want to answer.

Just before eight, Samantha took the elevator down to the clubroom, where a definite party atmosphere prevailed. Some of the women had already moved to their chairs and couches. She spotted the tops of Brooke and Claire's heads on the sofa they'd claimed for their own and was pleased to see the seat between them open. Edward shot her a smile when she entered, James handed her a glass of wine, and Isabella cocked her head and said, "The yooshall, me'lady?"

"Yes, thanks." She accepted the bag of popcorn and made her way down toward the front of the room.

"Is this seat taken?" she asked when she reached the sofa.

"Only by you," Claire said with a tap of the cushion. Brooke gave her a shy smile as she settled in between them.

"I see we're back to wine," Samantha said to Claire. "I

think you scared Edward away from the shandies and back to the straight and narrow."

"Works for me," Claire said. "I'm not planning to let any beer of mine get in the same room as a glass of lemonade anytime soon."

Brooke raised an eyebrow and smiled. But the smile was fleeting. Her brow furrowed.

Edward Parker took his place in front of the screen. "Welcome, ladies," he said, raising his arms and his voice above the din. Conversations ended and all eyes turned to the concierge. "I don't think you need any introduction from me tonight, but I do hope you'll stay for a bit afterward. We'll be having apple crumble for 'afters' with a choice of brandies."

There were murmurs of pleasure as Edward aimed the remote at the DVD player. "So now without further ado," he said. "I bring you episode three."

The theme music swelled as the concierge stepped out of the way. Downton Abbey appeared on the screen. Samantha gave a mental heave, trying to push Meredith and Hunter from her mind as she and every other person in the room leaned forward, eager and ready to be transported.

KEMAL PAMUK, THE TURKISH DIPLOMAT LADY MARY had been flirting with since they met at the hunt earlier that day, appeared in Mary's bedroom. Was he going to harm her? Was she actually going to flout propriety and . . .

The tap on Samantha's shoulder yanked her out of Lady Mary's bedroom with a gasp. Heads turned her way but only briefly. Even she was having a hard time tearing her eyes from the screen.

"Hey," Hunter whispered.

It took her a moment to come back to the present. When she did she could see what looked like panic in her brother's eyes. Worry creased his face. "Hey," she whispered back even as she girded her loins.

Claire and Brooke tore their gazes from the screen to look at her.

"Be right back," she said, and hoped this would be the case.

Samantha bent down so she wouldn't block anyone's view and led Hunter toward the door. No one paid them any mind. It seemed that Lady Mary was about to have sex with Pamuk. Samantha couldn't believe she was going to miss it.

When Hunter hesitated near the bar, she shook her head and motioned him out into the hall. He hugged her a trifle too hard.

She looked steadily at him, her heart already pounding with dread. "What's wrong," she asked. "Are you ill?"

"I wish." He said this quietly. A small snort of laughter followed.

Samantha considered her brother, waiting for him to explain. She saw his gaze sharpen. "Stop it," she said.

"Stop what?"

"Trying to figure out how to 'handle' me."

He looked surprised and she realized that she'd never called him on it before.

"Apparently whatever it is is more important than anything I might be doing. So go ahead and tell me now."

Again, she saw that she'd surprised him. Good. She was tired of always being on the receiving end of unpleasant surprises.

"The nanotechnology deal has gone south. There were some . . . irregularities. It's a little unclear who actually owns the patent. And there are questions about the stock that was issued. I have to pump in another hundred thousand dollars to stave off an SEC investigation into me and my backers."

She looked at him as his words sank in. "But Jonathan is one of your backers." Her head began to pound. "Does Jonathan know?"

He shook his head and dropped his eyes in the way he

had as a child. "I was hoping you could tell him. And ask him if he could make this one last investment to straighten things out."

She shook her head. *Oh, no.*

"It's only a hundred thousand," he said.

"Did you really just say that?" she asked. "When did one hundred thousand dollars become an *only* to you?"

"When you married Jonathan," he said simply.

She looked at her brother, really looked at him. Hated that he actually thought this was true. That in her attempt to take care of him and Meredith she'd simply gone out and married a lifetime bankroll. Was that what she'd done?

"No," she said. "Jonathan has done so much for all of us. He deserves better than that."

"He won't even miss it, Sam. It's like petty cash to him."

"No." She shook her head, adamant. And it wasn't just the money. She'd warned him the last time when he'd not only lost the money Jonathan had invested but dragged his name through the headlines that it absolutely couldn't happen again. Now he was talking about "irregularities" and a possible SEC investigation.

Hunter turned his head and she realized someone was in the hallway. It was Brooke and Claire. "Are you all right, Samantha?" Claire asked carefully. Both of them stared hard at Hunter.

She wasn't, not really. But she couldn't bring herself to say so. "This is my brother. Hunter, this is Claire and Brooke, friends of mine in the building."

He nodded but didn't waste even part of a smile. All of his focus was on Samantha. And getting what he wanted from her.

"Thanks for checking on me," she said to the two women. Her voice sounded wooden in her ears. "I'll be in in a minute."

"All right," Brooke said. "We'll get you an apple crumble and save you a seat."

"Thanks." She watched them leave. Through the glass she

could see them go up to Edward Parker. All three of them watched from within for several long moments.

"That was weird," Hunter said dismissively.

"No," she said. "I believe that was friendship." She was too bent on standing firm with Hunter to question why people she'd known for such a short time would wade into the middle of something even she didn't want to be a part of.

"So will you speak to Jonathan?" Hunter asked. "Just this one last time? I promise I'll never . . ."

She'd heard this promise far too many times to allow herself to believe it. "No."

"But you have to," he remonstrated. "I'll be finished. Ruined. We'll all be in the papers."

She looked him in the eye, forced herself to speak. "How could you do this? Have you even stopped to think what an investigation like this might mean to Jonathan and the firm?"

"But, the money would buy us time and it might help make that go away. And Jonathan knows a good opportunity when he sees it." He said this almost by rote. She could feel him trying to get her back on script; the one in which he asked, she agreed, and Jonathan gave.

"Oh, Hunter. Don't be ridiculous. When has Jonathan ever made money investing in your 'deals'? You've been his personal charity. And you've taken advantage of his generosity. We've all taken advantage."

He glared at her; his green eyes glass shards of dislike. But even as she watched, the dislike disappeared and was replaced with desperation. "People could go to jail, Samantha. I could go to jail. If it hits the papers . . ."

"This is finished," she said quietly. "I'll tell him there's a problem because he has to know. But I won't ask him to invest another penny or do anything but protect himself and the firm."

"You don't mean it," he said.

"I should have asked him to cut you off a long time ago. It's been unfair to him and it hasn't helped you at all."

He shook his head, dismissive and disbelieving. "You won't."

"I will," she said with all the certainty she could muster. "I want a half page from you explaining the . . . irregularities in this deal and the reasons why the SEC might become involved. And when this is taken care of I expect you to go out and get a job. A real one with a salary. Not a pie-in-the-sky, smoke-and-mirrors kind of thing. A real job so you can pay your own rent. Take care of yourself. And maybe even start paying some of the money back to Jonathan that you've lost."

The door to the clubroom opened and Edward Parker stepped out. "I'm sorry to interrupt, Mrs. Davis, but I wanted to see if you'd be coming in to join the discussion."

Hunter glowered at the concierge, but Edward Parker didn't seem to notice.

Samantha felt a small surge of relief. She'd said what she needed to say and Edward had offered an exit. "Thank you, Edward." She smiled a bit shakily at the concierge. "I'll be right there."

The concierge cast a look down his nose at Hunter. "If you're sure everything's all right?"

Hunter's mouth opened in a snarl. "Mind your own business or . . ."

Samantha drew herself up and squared her shoulders. "Yes, thanks." She swallowed but managed to raise an eyebrow at Hunter. "My brother was just leaving."

"Very good, madam," he said in a fair imitation of *Downton Abbey*'s butler, Carson.

"This is bullshit, Samantha," Hunter said as soon as the door closed behind the concierge. "How many people are going to come out here to try to protect you?"

She sighed, but she knew she couldn't retreat. "The better

question might be why these people feel I need to be protected from you?"

He continued to glare at her. She could tell he simply didn't believe she wasn't going to cave in and do what he'd asked.

"You need to go now," she said shakily. "I'll tell Jonathan about the problem in my own way. You've forced him into another untenable position. That seems to be a Jackson family specialty. But this is it. When this mess is cleaned up there will be no more backing from him." Then she said what she'd said to Meredith. "And in the meantime you better start looking for a job. One you can hold on to. Otherwise you'll be cut off completely."

"You can't mean . . ."

"Seriously, Hunter. The Jonathan Davis gravy train is over."

He sputtered at her for a moment in shock and disbelief. Then he whirled and strode down the hall to the elevator.

She waited until the elevator door closed behind him, breathing deeply, trying to regain her bearings. Edward Parker smiled gently at her as she entered the clubroom. Brooke waved her to an empty seat at the table between her and Claire Walker. A glass of brandy and a brimming dessert plate awaited her.

For a moment she let the conversation wash over her. There was laughter and an overarching atmosphere of goodwill, but Samantha felt immune to it.

"Evelyn Napier is cute," Mimi Davenport was saying, referring to the English diplomat. "Although Evelyn is not the most masculine name I've heard. I think Lady Mary should have paid attention to him."

"She only had eyes for Pamuk," one of the lit teachers called out.

"I don't blame her," Callan Ritchie said. "Kemal Pamuk was hot! Did you see the way Lady Mary perked up when she saw him?"

"Oh, God, I couldn't believe it when he died right there in her bed!" Callan's twin Logan added.

"I *hate* when that happens!" the white-haired Mimi Davenport threw in.

There was laughter.

Samantha turned to Claire. "He died in her bed?" she asked blankly.

Claire and Brooke nodded. "Oh, yeah. It was unreal," Brooke said.

"You need to see it for yourself, though," Claire added. "I bet Edward will loan you the episode."

Edward wrapped up the discussion and reluctantly, as always, the crowd began to leave. Brooke and Claire stood when Samantha did. She was relieved that they didn't ask what had happened between her and her brother; she could barely bring herself to think about it.

Edward Parker regarded her as they neared the door. "Everyone all right?" he asked, but his eyes were on Samantha.

"Right as rain," she said, though this was a blatant lie.

"Come on, we'll escort you upstairs," Brooke offered, her smile shy.

"Thanks," Samantha said. "But I'm fine." Or she would be. Just as soon as she found the strength to tell Jonathan what Hunter had dragged him into.

CHAPTER FIFTEEN

BROOKE PULLED UP IN FRONT OF BRUCE DALTON'S home and turned off the Volvo. The house, in the Candler Park neighborhood not far from Piedmont Park, was exactly the kind of house she would have chosen if she'd been in charge of their move to Atlanta. It was a Craftsman-style bungalow with a triangular gable roof and a deep shaded verandah. Flower beds and a lush green lawn framed the cozy structure and were in turn framed by the kind of white picket fence you might see in a children's fairy tale. It was exactly the kind of house they might have lived in if Zachary hadn't been so concerned with appearances.

Her stomach lurched at the thought of her ex-husband and his girlfriend's upcoming move into the Alexander and she attempted to push the thought aside as she climbed out of the station wagon and smoothed nervous hands down the side of her striped shirtdress. With unsteady steps she crossed the sidewalk and opened the gate then followed the curved concrete path to the broad steps and onto the porch.

"Mrs. Mackenzie?" The man who opened the bright

red door was of average height and weight with light brown hair and eyes and pleasant regular features. His smile was friendly and his hand, when he reached out to shake hers, was warm and dry.

"Yes. Mr. Dalton?"

"Call me Bruce." He stepped back so that she could enter and led her through the foyer into a spacious great room with windows that overlooked the side and backyard and wrapped around a gourmet kitchen. A fireplace, bracketed by built-in bookshelves, ran along one wall. Lantern-hung beams formed rectangles on the ceiling.

"Then I'm Brooke." She looked around, liking what she saw. "The house is beautiful. And the modern touches are really well blended."

"Thanks. The house had just been renovated when we bought it. We fell in love with the house's warmth and character, but modern plumbing and appliances make it even more lovable."

The furnishings were clean lined and modern but original pine plank floors were covered by brightly colored area rugs and white walls were dotted with family photographs and whimsical folk art.

He motioned her to a seat at the kitchen table. Light streamed in unchecked through a bank of double-hung windows. Outside a wooden playhouse was tucked in up against the fence, shaded by an ancient oak tree. A swing set dominated the opposite corner; it was quite elaborate with a monkey bar and slide and lots of things to climb around on. Ava and Natalie would have had a field day here. "The grounds are beautiful. Have you been in the house long?"

"No." He looked out the window to the yard. "We'd just moved in when my wife was diagnosed. We spent the first six months fighting her illness." He paused, then went on. "And the last six months trying to get used to being without her."

"I'm so sorry for your loss."

"Thank you."

Wanting to give him a minute, she reached for her tote bag. In an effort to look professional, she'd filled it with everything she could think of—tape measure, yellow pad, a barrage of pens and pencils, a few party supply catalogues that she'd found. There were also the hand sanitizer, wet wipes, tissues, juice boxes, and other detritus that went with motherhood.

She pulled out a yellow pad and set it on the table in front of her.

"So, um, Edward said you want us to plan a birthday party for your daughter?"

"Yes," he said. "Marissa's turning six and I want her to have a party." He smiled and she noticed a dimple slashing through one cheek. "I'm not all that sure what six-year-old girls want or like. And we really don't know many people here."

"Why don't you tell me a little bit about her?" Brooke prompted.

He thought for a few seconds. "Well, she's smart and a little bit of a tomboy. But I think she likes, you know, girly kinds of things, too. Like dolls. And . . . dress-up clothes."

"What shows does she like to watch?" Brooke asked.

"Hmmm, something with good luck in it. And one with a girl's name . . ." His voice trailed off. "And she has videos with some kind of a pet shop in them."

"Maybe *Good Luck, Charlie* on Disney and *Olivia* on Nickelodeon? Those are two of my girls' favorites. They're five and seven."

"Yes, that sounds right," he said. "And when she plays with her Barbie dolls she either dresses them up like a princess or sends them to climb Mount Everest in what we used to call 'hot pants.'"

She watched his face, liking the way the sadness lifted and his brown eyes lit up when he talked about his daughter.

"Edward said you'd like something simple, maybe in the backyard?"

"I just want her to have a good time. I'm open."

"Well, it looks like a great space. There's lots of room and plenty of shade. It's nicely confined so all your time won't be spent counting heads and worrying."

He watched her intently as she spoke. As if she were saying something that wasn't completely obvious.

She turned to look out the windows as she thought. "We could just do a really nice birthday picnic. You know, spread blankets under the trees. Have sandwiches and lemonade. Ice cream and birthday cake for dessert. And then we could include some kind of old-fashioned relay events like sack races and three-legged races."

"Instead of pin the tail on the donkey and clothespins in milk bottles?"

"Yes. Same idea. We'll keep them occupied, but they'll be working on something together in teams. And we could put out some arts and crafts in one area. My girls love to color and draw. Add a little glitter and it's a big-time treat."

He smiled. "I like it."

"And it'll be a little cooler by the first weekend in October." She could see it laid out in her mind. Thinking she should probably make notes, she reached back into the tote and felt around for a pen. She froze when her fingers encountered something soft and squishy. When she extracted her hand, four out of five of her fingers were streaked with chocolate.

Their eyes met.

"Breakfast?" he asked. His lips quirked upward.

Brooke sighed and felt heat stain her cheeks. "Unfortunately, no. It might be the remains of the Reese's cup Ava was eating at the park yesterday. Or it could be way older than that." So much for the professional presentation she'd been envisioning. "May I borrow your sink?"

"Of course." She sensed him trying not to laugh, but there was no help for it. She went to the kitchen and washed her hands thoroughly. Using a paper towel to dry them, she found the trash compactor and dropped it inside.

She came over to the table and reached back inside the bag. This time she came out clutching a half-eaten grocery store cookie. Which crumbled as they stared at it. "Good grief." She marched back to the trash compactor and dropped it inside. Bringing back a damp paper towel she wiped and de-crumbed the table.

When she returned to her seat she forced herself to meet his eyes. "Look, I don't know what Edward Parker told you, but I'm not a full-time concierge or anything. I'm just a mom. A mom who occasionally uses candy as bribery and then forgets to throw away the evidence."

He laughed. But she felt as if he were laughing with her, not at her.

"Frankly, I would say that makes you perfect for this assignment. Edward Parker sounded like a savvy fellow. He promised to find the right person for the assignment and I think you're it. All you have to do is plan the party you would plan for one of your daughters."

She thought about the expensive parties Zachary had insisted on once he'd started making money and building his medical practice. Chuck E. Cheese's. Six Flags Over Georgia. Renting a movie theater for a private screening. High tea at the Ritz—as if either Natalie or Ava had understood what was going on. Half the time he'd doubled the planned guest list in order to be sure their name—and his medical practice—would get in front of the mothers who lunched and Botoxed.

She was afraid Bruce Dalton was just being kind, but it wasn't as if she could just get up and leave. She'd promised Edward Parker she'd at least have this meeting and report back. And it was clear this man needed help.

She pushed aside her embarrassment and picked up her pen. "How many children will you be having?"

Bruce Dalton's face went blank. "I don't know."

"Do you want something small with only Marissa's close friends? Or something larger that includes her whole class?"

His brown eyes behind the glasses reflected his confusion. "I have no idea. Marissa doesn't really have any close friends. She's played at the little girl's across the street once or twice. And the babysitter we use took her to someone else's birthday party once when I had to be at a meeting." He looked down at his hands. "I never really expected to be doing this alone. I'm still trying to get used to the idea. And there are so many things that Chloe—that's Marissa's mother—just always handled. I'm afraid I've really been mucking things up."

Any thought of not planning and giving the sixth birthday of Marissa Dalton evaporated. "Do you have a class directory or anything?"

"Yes, I'm sure I must." He stood and moved over to a built-in desk that appeared stuffed with papers and miscellaneous—much like Brooke's tote bag.

She stood and moved over to the counter, perching on a bar stool where she had a better view. "If there's a neighborhood list, maybe you could pull that, too. So that I can get the little girl across the street's name and phone number. Her mother might be able to help me come up with a list of neighborhood children that we could invite, too."

"Oh. That's a great idea." Once again he said this as if she'd invented the wheel or discovered fire. "Yes, I think the little girl's name is Katie. And the mother is . . ." His forehead crinkled in thought. It was her turn to bite back a smile. Everything about Bruce Dalton shouted "absentminded professor." "Karen? Connie? Cathy? That's it. Cathy Banks."

"Great," Brooke said jotting the names on her yellow pad. She couldn't bring Marissa Dalton's mother back. Or even make her and her father's loss any less than the monumental thing it was. But she was going to put on the best birthday party picnic any six-year-old girl had ever had.

SYLVIE AND BRICK TALMADGE'S BACKYARD WAS roughly the size of a football field. A long, green, perfectly manicured rectangle, it had a pool and cabana, a tennis court, and an outdoor "kitchen" with a built-in grill and entertainment area. On this late Saturday afternoon in September, the Ole Miss–Mississippi State football game, which was playing on the big-screen TV, was currently in halftime.

Samantha sat on the Talmadge's back patio, sipping cocktails with the women who the world at large considered her best friends, but who had become friends by default—having married Jonathan Davis's friends. Out on the lawn, their barefoot husbands talked trash to each other while they tossed a football around.

Sylvie Talmadge was a statuesque blonde whose glory days as an Ole Miss cheerleader had resulted in marriage to Brick Talmadge, captain of the Rebel football team and one of Jonathan's childhood friends.

It was rumored that her pom-poms had been pried from her fingers to make room for the bridal bouquet before she headed down the aisle. But once joined to the aptly named Brick, Sylvie had channeled her earlier enthusiasm, and school spirit, into determined procreation. Given the bride and groom's gene pools, no one was surprised that all four of their children were blessed with blond good looks, impressive eye-hand coordination, and almost superhuman strength and stamina. Sylvie spent the years that followed cheering on their sons and daughters whom she enthusiastically ferried to football fields, baseball diamonds, and beauty pageants.

In contrast to the almost Amazonian Sylvie, Lucy Hammond Lee was small and curvy. Married to Jonathan's college roommate, Rock, Lucy had never met a social mountain she did not want to climb. Since her husband could, and did, trace his lineage to Robert E. Lee, Lucy had scaled and claimed Rock E. Lee with a flinty-eyed determination that could have landed her in the White House had she been so inclined.

Samantha, Sylvie, and Lucy had been brought together by their husbands' friendship. Not spending time with each other would have been impossible; disliking each other pointless. They saw each other frequently, but rarely without their husbands. All three women had married into old, wealthy southern families. The patent disapproval of their mothers-in-law was the glue that bound them.

"It's kind of hard to understand how she can love the children I produced so freely and dislike me so intensely. I mean I've been married to Rock E. for almost a quarter of a century. If I was only digging for gold I would have stashed and grabbed all I could and been gone a long time ago. It's downright insultin'," Lucy said in a familiar complaint.

There were murmurs of sympathy since "the boys" were far enough away not to overhear. Samantha sometimes wondered if Cynthia might have softened toward her if she'd managed to produce grandchildren like the others had. A soft Cynthia Davis was almost impossible to imagine.

"Brick says his mama wouldn't have approved of anyone he married, but after all these years she still talks about his high school girlfriend—who is now divorced and livin' just down the street at her parents'—like she walks on water." Sylvie took a long pull on her frozen margarita. "Sweet Jesus, just look at those boys." She was referring to Brick, Rock E., and Jonathan, who had taken off their shirts and were now running plays with much feinting and hilarity. "I must say Jonathan really stays in shape. Brick is not anywhere near as solid as he used to be. We may have to apply for some kind of name change." She sighed.

Samantha was fairly certain the nickname, a shortening of his given name of Brickland, had never had anything to do with his physique, but kept this observation to herself.

Modesty prevented her from agreeing that her own husband looked almost as fit as he had when she'd married him, but she had a hard time tearing her eyes from Jonathan's broad shoulders and rock-hard abs. It was easier to think about her husband's body than the conversation she needed to have with him. She hadn't wanted to bring up Hunter's latest business crisis on the phone. This afternoon when she'd picked Jonathan up at the airport they'd driven straight to Sylvie and Brick's and she hadn't wanted to spoil their reunion after almost a week apart. That's how big a wuss she was.

Talk turned to Sylvie and Lucy's children, who were now out of school, several of them married and producing grandbabies. Samantha smiled and nodded, but as always had little to offer. Neither Meredith nor Hunter had provided much in the way of bragging rights. And although she had been involved in raising them, she had not given birth to them. No, she didn't want to think about either of her siblings right now. Not Meredith, who had come home for her interview angry and had not yet heard from the Atlanta Preservation Board. Or Hunter, who might never forgive her for interfering with his revenue stream.

"Lord, I heard from Shelby the other day," Sylvie said. "You know she's got the twins now and she is at her wits' end. She told me that even with the nanny and Hildie in to cook and clean, she just can't keep up with things. I've been tryin' to think of what I could give her or do for her to help, but she is so particular."

Samantha looked at Sylvie. "What kinds of things does she need?"

"Oh, you know. Organizing. Planning. Errands. Whatever. Like when you're at a nice hotel and you just call down to the desk and say you need this or that."

An image of the elegant and sophisticated Edward Parker sprang to Samantha's mind. His willingness to take on Hunter on Sunday had surprised and warmed her. She liked and respected the concierge and would be glad to see his business expand—as long as the Alexander received its share of his attention. She thought about the mischievous sense of humor he displayed at the *Downton Abbey* screenings. Oh, he could handle Sylvie and Shelby all right; he'd have them eating out of the palm of his hand faster than ducks on the proverbial June bug. She could even see Brick puffing out his chest a little bit at the idea of a fancy concierge on the payroll. Samantha leaned closer to Sylvie and Lucy. "You know," she said casually, her fingers toying with the stem of her margarita glass. "I think I may have just the person to handle all of Shelby's pesky problems."

Maybe she could hire Edward Parker to handle hers. He could start with telling Jonathan that Hunter had once again lost a shitload of money and that anytime now the press and the SEC might be knocking on Jonathan's office door.

CHAPTER SIXTEEN

I T WAS POSSIBLE THAT PEOPLE WHO ACTUALLY knew how to cook found comfort in the act. Samantha had hoped this might be the case when she settled on the recipe for ossi buchin in gremolata, over which she'd planned to break the news of Hunter's latest financial disaster to Jonathan.

It was four forty-five p.m. and the knot in her stomach squeezed tighter. The veal was dry and leathery. The saffron rice, over which it was supposed to be served, was lumpy. And the gremolata had turned out to be a decidedly off-putting mixture of parsley, anchovies, and lemon rind.

With a last look at the clock, she dumped everything into the garbage and picked up the phone.

By the time Jonathan got home a bottle of wine was decanting and the condo smelled warmly Italian and inviting. She'd managed to shower and change into a simple black sheath that clung in all the right places and displayed just enough décolleté to hold her husband's attention without distracting him from the meal. She greeted him at the door with a gin and tonic and a smile.

"Welcome home." She went up on tiptoe to kiss him, then handed him the drink.

"Thank you." He dropped his briefcase on the foyer table and raised his glass in salute. "It's a relief to have a night in."

Samantha smiled and led him into the kitchen, but the smile was hard to hold on to. She felt a lot of things, but she was fairly certain none of them were relief.

"Mmmm. Something smells good." He glanced at the table, which she'd set for two, then at her. "Is it just us?"

She nodded, then busied herself stirring the rice, which she happened to know Giancarlo had cooked to perfection without a single lump or clump. It was clear that the grains in his kitchen did not have to resort to clinging together. In fact, they probably practically jumped into the boiling water at the honor.

Jonathan drained his cocktail and set the empty glass in the sink. "It looks like you've gone all out." He said this in all earnestness as if he actually believed she'd managed to produce the meal he was about to consume. He sniffed appreciatively. "Osso bucco?"

"Yes," she said. "And Italian wedding soup for starters."

"Fabulous," he said. "I'm starving."

"Good. If you'll pour the wine, I'll dish up the soup." She smiled though she couldn't imagine getting down a bite.

At the table she watched him dig into the first course with enthusiasm. "Delicious," he said. But she could feel him watching her. "Aren't you eating?"

"Oh, you know, I've been tasting all afternoon. I'm . . . going to save my appetite for the main course."

He nodded agreeably and reached for a slice of garlic bread. When he'd finished the soup he set his spoon down and took a sip of wine, looking at her expectantly.

This is Jonathan, she reminded herself. Not some ogre.

But still she couldn't seem to find the words that would start the conversation. She finished her first glass of wine before standing up to clear his soup bowl. The spoon clattered against the china and she startled.

"What's wrong?" he asked.

"Nothing," she said, but her voice quivered oddly. Keeping her head down, she dished up a bed of rice, then ladled the meat and sauce on top of it. The smell made her stomach roll. Her fingers felt thick and clumsy as she added perfectly grilled asparagus to both their plates. At the table she watched Jonathan eat. He closed his eyes briefly as he tasted the first bites.

"So," she said, her voice breaking on the word. "You haven't said much about your trip. How did it go?" She cleared her throat. "Is everything okay?"

"Yes." Jonathan looked up and finished chewing. "Andrew Martin is on board and the meetings in Boston went well. I shouldn't have to go back out to the West Coast for a couple of weeks."

"That's great." She moved the meat around her plate, not quite able to take a bite. Meeting his eyes proved equally difficult. "It'll be good to have you home for a while."

He continued to eat, clearly enjoying the meal, allowing her to steer the conversation. She told him about Meredith's interview and how right the position seemed for her. "I'm hoping she'll get the position. So that she can be a bit more . . . independent."

"Sounds good," he replied. "I'm glad Mother could be of help." He said this without irony, and she knew if she asked him, he'd do everything in his power to make sure Meredith got the job. That he would most likely do this without being asked. Because he was used to taking care of them. Jonathan took the last bites of veal, then dabbed at the corners of his mouth with the cloth napkin.

"Would you like a little more?" she asked hopefully, still not ready to dive into the subject that filled her mind. Maybe she should wait until he'd had dessert and had time to digest the meal. Maybe it would be better to talk after sex when both of them would be . . . more relaxed. His eyes skimmed over her bare skin and lingered on the rise and fall of her breasts.

"No, thanks." He topped off both their wineglasses and looked pointedly at the food on her plate, which she had spent the meal rearranging. "Why don't you tell me what's on your mind?" he said. "I appreciate the great food, but I feel kind of bad for enjoying it so much when you look so miserable."

She set down her fork and forced herself to meet his eyes. There was absolutely no point in putting this conversation off a minute longer. She'd been doing it all week and had gained nothing but completely frazzled nerves. Hunter was already furious with her—after he'd sent the one-pager he'd refused to return her phone calls. "It's about Hunter." She swallowed. "And the nanotechnology thing."

His jaw tightened and she knew just how wrong she'd been to put off bringing it up. He waited until she had no choice but to explain.

"Apparently there's a question about who owns the patent. There's something off about the stock issue and some of the other investors are . . . unsavory. Hunter's convinced that if he doesn't put in another hundred thousand dollars the whole thing will crash and the press will get hold of it." She swallowed again, the words stuck in her throat. "And the SEC seems poised to launch an investigation."

He didn't say anything but continued to watch her closely. His eyes gave nothing away and she felt a brief stab of pity for the people who'd sat on the other side of boardroom conference tables.

"I'm so sorry," she said in a rush, afraid that if she didn't, she'd swallow the words once again and never find the courage to speak them. "I don't want you to give him any more money, but it's all such a big mess. And I'm afraid that the firm's going to be dragged into it."

Something flickered in his eyes, but she couldn't identify it. He studied her closely, giving nothing away.

"I warned him the last time your reputation was threatened. But I . . . He wants to earn your respect; I know that's what he wants. But he just goes from one awful scheme to another. I told him there'd be no more money, that he had to go find a job, but I . . . I don't want you damaged and I don't want him to end up in jail."

"Jesus." He said this quietly, his eyes still on her. There was something new in them that she still couldn't decipher. Irritation? Disappointment? Weariness? Most likely it was all of the above.

"What do you want me to say?" His voice was clipped, his jaw tight. Whatever was going on inside was nowhere near as casual as his tone.

"I don't know," she admitted. She looked at her husband. The man she'd married out of fear and panic when she was barely old enough to understand what marriage was. His eyes had darkened until they were practically navy. There was that tick in his cheek again.

"I'm so sorry," she said again. "I should have put a stop to all of this a long time ago. Both he and Meredith have taken advantage." She resisted the urge to drop her eyes. "I feel like we all have."

She folded her hands in her lap to keep them from trembling. "I . . . I'm sorry. I know that's completely inadequate, but I am." She made herself meet his eyes. "I know you must be so angry."

He shook his head, ran a hand through his hair. "Being angry at Hunter is like being angry at a tornado for turning counterclockwise. He's a born gambler just like your father." He hesitated and Samantha knew he was thinking of her father's theft. How seriously he'd damaged the law firm that Jonathan had inherited and given his life to rebuilding. "He really believes that each venture is going to be the big score," Jonathan continued. "I'm not angry at Hunter. I understand where he's coming from and what motivates him. And I'm certainly not going to let him go to jail."

His eyes clouded and she began to understand. Knew she'd had good reason to avoid this conversation. "You're angry at . . . me." She said it quietly as if speaking softly would somehow soften the blow.

He nodded. "I'm angry that after twenty-five years of marriage you could actually be unable to eat a meal you've gone to great lengths to pretend you've cooked, because you're afraid to talk to me." The tick in his cheek became more pronounced. "I'm angry and disappointed," he said, looking both. "Because it's so obvious that you don't understand me, or my motivations, at all."

TWO WEEKS LATER, ON THE MORNING OF MARISSA Dalton's birthday party, Brooke awoke long before her alarm. For a time she lay in bed examining the day that lay ahead and going over the past weeks, which had been as turbulent as a propeller plane caught in a bank of thunderstorms. The pleasures of planning the "princess picnic" were the highs— the time spent dreading Zachary and Sarah's move into the Alexander, which would also take place today, had provided the stomach-churning drops.

With a potential guest list compiled with the help of the Daltons' neighbor across the street, Brooke had sent out invitations to the girls in Marissa's class and in her neighborhood and received a reassuring number of RSVPs. Last night she'd used cookie cutters to turn the picnic sandwiches into stars and hearts, loaded the art supplies and goody bags into the station wagon, and triple-confirmed the castle-shaped birthday cake, which she'd pick up on the way.

Bruce Dalton had insisted she bring Natalie and Ava to Marissa's party and the girls had shopped enthusiastically for a birthday present for the little girl they'd never met, asking questions the entire time.

"How come her mommy isn't giving her a birthday party?" Natalie had asked.

"Because she doesn't have one, sweetie. Her mommy was sick and had to go to heaven."

The girls were stunned that someone could not have a mommy. Missing fathers peppered the landscape at the private school they attended and, of course, there was the largely absent Zachary to let them know exactly what that felt like. But it clearly had never occurred to them that a mother might go away and not come back.

"Are you feeling okay, Mommy?" Ava had laid a chubby hand on Brooke's arm as they walked the aisles of Target's toy department, and Brooke knew she wasn't asking about her emotional well-being, but her plans to continue breathing.

"I feel great, sweetheart," Brooke said carefully. "And I'm not going anywhere." She hefted Ava up into her arms and planted a kiss on her forehead. "But that's why Marissa's daddy asked me to help plan Marissa's birthday party. And we're going to be extra sure she has a good time since she's new here and doesn't know a lot of people yet."

Natalie nodded sagely. "I me-member when we didn't know anybody at our school. It feels so sad."

Brooke reached down to squeeze her oldest's hand. The move to Atlanta had been hard; the lessons learned when Zachary left them harder still. "It's good to look out for other people who might need help to feel better," she said to both of them. "That's called empathy." She felt her heart rise in her throat. "And it's a good trait to have."

It had been a great teaching moment and she was proud of her children. But at this particular moment Brooke was most thankful that they'd be out of the Alexander today while Zach and Sarah moved into it.

The girls, however, were fascinated with the idea of their father a mere floor away and couldn't leave the topic alone.

"Will Daddy really live in the building when we get back

from the birthday party?" Natalie asked over her bowl of Cap'n Crunch.

"Does Sarah have to come with him?" Ava wanted to know.

"Why can't he just live here with us?" Natalie asked.

These were all very good questions. For which Brooke had no good answers. She was relieved when they were struck dumb with admiration for the turret-topped birthday cake they retrieved from the bakery. A castle that Brooke thought bore a striking resemblance to Downton Abbey; except for the Rapunzel-haired figure peering out from the turret window.

"Oh, Daddy, look at the castle!" Marissa Dalton's squeal of joy at her first sight of them and her birthday cake pushed all thoughts of Zachary and his girlfriend out of Brooke's mind. The smile that split Bruce Dalton's face at his daughter's excitement set the tone for the rest of the day.

The Daltons' backyard was green and lush and perfectly shaded. Leaves stirred in the early October breeze as Marissa, Natalie, and Ava raced outside to watch the castle-shaped bounce house put into position and inflated. While they "tested" the castle's bounce-worthiness, Brooke set up the arts-and-crafts stations, decorated the help-yourself lemonade stand, and arranged the cake on a table in the screened porch where everyone could see it but insects couldn't get to it.

As the guests arrived Marissa handed each little girl a pink or purple princess scepter and crown, and directed them to the arts-and-crafts tables where they could decorate them. The mothers who stayed congregated around a table Brooke had set with iced tea and fancy finger sandwiches. Many of them seemed keen on getting better acquainted with Bruce Dalton, who at times looked alternately pleased and panicked at their attention.

Marissa's purple princesses had trounced the pink team in egg carrying and the three-legged race, but lost the sack race when Brooke called a temporary halt to the relay races so that the picnic lunch could be served. The girls buzzed happily as they found seats on the blankets that had been spread beneath the trees.

"You've done an incredible job." The girls were munching on their sandwiches and drinking their lemonades when Bruce Dalton came up beside her. "I haven't seen Marissa so happy since . . . well, not for a long time. Everything's been just right."

Brooke glowed at his praise. The party was going well. She was gratified to see Marissa in the center of what looked like a great circle of friends-to-be; a circle her own two had been cheerfully drawn into.

"Thank you," she said. "I'm so glad she's having a good time." Out of the corner of her eye she saw the mothers watching Bruce Dalton and couldn't blame them. He was a nice man with a gentle, reassuring warmth. As she surveyed the interested females, she hoped he'd fall into sympathetic hands.

"The Princess Wars was sheer genius," he continued, his eyes on his daughter. "It's the perfect blend of princess and tomboy."

Brooke blushed at the compliment but felt an internal glow at the truth of it. Everything about the party, and Bruce Dalton's approval, made her feel good. "I think it's time to let Marissa blow out her candles. After the cake we'll try to burn up a little of the sugar high in the bouncy castle and with one or two more relay events before we declare the winning princesses."

"Sounds good," he said, flashing her a smile and motioning to Marissa. Together they led the way to the porch where Brooke lit the sparkler at the top of the cake's front turret.

Later, when the yard had been cleaned up, the bouncy castle retrieved, and her own children finally convinced it was time to leave, Bruce Dalton and his daughter walked them out to the driveway and helped them load the car.

He watched her strap the girls into their seats, then opened Brooke's door for her. "Thanks so much," he said as he closed the door, then leaned in the open window. "We both really appreciate everything you've done."

"It was my pleasure," Brooke said, meaning it.

"Well, I hope our paths cross again," he said, his eyes warm. "And I hope it's soon."

The Daltons watched as she backed the Volvo down the driveway. They hadn't even gone a block before Ava's and Natalie's heads began to bob with exhaustion. Moments later their chins fell to their chests in sleep. Equally weary, Brooke headed back to the realities that awaited them at the Alexander. She drove slowly and carefully, trying to shore herself up with the satisfaction she'd felt today, knowing she'd need every shred of confidence she could muster.

Turning onto Peachtree, she was relieved to see that there was no evidence of a moving van. As she carried Ava inside and held Natalie's sticky hand in hers, she told herself she was strong enough to handle whatever lay ahead. She yawned as Natalie pressed a sticky finger to the elevator call button and reminded herself that all was not yet lost.

She might not yet know how to deal with her ex-husband and his girlfriend living a floor away. But she apparently knew how to throw one hell of a princess wars picnic birthday party. Maybe something good could come of that.

CHAPTER SEVENTEEN

WITHOUT A JOB TO GO TO OR A CHILD TO GET off to school or cook meals for, Claire's days were large amoeba-like spans of emptiness, which she tried, but failed, to fill. They consisted of long bouts of concentrated procrastination, which Claire told herself were actually opportunities for her subconscious to work out the story problems, but whatever she called the hours she wasted, they did nothing to produce pages or much of anything but panic.

She walked at least once a day, sometimes with Brooke, who was intent on staying out of the building as much as possible and who scurried across the lobby with her head tucked into her shoulders like a turtle afraid of exposing too much of itself out of its shell.

On the bright side, it was October and the leaves had turned vibrant reds and golds and the temperatures were mild so that any sweating over the manuscript was figurative and not literal. She could, and did, spend hours out on her balcony scribbling in her journal and staring out over

Peachtree, but the book idea she'd once seen such promise in felt as empty and ill-defined as her days.

The characters that inhabited Downton Abbey had become almost as real to Claire as the women she watched it with. And far more real than her own characters, who refused to be coaxed out of her mind and onto the page. In just a few minutes she'd head to the clubroom for her Sunday-night fix.

Over the last two Sundays she'd watched Anna and Bates fall in love with each other despite some dark secret that kept him from being free, seen sparks fly between Lady Mary and Matthew Crawley, and watched Lady Sybil begin to notice just how attractive the Irish chauffeur was. Then there was poor Edith, who had stirred the pot by writing a letter to the Turkish embassy that would presumably implicate Mary in Kemal Pamuk's death.

The plot had been thickening and the story lines racing forward at a pace that Claire couldn't help admiring even as she compared its graceful dance to the fumbling, halfhearted steps of her own manuscript.

The phone rang, the sound so rare that it startled her. "Hello?" she answered tentatively.

"Claire?" The voice was young, with a pronounced New York accent that seemed vaguely familiar.

"Yes?"

"It's Erin. Erin Galloway. Your publicist at Scarsdale."

"Oh." Claire stared out over the balcony railing, trying to make sense of this. All authors at major publishing houses were assigned an in-house publicist. How often you heard from that publicist and what he or she actually did for you depended on how high up you were on the food chain and the publisher's perception of your potential moneymaking ability. With only two modestly successful books to her credit, Claire figured she was little more than a minnow in the vast sea of publishing. An insignificant form of bait; potential chum for the sharks.

"I'm sorry to bother you on the weekend," the publicist said. "Especially on a Sunday."

"Um, no problem." Claire studied the traffic down on Peachtree, searching for some sign that hell had, in fact, frozen over. But although the light was fading, the sky was still clear. A soft breeze teased at a flag that hung off a nearby building.

"My boss asked me to call you," Erin continued. "Because there's a bit of an emergency that we, um, well, that I thought might actually work in your favor."

Claire was fully tuned in now, though she couldn't imagine what sort of publishing emergency she might be able to assist with.

"Well, the thing is, LeaAnn Larsen is scheduled for a book signing at the Barnes & Noble in Midtown," the publicist said. "The one at Georgia Tech. I believe that's somewhere near you?"

"Yes." Claire still didn't understand. LeaAnn Larsen was a huge name in futuristic romance. That was to say she was a whale-sized fish in the publishing sea who could draw huge crowds to any bookstore a limo dropped her off at.

"Well, she's scheduled for a highly publicized signing there on Tuesday night."

Claire couldn't imagine what this had to do with her. Larsen was a favorite of women of all ages, who couldn't get enough of the former Navy SEALs, propelled into the future, who were the heroes of her books.

"That's great," Claire said. She glanced at her watch and saw that it was almost eight. She didn't want to be late for the *Downton Abbey* screening or to claim what had become her, Brooke, and Samantha's sofa. "But I don't really understand why . . ."

"LeaAnn's unable to do the event. We thought you might like to appear in her place."

Claire waited for clarification, certain she must have misheard or misunderstood. There was nothing but silence on the other end.

"Me?" Claire asked. "You want me to show up in LeaAnn Larsen's place? You do know who you called, right?" Maybe Erin had dialed the wrong number. There were plenty of better-known writers in Atlanta, at least half a dozen of whom were published by Scarsdale.

"Yes," Erin replied.

"But why?" Claire asked.

There was another silence.

"Because no one else was available," Erin admitted, her tone apologetic. "And the bookstore is really upset that they've advertised the event so heavily and won't have an author there."

Claire left the balcony and went inside. "This doesn't make sense. We're not exactly interchangeable. No one who shows up to see LeaAnn Larsen is going to be excited to see me instead. None of them will have ever heard of me. I'm . . ." She stopped just shy of calling herself a nobody, though in reality the minnow analogy might have been an exaggeration. In sea-of-publishing terms she was more like plankton.

They were offering the store a bone. A raggedy, over-chewed, and not very interesting bone, but a bone none-theless.

"If you can make it, we'll try to get some extra copies of your books there. And the store will be pulling in whatever copies they have at other Atlanta locations."

"This really doesn't seem like a good idea," Claire said.

Nobody in their right mind would agree to show up to face an unhappy and disappointed crowd. With the event two days away she wouldn't even be able to rally anyone who'd ever heard of her. Claire could hardly breathe. In the suburbs where she'd lived for so long, given enough lead time, phone calls to friends and acquaintances, and an email to her local readers she might have produced a respectable number of friendly faces. But here in Midtown where she knew practically nobody? She'd be lucky if she could talk the homeless guy on the corner into showing up on such

short notice. Even if she threw in a meal and a pack of ciga-
rettes.

"Oh, I don't think . . ." she began, knowing it would be
awful—and the last thing she needed right now was to feel
worse about herself. Plus she'd be far better off spending the
next two days writing instead of bracing herself to face a
hostile and disappointed crowd. "Listen, Erin, I appreciate
the thought, but I really don't think this is going to work."

"Please?" The woman's New York accent had softened,
the word unaccustomed on her lips. For some reason Claire
didn't understand this was important to the young woman
she'd never even met in person. "The thing is, the store has
threatened to never host another event for Scarsdale again if
we don't send someone in LeaAnn's place." There was a brief
pause. "If I don't get one of our authors there, my days in
publicity will be over. My boss has made that pretty clear."

Claire had no idea what to say to this.

"I mean, it would only be a couple hours of your time."

Just long enough to be completely humiliated and set her
writing back another week or two. As if she were writing now.

"Okay," Claire said barely able to believe she'd agreed even
as the young publicist offered her undying thanks and abject
gratitude.

Determined not to think about the potential fiasco she'd
just agreed to, Claire grabbed her purse. Eager to lose herself
in the world of *Downton Abbey*, which was far, far, more
attractive than her own, Claire closed and locked her door
behind her and headed down the hall.

WHEN BROOKE ARRIVED IN THE CLUBROOM JUST
after eight, Isabella, James, and Edward Parker greeted her
warmly. "Welcome, mum," Isabella said with a proper curtsy
and an elegant "It's quite lovely to see you again." James
handed her a glass of wine with a formal bow.

"You made quite an impression on Mr. Dalton," Edward said as Brooke took a small sip of wine and contemplated the tiny mincemeat and shepherd pies that had been set out on the table. "He and his daughter were absolutely thrilled with the princess picnic birthday party yesterday. In fact, I believe he'd like to hire you to handle some other things. Would you be open to that?" His brown eyes were warm, his smile friendly.

"Oh, yes." Brooke felt her cheeks heat at the thought. Bruce Dalton's compliments and Edward Parker's confidence in her were a balm to her bruised and battered ego.

The Ritchie twins and their mother arrived, flashing their identical smiles of hello. The feisty Mimi Davenport followed. Soon they were talking, heads bent, to Sadie Hopewell and Myra Mackelbaum.

The door opened and Samantha Davis entered. "Hey," she said with a smile that managed to include both Brooke and Edward Parker.

At a raised eyebrow from the concierge a glass of wine and a plate of appetizers were quickly placed in Samantha's hands. "Thanks," Samantha said easily, not at all surprised by the prompt attention. Together they headed toward the sofa, which Claire had already claimed.

"How did the party go yesterday?" Claire asked as they settled into their usual spots.

"Great," Brooke said.

"And the *doctor's* move into the building?" Samantha asked.

"Well, fortunately I missed it," Brooke replied. "But we bumped into them in the lobby this morning fresh from their run. Their exercise clothes are color coordinated. They looked like Workout Barbie and Marathon Ken."

Samantha grimaced. "I do not understand why that woman would want to live in the same building as her boyfriend's ex-wife."

"To rub Brooke's nose in it?" asked Claire.

"Her mere existence already does that," Brooke said. "And honestly, I don't see either of them wasting a moment's thought on me. I seem to be a nonentity in both of their minds." Oh, God, was that her sounding so pathetic?

"It sucks," Samantha agreed. "But I think we should try our best to look at the positives in the situation."

"Which are?" Brooke asked.

"Well, it's certainly going to make it more likely that Natalie and Ava will spend time with their father," Samantha said.

"And the drop-off/pickup time will be way shorter," Claire added.

"True," Brooke agreed. And if she did find a job or accepted more projects for Private Butler, Zachary might be more flexible about taking the girls if they were just a floor away.

"The building's pretty spacious," Samantha pointed out. "There are lots of people I never see coming or going."

Brooke nodded, but she knew how these things worked. Just because she didn't want to see either of them she was bound to run into Barbie and Ken every time she stepped out of her apartment.

"Is everything okay with your brother?" Claire asked Samantha and Brooke realized that Samantha hadn't so much as mentioned him since the night two weeks ago when they'd argued in the hall.

"No, not really," Samantha said, a frown creasing her forehead, something Zachary would have been quick to discourage.

Brooke waited for an explanation but that appeared to be it on the subject. Samantha Davis had proved surprisingly friendly and interested in her and Claire, but she didn't offer a lot of details about herself. Once again she deflected and turned the subject. "You have a strange look on your face," she said to Claire. "Is everything okay?"

Claire drained her glass and set it on the cocktail table,

but she didn't go for another. Brooke had noticed that ever since the shandies, she'd been careful about her alcohol consumption. "Yes."

"But?"

Claire just looked at her.

"The way you said that it sounded like a disclaimer was coming," Samantha said with a shrug.

Brooke nodded her agreement.

Claire sighed. "Well, for one thing my book isn't moving forward anywhere near as quickly as I'd hoped." She hesitated before continuing. "And I've been asked to do a book signing Tuesday night at the Georgia Tech B&N."

"But that's good, right?" Brooke asked, not understanding why Claire seemed so uncomfortable. "Isn't that how authors promote a new book?"

"Yes," Claire said. "But my last book came out more than a year ago. The only reason they asked me is because LeaAnn Larsen had to cancel at the last minute."

"I think I've heard of her," Samantha said. "She's a pretty big name, isn't she?"

Claire nodded, her expression glum.

"I love her books," Brooke said. "Those Navy SEALs are . . . dreamy."

"I know," Claire said. "My daughter used to devour them. But I don't write Navy SEALs past, present, or future. I write romances set in seventeenth-century Scotland."

"So why is this happening?" Samantha asked.

"We're with the same publisher, although, that's kind of like saying we're both cars when I'm a PT Cruiser and LeaAnn Larsen is a Rolls-Royce. But somehow the store thinks any author is better than no author."

"And you don't think so," Brooke said.

Claire shook her head. "LeaAnn Larsen's fans are bound to be royally pissed off. And it's not like I have fans that are going to show up with only two days' warning. My local audience lives out in the suburbs and seems to have an aversion to driving through the 'circle of fire' that is Highway 285 to come in town."

Samantha laughed. "I'm sure you must have fans ITP." She used the term for inside the perimeter.

"Well, there may be some. But I'm not exactly a household name. Had you ever read or even heard of either of my books before we met?"

"No," Samantha conceded.

"Me, either," Brooke admitted. "But I'd like to read you. I've never known a real published author before."

"Good," Claire said drily. "If you're not busy Tuesday night, you two can come circle the wagons around me and protect me from the angry Larsen fans."

"Of course we will," Samantha said as Edward Parker moved toward the front of the room. The chatter began to die down.

"Absolutely," Brooke added. "We'll both be there. And, who knows, maybe those Larsen fans will give your books a try and realize what they've been missing."

Chapter Eighteen

LEAANN LARSEN'S FANS KNEW EXACTLY WHAT they were missing. And that was LeaAnn Larsen.

When Claire arrived at six forty-five a line of Larsen's fans already stretched out the front door and snaked around the block. They eyed her impatiently as she walked by them with her poster for *Highland Hellion* bumping against one knee and her tote bag stocked with bookmarks, "autographed by the author" stickers, pens, and a "please join my mailing list" sheet stuffed inside. The looks got angry when she entered the store and walked past the fans who'd shown up early enough to be at the head of the line.

A woman detached herself from the information desk and hurried over to Claire. "I'm Dee, the customer relations manager." She looked briefly over Claire's shoulder and her lips trembled. "Thank God you're here."

"Hasn't anyone told them she isn't coming?" Claire asked through dry lips.

"Um, no. We drew straws and did rock/paper/scissors, but none of us could agree on who would tell them."

The jostling of the crowd grew more pronounced.

"Where is she?" one of them called out. "Where's LeaAnn?"

"And where's Blade?" another yelled, referring to one of Larsen's most popular former SEAL heroes. "I heard she always brings a hero with her."

Jesus. Claire was afraid to turn around. If there'd been another author within hailing distance, she would have been in a heated round of rock/paper/scissors herself right now.

"Come on," Dee said reaching for Claire's poster. "Let me get you set up." She snuck another look over Claire's shoulder and a shudder ran through her.

"What?" Claire asked.

"Nothing." The CRM swallowed and averted her eyes. She took Claire's arm and began to lead her toward the signing table. "Would you like something to drink?"

The crowd began to murmur and not in a friendly/happy way. Claire felt like a Christian about to be fed to the lions. "Only if it's alcoholic and fast working."

"Sorry." The CRM did, indeed, look sorry. In fact, she looked like she might burst into tears at any moment. Claire knew the feeling.

They reached the table but neither of them turned to face the now-muttering crowd.

"Hey, where's LeaAnn?" a voice cried out.

"Who's that?" another yelled.

"Are you ready?" Dee asked quietly.

Claire shook her head gently. "Not really," she said. She'd had signings where the only people who approached her table were looking for directions to the bathroom or the information desk. When you weren't a big name book signings were a total crapshoot—sometimes a respectable number of actual readers came and sometimes even your immediate family didn't show up. But she'd never before been afraid for her safety. Maybe if she just turned and left now, no one, especially her, would get hurt.

Dee ignored her comment. Still holding Claire's arm, she

led Claire to the chair behind the signing table. The CRM might be young and thin, but she had a grip like a vise. Still, you might lead a frightened author to a signing table but that didn't mean she had to sit. Claire hovered behind the chair studying the crowd, who had now pushed past the stanchions and were studying her back.

With shaking hands Dee set the poster on the table and opened the back flaps so it could stand on its own. There was silence as the fans at the front of the line took in the book's cover and read the title and the author's name. Some of their mouths moved with the effort, but that might have been because they were battling their disbelief. Another store employee wheeled over a cart stacked with books. He propped a copy of *Highland Hellion* and one of Claire's first book, *Highland Kiss*, in front of one of the stacks so that their covers could be seen.

"What kind of bullshit is this?" a girl in a Georgia Tech T-shirt cried. "I cut my Lit class to come here."

"This is bogus," someone else shouted. "I didn't stand in line for an hour to see somebody I never even heard of!"

There was chaos as the front of the line broke ranks. Claire braced for a frontal assault but the majority of the surge was backward toward the exit.

"Where are the frickin' Navy SEALs?" a woman who found herself unexpectedly at the front asked. "I promised my daughter I'd get a picture with one of the Navy SEALs!" She held up her camera. The flash accidentally went off.

Once the pushing started the crowd surged and retreated, looking much like a cell attempting to divide as people at the front tried to leave and people at the back, who couldn't see what was going on, pressed forward. Each new batch that landed at the front read the poster, glared at Claire, and shouted out either their disappointment or anger before clawing their way back toward the entrance.

"Gosh, maybe we *should* have canceled," Dee said. "We voted on it a bunch of times but it was always a tie."

"What, you didn't rock/paper/scissors it?" Claire dead-panned. Her heart was racing in her chest, and her mouth was horribly dry, but the fear was receding. So far she'd received a lot of angry looks and a good bit of disdain, but no one had seriously threatened bodily harm. Yet.

An older woman was thrust forward by the surging and receding crowd—like a seashell deposited onto the beach by the ocean's tide. She teetered precariously for a moment, her glasses askew, her fluffy white hair puffed out around her head. Slowly she regained her balance, steadying herself with her cane.

Claire stepped around the table and the cart of books when she recognized the woman. "Mrs. Davenport? What are you doing here?"

"My word!" The older woman brushed off her silk blouse and straightened her pearls. "I got a phone call about your book signing and I must say you've got quite a crowd." She looked around, her forehead creasing in confusion. "But I don't understand where they were putting the seals. Is there a tank somewhere in the store?"

There was another tidal strength surge and Sadie Hopewell and Myra Mackelbaum landed near Mimi Davenport.

"Goodness," Myra said, running a hand over her hair. "I had no idea we'd have to fight our way inside."

Sadie blinked several times, taking it all in. "Did they really say there were seals here?" She turned to Claire. "Are you a nature writer, dear?" she asked.

"No," Claire said, far closer to laughing than she would have thought possible just ten minutes ago. "I write histori-cal romance. Set in the Scottish Highlands."

"You've gotta love a man who can wear a kilt," Samantha Davis said as she stepped through what remained of the original crowd. As usual, every hair was in place. Her jeans, white T-shirt, and blazer looked completely unruffled and casually elegant. "I hope you're planning to sign some books," Samantha said. "Because I'm looking forward to reading your work and both my sister and my mother-in-law asked me to pick up autographed copies for them."

The CRM straightened beside Claire, flashing what could only be called a relieved smile. "Well then, I guess we have ourselves a signing." She bustled around the cart and table and pulled out the chair. "Ms. Walker?"

The crowd had diffused now so that it was possible to see individuals. Claire felt a reassuring glow as Brooke Mackenzie stepped up behind Samantha, giving Claire a friendly wave and a warm smile. Edward Parker, James, and Isabella, who was not sporting her upstairs-maid attire but seemed to have brought her attempts at a British accent with her, moved through the milling group to stand behind Brooke in what was beginning to look like an actual line. "'Ello, 'ow ya doin', guhv'nor!" she proclaimed to a bookstore employee.

An unhappy LeaAnn Larsen fan clutching a book with a Navy SEAL on the cover walked up to the concierge. Claire couldn't hear what the woman said, but she heard Edward Parker's reply. "I understand, madam," he said in his crisp, elegant accent. "But I highly recommend this author." He leaned down to hear her response. "No, I don't believe there are any seals in her stories."

Isabella bobbed her head and offered the woman a curtsy. A few others who'd come for LeaAnn Larsen shrugged and joined the line as Claire took the proffered seat and quickly unpacked her bookmarks and autograph stickers. Dee and her coworkers moved copies of *Highland Kiss* and *Highland Hellion* off the cart and onto the signing table. Claire looked up and spotted the Ritchie twins and their mother. Melinda Greene and her partner Diana were right behind them.

Claire wasn't sure if it was Brooke or Samantha or both who had put out the word, but practically the whole Sunday-night *Downton Abbey* group seemed to be here. Claire felt a smile stretch across her face.

"Well then," Dee said, ushering Mimi Davenport up to the table. "I think it's time for the signing to begin."

* * *

EDWARD LED EVERYONE BACK TO THE ALEXANDER
clubroom for champagne and chocolates after the signing.
He was gratified by how many of the Sunday-night group
had made it to the bookstore. Many of them had brought
friends and acquaintances. Claire Walker's "fans" had proved
less . . . vocal . . . than the originally scheduled author's readers, but they'd numbered close to thirty and Edward had
noticed that almost everyone, including himself, had bought
multiple copies.

Even Mimi Davenport, who'd almost "accidentally"
walked out of the store without paying had bought several
copies for her daughters and daughters-in-law.

"To the Alexander's full-time and soon-to-be-famous
author!" Samantha raised her glass of champagne in toast.

"Hear! Hear!"

"Woo-hoo!" Logan and Callan Ritchie hooted.

They clinked and drank. Isabella passed trays of
desserts—all of them covered with, filled with, or made of
chocolate—with commendable restraint and only a few bobs
and curtsies and one lamentable, "Bottoms up then!"

Edward was pleased at the increasing ease with which the
women who'd become regulars interfaced.

"I want to thank all of you for coming to Barnes and
Noble tonight," Claire said over her raised glass. "I was
thrilled that you took the time to come out and I appreciate
you buying my books. I think you saved me from what would
have been a horrible ordeal."

"Is she talking about the seals?" Mimi Davenport asked
putting a hand up to cup her ear.

"No, Mrs. D," Isabella said. "She said ordeal!"

Claire aimed a smile at Brooke and Samantha. Edward
was glad to see that she'd guessed who'd organized the evening. He'd been watching the three women begin to bond
over the past weeks and thought Samantha Davis, Brooke

Mackenzie, and Claire Walker made an interesting combination.

"It meant a huge amount to me that you came. And I think the customer relations manager was pretty relieved, too." Claire raised her glass to her lips and took a long drink.

Edward watched the women fall into chattering groups. In less than a week they'd screen the last program of season one. Then it would be on to the second season. His uncle had tried to tempt him again with a sneak peek at season three, but Edward looked forward to watching it here in January. Hopefully with this same group.

Slowly the room began to empty. As Isabella and James began to tidy up, Samantha Davis turned back from the doorway and came over to speak with him. "I wanted to thank you for organizing the spread." She nodded to the table where Isabella and James were packing up what remained of the desserts and bottles of champagne. "I was glad we had such a good turnout."

"Yes, you certainly know your way around a, what did you call it, a phone tree?" Edward said.

"Everyone has to be good at something." Samantha laughed. "You can't serve on as many committees as I have without learning how to use a telephone to its fullest."

"Well, you're a maestro," Edward replied. "And I've been wanting to thank you for the referral to Sylvie Talmadge and her daughter. I've put one of my people full-time on servicing them, and I checked in several times last week to reassure them that they have our undivided attention."

"Perfect," Samantha said. "I knew you'd have them figured out in no time."

"People are people," he said smoothly. "Everyone wants to feel cared for and important."

"Yes."

"Well, I appreciate your confidence in me and my business as well as the referral. I hope you'll let me know if there's ever anything I can offer in return."

He didn't think there was a lot she didn't or couldn't have, but her eyes lit up.

"Do you mean that?" she asked.

"Yes, of course," he replied. "Is there something you need?"

She hesitated but only briefly. "Would you consider interviewing my brother for a position in your company?"

He kept his features schooled to mask his surprise. "Hunter?"

"Yes, he's really good in sales. We do know a lot of people who might appreciate your services. Perhaps he could serve as a sales representative as you continue to build Private Butler."

"I don't really have a sales spot per se. I've done most of that and, of course, we rely largely on referrals and word of mouth." He hesitated. "I'm not sure I'd have anyone selling my company who hadn't worked in it." He looked at her, weighing his words. "If he were willing to learn the business from the ground up . . . spend some time as a concierge . . . it could turn into something more."

"It could work," she said carefully. "Assuming you'd be willing to take him on. I . . . ." She paused. "I don't want to put you on the spot."

Edward thought about the young man's sense of entitlement. The way he strutted through the building, expecting others to take care of his every need. "Is he interested in this?"

"I don't know," Samantha said. "But I don't see why he wouldn't be. You have a real business and he'd have a chance to get in on the ground floor."

"It's also hard work, and there's not much glory in it," he said quietly. "The customer is always, always right." Once again he weighed his words. "If you'll forgive me for saying so, I'm not certain he'll be happy taking orders instead of giving them."

"You are an astute judge of character, Edward," Samantha Davis said. "I respect that about you. But he's looking for a job—or at least he's supposed to be. And his time is running out."

"I'll be glad to introduce him to the business and give him some projects. I thought he was more of a financial person . . ."

Samantha frowned. "That hasn't gone as well as it might. He needs a new direction. I'll speak to him and ask him to set up an appointment."

"That would be fine," Edward said, keeping his true thoughts to himself. But as he drank the glass of champagne that had gone quite warm in his hands, he found himself hoping that Hunter Jackson would turn his nose up at Private Butler. If ever he'd met a man that seemed ill suited for cheerfully serving others, it was Samantha Davis's brother.

Chapter Nineteen

"Y OU WANT ME TO WHAT?" HUNTER SNAPPED AT Samantha. She'd invited him out to lunch in hopes of avoiding an ugly confrontation, but her brother looked at her as if she'd just suggested he strip naked and stake himself out on an anthill.

She kept a smile on her face and her voice low. When the waiter looked as if he were headed their way to check on them, she shook her head slightly to discourage him. "I want you to call Edward Parker and make an appointment to talk to him about opportunities at his company."

"The man is a glorified servant," he said nastily. "And I don't care where he got his accent or the stick up his butt. The answer is no."

"No is not an option, Hunter."

"It would be if you'd convinced Jonathan to save the nanotechnology deal."

"Apparently there was nothing to save," she said. "Except your ass. Which Jonathan has done for the very last time.

It's a miracle he was able to satisfy the SEC and keep things out of the paper."

"This is bullshit," he said in what could only be called a snarl. But at least it was a low snarl.

"No," Samantha said determined to stay on point. "It's reality. Your reality."

"You talked him into cutting me off." Hunter picked up his highball glass and looked up and around for the waiter, who made a hopeful step toward the table. When Hunter looked down at his plate, she warned the waiter off with another small shake of her head. The man turned on a dime and headed back into the kitchen.

"It didn't take much talking," she said to Hunter. "And he's kept you out of jail. Which is more than you deserve."

He looked at her with real hatred. "Good God, what has happened to the service here? I don't even see our waiter."

Samantha shrugged. The last thing this conversation needed was more alcohol.

"I'm not going to go out and try to sell some flaky concierge service," Hunter snapped.

"Private Butler is a real business," she said. "And what you do for the company would be up to Edward Parker."

"You've got to be kidding."

"No." Now Samantha wished she could have another glass of wine. Or two. She hoped the waiter stayed scarce; she was using up all her willpower not backing down from Hunter's anger. "You're welcome to apply for other jobs you feel are more suited to you." Were there still financial positions for people who'd frittered as much money as Hunter had? "But didn't you learn anything from Dad?"

"I learned that working for a paycheck is only for chumps. When did our father ever do that?"

"Oh, Hunter," she said. "He was a gambler and a thief who stole from his partners and died trying to escape a mess he couldn't talk his way out of." And he'd taken their mother with him. "I think there's a lot more honor in working for a living than there is in stealing. Or letting someone else support your pipe dreams."

"That's easy for you to say."

Samantha bit back the angry words she wanted to hurl at him. What was the point? Neither her brother or sister had any idea of the guilt she felt for marrying Jonathan for so many selfish reasons. Or bothered to wonder what she might have done with her life if she hadn't spent so much of it taking care of them. "You really never give me the benefit of the doubt, do you? You're so occupied with yourself you have no idea what goes on in my life."

He didn't answer. But he did make eye contact with the waiter, holding up his empty glass so there could be no question what he wanted. He didn't ask Samantha if she'd like another drink.

"I expect you to make an appointment with Edward Parker," she said. "If you don't, I will personally cut off your credit cards and close your bank accounts and let Jonathan know that you won't be needing the apartment anymore."

"You wouldn't."

"I would," she said. "And I will."

"Is there anything else?" It was a dare. Once again she refused to back off.

"Yes. We're going to be celebrating Meredith's new job at the Atlanta Preservation Board. You're not the only one who's expected to pull their own weight. I'm making a reservation at Four Seasons for Friday night and I want you to join us."

"Well, apparently your wish is now my command," he said in the nasty tone that he'd perfected at her expense over the years. "I'll check my calendar."

Once she would have dissembled. Apologized for making him feel that way. Told him that wasn't how it was at all. Offered to change the date if there was a conflict. But he'd crossed the final line in his dealings with Jonathan. And

Samantha was deathly afraid that if she let Hunter continue down his current path, he'd end up disgraced and dead like their father.

"Good. I'll text you the time as soon as I've made the reservation. It would be great if you'd already spoken to Edward Parker by then so that you can share your good news, too."

The waiter was headed their way with Hunter's drink, but it was clear to both of them that the meal was over. She paid the check and left him nursing the whiskey and soda. Along with his anger at her.

THAT FRIDAY MORNING BROOKE APPROACHED THE lobby head down, eyes on her feet, moving at a relatively fast pace so as not to see—or have to acknowledge—Sarah Grant should they end up in the lobby at the same time.

"Mrs. Mackenzie?"

She stopped and turned at the sound of Edward Parker's voice. He crossed the lobby. As always she felt slightly unkempt in front of the smartly pressed concierge. "Hi," she said. "How are you?"

"Fine, thank you. And you?"

"Good." Okay, it was a lie; a somewhat pathetic attempt at the "smile and the whole world smiles with you" philosophy that had led some sadist to invent the smiley face, but a small part of her hoped it would work. "Did you want to talk to me about something?" She couldn't help darting a look around the lobby. She didn't want to be caught unawares by Barbie and/or Ken.

"Yes, actually," the concierge said. "I've had a request for your services."

"My . . . services?"

"Yes. Bruce Dalton called. I know I mentioned how happy he was with the birthday party for his daughter."

This time the smile planted itself on her lips of its own

accord. She was almost embarrassed by how good it felt to receive a compliment. The check the concierge had left in her lobby mailbox had also been wonderful. It was the first money she'd earned since their move to Atlanta.

"He'd like to hire you to take his daughter clothes shopping. It seems he doesn't feel, er, equal to the task." Edward smiled. "Is that something you might be willing to take on?"

"Really? He asked specifically for me?"

"Yes," Edward Parker said. "You and your girls apparently made quite an impression on both of them."

"That would be . . . great," Brooke said.

"Good. All you need to do is call Mr. Dalton to set up a mutually convenient time and then keep track of your hours and mileage. I'll handle the billing once Mr. Dalton deems her wardrobe complete."

"Okay." Brooke blushed again but was already sorting through the girls' schedule. Maybe she could take Marissa shopping next Tuesday or Thursday when the girls stayed after school for music. Or maybe it would be better on Wednesday when Zachary was supposed to pick them up for dinner and to spend the night. Without thinking she went up on her toes and threw her arms around the concierge. "Thank you," she heard herself gush. "Thank you *so* much."

Edward Parker smiled cautiously and gave her a hug in return. "I'm very happy to have someone so competent and enthusiastic covering the 'mother sphere' for Private Butler." He gave her a friendly pat on the back and she almost whimpered at how nice it felt to have someone who thought well of her touch her.

Someone cleared his throat behind her and she jumped in surprise.

"Am I interrupting something?" The voice was smooth and southern. Somehow the speaker managed to insert a great deal of condescension into the polite inquiry.

Edward Parker stiffened and dropped his arms, but his face gave no indication of surprise or irritation.

Brooke turned and saw Samantha Davis's brother studying the two of them. In the daylight, unlike in the darkened hall outside the clubroom, Brooke could see just how attractive he was. She could also see the anger in his green eyes and the nasty smirk on his lips.

"Well, thank you again," Brooke said to Edward. She bobbed her head at Hunter Jackson, but Edward could see how uncomfortable the young man had made her.

Edward felt his mouth tighten in disapproval at Jackson's trampling of what had been a lovely, and innocent, celebratory moment. "My pleasure," he said to Brooke. "I'll look forward to hearing how the outing goes."

He gave himself a moment before turning his attention to Samantha Davis's brother. Both of them watched Brooke Mackenzie skitter away.

"It must be like shooting fish in a barrel for you here," Jackson drawled. "All these mousy, grateful women creaming over that accent of yours."

The expression on Jackson's face was expectant as he waited for Edward's reaction to the vulgarity. When Edward said nothing the green eyes narrowed. "Or maybe that's not what floats your boat?"

Edward simply stared back, which afforded him the satisfaction of seeing Hunter Jackson shift uncomfortably from one foot to the other.

"I didn't invite you here to discuss my sexual preferences or activities," Edward said finally. "And for your information Private Butler staff never service the clients in that way." He could feel Hunter resisting the urge to look away. "Never."

"But you didn't really invite me did you?" Jackson said. "You owe my sister a favor and you want to impress my brother-in-law. You had to take a meeting with me." Jackson looked far too smug by half.

"Is that what you think we're doing?" Edward asked. "Taking a meeting? Because I rather thought I was interviewing you for a possible position within my firm."

Hunter Jackson broke eye contact first, but he masked his retreat with a look of utter contempt. So far Edward had seen little of the charming salesman Samantha seemed to think dwelt somewhere inside her brother. "It seems we're wasting each other's time then, doesn't it?" Edward said, glad to put an end to it. He turned to go.

There was a long beat of silence before Jackson reached out, his hand stopping just short of Edward's sleeve. "No. Wait." He dropped the sneer. "I'm supposed to be making a good impression on you and I've already crashed and burned." He offered a self-deprecating smile. One that actually reached his eyes. "I'm sorry. Maybe we could start over?"

The change in demeanor was swift, hinting at a host of Hunter Jacksons buried beneath the prep-school, too-wealthy-for-his-own-good façade.

"Do you really think it's possible to erase a first impression and replace it with another?" Edward asked, almost curious to hear the answer.

"No, not really," the younger man conceded. "But I'm hoping *you* do." There was a good bit of bravado in the smile that accompanied Jackson's answer. When Edward didn't respond Hunter straightened his shoulders, smiled broadly, and offered his hand. "Hunter Jackson," he said smartly. "It's a pleasure to meet you." His handshake was firm but not bone crushing. His eyes met Edward's with what looked like sincere enthusiasm. "I've heard great things about Private Butler and I appreciate you taking the time to speak with me about opportunities within your organization."

The handshake ended but Jackson maintained eye contact. The smile remained in place. There was not a speck of con-descension or sarcasm in evidence. Even Edward, who prided himself on the ability to read others, wouldn't have suspected how much anger and hostility lay beneath Jackson's smooth surface if their initial conversation hadn't taken place. The man could act. How long he could stay in character—and what actually lay beneath the roles he played—was another question altogether.

"Come along then," Edward said. "Let's talk in my office."

They crossed the lobby. As they neared the concierge desk Isabella dropped a curtsy in their direction. "'Allo, guhv'nors!" A look of longing showed on her face when Hunter Jackson flashed a smile at her. Isabella blushed but nonetheless stuck out her hand when Edward introduced them. "Sorry. I've been working on my accent for the *Downton Abbey* evenings."

Edward studied the young man. He was extremely attractive and knew it. More to the point, he was used to using his looks to his advantage, but Edward would be a hypocrite if he pretended he hadn't done the same. One used the assets at one's disposal. Not to do so would be foolish.

Isabella turned scarlet when Jackson held her hand a bit longer than necessary. "I'm a . . . an actress," she explained, then looked at Edward nervously. "But I'm learning the concierge business, too."

"I would imagine the fields have quite a lot in common," Jackson observed drily. The laugh that followed made it difficult to detect hidden levels of sarcasm. Isabella's face lit up at the sound.

Edward led the young man into his office and ushered him into the seat opposite the desk. He watched Jackson take in his surroundings, the diploma from Cornell, the photos of Edward with select celebrity guests that covered a small section of one wall. Now that he'd stopped trying to shock and offend, Hunter Jackson's face was even more pleasant to look upon. He crossed one leg over the other and folded his hands in his lap. The boy had a lot going for him. He was young, attractive, and well spoken. He dressed beautifully and knew how to look a person in the eye. His family's contacts were significant. But none of this mattered if Jackson couldn't control his tongue or rein in his attitude for sufficient periods of time.

There was no question that Samantha Jackson Davis had

a blind spot when it came to her siblings. Edward thought about his grandfather and his twin as well as his own brother, Bertie. If your own family couldn't overlook your shortcomings, who could?

"Let's cut to the chase, shall we?" Edward said. "You're here under duress. And I'm interviewing you as a favor to your sister."

The green eyes telegraphed surprise at the admissions, but Jackson remained silent.

"I also know that the concierge business is pretty far removed from what you've been doing."

Jackson nodded but still didn't speak. Edward gave him several points for knowing when to remain silent.

"So, I have to ask myself are you here for any other reason than to satisfy your sister. And if so, what, in fact, you bring to the table."

Jackson looked shocked that anyone would question him, but hid it quickly. "Okay," he said. "I guess under the circumstances those are fair questions." This time he studied Edward, taking his measure. "I'm here to get Samantha off my back. And I don't know anything about serving others." He practically shuddered on the last two words. "I can't say that I have any real interest in doing so." He paused, still maintaining eye contact. "But apparently I need a job. And I can talk pretty much anyone into pretty much anything. I don't think there's any item, concept, or service I couldn't sell. If I decided to." Jackson's words had been chosen with care, but his body had opened slightly, his gestures had become less guarded.

It was time to explain Private Butler in terms the younger man might understand. "For the last four quarters there's been huge growth in the personal services sector. And far more growth is being forecast. Everyone's rushing around at top speed; even the wealthy feel the push-pull of it. Every reliable survey indicates that the one thing people desperately need in their lives is more time."

The green eyes flickered and Edward could tell he had

Jackson's full attention. "We give our clients that extra time. Plus an attention to detail and a degree of pampering that most—even the ultra wealthy—do not allow themselves." He paused to let this sink in. "My family has been 'in service' in one way or another since the early nineteenth century. It's an honorable profession, which requires skill and finesse and at times the ability to bend others to one's will without them even sensing it."

A small smile tugged at Hunter Jackson's lips.

"Yes, just like in the field you've come out of. In any field really." Edward smiled. "We're not selling birthday planning, though Mrs. Mackenzie just put on a bang-up party for a new client's little girl. Nor are we selling errand running or personal shopping, though I have several part-time employees who excel at this." He was pleased with how carefully Jackson seemed to be following. "Our job, our goal if you will, is to make their lives better."

"You're selling the sizzle, not the steak," Jackson said, nodding.

"Exactly," Edward said. "The Private Butler tagline is 'Making Your Life More Civilized, Whatever It Takes.' The subtext is the same as that hair color company that uses, 'Because You're Worth It.'"

"It sounds like a way easier sell than what I'm used to," Jackson said. "I don't think I'd have any trouble at all selling Private Butler."

"Yes," Edward said, watching Hunter's face carefully. "In time, I'm sure you could."

"In time?" The objection came swiftly. The green eyes flashed with anger. Hunter Jackson's true self could be hidden but it was never far from the surface, where it simmered waiting to erupt. "I've been selling far more complicated concepts for years now. I—"

"I understand all that," Edward interrupted calmly. "But this is my company and my reputation. There is not one without the other."

Edward waited for the protest he could see forming on Jackson's lips. It took a few moments, but Jackson managed to squelch it. It was good to know he had the capacity to think before speaking when the occasion demanded it.

"No one who hasn't worked in the trenches and learned firsthand what Private Butler is will ever represent me or my company. And not to put too fine a point on it but it's a matter of 'my company, my rules.'"

Edward paused waiting for another protest, which would, as far as he was concerned, conclude this interview. Jackson remained silent. As Edward watched, the other man's tight jaw loosened.

"If you're interested, I'll assign you to the entry-level projects I think you're best suited for and will train you as I have the others."

He waited, watching Jackson carefully as he did so. "Is that something you can live with?"

Edward wasn't completely sure what Jackson's answer would be. Finally Jackson nodded. "Yes." He stood and extended his hand. "I'm ready to start whenever you are."

Edward stood and shook the younger man's hand. He gave him paperwork to fill out and walked him out to the lobby.

Jackson stopped briefly at the concierge desk to flirt with Isabella. The girl's giggle had nothing British about it and she blushed crimson when she noticed that Edward was watching.

But as he watched Hunter Jackson leave the building Edward wasn't thinking about Isabella. He was thinking that Hunter Jackson had a lot to offer. That with the right training and supervision it was possible that he could become a true asset to Private Butler. But Edward Parker had not just fallen off of the parsnip truck. He mustn't allow himself to forget that Hunter Jackson was a person one should never turn one's back on.

CHAPTER TWENTY

BY FRIDAY AFTERNOON CLAIRE'S RELIEF AT THE salvaging of her book signing had begun to dissipate. Thanks to the *Downton Abbey* posse, disaster had been averted. She'd sold enough books to walk out of the store with her head up. It had not, however, improved her focus on the book she was supposed to be writing or eliminated the guilt she felt at the breadth and depth of her procrastination. In the days since, she'd sat and stared at her computer screen for maybe two or three hours each day, struggling to envision her heroine, now named Alana, whose goals and motivations continued to elude her and whose name she could not yet fully commit to. Claire's mind felt as close to blank as it was possible to get without going on life support. That is to say she produced what might charitably be called . . . nothing. No matter how many times she asked herself what Nora would do, she could not bring her brain to heel or will her fingers to pick out the letters that would turn into the words that would allow her to begin.

This time when Claire's phone rang she recognized the

New York phone number as that of her agent, Stephanie Rostan. Its appearance on her caller ID was rare; her agent did not dodge her as some agents dodged smaller, lesser-known clients, which she was. But she didn't call to chitchat, either. Theirs was a business relationship. They communicated largely via email and talked only when there was something to talk about—a contract clause, a manuscript delivery date, a question about language.

"Hello?" she answered tentatively.

"Claire?" Stephanie's voice was quick and clear, her manner direct. She was not unfriendly, but she didn't pretend to the warm fuzziness that might allow an author to think he or she was in a business where anything but the marketability of the final product truly mattered.

"Hi, Stephanie," Claire said. "How are you?"

"Good. You?"

The pleasantries, such as they were, out of the way, her agent came to the point of the call. "Scarsdale is grateful that you stepped in Tuesday night. Wendy McCurdy called me," she said, naming Claire's editor at Scarsdale. "She's eager to read what you've got on the new book. They've had a slot open up for next November, which would get you on the shelves almost five months earlier than we expected. You could have that slot if you can deliver a complete manuscript by June first."

Claire may have stopped breathing. Surely that was what was causing the lack of oxygen to her brain. "I'm sorry. What did you say?" Claire's heart pounded and her mouth had gone dry. She hadn't even committed to her character's names or completed a serious character sketch.

"You definitely want to jump on this while they're feeling grateful and have you on their mind," the agent said. "It's a very good thing you're writing full-time now. How soon can you get the synopsis and first three chapters to Wendy?"

It had never before occurred to Claire that being in her publisher's thoughts could be a bad thing. She'd flown underneath their radar for so long she could hardly process this.

"Claire?"

Claire's brain was racing now, but not in any discernible direction. She knew the right answer was "next week" or even the week after that, but that, of course, was impossible. "Um, I'm not sure how long it'll be until I have something that's ready to be looked at," she finally said. "I'm, um, waiting for a few things to gel in my mind."

There was a silence, but it, too, was quick and efficient. Stephanie Rostan needed nowhere near as long as Claire did to regroup.

"Why don't you send me what you've got and I'll take a look at it?" Stephanie said.

This was an unprecedented offer. Rostan had been an editor before becoming an agent, so her feedback would be valuable. If, in fact, there were anything to offer feedback on.

Claire began to pace her apartment, the phone pressed to her ear, her thoughts jumbled and uncertain. This was the opportunity she'd been waiting for. Somehow all of the publishing stars had miraculously aligned. And she was nowhere near ready to take advantage of it.

Should she tell Stephanie what was going on? Or rather what was *not* going on?

What would Nora do? The question caused a knot to form in the pit of her stomach. Nora would not be in this mess. Nora would have been writing her twenty pages a day every single day and would be only too happy to send off whatever her agent or editor wanted to look at.

No. Claire stifled the admission of writer's block and panic that threatened to spill out. Admitting what was going on would not be the relief she coveted. It would be a mistake.

Her agent was not her friend. To be too honest about her lack of progress would be a fatal error; one her career might never recover from.

The silence spooled out between them. Too much silence could be just as damning as too many words.

"I want to read over what I've got and play with it a bit,"

Claire finally said, feeling out and weighing each word. "I'll let you know when I'm ready to send it."

It took an immense act of will not to allow this last statement to turn into a question. And an even greater one to hang up without adding an apology or an attempted clarification.

In real life as on the page, there were times when less was, in fact, more.

NOT A SINGLE PERSON SKIPPED THAT SUNDAY NIGHT'S screening of the final episode of *Downton Abbey*'s first season. Samantha arrived ten minutes early and found the clubroom already abuzz with excitement. Everyone from Mimi Davenport to Callan and Logan Ritchie were already huddled around the drinks and hors d'oeuvres, fortifying themselves for the occasion, debating which story threads might be tied up and which would be left hanging to lure them back in.

"I can't wait to see what's going to happen to Anna and Bates," Melinda Greene said.

"And what comes after that kiss Mary gave Matthew," her partner Diana added.

There was laughter as drinks slid down throats. Plates were emptied and refilled.

"What is this?" Claire sniffed her drink tentatively. "That's not lemonade I smell in there, is it?" She eyed the bellman in his livery.

"No," James replied. He shook his head. "Absolutely not." He looked to the concierge for backup.

"It's Pimm's Number 1," Edward said. "It's a mixture of dry gin, liqueur, fruit juices, and spices. It was created in 1859 and to this day the recipe is so secret that only six people know exactly how it's made." He'd dropped his voice to illustrate just how hush-hush a thing the recipe was. "We also have Buck's Fizz—champagne mixed with orange juice—what you would call a mimosa." He smiled at Claire.

"I've made a vow that lemonade will never again darken a Sunday evening screening. So you may drink assured that there is not a shandy in sight."

"Why, thank you, Edward. That's very civilized of you," Claire teased.

"My pleasure, madam."

"Cheers then!" Claire raised her highball glass and clinked it against Edward's, Brooke's, and Samantha's. Isabella came up to them with a tray of English cheeses and water crackers. The other hors d'oeuvres were less easily identifiable.

Samantha peered more closely at what looked like sausage bites and . . . "Is that mashed potato?"

"It's that all right." Isabella curtsied smartly and bobbed her head. "If you're feeling a bit feckless it'll be bound to 'it the spot."

"That's 'peckish,'" Edward sighed. "Meaning a bit hungry, as opposed to worthless." His tone was beleaguered, but his lips twitched. They had discovered that Edward Parker's formality ran bone deep, but his marrow was warm and soft and infused with a decided naughtiness. "Isabella's accents are evolving and developing nicely," he continued. "Sometimes her word choice is a bit . . . dicey."

"This is a version of bangers and mash," the concierge explained. "A miniature version. I do hope I won't be struck dead for playing around with such a traditional dish. Normally you'd be served a heaping plate of it. Tonight all you have to do is dip the sausage bit into the mashed potato and . . ." The concierge popped the potato-covered sausage into his mouth and chewed it with polite relish.

Samantha and the others did the same.

"Yum," Brooke said.

"Ditto," Samantha said as she savored the appetizer's combination of warm gooiness and firm chewiness. "I've always been a closet meat and potatoes junkie. This hits all my favorite food groups."

"I've never met a food group I didn't like," Brooke admitted as she chewed the mini banger and mash. "But at the moment I choose to believe that this delicious meat-and-potato moment is going to be too brief to do real damage."

"Well, if it does, we'll just have to burn it off on the elliptical," Samantha replied though, in fact, she had no idea whether Brooke had been on the machine since their first encounter. Nor did she know how Brooke was dealing with having her ex-husband and his girlfriend in the building.

"You'll most likely burn it off shopping," Edward said to Brooke. "I understand you've scheduled a shopping expedition with Marissa Dalton."

Brooke blushed. "Yes. We're going on Wednesday." Her voice held both enthusiasm and embarrassment; it was hard to separate them out. Samantha promised herself she'd take the time to reach out to Brooke. At the moment she would have liked to reach out to Edward and ask whether he'd heard from Hunter, but she was afraid that the answer was no.

"Was your publisher pleased with your signing event?" Edward asked Claire, pulling her into the conversation. He really was a master at making everyone feel included.

"Yes," Claire said. "Thanks to you all, I seem to be a somewhat larger blip on the radar screen up in New York." She smiled, but her tone sounded far more worried than satisfied.

"Isn't that a good thing?" Brooke asked.

"Yes. It's supposed to be." Claire nodded and flashed another smile. But something didn't quite jibe.

Looking up, Samantha noticed that people had begun to move toward their seats. Claire and Brooke went to the bar for refills while Samantha stayed with Edward, debating once again whether to come out and ask about Hunter.

"Your brother came by Friday to discuss Private Butler," Edward Parker said, ending her internal debate.

Unable to trust her voice, she watched his face. When it came to her siblings, she'd learned to hope for good news but brace for the bad.

Edward gave her a white-toothed smile. "It went well. Better, I think, than either of us expected," he said, putting her out of her misery.

"That's great," she said, trying to mask her sigh of relief. "I hope that something mutually beneficial will come of it."

"That would be nice," the concierge said in an equally casual tone. But there was something in Edward Parker's eyes that made her suspect he could see right through her to the embarrassingly frantic happy dance that was taking place inside her.

THEY WATCHED THE LAST EPISODE OF SEASON ONE in a delicious silence as one after another of the elegant soap opera's story lines played out. Lady Mary came back from the London season no longer the desirable debutante she'd once been. In a move that owed much to Margaret Mitchell's Scarlett O'Hara, Lady Mary ruined her sister Edith's marriage prospects while dampening Matthew's affections. Mrs. Patmore's eyes were worse, which made cooking for both family and staff at Downton a serious problem, and a newfangled device called a telephone was installed.

There were gasps as the bitter and ever-nasty O'Brien ended any hopes of an heir that might supplant Matthew Crawley. There were sighs as what began as a garden party ended with Britain at war with Germany.

They sat quietly, barely moving, through the closing credits and the very last note of music. Edward Parker turned off the screen and gently raised the lights. He smiled at them, patiently waiting as they drifted slowly back to the present.

"I've enjoyed our first season together," he said with real warmth. "I hope you'll stay for a bit. We've got sticky toffee pudding and brandy for 'afters.' And I think we'll take just one week off before we begin season two."

There were groans and protests.

"That will allow us to end just in time for the holidays.

Which will leave us ready when the brand-new season airs in January on the Atlanta PBS affiliate."

They stood and stretched, then moved toward the tables where dessert had already been set up. As had become their habit they carried plates and snifters to the conference table. Samantha, Claire, and Brooke took seats together.

"Thank God we start season two right away," Claire said. "I don't think I could wait a year to see what happens next."

"I know. It's been hard enough to get through the whole week," Brooke agreed.

"I can't tell you how tempted I've been to order season two and then just pretend ignorance when we start back here," Samantha said, only half joking. "Except that I'd have to make sure it arrived in a plain brown wrapper." She shot a look of feigned worry over her shoulder toward Edward Parker.

"Or went to a PO box," Brooke added.

"Or a secret drop box, which you could only access in a trench coat in the dead of night," Claire said.

Samantha bit back a smile. "Leave it to the writer in the room to come up with the most complicated scenario."

Brooke laughed.

"I heard that," Edward said. "Delayed gratification is a character builder."

"So are natural disasters," Samantha replied. "But no one would intentionally experience one."

"I should perhaps warn you that the PBS affiliate has been airing repeats," Edward said. "But I assure you you'll enjoy the experience more if you watch them in order."

He gave them all a mock stern look. "Perhaps we need to institute our own abstinence campaign." He said this in the driest of tones, but an almost impish smile played around his lips. "I could get each of you to swear a pledge."

"Oh, my God," Samantha said as laughter erupted around the table. " 'Just say no' is about to take on a whole new meaning!"

Everyone was reluctant to leave and the good-byes were long and drawn out. Samantha, Brooke, and Claire lingered longest, only leaving the clubroom when Isabella and James had finished cleaning up and left. Edward said good night and locked the clubroom door. The three women lingered in the hallway near the elevator.

"It's so weird to go home to an empty apartment. And even weirder to think the girls are sleeping just a few floors away," Brooke said.

"I know. I still find myself thinking I need to get home for Hailey even though I don't," Claire said. "I can't imagine what it would feel like racketing around our old house in the suburbs all by myself. I feel kind of like one of the three bears saying this, but at the moment my studio apartment feels 'just right.'"

Samantha thought about her palatial apartment and the man who'd provided it. Relations between her and Jonathan had normalized, but Jonathan's accusation that she didn't know him at all still hung in the air between them. She'd caught him looking at her, some question that he didn't ask and that she was afraid she couldn't answer, in his eyes. If it hadn't been for Hunter . . . but if it hadn't been for Hunter and Meredith, would she even be married to Jonathan?

"Are you really doing another job for Private Butler?" Samantha asked Brooke, the thought of Hunter pulling her back. "I thought the birthday party was a onetime deal."

"So did I," Brooke said. "But the money's great. And the Daltons are . . ." Her voice trailed off. "Well, I'm glad I have a chance to fill in some gaps for Marissa now that her mother's gone. And I have to admit the idea of her father trying to navigate a girls' clothing department, well, I can't decide if it makes me want to laugh or cry."

Samantha thought about Hunter again. She was relieved that Edward Parker was going to give him a chance. But as much as she'd pushed for this, she couldn't quite picture what kinds of tasks he might be assigned to. "My brother's going to be doing some work for Private Butler, too," she said.

"Oh?" Brooke's expression became more guarded. "I ran into him while I was talking to Edward in the lobby."

"I thought he was an investor/entrepreneur of some kind," Claire said. She and Brooke exchanged looks, and Samantha remembered how they'd come out into this same hallway to try to protect her from her own brother.

Samantha considered her answer. She'd spent so many years and so much energy presenting her brother's failures in the best possible light. Even with Sylvie and Lucy, she'd shared the auspicious beginnings of each new venture, then skimmed over the ugly endings and mounting losses. But all of that was over. And she was so very tired of pretending.

"He's invested other people's money in all kinds of things. And he's lost pretty much every penny." The words were out before she could reconsider. "I'm hoping Edward will be able to help him harness his skills a little more productively." Making the admission aloud was oddly liberating.

"If anyone can harness anything, it's Edward Parker," Claire said firmly.

"It's true," Brooke agreed. "Private Butler and Edward Parker have stellar reputations. I'm really excited about doing these jobs for the Daltons."

"Well, Hunter can be a handful," Samantha said. "He's so persuasive. That's why he's always been so good in sales. But he has a real problem answering to others." Oh, God, had she really said these things aloud, too? She studied Claire and Brooke's faces and saw no judgment or censure there.

"Well, my money's on EP," Claire said. "He always seems so cool and collected. And he handles his clients with kid gloves. But I don't think he takes any shit off of anyone."

"Claire's right," Brooke said. "It could be a great introduction to a whole new business for your brother. And Edward Parker can take care of himself."

Brooke stifled a yawn. Claire and Samantha automatically

followed suit. Embarrassed by how much she'd said, Samantha pushed the elevator call button. "I hope so."

Claire surprised Samantha by giving her a hug. "It'll be okay," Claire said. "Sometimes as a parent you have to step aside and let your child fall and scrape his knee. That's how they learn."

"Hunter's not exactly a child anymore," Samantha said ruefully. "I just hope it's not too late to try to force him to turn things around."

"It's never too late to do the right thing for the people you love," Claire said. "And a parent—or parent figure—is allowed to change her mind. Lord knows I did a ton of that and Hailey seems to have survived it."

The elevator arrived. Claire turned and headed down the hall to her unit. Brooke and Samantha stepped onto the elevator and pushed their respective floors.

When the doors opened on nine, Brooke held the door open for a moment. "It'll be okay," she said softly. "It will." She hugged Samantha carefully as if she were afraid the hug might not be returned or welcomed. "And you can give me or Claire a call if it's not."

"Thanks." Samantha rode up to the twelfth floor and tiptoed into the apartment, embarrassingly grateful for the hugs and the support. In the bedroom she found Jonathan asleep. Gently she removed the reading glasses that had slipped low on his nose and pried loose the business journal still clutched in his hands.

"Hey," she said softly, pulling the covers up over him and turning off the bedside lamp. His eyes remained closed, his breathing regular. But as she placed a good-night kiss on his forehead, his lips turned up in a smile.

CHAPTER TWENTY-ONE

B ROOKE HAD PLANNED THE DAY WITH THE KIND of precision normally reserved for a Swiss timepiece and military invasions of foreign countries. By the time she picked the girls up from school, the condo was spotless, Darcy had been "speed walked" and the girls' overnight cases were packed and sitting by the door. There was nothing left to do but feed them a snack, hear about their day, and deliver them up to Barbie and Ken's apartment, where they would eat dinner and spend the night.

"Here, let me get that." Brooke wiped Ava's chocolate-smeared face and brushed the cookie crumbs off of her T-shirt. "I think you're supposed to eat these cookies, not wear them, baby," she said when she'd eliminated the snack remnants. "Do you want me to check your homework, Natalie?"

"I don't have any," Natalie said her attention focused on the cookie on its way to her mouth.

This was unlikely. Although Natalie was only in second grade she almost always had a math sheet or two and a reading assignment. "Natalie." She gave her the "I'm your mother" look, but Natalie didn't seem at all concerned. She washed the cookie down with a long gulp of milk. "Daddy said Sarah can help me. 'Cuz she knows all about big budgets and spending money."

Brooke stopped the frown before it could form. Sarah's spending habits were none of her concern. If Zach and Sarah were willing to help with homework, she should be glad, not irritated. More time with their father was a good thing for the girls and far more important than any discomfort Brooke might feel.

Right.

Brooke glanced down at her watch. She'd arranged to meet Marissa and her father at Lenox Square mall at six thirty and reaching Buckhead during rush hour could be a long and agonizing process. "Okay then," she said. "Let's potty up and I'll take you upstairs."

There were no protests and so at five thirty she closed the apartment door behind them and didn't even scold when the girls raced down the hallway to be the first to push the elevator button.

On the tenth floor Brooke found herself following the girls who, unlike her, knew exactly which door they were looking for. In front of number 1012 Natalie pressed a finger to the buzzer and went up on her tiptoes to try to see in the peephole.

Nobody came to the door.

Natalie and Ava turned to Brooke.

"Go ahead and ring again, Natalie. Maybe they didn't hear the bell."

Natalie rang again, pressing harder this time. Brooke stepped closer and heard the peal of the bell inside. What she didn't hear were footsteps. Or the sound of a hand on the knob.

Shit. Brooke glanced down at her watch. It was 5:42. "Let me call Daddy and see what's going on." Not wanting to upset the girls, she tried not to look as pissed—or worried— as she felt. She'd spoken to Zach on Monday to confirm tonight's details and he'd raised no objections or concerns about the timing.

She stood in the hallway, her cell phone pressed to her ear, listening to the hollow ring of Zach's cell phone. Then she listened to his cheerful recorded greeting as she was routed to voicemail. After leaving a terse message to call her right away, she dialed his office, which had apparently already closed for the day.

She debated whether to call the emergency after-hours number, but she had no idea who was on call tonight. She only had a 30 percent possibility of reaching Zachary instead of one of his partners.

Ava tugged on her hand as Brooke tried to figure out her next steps. Both girls were staring at her, waiting for her to do . . . something.

Brooke's watch read five fifty; she'd planned to be in her car and on the road right now. The only thing predictable about Atlanta traffic was that it would be heavy. The rate of—or lack of—forward movement was an unknown that would only be discovered when you were in the thick of it with no means of retreat.

Shit! She had no idea what to do. Fragments of ideas sprang to mind, none of them helpful. She thought about Claire Walker's offer to watch the girls if she had to work. She'd seemed sincere and had even insisted that Brooke put her number in her cell phone. But how could she just call at the last minute like this and expect her to drop everything to watch her children?

"Mommy," Ava crooned. "Where's Daddy?"

Brooke's armpits were damp and the waistband of her slacks dug into her waist. She'd felt obliged to dress as professionally as her wardrobe allowed, but now she regretted the long sleeves of the cotton button-down shirt and the too-tight pants.

"I don't know, sweetie, he's probably on his way home right now." *Or not.* "But I need to go to work." Brooke had intentionally not told the girls that she was taking Marissa Dalton shopping, knowing they'd want to come along. Maybe she should call Bruce Dalton and see if she could bring the girls after all. But he'd be put on the spot and feel compelled to say yes. And how much could she focus on Marissa and make the trip all about her if she had the girls with her?

Damn Zachary and his girlfriend. They could be anywhere right now, doing anything. Even if she reached them she had no idea how long it might take Zachary to get back here. Assuming that he would even drop whatever he was doing.

Ava plopped down on the hall floor. Natalie slumped against the wall.

Should she call Bruce Dalton and at least let him know she was running late? Maybe ask if they could move their time back a bit? She looked down at her wristwatch again and knew it was too late for that. He and Marissa would have already left their house. Just as she should have.

Swallowing back an oath, she dialed Claire Walker's number.

"'Lo?"

"Claire? It's Brooke. Brooke Mackenzie."

"Oh. Hi. What's going on?"

Brooke turned her back in an attempt to keep the girls from hearing. "I'm, well, I'm . . . you mentioned you might be able to watch the girls if I ever found myself in a pinch."

There was silence on the other end.

"I've just brought the girls up to Zachary's because I have a job for Private Butler. Only neither Zachary or Barbie, I mean Sarah, are here."

She felt the girls' eyes on her and turned so that she could see them. Ava dropped her head into her hands. Natalie opened her overnight case and began to paw through it.

"Oh, gosh," Claire said. "I'm so sorry, but a friend from my old neighborhood is actually here in Midtown and I'm on my way right now to meet her for dinner. If she weren't already here, I'd cancel so I could keep the girls. Really, I'm . . ."

"No, don't apologize." Brooke was embarrassed even to be asking, but she didn't know what else to do. The girls looked up at her through eyes that reflected their disappointment. "That's all right, I'll just . . ." What? Call Bruce Dalton and tell him she wouldn't be able to make it after all? She didn't want to disappoint Marissa. Or Edward Parker, who had a company's reputation for reliability to maintain.

"Why don't you try Samantha?" Claire said interrupting Brooke's thoughts. "I ran into her in the elevator just a little while ago. I'm pretty sure she's home."

"Oh, I couldn't possibly . . ."

"I don't think she'd mind at all," Claire said.

"But it's dinnertime and the girls haven't eaten and—"

"I'm sure the woman has food in her apartment," Claire said, cutting her off. "And the worst she can say is no."

"But . . ."

"It's a job, Brooke. It's important. If Samantha's at home, I'm sure she'll be glad to help you out. Wouldn't you do the same for her?"

The answer, of course, was yes. But unlike Brooke, Samantha had a husband and a social life. Even if she were at home she was probably getting ready to go out.

"Just ask," Claire said. "And if she can't, she can't."

It sounded so logical but Brooke couldn't even imagine asking. Or Samantha agreeing. And how would the girls feel about being left with someone they barely knew? "Okay. Thanks."

Brooke hung up without thinking to ask for Samantha's number. She began to punch in Claire's number to ask for it, then caught a look at her watch. It was ten after six.

"Oh, what the hell." Brooke grabbed each of her daughter's hands, pulled them to their feet, and sprinted for the elevator. The Davises only lived two floors up.

AS QUIETLY AS SHE COULD, SAMANTHA PUT THE LEFTover spaghetti and meatballs into the refrigerator. With Natalie Mackenzie's help she loaded the dinner dishes into the dishwasher. Both of them listened to the rise and fall of

Jonathan's voice as he read a bedtime story to Ava on the family room couch.

"Thanks," Samantha said to Natalie when the kitchen counter had been wiped down. "Do you want to go lie down until your dad or your mom can get here? We have an extra bedroom with two beds in it."

Natalie shook her head, a none-too-gentle movement that sent her mushroom cloud of red hair brushing across her sturdy shoulders. "Could I maybe just go listen to the story Mr. Davis is reading Ava?"

"Sure," Samantha said. "We'll both listen."

They moved quietly toward the couch where Jonathan was in the middle of what Samantha thought might be his second time through Ava's dog-eared copy of *Stellaluna*. Ava's head kept nodding downward and jerking back up as she fought to remain awake.

Each time he stopped, Ava dragged her chin off her chest, opened her eyes, and asked if he'd please read some more.

Each time he complied without so much as a sigh or a word of complaint, her heart did a strange little summersault in her chest. He'd been the perfect host, welcoming the children in when Brooke arrived with them so unexpectedly, entertaining them through dinner, and then readily agreeing to read Ava the book she'd dragged out of her My Little Pony overnight case.

But then he'd always had an affinity for children. Even at twenty-seven when he'd married Samantha and taken on the role of father to the eleven-year-old Meredith and nine-year-old Hunter, he'd had a gentle patience with them that exceeded Samantha's.

He smiled as she and Natalie settled on his other side and he became more animated, acting out the parts of the lost fruit bat and the baby birds as he read. The curtness with which he'd been addressing Samantha since they'd discussed Hunter's latest financial debacle had disappeared.

As she listened to the rise and fall of his voice, Samantha felt a keen pinch of regret that she'd never been able to give him the children they'd both wanted. He'd never thrown her infertility up at her or used it against her in any way. But he hadn't supported Samantha's desire to adopt. He'd caved to his mother's horrified objections at the idea of someone without Davis blood carrying the Davis name, even as she'd complained over the lack of an heir to carry it on.

A rueful smile tugged at her lips. If this were *Downton Abbey*, Hunter would undoubtedly be arguing in favor of an "entail" and angling to land the part of Matthew Crawley.

It was after nine, and both girls crumpled in sleep on either side of Jonathan when a quiet knock sounded on the front door. The flickering light from the television cast light and shadows over their sleeping faces.

"I'll get it," she whispered as she eased off the sofa and gently repositioned Natalie's now-heavy limbs.

Brooke was already apologizing when Samantha opened the door. "I'm so sorry," she said as she stepped inside. "I finally heard back from Zachary at eight thirty. He and Sarah drove up to Highlands to play golf with friends and to see the foliage and were invited to stay for dinner." She drew a deep breath of outrage, her body practically vibrating with anger. "I just can't believe he did this to them. Or me." She grimaced. "I'm so sorry we intruded on your evening."

"It's all right," Samantha said. "Really. They were a pleasure."

"Oh, I'll bet your husband just loved the whole thing." This was accompanied by an eye roll.

"You'd be surprised," Samantha said. In many ways the girls' presence had smoothed out the rough edges of their disagreement. It was hard to be angry or distant with such sweet neediness right there in front of you. "How did the shopping trip go?"

"I know Marissa enjoyed it. I got her completely outfitted, including some winter things and this adorable red winter coat." She dropped her eyes. "And I think Bruce was happy with how happy Marissa was."

"And you?" Samantha asked noting the way Brooke flushed every time Bruce Dalton's name was mentioned.

"Well, it would have been great if I hadn't been so worried about where Zachary was and why he hadn't even called. And then I kept picturing the girls here driving you both crazy. I'm sure the last thing you expected to do tonight was babysit." She said this as if it were akin to being flayed alive.

"Like I said, it was no problem." Samantha led Brooke through the kitchen and into the family room. From there they could see the back of Jonathan's head. It looked as if he sat alone on the couch. "We like children."

Brooke came to a halt as they rounded the sofa. Her mouth dropped open as she caught sight of her daughters on either side of Jonathan, collapsed against him like little red-headed bookends. The book he'd been reading lay open-faced across one muscled thigh. Jonathan winked at Brooke in welcome and laid a warning finger against his lips. "Let's not wake them up if we can help it," he said softly. "I like *Stellaluna* as much as the next man. But after the first time through it's kind of hard to get the bat and bird voices right."

When Brooke and the children had gone, Samantha locked the front door and turned out the foyer light. Not waiting for an invitation, she settled next to Jonathan on the sofa.

"Thanks," she said. "You're a good man, Jonathan Davis." She laid her head on his shoulder and rested her hand on his thigh. "And you read a mean *Stellaluna*." His thigh tensed beneath her hand, and she was afraid for a moment that he would shrug away from her. But she felt him expel a breath of air as his arm slipped around her. He pulled her tighter against him.

"We aim to please," he said quietly, and she thought she heard an uncomfortable note of irony. But then he shifted and pressed her back into the cushions. When his lips found hers and he began to undress her, she almost convinced herself that she had imagined it.

CHAPTER TWENTY-TWO

EDWARD ARRIVED AT THE ALEXANDER ON THURS-day morning to find Hunter Jackson in the lobby flirting with a clearly enamored Isabella. Edward looked the young man over and could find no fault with his sharply creased gray pants and blue blazer, which he'd paired with a crisp white collared shirt and red tie. His demeanor when he spotted Edward fell shorter of the mark. Rather than "snap to," he gave Isabella a last overly familiar wink, straightened quite slowly, then sauntered toward Edward.

"Good morning." Jackson's tone was friendly enough, but the bob of the head was regrettably casual for someone reporting for his first day on a brand-new job.

"Good morning," Edward said smartly, hopefully demonstrating the importance of one's demeanor. "Shall we?" He motioned his head toward his office and kept walking, expecting Hunter Jackson to follow.

Edward did not remove his jacket but motioned Hunter into the supplicant's seat before taking his own behind his desk. "I appreciate your punctuality," he said without preamble. "My plan is to expose you to the different levels of service we provide our clients. I have chosen a number of tasks for you to perform that should help illustrate this range."

"Yes, well, I have some ideas for raising Private Butler's profile. I've also made a list of potential corporate clients I can approach." Jackson's words were businesslike and well thought out, but he was slouching in his chair as if hashing something out with a colleague. Only the telltale leg movement gave away his nervousness and/or irritation. Edward wasn't certain which.

Edward folded his hands on his desk as his uncle Mason often did before imparting an important point of clarification. "Good. We'll take a look at that together after you've had some time to get acclimated to our services and company philosophy."

"I'm sorry?" Jackson said, looking genuinely confused.

"You won't be calling on people until you have a clear understanding of the services we offer and the manner in which all employees of Private Butler conduct themselves. I'll also want to make sure you completely grasp the underlying philosophy on which the company is based," Edward explained.

"Really?"

"Yes," Edward replied. "Really."

They stared at each other for several long moments. Long enough for Edward to note the flare of anger and astonishment that sharpened Jackson's features and see him hide the reaction in the depths of the green eyes. Jackson looked away first. "But isn't that a waste of my connections and experience?"

"For the moment it may seem that way," Edward conceded. "But it's hard for even the most accomplished salesperson to sell or market something he doesn't fully understand."

"With all due respect," Jackson said. "Your business isn't all that complicated."

As usual, any sentence that began with "with all due

respect" included almost no respect at all. Edward shrugged off his irritation and kept his tone pleasant. Just as Hunter Jackson needed to learn to do.

"I promise you there are things to be learned. Important things."

"I'm all ears, then."

"Very well," Edward said, even though Jackson seemed more insolence than ears. "This is how we shall begin. For the next week you'll take on small tasks for a variety of our clients. No matter how small the task, it will be treated as if it were of the utmost importance, because to us, to this company, it is.

"We are time-savers. Convenience givers. We make our customers feel good about spending money for others to do what they could, in fact, do for themselves if they had the time or the inclination." He paused to allow the message to sink in. "We make people's lives easier. Period. There's nothing we won't do—as long as it's legal and ethical."

He paused again both for emphasis and because he wanted to make sure Jackson heard what came next.

"This morning you'll handle these requests for two of our long-term clients. After lunch you will explore these travel-related issues for Emily Redding." He handed Hunter Jackson a typed form with the pertinent names and addresses.

"You actually expect me to pick up and deliver someone's dry cleaning?" Jackson asked.

"Yes, of course."

"And take a package to the UPS Store?"

"You'll also be hiring a cleaning company for the Ritchies. There's a potential list attached. And picking up Grace Anthony's dog from the groomer's."

"But these are *errands.*" The horror in Jackson's voice indicated that this was a veritable crime against nature.

"Yes." Edward maintained eye contact. "And quite menial ones at that. For which we are paid." He watched Jackson process this shocking turn of events. "If you handle these assignments without any trouble, tomorrow you'll keep an appointment with James Culp to select a gift for his wife Alicia's sixtieth birthday. I have a questionnaire I often use to elicit enough information about the recipient to make it truly special."

"You're kidding."

"No." He had in fact been planning to give this assignment to Brooke Mackenzie, who wouldn't need a form or prompting of any kind, but the point here was to teach Hunter Jackson the scope of what Private Butler offered from the seemingly insignificant to the mundane to the life changer. To make him understand that no request from a client was more important than another. And perhaps to make him stop and think about what it meant to give thought to another human being's needs or wants above his own, which Edward suspected would be the hardest lesson of all.

"If you have any problems or questions you can call me on my cell phone." Edward handed the younger man a business card. "Otherwise I'll expect you back here by four p.m. to fill me in on how things went."

"You want me to come back here to report how the errands went?" Jackson asked, apparently unable to grasp the concept.

"Yes, of course," Edward replied.

Jackson nodded but didn't speak. The sheaf of papers in his hands trembled slightly with what Edward suspected was suppressed anger. Suppressed was good. This business was all about controlling one's personal thoughts and emotions.

"And while you are representing this company in any capacity whatsoever, you must be aware of the signals your body language may be sending."

"Is that right?" Jackson asked.

"Yes. Slouching as you are right now is never appropriate. It demonstrates a lack of interest in what's being communicated as well as a lack of focus in general. When you meet another person's gaze, you don't want to show emotions or judgments that you are then forced to mask."

"Is that right?" Jackson asked again. His tone of voice was

far too terse, but he had already straightened in a far more acceptable manner.

"Yes," Edward replied calmly. "Your voice and what it gives away is also critical. Private Butler employees never challenge the client in any way. The client is always, without exception and without argument, right."

"How unsatisfying." Jackson's response was offered without inflection or emotion, but the green eyes were icy sharp. Yet another window into his true thoughts that the young man would need to learn to keep shut.

"Being a concierge means focusing on the customer's satisfaction above all else," Edward said. "To use a sexual analogy, we want the customer completely and utterly satisfied. We don't want them faking an orgasm so to speak and then not calling us again. *Your* satisfaction is not required."

THE CELEBRATORY DINNER THAT NIGHT FELT A BIT like a Hollywood film in which all of them had been cast and expected to perform. Although Samantha could see the anger and resentment in their eyes, Hunter and Meredith played the roles of the newly and happily employed; Jonathan acted the genial if distracted host while Cynthia played the crusty but loving matriarch, which allowed her to work in more than a few slap downs while pretending to be supportive. Samantha was the proud "parent" who pretended the smiles were real and the future rosy.

By the time it was over and they'd dropped Cynthia off at Bellewood, Samantha's jaw hurt from the forced smiling. Every last nerve stood on end.

She watched Jonathan's face in the spill of passing streetlights, the planes and angles falling in and out of shadow going back over how little he'd spoken at dinner. In fact, she'd barely heard his voice since the other night when he'd read *Stellaluna* to the Mackenzie girls with such warmth and feeling.

"Thank you for the dinner," she said.

"My pleasure," he replied.

More streetlights and more silence followed. They were alone and yet they were still playing their parts. Apparently no one had approved the scene and called "cut."

"Did everything get settled on the nanotechnology thing?" she asked, needing to break the silence and because if she didn't ask now, she suspected she'd never really know.

"Yes." His eyes remained on the road. His tone was even but there was no missing the note of dismissal. It was a note she'd learned to heed, always afraid of overstepping her bounds. But she needed to know how much damage had been done.

"That's it?" she asked. "One word to cover what had to be a huge hassle and expense?"

"What else do you want to know?" he asked simply.

"Was it expensive? Did it take a lot of your time?" *Are you still angry with me?*

"Yes."

He didn't look at her. But she could feel the stiffness of his body, the tension in the large, capable hands that held the wheel.

There were so many questions she'd never asked. She'd tread so carefully, always afraid that if she went too far, asked for too much, he'd realize she wasn't worth it. This approach had seen them through twenty-five years as husband and wife. But it had not made them equals. As they had in tonight's "movie" they'd played out the roles they'd created in their own long-running production. She had always been the supplicant to his munificent provider.

"We may not always show it," she said. "But we all appreciate what you've done for us."

He continued to stare out the windshield and she thought that was going to be the end of it.

His voice, when he finally spoke, startled her. "It's funny, isn't it, that after all this time the three of you are still 'us' and I'm . . . I don't know, Samantha, what exactly am I to you?"

"What . . . what do you mean?" Her voice sounded timid and afraid even in her own ears.

He turned and looked at her. She forced herself to meet his eyes, tried to see what they held. But they were lost in the shadows. "I'm so tired of your gratitude," he said. "The way you think you have to please me all the time."

Samantha sat, frozen, unsure what to say. She searched his face, trying to figure out what he wanted to hear.

He shook his head and gave a rueful snort. "I rest my case. You're too busy trying to figure out what I want you to say to even consider saying what you actually think and feel."

They were at the Alexander before she realized it. He pulled the car into the parking garage.

"But I can't help being grateful," she said. "My God, Jonathan, you saved us from complete ruin. You became a parent to a nine- and eleven-year-old at the age of twenty-seven. No matter how difficult they've been, you've treated Hunter and Meredith like your own flesh and blood. You've bailed them out over and over again."

He parked and turned off the car. They sat in the dimly lit concrete structure.

"I can barely let myself think about how much they've cost you. How much we've all cost you. All the things you've given up. How can I *not* be grateful?" she asked.

He closed his eyes briefly, then opened them. She could see them more clearly now, but they remained dark and unreadable. "I don't know, Samantha," he said. "I only know that I'm no longer sure whether gratitude is really enough to hold a marriage together."

He got out of the car. Despite the things he'd said to her he walked around and opened her door. But Jonathan Davis's manners had been hardwired into him at birth. She knew better than to read anything into them.

They entered the building and crossed to the elevators in

silence. He held the door open as she entered. He didn't say another word as they rode up to the twelfth floor and disembarked.

Her thoughts skittered about, jumbled and unclear. Maybe if she found the right words she could turn this around. But her fear of saying the wrong thing; the possibility of spewing her deepest feelings out into the silent abyss that now surrounded them and having them found lacking or, worse, unreciprocated, made her swallow them back.

"Jonathan, please . . ."

He looked down at her, watching her carefully, waiting for she didn't know what.

"Just tell me what you want. I don't know what it is you want from me," she said.

"I know." His tone was as sad as his eyes. Both were filled with regret. "That's the problem, isn't it?"

She watched him, mute, as he pulled things from the closet and dropped them into his carry-on bag. "I've got meetings scheduled out in LA on Tuesday and Wednesday. I think I'll head out in the morning and get in a few days of golf—unwind a little bit—before then." It wasn't a question.

Tears clogged her throat and dampened her eyes. She had the oddest flash of Rhett Butler packing and leaving Scarlett O'Hara in the final scene of *Gone With the Wind*. She had an embarrassing urge to cry, "Oh, my darling, if you go, what shall I do?" just as Scarlett had asked Rhett. Except that she was horribly afraid that if she did, Jonathan would quote the modern equivalent of Rhett's famous words back to her.

The last thing Samantha could bear to hear from Jonathan at the moment was, "My dear, I don't give a damn."

CHAPTER TWENTY-THREE

WHEN SAMANTHA WOKE THE NEXT MORNING the apartment's silent emptiness told her that Jonathan had already gone. Feeling as hollow inside as the apartment, she turned her head and opened her eyes in search of some proof that he had left something for her beside the memory of his disappointment. But there was no note on the bedside table and no comforting scent of coffee already brewed. Samantha pulled the sheets up over her head and closed her eyes, but there was no wishing herself back in time or even back to sleep.

Her mind replayed last night's conversation and pinpricks of panic pierced her. Jonathan had sounded so disappointed in her, in them. Disappointed enough to leave.

"Stop it." She said this aloud even as she threw off the covers and sat up, swinging her legs over the side of the bed. "He's upset and he left a few days early. He didn't *leave* leave." But it was so unlike Jonathan to be poking and prodding her feelings like that. If he hadn't taken her by surprise, she would have come up with something better than how *grate-*

ful she was. She rubbed her feet over the carpet. But would she have opened herself to that kind of hurt? Their whole marriage had been a bargain. How could she admit to feelings she shouldn't even have and then face his pity or have to hear him apologize for not returning them?

She glanced at the clock and was almost sorry she had no workout scheduled this morning. Physical exertion might burn off some of the worry and having someone—anyone—push her would be a good thing right now. She began to swing her legs back onto the bed. Her hand was already reaching for the covers when she stopped. "No!"

She'd have one cup of coffee and then she'd get out of the apartment. Maybe she'd jog to the park and back before she had to shower and dress for the day. What she couldn't do was sit here worrying. She and Jonathan had been married for a long time. Like any married couple they had arguments and problems. Normally she was able to smooth things over before anything could fester or grow out of proportion.

Because she was afraid she would appear ungrateful. Which might cause Jonathan to question why he had married her at all.

The pinpricks became sharper, blooming into full-fledged panic. She raced into the closet to make sure Jonathan's things were still there. *Don't be silly. He's upset and he left for a few extra days to think. That's all.* But what if his thoughts led him to decide their marriage wasn't worth saving?

She was out of the apartment and jabbing at the elevator call button as if wolves were nipping at her heels. When she stepped in for the ride down she tried to think calming thoughts, but the panic seemed to be sucking up all the gray matter and blotting out rational thought. Just as it had when her father's disgrace and her parents' deaths had left her not only penniless but responsible for her brother and sister.

Nerves jangling, she groaned aloud when the elevator stopped on the tenth floor. Because she apparently wasn't feeling quite horrible enough, when the doors slid open Zachary Mackenzie stepped on.

Samantha's lips clamped together. His opened wide in a happy smile.

"Hello," he said jovially. "I'm so glad to see you. I've been wanting to thank you for watching the girls the other night."

Irritation ignited into anger and mingled with the panic, creating a toxic brew. He looked at her expectantly. She didn't trust herself to speak.

"You know, Natalie and Ava Mackenzie?" he prompted. "I understand they spent the evening with you and your husband."

"Yes," she answered. The fury bubbled in her veins and sought release. It was a relief to let it out. "Because you'd forgotten them."

"Well, not exactly," he said with what she knew was meant to be an ingratiating smile.

She stared at him. "Not exactly, how?"

"It's just that I'm not used to taking them on weekdays," he said, as if this explained everything. "And we were invited to play golf up in Highlands with the Oglethorpes; they're an old Atlanta family. Maybe you know them?" He shrugged when she didn't answer. "Time just got away from us." He seemed so smugly happy with himself. Oblivious to the fact that she, whom he seemed so eager to impress, was about to erupt and rain molten lava all over him. The man might know how to improve bodies and faces; if he knew how to read them he'd be pressing the emergency button and trying to escape.

"You know how it is," he said.

"No," she said sharply. "Actually I don't. In fact, I can't imagine how anyone could forget his children. Or leave their mother in such a difficult situation. Especially not in order to play a round of *golf*."

He fell back a step. "Well, now, I . . . I mean it was Sarah who committed us. I mean we . . ."

Samantha just looked at him, glad to see *Doctor* Mackenzie stumble over his words and then grind to a halt.

"Sarah?" she asked as if she'd never heard the name before.

"My . . . girlfriend. We live in 1012 now. Just two floors below you and your husband." He swallowed but stayed where he was. "Maybe the four of us could get together sometime and . . ."

The man was a social climber *and* a moron. Who seemed to believe that she and Jonathan had taken care of his children as part of some random act of kindness.

"Your children are lovely," she said. "We were glad to have them over."

He perked up at that. "Yes, they are sweet, aren't they? But it's Sarah and I who . . ."

There was still a small sliver of her brain that knew her anger at Zachary Mackenzie wasn't only about his bad behavior, but at the moment she didn't care.

"Brooke is a friend of mine and I was happy to help her out. In fact, friendship is very important to me. Doing the right thing is very important to my husband. I doubt he'd be interested in socializing with anyone who could allow a round of golf to push their children right out of their mind."

He stared at her, speechless, as the elevator reached the lobby.

When the doors slid open she nodded as regally as she could then swept out of the elevator, channeling not just Scarlett O'Hara, but *Downton Abbey*'s Countess Cora, Lady Mary, and the dowager countess all rolled into one.

THAT FRIDAY AFTERNOON BROOKE MACKENZIE FOLlowed Bruce Dalton into his daughter's bedroom. She stood beside him and examined the space, taking in the toddler-sized bed with the Kermit and Miss Piggy sheets and the nursery rhyme wallpaper. A Little Tikes table and chairs sat near one wall. An army of stuffed animals littered a Humpty Dumpty area rug.

"Marissa says it's a 'baby room' and wants a big girl one," Bruce Dalton said. "I have no idea what that means or where you get one."

A smile tugged at Brooke's lips. "You don't typically go out and buy a whole room," she explained. "It's more a matter of choosing things that she likes and making them all work together. Natalie and I did her room over together when she turned six." Her smile faltered a bit. The redecorating process had barely begun when Zachary moved out. "Ava's already started clipping pictures out of magazines to make a poster board of all the things she likes. It's a fun art project and it's a good jumping-off point." She studied Bruce Dalton's face, liking the simple earnestness to please his child that she saw there. The kindness that seemed to be wrapped up in the brown eyes. His desire to be a full set of parents. "You could probably do it together if you wanted to. I could advise or consult along the way."

"I hate to sound like a wuss, but I didn't even realize until recently that there were so many shades of pink and purple. Chloe was the designer in the family." His smile faltered. "I know if she were here the room would already be done." He reached down and picked up a fuzzy white bunny rabbit that had seen better days and set it gently on the bed. "I hate to keep leaning on you, but would you be willing to redecorate the room with Marissa? I know I could hire an interior designer to do it, but you know her better than a stranger. You can help her pick out what she likes, not just what goes together, and you can relate as a mother . . . Does it seem odd to be trying to turn it into a semblance of a mother-daughter experience?"

"No, of course not. I understand completely. It's not every man who would be as sensitive to his daughter's emotional well-being." She knew this from personal experience.

"Then you'll do it?" The relief in his voice was unmistakable.

"Absolutely," she said. "And maybe you can come along

so that you can share the experience with Marissa. I'm sure she'd be glad to help educate you to the nuances of pink and purple."

"Okay," he agreed. "As long as I'm not the final decorative decision maker, I'm in."

She got a bit more caught up in his easy smile than she'd meant to and reached for her tote bag. "Is it all right if I look around and make some notes?" She pulled out her pad and pencil, grateful that this time no half-eaten food fell out.

"Sure." His cell phone rang and he glanced down at it. "Sorry, I've been waiting for this call. Will you excuse me?"

Bruce headed out of the room. A door, presumably to his office, closed.

Brooke studied Marissa Dalton's bedroom, quietly taking in the space and comparing it to the little girl she'd just begun to know, and jotted down whatever came to mind. In the closet Brooke found the outfits they'd bought on their shopping trip hanging neatly, the new shoes lined up beneath them, and felt a warm glow at the thought of Marissa liking them enough to arrange them with such care.

The doorbell rang and she hesitated, expecting to hear Bruce head for the door. On the second peal, she debated whether she should answer it. On the third, she headed for the door, her only thought to stop the noise from interrupting his business call.

The woman on the front step was tall and blond with a perfect pair of breasts and an unlined face that Brooke recognized as the work of a first-class plastic surgeon. She wore a very short tennis skirt that exposed long, muscled legs and a body-hugging sleeveless tee that showed off toned arms and her two best features, which were significant. Like Sarah, she was the anti-Brooke; the very version of womanhood that Zachary created in the operating room and had traded her in for. Apparently the woman also cooked. Though it didn't look like she ate. She held a disposable casserole dish in her hands. "Is Bruce here?"

"Yes," Brooke replied. "But he's on the phone. Can I help you?"

The woman looked Brooke up and down. "No, thanks. I'll just bring this in for him." She raised the aluminum foil–covered dish. "He and Marissa just love my cheeseburger casserole." She stepped around Brooke and sashayed into the kitchen. "Are you the new housekeeper?"

"Um, no."

"Because I heard he was looking for one."

She set the foil-wrapped offering on the counter. Big blue eyes skimmed over the stainless-steel appliances and the well-appointed family room. An avaricious gleam lit them.

"Do you have any idea how long he's going to be on the phone?"

"No."

The blonde looked down at her Rolex and pouted prettily; a look Brooke suspected she used to good effect and as often as possible. Brooke was tempted to warn her that if she kept it up she'd need those collagen injections more frequently.

The woman sighed in disappointment. "Tell him that Monica stopped by," she instructed in a tone that indicated that although Brooke might not be the housekeeper, she had "employee" written all over her. "And that I'll try him again later." Without waiting for a response, she turned with a swirl of her tennis skirt and showed herself out.

Brooke, used to being summarily dismissed, jotted a few more notes on her pad and was debating whether to simply leave a note and go when Bruce appeared.

"Sorry," he said. His hair stood up on end as if he'd been running his hand through it. His smile was a bit crooked. "I just closed on a commercial building in Smyrna and there were a few details that needed to be clarified."

"No problem." Her eyes met his. There was something endearing about his rumpledness. "Oh, Monica came by to see you. She left a casserole." She watched him closely interested to see his reaction.

"Ah," he said, giving nothing away. "We didn't know many of our neighbors before Chloe got sick. But the neighborhood caring committee set up food delivery in those last months. Some of them still bring food." He opened the freezer. Rows of disposable casseroles like the one Monica had delivered were packed tightly inside. "I haven't had the heart to tell them that I've always been the primary cook in the family. They seem so eager to feed us."

That wasn't the only thing Monica was eager about.

"Truthfully, neither of us has been able to face a casserole since Chloe died. I'm afraid to throw them out in case someone sees them in the garbage." There was the smile again. "I'd be happy to send some home with you if you think the girls would like them."

"Oh." Brooke could just imagine Monica's reaction if she ever found out that the "help" had gone home with the cheeseburger casserole meant to win over the handsome widower. "Actually, that would be great. I'm a pretty utilitarian cook—you know, an assembler of ingredients—it would be nice to have a meal ready to pop in the oven. And a man who can cook? I think that belongs in the fantasy category for most women."

"Well, a little fantasy never hurt anyone." He smiled. "In fact, why don't you let me cook you a meal one night?" He must have seen her confusion because he added, "I was thinking something elegant. You know, adult. Just for the two of us."

"Oh." Surprise and pleasure sent heat rushing to her cheeks. She practically felt them turning scarlet, which was not a good look for any redhead. "I don't know. I haven't really been . . ." She stopped, horrified that she'd been about to tell him that she hadn't had a date—or even a real conversation with a man—since Zachary walked out on them.

"If you'd rather, we can make it a family dinner," he said. "Maybe next Saturday?"

"Oh." Relief and disappointment coursed through her.

"Sure. That would be great. Maybe I can bring a poster board and some magazines and Marissa and Ava can work on their room collages." She flushed, afraid that he'd think she was planning to bill him. Should she tell him that wasn't what she'd meant? But how exactly would she do that?

"That sounds perfect," he said, wiping out her worry with the warmth of his smile. "Shall we plan on six o'clock?"

She stammered her agreement and let him walk her to the door. It was only after she'd settled the two casseroles he'd insisted she take on the floor of the Volvo and backed out of his driveway that she realized that Bruce Dalton—the man who could have, and possibly had had the perfect Monica—had offered to cook for her.

Chapter Twenty-Four

THE PROBLEM WITH WRITING—OR IN CLAIRE'S case *not* writing—on a full-time basis was that the work never went away. Even on a beautiful Saturday like this one, it sat there waiting for you, haunting you, far too insistent to ignore. She knew writers who, like Nora, met a page count each writing day and then mentally clocked out until the next. Perhaps if she were being at all productive, she, too, might learn to do that. At the moment no matter what she was doing or where she went, she was hyperaware that she had not yet produced pages that she could send to her agent. But no matter how insistently her computer's blank screen haunted her or how much of the dining room table she littered with scribbled thoughts and notes, she couldn't fool herself into believing she was actually doing something. You could force a writer's butt into a chair, but you couldn't make her think.

Claire stared out the French doors of her apartment trying to understand how her greatest escape had become the thing she most wanted to escape from. The balcony beckoned, but she'd already spent close to an hour out there this morning catching up her journal and it was easy to get distracted outside. For the next twenty minutes she debated whether to carry her laptop out onto the balcony before finally deciding against it. But though she managed to keep her butt in the chair, she couldn't resist calling Hailey.

"Hi, Mom. How's it going?" The sound of Hailey's voice was like a gift from the gods. And if she strung out the conversation long enough, she could have a break from pretending to work.

"Great. It's really going great."

"How many pages did you write today?" Hailey asked.

Claire hesitated. The few times she'd lied to her daughter it had been to protect or spare Hailey, not to make herself look better.

"That bad, huh?" her daughter asked. "Maybe you need to go out and take a walk to clear your head?"

"That's a good idea, Hailey," she said. Unfortunately, she'd already done that first thing in the morning when she'd been certain she'd come back energized and ready to get down to work. It was such a glorious day—all bright blue sky and pulled white clouds—that she'd barely been able to force herself back inside. "But what I really want to do is hear about you."

As she'd hoped, Hailey was diverted and chatted happily for at least fifteen minutes about her classes, her job in the library, which was apparently still a bit "lame," and the boy she'd met in her creative writing class, who wasn't. Claire hung on each word, asking a new question anytime she sensed Hailey bringing the conversation to a close.

"Sorry, Mom," Hailey finally said. "I know I'm cutting into your writing time. I'll let you get back to work."

Claire barely resisted begging her daughter not to hang up. "Okay, Hailey. Take care of yourself."

"I will, Mom."

"And keep me posted."

"Good luck with the proposal. I know it'll be great." Hailey hung up.

Claire looked at the blinking cursor. All alone in the top left corner of the great big blank screen. Her brow furrowed. Was that an SOS it was blinking out?

She pulled up Facebook mostly just to fill the screen, posted something cheerily vague to her author page, then clicked through her personal page.

Standing, she paced the apartment first in one direction and then the other. She stood for a few minutes with her nose pressed against the glass of the French door. But she was very careful not to step outside.

She was trying to force herself back to the computer when she saw a message arrive.

Are you working? Karen's message asked.

Yes! she typed back, exclamation point and all.

Don't lie to me. I can tell. Karen had been writing two books a year for the last four years, each one better than the last. As her body of work grew, so did her readership. Claire was really excited about her longtime critique partner's success, but her productivity level left Claire feeling like a slug in comparison.

Not lying, Claire lied. *Writing up a storm. My fingers are practically falling off.*

Then why are you answering messages?

Only yours, Claire replied. *I seem to remember a blood oath never to ignore communication from my critique partners.*

Karen ignored this. *Crap can be fixed, blank page can't. Get to work.*

Okay, Claire typed. *Will vomit heart and soul onto many pages ASAP.*

Too messy, Karen typed back. *Use fingers. Easier to read.*

Ha, Claire typed back, getting into the conversation. *Now you tell me!*

Claire waited for a response, but Karen was gone. Undoubtedly to finish the day's chapter. Or possibly the second.

Susie's message arrived about ten minutes later. She knew

this because she'd been staring at the screen watching the minutes elapse. Susie tended to lean toward positive motivation rather than tough love, and she had a penchant for inspirational quotations.

Waiting for pages to critique, Susie typed. *How's it going?*

I'm too busy staring at screen to write, Claire typed quickly. *Hoping for inspiration.*

Jack London says not to wait for inspiration. Advises you go after it with a club.

Are Jack and club available? Claire replied.

Ha!

She was considering adding an LOL, but Susie was gone almost as quickly as Karen. Undoubtedly to write a chapter that Claire would wish she'd written when she read it.

Claire groaned aloud just so she'd feel like something was happening. She emitted a primal scream, but kept it quiet so she didn't bother any neighbor who might be taking a late-afternoon nap. This thought had her eyeing her bed. Which would be the perfect place for a person who felt as slug-like as she did right now. She could just lie there for a little bit reading one of the *Downton Abbey* books. Surely that would inspire her.

Her cell phone rang and she practically leapt on it. "Hello?"

It was Brooke. "I hope I'm not interrupting anything."

"No," Claire said too quickly. "Not at all. What's going on?"

"You won't believe this," Brooke said almost as quickly. "Because I don't. But Zachary just showed up out of the blue an hour ago and asked if he could take the girls for the weekend. The *whole* weekend."

"But why?" For the first time that day Claire's brain seemed fully engaged.

"I don't know. But he was apologizing all over himself for screwing up and forgetting to pick them up on Wednesday. He claimed he wanted to make it up to them. And me. I think they're going up to the mountains."

"Seriously?" Claire asked.

"Yes. And then he told me to be sure to let my friend Samantha know. Probably still trying to kiss her ass. But it's weird, huh?"

"It is, but in a good way."

"So, all the sudden I have all this free time," Brooke continued. "And I'm kind of going through *Downton Abbey* withdrawal."

Claire laughed, her mood lifting. "I know what you mean."

"So I was thinking it might be fun to borrow the season one video from Edward and maybe order pizza for dinner." There was a pause. "Unless you're going out. Or really busy working. I mean I know this is last minute and everything."

Claire was almost embarrassed by how wonderful this sounded and how eager she was to have a reason to stop pretending to work. Pretending to work was even more exhausting than the real thing. "I'm in," she said. "And I've got a bottle of white wine I can bring. Did you call Samantha?"

"Gosh, no," Brooke said. "I mean it's Saturday. I figured she and her husband probably had plans."

This, of course, was what single women always assumed about married ones, but that didn't make it true. "They might," Claire agreed. "But let's at least invite her. I can call if you want while you get the video."

They worked out the details and agreed to five thirty at Brooke's. Claire jumped up from the computer with a new sense of purpose. Picking up the phone, she dialed Samantha Davis's number and put a second bottle of wine in the refrigerator to chill.

SAMANTHA COULDN'T BELIEVE HOW GRATEFUL SHE was to get Claire Walker's call. No, not grateful. Even thinking the word made her stomach knot up. Glad was better. She was glad and relieved to have something to do instead of sitting in her apartment worrying about why she hadn't yet heard from Jonathan. Last time she'd had a weekend to herself she'd reveled in the experience. This time she felt abandoned and frightened. A good dose of *Downton Abbey* and lady friends might never appear on a prescription, but at the moment it felt like just what the doctor ordered.

She raided the wine supply for two nice bottles of red and pulled a bakery box of Giancarlo's chocolate chip cannolis from the freezer. Ten minutes later she was standing in front of Brooke's door, a bottle of wine tucked under each armpit and the bakery box in her hands. She had to poke her elbow into the doorbell to ring it.

"Hi. Can you take the box?" Samantha said when Brooke opened the door. "I think one of the bottles may be starting to slip."

"Oh, my gosh!" Brooke took the box while Samantha clamped her arms more tightly against her sides.

"I'm not sure direct body heat does good things for a wine, but I never can seem to find those carriers I know we have somewhere," Samantha said.

"It won't bother me," Brooke said. "Zachary spent long amounts of time reading and discussing wine with anyone who would hold still long enough. But I'm not a picky drinker. Or eater, for that matter."

"Ditto," Samantha said when they reached the kitchen.

"I'm glad to hear it because I ordered an extra-large pizza. I think it's called everything but the kitchen sink." Brooke smiled.

The doorbell rang and Brooke went to let Claire in. Samantha opened a bottle of the red and looked around the kitchen, which was all sharp angles and shiny surfaces. The appliances were top-of-the-line and custom fitted. The space was expertly done, but it wasn't at all what Samantha would have expected from a woman who exuded such a sturdy earthiness.

"Hey." Claire set two bottles of white wine next to the

reds. "I see great minds think alike. At least we won't have to make a liquor run."

"Well, if we do it's only a matter of floors," Samantha said. "Jonathan has a wine closet outfitted with a backup generator." The minute she brought up his name, she regretted it. Even thinking of Jonathan caused the strangest twinge in her chest. She turned as if considering the kitchen for the first time. "This is really state-of-the-art," she said, motioning to the Sub-Zero refrigerator and Wolf ovens. "Do you like to cook?" Samantha's thoughts turned to all the meals she'd pretended to cook for Jonathan over the years and she felt a stab of regret that she'd never really learned.

Brooke's nose wrinkled. "Not really. I mean I put food on the table on a regular basis, but this is not the kitchen I would have chosen to do it in. Zach hired an interior designer to do the whole apartment. He wanted the best of everything and he got it. But none of it is exactly kid- or user-friendly." She hesitated briefly. "I was in Bruce Dalton's kitchen yesterday—he's asked me to help Marissa do over her bedroom. Now that's a kitchen meant for a family to live in. And he cooks. He invited the girls and me over for dinner next Saturday." She blushed with what looked like pleasure.

"Grab him," Claire said. "I'd be all over a man who can cook."

"I think the women in his neighborhood are already all over him. They keep bringing him food. And they don't wear a lot of clothes when they deliver it."

"Well, he invited *you* for dinner," Samantha said.

"I think a man cooking is sexy," Claire said. "Who needs *Fifty Shades of Grey*? Give me a guy in a chef's toque any day. Add some vacuuming and dusting and it's downright orgasmic."

Samantha laughed while Claire began to open the wine. Brooke pulled wineglasses out of the cupboard.

"Did you know that Zach took the girls for the whole weekend?" Brooke asked Samantha.

"No."

"And he wanted me to make sure you knew it." Brooke was watching Samantha's face.

"Really?" Samantha asked casually.

"Why is that?" Claire asked.

There was a silence while Samantha debated how much to divulge. The emotional mess she'd been yesterday morning was just one more aspect of the problems with Jonathan that she didn't want to think about. But that didn't mean she regretted setting the *doctor* straight. "Well, we did run into each other in the elevator yesterday," Samantha said.

"And?" Brooke asked.

Samantha shrugged. "And I may have called him out on forgetting the girls Wednesday night." She turned her attention to the wine. "Do you want red or white?"

Brooke laughed. "Fine. I guess I don't need all the details. I'll have red." She steadied a glass while Samantha poured. All three of them held up their glasses. "To Samantha, who apparently shamed Zach into spending time with his daughters and who made this evening possible," Brooke toasted.

"To Samantha!" They clinked and drank.

When the pizza arrived, they filled paper plates with slices and carried them into the family room, which was also a sophisticated contemporary showcase built around a massive big-screen television. They settled on the Roche Bobois cream leather sectional and chowed down.

"Wow," Claire said. "Zach must have hated leaving that television set behind."

Brooke smiled somewhat grimly. "If he hadn't had it so completely built in, I'm sure it would have been the first thing he moved upstairs. It's way too big. Even Winnie the Pooh looks scary at that size." She looked around and sighed. "Everything about this place is too polished, too cold, and too uninviting."

Samantha was very careful not to react. She saw Claire doing the same.

"I know," Brooke said. "Just like Zach." She held up her slice of pizza. "I have to confess, sometimes I get this almost irresistible urge to mess everything up. You know, rub a greasy finger on the leather. Drop a pepperoni in the carpet. Is that childish?"

Samantha edged the glass of red wine she'd set on the cocktail table a little closer to the center. The carpet was a plush pile in a very pale cream.

"When Daniel and I got divorced, I maxed out my credit cards redecorating when I definitely couldn't afford it. Just to feel like I was starting over," Claire said. "Which was not only childish but stupid. It took me years to pay off that card."

Once again Samantha's thoughts turned to her absent husband. "When Jonathan and I got married I was only twenty-one and he was twenty-seven. And we had my brother and sister to raise. There wasn't a lot of opportunity for childish behavior."

"I guess I could have let Zach buy the condo for him and Sarah," Brooke said. "But as much as this place isn't me, I couldn't bear to think of them in it. Plus I had no confidence that we'd be left with enough to buy something else." Brooke wrinkled her nose again. "Sorry. That's probably too much information." She finished off her glass of wine. "I know you didn't come here to hear all about my ex-husband."

"Well, I'm happy to hear whatever anyone wants to share," Claire said. "As long as I don't have to stare at a blank computer screen while I do it."

"What does that mean?" Samantha asked.

Claire shook her head. "It means now that I have my editor and agent's full attention, I can't seem to think straight enough to figure out the book I thought I was going to write."

"You mean like writer's block?" Brooke asked.

"I'd have to have started writing to be blocked," Claire said. "I can't even seem to get my idea solidified."

"That doesn't sound good," Brooke replied after chewing thoughtfully.

"It's not. I was a lot more productive when I was working full-time and taking care of a child by myself," Claire said. "It's kind of like winning the lottery and then not being able to figure out what to buy with the money. I have all this time now and I can't seem to stop squandering it."

Their shoes off, they padded through the deep pile carpet and into the kitchen to refill their plates and glasses.

"How about you, Samantha?" Claire asked, flipping open the pizza box. "We're both pissing and moaning over here and you haven't said a word of complaint."

"That's because she's married to a gorgeous and successful man who is willing to read *Stellaluna* multiple times to small children he's never met before," Brooke said topping off their glasses and reaching for a slice of pizza. "How many years have you and Jonathan been married?"

"Twenty-five," Samantha said. "Almost twenty-six." Once that might have been a boast. Now it sounded long and hollow.

"Wow!" Brooke said.

"You certainly seem to have hit the matrimonial jackpot," Claire agreed.

"Like I said," Brooke crowed. "Twenty-five years and no complaints. Maybe we should call Guinness World Records."

"Or Ripley's Believe It or Not!" Claire added, looking at Samantha sharply. "What do you say to that, Samantha?"

Samantha smiled and kept silent, which was what she'd always done when Sylvie and Lucy complained about their spouses or their marriages. Even when her mother-in-law had gotten in her swipes at her dearly departed husband. Of course Samantha had nothing negative to say. Because she was too damned grateful to Jonathan for marrying her in the first place.

Claire Walker and Brooke Mackenzie weren't Sylvie and

Lucy. Both of them watched her and waited for her to say something.

Samantha felt the oddest urge to tell the truth. To confess that she hadn't heard from her gorgeous and successful husband in a whole week and that she was afraid that calling him would only make things worse. But a lifetime of holding her fears as close to the vest as she did her feelings smothered that urge. "Are you kidding?" she finally said. "I say it's time to open another bottle of wine and let the *Downton Abbey* marathon begin."

CHAPTER TWENTY-FIVE

BROOKE WOKE ON SUNDAY MORNING AND PAD-
ded into the kitchen to turn on the coffeemaker. Her
head throbbed slightly from the wine they'd drunk the night
before, her stomach felt unpleasantly full from the steady
stream of junk food, and her mouth was as dry as a patch of
the Sahara. But while her physical reactions to the late night
Downton Abbey marathon were negative, they were accompanied by an unexpected and unfamiliar sense of well-being.

With a yawn she wandered into the family room and
found Claire and Samantha still asleep on the massive sectional they'd nodded off on. Claire lay on her stomach, her
face buried in a silk pillow. Samantha lay on her back on the
opposite end of the "L," her arms thrown out in abandon-
ment, her dark hair hanging off the side. A steady and not
exactly ladylike snore escaped her open mouth with each rise
and fall of her chest.

Without comment Brooke dropped onto the nearby club
chair, propped her bare feet on the ottoman, and drank her
coffee while she contemplated the room. Empty wine bottles

and glasses littered the cocktail and end tables. The pizza box sat open on the carpet, its lid propped up against a floor lamp. The bakery box, from which every delectable crumb had been scraped clean, lay on the floor near one of Samantha's hands.

Morning light slatted in through the shutters. Brooke sipped her coffee and considered the mess; she couldn't help smiling when she imagined leaving the room this way so that Zachary would be forced to see it when he brought the girls back.

They'd watched five of the seven episodes on the *Downton Abbey* DVD, pausing only for food and potty runs. Somewhere around three a.m. Samantha had fallen asleep. Shortly afterward Brooke had returned from the bathroom to discover Claire curled in a ball with her back to the television. Seeing no reason to wake them Brooke had turned off the TV and the lights and gone to bed.

Claire rolled onto her back but her eyes remained closed. "Where am I?" she asked.

"On my couch," Brooke replied.

"What's that awful noise?" Claire yawned.

"Samantha."

"You're kidding." Claire's eyes opened.

"Nope."

Claire sat up and rubbed sleep from her eyes. "Is it wrong of me to be so tempted to get out my phone and shoot a little video?"

"It is since we promised that 'what happens while watching *Downton Abbey* stays with *Downton Abbey*,'" Brooke said.

"We're not actually watching *Downton Abbey* right now," Claire pointed out with another yawn.

"True," Brooke agreed as Samantha gave another less than ladylike snort. "But we were. And we still have two episodes to go." She scrubbed at her own eyes and smiled. "I don't have anywhere I have to be. Do you?"

"Well, I know where I should be. And what I should be

doing there," Claire said. Her smile dimmed. "But someone would have to drag me out of here first. I made it through the marathon so far. I'm not dropping out now."

Samantha inhaled sharply, then emitted a final explosive snort. Her eyes blinked open.

Brooke and Claire laughed. "God, Jonathan really is a saint," Claire said.

"What's so funny?" Samantha didn't move, but her eyes were blinking rapidly.

"I just uploaded video of you snoring to YouTube," Claire deadpanned.

"You did not." Samantha turned her head and looked at Brooke. "Did she?"

"No, she didn't. But it's a good thing you woke up when you did. She was lobbying hard for the opportunity. I'm not sure I could have held her off much longer." Brooke laughed, almost embarrassed by how great it felt to have friends here in the home that had never felt really hers.

"I can't believe we slept here," Samantha said, stifling another yawn. For the first time Brooke noticed dark shadows beneath her eyes. "Did we even talk about going home?"

"No. You just sort of dropped out one at a time. I barely made it to my bedroom," Brooke said.

"Yeah," Claire said, hugging a pillow to her stomach. "I think I made it right to the point where Edith was writing the letter to the Turkish ambassador."

"The last thing I remember is Maggie Smith letting Molesley's father win the flower show." Samantha hugged her knees to her chest and rested her chin on them. "God, I haven't been to a slumber party since eleventh grade." She sniffed. "Is that coffee?"

Brooke nodded. "Can I pour you a cup?"

"God, yes," Claire said. "But I need sustenance. Do you want me to make a doughnut run?"

They looked at each other. All of them were rumpled. Hair stuck out every which way. No one seemed to care in the least. Brooke's headache had already begun to recede and she felt the first stirrings of hunger. After last night's feeding frenzy there seemed no point in counting breakfast calories. "I'm ready to watch *Downton Abbey*," Brooke said. "If you all can live with toaster waffles, I think I have a box of Eggos in the freezer."

AT THE END OF HUNTER JACKSON'S FIRST WEEK AT Private Butler, Edward felt a little like Rex Harrison's Professor Higgins in *My Fair Lady*. Only instead of producing a lady from a flower girl he was trying to turn an overprivileged peacock into a self-effacing concierge.

Hunter Jackson had completed all the errands and tasks he'd been assigned. Though Jackson's automatic response to Edward's authority too often resembled that of a teenager to an irritating parent, the clients Jackson had been assigned to assist had seemed satisfied. As the week wore on Jackson's demeanor became quite proper bordering on formal. At times Edward suspected the young man might actually be doing a parody of Edward; that in this case imitation was not the sincerest form of flattery. But it was hard to know for certain. In the end Edward dismissed these thoughts as uncharitable and reminded himself that what Jackson thought was not his concern as long as his actions and behavior remained acceptable.

At the moment, Jackson sat across from Edward's desk, his back straight, his attention focused on Edward.

"I heard from Mr. Culp," Edward said. "He tells me that you've suggested a party and a private family cruise of the Greek Isles for his wife Alicia's sixtieth that will include all of their children and grandchildren."

Hunter nodded. He smiled quite modestly.

"How did you come up with the idea?" Edward asked, curious.

"Actually it was your questionnaire," the young man said.

"I felt kind of silly pulling it out when I met with Jim the first time. But once he started answering the questions it seemed clear that a trip was in order and since money was no object . . ." Jackson shrugged. "Well, I thought why not go all out?"

Edward winced at Jackson's use of the client's first name and the allusion to Culp's wealth. But the younger man had made great strides. And he didn't think all of his enthusiasm was feigned. "You've done well," Edward said. "But we do need to be careful not to be overly familiar with the clients. And we certainly never call them by their first names."

Jackson stared at him as if he were daft. But the look was brief. "All right." Then as Edward reached inside his breast pocket for the week's assignments, Jackson said, "I have a few ideas about marketing that I thought I'd run by you. And it occurred to me that Private Butler might be a perfect candidate for franchising. I know someone down in the Keys who's a specialist in that field." Jackson leaned forward eager to press his point.

"Let's not get ahead of ourselves," Edward said, cutting him off and handing an assignment sheet across the desk. "Perhaps in another few weeks once you've gotten a bit more acclimated, you might share some of your thoughts on marketing with me. But Private Butler will never be franchised. That's not what this company is about. This business is personal—personal service, personal attention, personal integrity. That's not something that can be franchised."

Jackson's jaw set and he dropped his eyes to skim the listed dates, times and assignments. Clarence Fitson, who had just turned ninety, needed a ride to his tailor for a fitting. Mimi Davenport had requested a driver/escort to visit her sister in Nashville.

"What is this?" Jackson bit out. "A remake of *Driving Miss Daisy*?" Jackson's calm began to evaporate. It disappeared completely when he reached the final item. "You actually expect me to take someone's child to Mommy and Me?"

he asked. His eyes reflected a toxic mixture of anger and horror.

"Well, it's not just anyone's child," Edward replied coolly. "It's a friend of your family. Sylvie Talmadge's granddaughter, in fact."

Jackson's face turned a mottled red. "You cannot be serious," he said. "I'll be a laughingstock." His gaze sharpened. "This is an attempt to get rid of me, isn't it? You want to see just how much humiliation I can take before I tell you to, what's that expression? To sod . . ."

"Sod off?" Edward completed the phrase for him.

"I'm telling you, you are completely wasting my talents on this bullshit," Jackson said. "You can't possibly expect me to do this crap."

Edward noted the double excremental expletive, but said nothing.

"I could be making you money," Jackson railed, somehow managing not to raise his voice. "Putting together investors to franchise your business. And you want me to take a child to play with other . . . *children*?" The last was clearly intended as an expletive. But at least there was no excrement involved.

"As I said earlier, I might be willing to discuss your ideas in due course," Edward said reasonably. "Assuming you can follow directions and represent Private Butler in the manner I've proscribed. Until then, I need you to simply take care of these clients. And I'd also like you to pinch in for Isabella. She has an audition tomorrow afternoon and needs someone to cover for her. You two seem quite friendly. It occurred to me you might be willing to help her out."

The gritting of teeth wasn't a good look for young Jackson. But he did manage to swallow back whatever invective he'd been planning to hurl. "Is that all?" he asked tightly.

"Yes, that will do for now," Edward said unperturbed. He stood, forcing Jackson to do the same and leveled a look at the younger man that said, "I am the boss. You are not."

If Hunter Jackson couldn't come to terms with this, he would be gone.

Jackson turned and stormed off. But he did it with perfect posture and without uttering a single expletive. Surely that was progress of some kind. Something might be made of the boy after all. Perhaps the rain in Spain didn't only fall on the plain.

ON THE DALTONS' DOORSTEP BROOKE RAN A HAND over her hair, which she'd desperately tried to tame, and tugged on the angular hem of her new blouse. It was a little snugger than she was used to with no extra fabric to hide beneath. But its graduated hem hung low on her hips and made her short, stocky body appear longer and leaner. The saleslady had assured her that the drop waist was in fact slenderizing and that the deep gray color turned her hazel eyes to smoke. Brooke had bought it immediately not even caring if the woman was exaggerating; it made her feel attractive and it was a world away from her usual beige.

An image of the lovely Monica standing on this same welcome mat in her short tennis dress arose in Brooke's mind and she did her best to banish it. But Brooke was relieved that this was a family dinner and not a date; she sincerely hoped that would keep the comparisons to the casserole women out of her mind and Bruce's.

Natalie and Ava juggled magazines and poster board in their arms as Brooke rang the doorbell. Footsteps sounded and the door opened to reveal Marissa. Her father stood behind her.

The girls' greetings were hurried and effusive. Before Brooke could gather herself all three of them had raced off to Marissa's room to help Marissa begin her collage.

"It doesn't look like they need us," Bruce observed as he closed the door.

"No," Brooke agreed, still trying to control, or at least

hide, her nervousness. "Natalie and Ava were thrilled with the idea of showing Marissa what to do. I suspect we'll have to pry them out of her room when dinner's ready."

"Sounds good to me," he said. "Will you have a glass of wine?"

"Gosh, we've been here at least two minutes," Brooke teased. "I thought you'd never ask."

"Come on. You can talk to me while I finish dinner."

Following him through the family room, she saw that the kitchen table had been set for five. The silverware and dishes looked like everyday, but a brightly colored cloth covered the table and a vase of fresh picked flowers sat squarely in the middle. Carefully labeled place cards had been written and illustrated for each of them.

"The table looks lovely," Brooke said.

"Marissa was in charge of decorations. And she helped me bake the dessert," he replied.

"Homemade dessert?" Brooke said. "I am impressed." And pleased and thrilled. "What is it?"

"Sorry," he said. "It's a surprise. I had to do a pinky swear that I wouldn't say anything in advance."

"Ah, well," Brooke said as she slid onto the bar stool and settled in at the kitchen counter. "I know just how binding a pinky swear is. So I won't even ask if it's animal, vegetable, or mineral . . ." She raised an eyebrow as if waiting for him to fill in the blank.

"Sorry." He mimed zipping his lips.

"Fine." She pretended annoyance but was incredibly moved by the idea of a man who would understand the importance of a promise made to a child. "I guess I'll just have to live with the anticipation."

"That can be a good thing," he said. "White or red?" He held up a bottle of each and she opted for the red. A wheel of warmed Brie surrounded by crackers and apple slices had been arranged on a glass platter. Brightly colored enamel bowls filled with mixed nuts, Goldfish, and other nibbles dotted the counter. He poured them both a glass of red wine. After setting hers in front of her he raised his in salute. "Welcome. I'm very glad you all could join us tonight."

"We're honored to be here," she said in return. There was something about the sincerity of his smile and the appreciative glint in his eyes that made her feel not only welcomed but attractive. She sniffed appreciatively. The scent was warm and tomatoey with a hint of meat. "Is the main course hush-hush too? Because I think I might be able to guess this one."

"Marissa requested my world-famous spaghetti and meatballs." He turned to her. "It's not particularly fancy or gourmet. I hope that's all right with you?"

"It's perfect. My girls will love it. We all will."

The talk between them was easy and punctuated with appearances from the girls.

"Look, Daddy! I picked all purple things. Do you like these pillows?"

Marissa carried the poster over and put it up on the counter. Natalie and Ava were right behind her. "Do you think I could have purple walls, too?" Marissa asked.

"Well, I personally have always been a big fan of purple. It's the color of royalty, after all," Brooke said.

"Oh, Mommy, we should bring Missa our copy of *Princess Prunella and the Purple Peanut* to read," Ava said. "I know she'd like it."

When dinner was ready the girls washed their hands without protest and took their seats eagerly. Marissa and her father served and cleared away.

"No," Bruce insisted when they tried to help. "You're guests. The only thing you have to do is enjoy the meal."

Brooke felt a goofy smile take over her face. She couldn't remember a time when Zachary had been remotely tempted to wait on her. "Gosh, I feel like a queen tonight," she said. "Maybe *I* should have worn purple."

"You deserve to be waited on," Bruce said.

She nodded regally. "Why, thank you, kind sir," she said,

trying to keep things light. What did that say about her that such simple kindness made her eyes tear up? "I hereby name you the royal chef. You may feed me and my princesses anytime."

"Done." He gave Ava and Natalie a wink then he and Marissa huddled together at the back counter obscuring Brooke, Natalie, and Ava's view. A few whispered, giggling moments later father and daughter turned. Marissa held a plate aloft. Bruce held two.

"Your majesties," he said as they placed the desserts in front of their guests. "Bon appétit."

Each plate held a still-warm slice of apple pie topped with a heaping scoop of French vanilla ice cream. "Oh, my gosh." Brooke closed her eyes as she took the first bites. "This is delicious. Did you two really make this pie?"

Marissa nodded happily. "I got to peel some of the apples and help make the crust. It was my mommy's favorite dessert. Daddy always made it for her birthday and special 'kashuns."

Natalie and Ava pretty much Hoovered up every morsel of the pie. Brooke saw Ava grasp her plate with both chubby hands and reached out just in time to keep her from tilting it up so that she could lick the last bits of ice cream–soaked crust.

Holding back a smile, but without saying a word, Bruce cut and served everyone another smaller sliver. Natalie pronounced it the best dessert ever. Ava sent Bruce a look of abject adoration.

By the time Brooke and the girls had been handed into the car and invited to come back soon, Brooke had experienced more than a few adoring thoughts herself.

Chapter Twenty-Six

Tに the invitation to Bellewood for Sunday brunch was actually more of a summons than an invitation. Samantha had canceled her regular Wednesday lunch with her mother-in-law pleading a headache, which wasn't a stretch at all and had known that at some point she'd have to see and speak with Cynthia. But after more than a week with nothing more than the curtest of informational texts from Jonathan, the last thing Samantha wanted to do was spend time with his mother. Nonetheless she dressed and drove to Buckhead, checking both text and email in hopes of a message—a real message—from Jonathan as she drove.

Jonathan had traveled extensively on business over the years, but his absence had never felt this intentional. Nor had he ever communicated so . . . sparsely. For more than half of her life he'd been there, steady and sure. A sturdy rock to lean on. A port fit to weather any storm. The emptiness inside her had grown so cavernous that she'd begun to imagine she could hear an echo.

She was relieved when she saw Meredith's and Hunter's cars in the drive assuming that with all three of them there, her misery would be easier to hide.

"Hello, Miz Davis," Zora said as Samantha stepped into the foyer. "They're all in the living room. Brunch will be ready in just a few minutes."

Samantha caught the scent of biscuits just out of the oven, which Doris, the Davises' longtime cook, would serve with a choice of honey or sawmill gravy. Samantha knew the sideboard would groan under the weight of chafing dishes filled with scrambled eggs, bacon, ham and sausage, fried potatoes, and cheese grits, all of which would be washed down with copious amounts of chicory-flavored coffee.

The thought of so much food made her feel physically ill.

"My, you look done in," Cynthia said in greeting. "Aren't you feeling well?"

"I'm fine," she said, though it had taken double the usual amount of concealer to try to disguise the dark puffy circles under her eyes. "I'm sure it's just allergies. You know how I react to ragweed." This was a safe thing to ascribe any illness to in fall in Atlanta, which was second in swollen nasal passages only to the golden shroud of pollen that covered Atlanta every spring.

Samantha accepted hugs from Meredith and Hunter but was too weary to search their faces for warning signs of unhappiness, irritation, and unknown agendas.

"Where's Jonathan?" Meredith asked idly.

"He's out of town on business," Samantha said lightly.

Cynthia looked at her sharply. "And when do you expect him back, dear?"

"I'm not sure," Samantha said.

Samantha sensed her mother-in-law's antennae quivering. Hunter, too, was tuned in while pretending not to be.

They helped themselves from silver chafing dishes on the sideboard and settled into their usual seats. Samantha's eyes strayed to Jonathan's empty place at the head of the table. The house she'd grown so used to felt colder and less welcoming without him in it.

When they'd all been seated, Cynthia lifted her fork in signal that they could begin. "How are things at the Preservation Board?" Cynthia asked.

"Good," Meredith replied. "It's just that compared to New York, Atlanta's practically provincial. And the preservation laws don't have the same kind of teeth that Charleston and Savannah's do."

"But still it's a great opportunity," Samantha cut in when she saw Cynthia stiffen in her seat. "You're very fortunate that Cynthia had connections there."

"Yes, that's true," Meredith agreed, though nowhere near as speedily as Samantha would have liked. "Very lucky."

"And how is that young man in New York?" Cynthia inquired casually. Except that Samantha knew it for the jab that it was. "Do you think he'll be coming down to visit?"

"Maybe later this fall," Meredith said. "It doesn't look like he'll be able to get away from work as soon as he'd hoped."

Hunter raised an eyebrow at his sister, a silent taunt.

"Oh, and your relationships are so significant?" Meredith's chin shot out mulishly. "When's the last time you dated anyone with enough brain cells to carry on a conversation?" She paused briefly as if the question were something other than rhetorical. When she got no reply she continued. "And frankly, your current job is driving and errand running. You have no room to talk."

"That shows what you know," Hunter retorted. "I've already spoken with Edward about the concept of franchising Private Butler. The service sector is the only one on the rise in this economy. There's real money to be made for the smart investor."

For once Samantha let the barbs fly without any effort to stop or soften them. In truth they barely registered. For the moment her siblings were employed and not in crisis mode; which was more than could be said for her.

"I ran into Sylvie Talmadge the other day and she told me how impressed she was with the company Hunter's with," Cynthia said. "What is it called again?"

"Private Butler," Samantha said. "Edward Parker, the Alexander's concierge owns it."

"Hmmm," Cynthia said. "Private Butler. It has a nice ring to it."

"Well, I ran into Shelby Holcomb," Meredith said naming Sylvie's daughter. "She told me Hunter took her daughter Riley to Mommy and Me." She laughed derisively. "And didn't you drive some ninety-year-old man to his tailor?"

"That ninety-year-old man has a major stake in Coca-Cola and the Home Depot," Hunter shot back. "He understands investments." Hunter laid down his fork and knife. "Edward and I agreed I'd get the feel of the day-to-day of the business first as a prelude to building the brand and other . . . opportunities."

Samantha was relieved that Hunter seemed so positive about the work he was doing. Maybe this association with Edward Parker and Private Butler would be just what her brother needed. Her eyes strayed to Jonathan's empty seat and she wished again that her husband were here. As she moved the food around on her plate, she reminded herself that the phone worked both ways. She could call Jonathan from the car on the way home and at least hear his voice. Except that she was afraid he wouldn't answer; or worse, fail to return her call.

Samantha looked up, caught her mother-in-law watching her, and slid a large bite of egg and grits into her mouth, then tried to look happy—and hungry—while she chewed it.

"You willingly escorted that little terror to a playgroup and hung out with the other mothers?" Meredith asked Hunter in disbelief.

"Research, my dear sister. Research. That's the key to finance and business development; an important step, which is so often overlooked. And which you clearly know nothing about."

"Well, then," Cynthia said, turning her attention back to the others, "if you'll bring me some cards, Hunter, I might begin making some referrals when it seems appropriate." She smiled quite regally. "Now that we've sorted all that out, perhaps we should have some of Doris's peach cobbler?"

With the meal finished and the plates cleared, Hunter and Meredith kissed Samantha and Cynthia good-bye and departed. Samantha stood in the massive foyer preparing to do the same. Her mother-in-law laid a hand on her arm as Samantha reached for the door. "I hope you'll forgive my butting in," Cynthia said in an apologetic tone that was most unlike her. "But I heard from Jonathan yesterday. I've never heard him so uncertain about his travel plans."

"Yes." Samantha searched her mother-in-law's face for some sign of what Jonathan might have said even as Cynthia searched hers.

"I know from personal experience that it can be dangerous to leave even the most steadfast of husbands too long on their own," Cynthia finally said as if Samantha had been invited and refused.

"I'm sorry?" Wherever this conversation was headed, Samantha was pretty certain she didn't want to go there.

"Yes, dear, so am I." Her tone had turned alarmingly sincere. "I never wanted him to take on so much responsibility at such an appallingly young age and certainly not after your father practically destroyed the firm," she said. "Jonathan never could resist an injured animal. Or a pretty girl in distress." She sighed. "But still, one hates to see any marriage founder."

Founder? Jesus. Samantha focused on keeping her breathing regular and the fear off her face. Had Jonathan told his mother he was unhappy? Had he confided his feelings in her?

Or had his extended absence and the vagueness of his return sent her on this fishing expedition?

She looked her mother-in-law in the eye. Samantha had no idea what to say any more than she knew how to rectify the situation. But one thing she was *not* going to do was discuss her marital problems with Cynthia. That would be way too much like inviting the fox into the henhouse. "Thank you for your concern and for brunch," Samantha said. "Everything was delicious."

With what she hoped would pass for a gracious smile, Samantha let herself out. But all the way home she replayed her last conversation with Jonathan. He'd said he wanted to know what he was to her, how she felt.

Samantha would have laughed if it hadn't been so tragic. The thing was she'd just begun to realize what she wanted from Jonathan, was almost shocked at how much she wanted it. But she wasn't at all certain what he wanted from her.

Or if, in fact, he wanted anything from her at all.

THAT NIGHT WHEN THE FIRST EPISODE OF SEASON two ended, Claire, Brooke, and Samantha picked up plates of raspberry tarts and snifters of brandy and joined the rest of the group around the table.

"Thank God Bates proposed to Anna," Brooke said as they took their seats.

"And I love that Branson proposed to Sybil!" Samantha added.

"That was so Ashley Wilkes of Matthew to ask Mary to look out for Lavinia if he dies," Claire observed. "Do you think they mean for Mary to be an Edwardian version of Scarlett O'Hara?"

Edward Parker looked on like a proud father as the group debated this question without his prompting.

"I can't believe Thomas intentionally shot himself in the hand so that he could leave the front," Brooke said, squinching her face in disgust. "Ugh."

"I guess he didn't think of dressing up like a woman to try to get a discharge like Corporal Klinger did on *MASH*," Claire said. "I used to love those reruns."

"The British think dressing up like a woman is funny, not crazy," Mimi Davenport observed. "My husband loved that English comedian Benny Hill's show. He used to dress up all the time." She looked at Edward. "No offense intended," she said with a bob of her white head.

"None taken." Edward smiled. He waited while the conversation played out, then motioned to Isabella and James, who began to hand out sheets of paper and pencils. "Now that we've all had a bite and quenched our thirsts I think the time is ripe for a little quiz."

There were groans at this.

"Oh, no, I always freeze up on tests," Brooke said.

"I guess it's a good thing we had our marathon last weekend," Claire said. "It'll be fresh in our minds."

"I don't think anyone's going to be flunking out of Sunday-night screenings," Samantha said.

"No, no one will be flunking out," Edward said with a smile. "The quiz is quite clever. I found it posted on the WETA Television website. It's designed to tell you which *Downton Abbey* character you are. The results can be quite . . . surprising.

"Please let Isabella and James know if you'd like more to eat or drink as they come around. Then I'll give you time to take this small, but illuminating quiz."

Edward began to pass out the questions and Claire felt Brooke relax beside her. There were giggles as the tongue-in-cheek nature of the quiz became apparent.

"As you can see it's impossible to fail this quiz," the concierge said with a smile. "But I'll read the first question aloud, just to help you get started." He held up the list he'd printed from the WETA website. "All you need to do is fill in the correct bubble."

"I have a whole weekend to myself!" he read, "I'm going to:

What's a weekend?

Find some poor soul to help

Attend a political rally

Make plans to ruin my rival's life

Stay alone in my room and read

Attend a jolly good foxhunt, followed by billiards and cigars

Get ahead on next week's work."

They laughed as they filled in the bubbles and chattered amongst themselves. Edward, clearly pleased, watched from the head of the table. When the majority had finished, he asked for a first volunteer. Mimi Davenport raised her hand, then handed him her sheet.

"All right then, let's see about you, Mrs. D," he said as he scanned her answers and compared them to what looked like some sort of answer key. "My goodness, Mrs. Davenport. You're apparently Bates, valet to Lord Grantham."

He smiled wickedly while laughter filled the room, then read the description from a sheet of paper. "You probably have a secret identity or are lying about your past to someone you care about, but at least you feel really bad about it. On the plus side, you're loyal and hardworking and you'd never rat anyone out to the boss, even when they really deserve it. Noble and a bit mysterious, you're a genuinely decent person—and everyone's wondering when you're just going to tell that nice Anna girl how you feel."

The group erupted with laughter as Mimi Davenport stood and took an exaggerated bow.

"Not my words, mind you." Edward raised his hands in disclaimer. "I downloaded these character descriptions from the WETA website."

They passed their tests toward Edward, all of them eager now to see which character they were. "It's all right, Mrs. D," Edward said as he sorted through them. "I'll confess I wasn't who I expected to be. I assumed I'd turn out to be Carson, but I could hardly have been further off."

"Who were you?" Samantha prompted.

"I don't know if I should say." Edward feigned reluctance. "It is a bit embarrassing."

There were hoots of encouragement.

"All right then. Here it is word for word from the WETA Television site." He cleared his voice dramatically, amping up his accent. "You are Violet, Dowager Countess of Grantham."

He raised an eyebrow in elegant imitation and waited for the laughter to die down.

"You're the imperious, aristocratic head of your family who (almost) always gets her way, and you don't suffer fools gladly," he read. "Though you're often bossy and arrogant, you're surprisingly adaptable and exceptionally loyal to the people you love. By the way, you also get all the best lines, so we hope you're ready for immortality, but you should really look up the definition of 'weekend.' "

CLAIRE SIGHED AS EDWARD PARKER FINISHED READ-ing the description, which was wonderfully phrased and hysterically funny. She felt total envy for whoever had penned it and the other character descriptions, which Edward began to read aloud as women handed in their papers. But then at the moment she envied the person who'd written the advertising copy on her box of Frosted Mini-Wheats. It seemed that everyone could express themselves better and more rapidly than she.

"What's wrong?" Brooke asked as the evening came to an end and they left the clubroom together.

"Hmm?" Both Claire and Samantha looked up and answered at the same time.

"You're both off," she said as they lingered in the hallway. "And I don't think it's because you ended up as O'Brien and Thomas."

"Easy for you to say since you got to be Lady Cora," Samantha said, but there was something in Samantha's voice that Claire couldn't quite identify.

"Well, I might have fudged the answers just a little," Brooke admitted.

"Me, too," Claire admitted. "But I still ended up below stairs."

"Well, at least you were female," Samantha said. "I mean Thomas is a fascinating character. But he hasn't got a shred of moral fiber or anything that resembles a conscience."

The hallway had cleared. Edward Parker locked the clubroom door and said his good nights. They continued to linger.

"Why don't we go outside to the pool?" Claire suggested. "It's really gorgeous outside tonight." She led them out the door and over to a trio of chaises. The pool's surface rippled under a light breeze. A large magnolia tree that rose near a corner of the pool deck swayed softly. The night sky was dimpled with stars. "The neighborhood pools out in the suburbs are emptied after Labor Day. I like that this one's heated and maintained year-round."

They sat in the silence with just the occasional car horn or traffic noise to remind them that they were in the city.

"All right." Brooke sat up straighter in her chaise and folded her arms across her chest. "Are either of you planning to tell me what's wrong?"

Surprised by the note of command, Claire turned to look at Brooke. Samantha did the same. Neither of them spoke.

"I mean, you've both been holding my hand since Ken

and Barbie moved into the building. Samantha took care of my children at a moment's notice and, I think, told Zachary off on my behalf. While you"—she nodded at Claire—"have offered to help, given me advice, and propped me up in general." She paused, but she didn't stop. In fact, she seemed to be gathering steam. "I'm not a charity case. And I hate that now when I can see that you're both struggling in some way, you're just blowing me off. I mean it's insulting. I appreciate your friendship and your support. But those things don't work when they're one-sided."

Brooke stopped talking but her words hung in the October air as if written there in capital letters, impossible to ignore. Claire cut her eyes to Samantha, who had gone still, the expression on her face far less certain than Claire had ever seen it.

"Nothing's wrong in my world," Claire finally said, feeling oddly protective of Samantha. "If you don't count the fact that I've started dodging calls from my agent and my editor, which believe me is unheard of for someone at my lowly rung on the publishing ladder. I'm also lying to my daughter—who has her act far more together than I do. I've been pretending I'm actually writing a book when I haven't written the first word. In fact the only thing I'm writing in is my journal—lots of Claire Walker and friends present day—and almost no great love story in the Scottish Highlands. It feels like ancient history . . ."

This got a laugh as she'd intended. She only wished that it was actually funny and not so frightening. "I just don't seem capable of doing what I came here to do." She hesitated. "And I'm not even sure anymore that I want to." The truths spilled out of her mouth without benefit of editing. "I'm running through my money twice as fast as I expected. And I have absolutely nothing to show for it." She was embarrassed to feel tears gathering behind her lids. All those years of staying strong for Hailey blown to bits.

"You've got us," Brooke said quietly.

Samantha nodded. But she didn't quite make eye contact.

"Thanks." Claire expelled a breath of air, drew one in. "That would make you my silver lining."

Their eyes turned to Samantha, who shifted uneasily on her chaise. Her forehead creased slightly as if she were conducting some sort of internal debate. In the end she shrugged. "Sorry," she said apologetically. "All I have to throw in the pot is that Jonathan's out of town a little longer than usual." She looked out over the wall at the magnolia while the two of them waited for her to go on.

"That's it?" Brooke asked. "That's all you've got?"

Samantha shrugged, but Claire couldn't help thinking that the casual gesture seemed to take an awful lot of effort. "That's it."

"So, it's just Claire and I who are battling right now? Everything in your world is just hunky-dory?" Brooke tried again.

"I didn't mean it like that," Samantha said. "I just wasn't raised to air my dirty linen in public. And believe me, there's been plenty of it."

"Oh, so you're above all that?" Claire asked.

"I didn't mean it that way, either," Samantha said.

"Why don't you tell us how you *do* mean it," Brooke said. "So we can understand. And maybe even help?"

"I appreciate the offer, but . . ." She shook her head. "Sometimes putting things into words makes them almost too real, you know?"

Claire did. "Yeah. At the moment I'm pretty horrified at all the things that came out of my mouth. I mean, I turned my whole life upside down to come here and write this book. I have the gift of a year—a chance to finally fulfill a dream— and I can't even seem to get started." She looked straight at Samantha. "I may not be able to summon them at will, but I understand how potent words can be."

Brooke smiled sadly and looked down at her watch. "Well, I guess it's getting kind of late. We should probably head in now."

As they rose, Claire studied Samantha, she of the perfect life and the marriage that had lasted for more than a quarter century. She wasn't sure what "longer than usual" meant and couldn't remember the last time she'd seen Jonathan Davis in the building. But Claire didn't want to pry into something Samantha so clearly didn't want to talk about. Life in a suburban swim-and-tennis neighborhood had often felt like living in a fishbowl; that constant scrutiny had been one of the things she'd been eager to escape.

They walked inside and stopped in front of the elevator. But this time as Samantha pressed the elevator call button Claire knew that Brooke had been right. Like a duck who appeared to float serenely on the lake's surface, there was a lot of frantic paddling going on beneath Samantha Davis's perfect surface.

Chapter Twenty-Seven

EDWARD'S OFFICE PHONE RANG AT PRECISELY FIVE fifteen p.m., which made it ten fifteen in England. Edward didn't need the caller ID to know who was calling. Leaning back in his chair, Edward propped his shoes up on his desk and answered.

"Hello, lad," his great-uncle Mason's voice sounded firm and fine with no hint of the number of pints he might have consumed at the Hungry Fox that night. "How are things?"

"Good," Edward replied. "Almost too good."

"No such thing."

"No, but I'm scrambling to keep up. And I'm not a happy scrambler," Edward replied.

Mason laughed. "That you're not. You're a damned planner just like your grandfather, always so meticulous, dotting all those i's and crossing all those t's. I'm exhausted just thinking about it."

"You're exhausted because you're eighty-eight and you're still helping out at the pub every night," Edward said reasonably.

"Don't even like to think of the place having to get by without me," Mason replied. "Your brother's always happy—and grateful I might add—to see me. Unlike some people I know."

"How many plane tickets have I sent you?" Edward countered as he always did to this jibe. "And how many times have you actually come over here?"

"Once was enough, thank you very much," Mason grumbled. "Can't follow those damned accents. Every word stretched out into infinity. They talk so slow down South a body could drop dead from boredom waiting for a sentence to end."

Edward laughed. He'd had to interpret for both sides of a conversation during Mason's only visit to Atlanta.

"It would be better if you came home for a visit," Mason said. "In fact, an old friend of yours was in the Fox tonight asking about you."

Edward closed his eyes, knowing from his uncle's attempt at nonchalance exactly who he was talking about.

"She looked fine. Beautiful really," Mason said. "Her husband's died, Eddie." His great-uncle used the nickname when he most wanted to make a point. "Almost a year ago now. She's come home to take care of her mother. This could be your opportunity to win her back."

Edward sighed as a picture of Julia Bardmoor formed in his mind. She'd been tall and lithe and beautiful in her wedding gown, which was what she'd been wearing the last time he'd seen her. Her blue eyes had shimmered with tears when she'd left him at the altar all those years ago; as unable at the last to commit to a nomadic life of hotel postings across the United States as Edward had been to give them up to have her.

"I saw the look in her eyes when she asked about you, lad," his great-uncle said softly. "It's not too late." He hesitated. "It's never too late for love," he said quite dramatically.

"Said the confirmed bachelor as if he had a clue what he was talking about," Edward said. "Have you started writing Hallmark cards on the side?" He laughed, trying not to notice the hollowness of the sound. "I'm a lot more likely to listen to your advice if you choose a subject you know something about. Say drinking. Or causing trouble. Or . . ."

"Fine," Mason said. "So tell me how things are going with that Hunter person you've taken on."

"Oh, I'm working on whipping him into shape," Edward replied. "He's bright and so far he's taken what I've dished out. At the moment he's focused, though I'm not sure he's grasping the reasoning behind things. Between his sister and her mother-in-law's referrals, business is booming. Hence the scrambling to add staff I mentioned earlier."

"And the screenings?" Mason asked. "Have you started season two?"

"Yes," Edward said. "We're two programs in and the group's grown even larger."

"Well, season three is a corker. In the episode last night Shirley MacLaine told Maggie Smith to—"

"Oh, no," Edward cut his great-uncle off. "Don't do it. I am not listening to this. I've forbidden the ladies to skip ahead. I'm not going to betray them by getting a blow by blow from across the pond or anywhere else."

"Ach. You and your straight and narrow," Mason complained. "It's just a television program. I really don't see the harm."

"It's not about the program," Edward said. "It's about keeping my word. And not taking shortcuts. Who was it that taught me that 'a good name is better than bags of gold'?"

"No need to go quoting Cervantes on me. And I'm fairly certain that was your grandfather's favorite quote, not mine."

Edward's cell phone rang. Glancing down he recognized James Culp's phone number. "I've got a client calling," he said. "I've got to ring off. But I'll be speaking to Mum and

Dad over the weekend. Perhaps we'll have a word then. But none of those words can be about the new season of *Downton Abbey*."

"All right," Mason said. "But I still think you should consider a trip home sometime soon before someone else snatches Julia up again."

"Right," Edward replied. "If I suddenly decide that I can't survive another day without a wife, I'll consider it." A picture of Julia fleeing the church and him, her head bent, her long white veil billowing out behind her, rose in his mind. The picture was sharply focused, its colors so bright that the image was every bit as painful today as it had been when it was formed.

"THREE DOWN, ONE TO GO." BROOKE STEPPED BACK and set her paintbrush on the edge of the painter's tray to survey Marissa Dalton's bedroom. "What do you think? Is it too much purple?" She'd debated whether the color would be best as an accent, but Marissa had been so in love with the deep plumy shade, they'd decided to use it as the base color. The fourth wall had been taped off to be painted in floor-to-ceiling stripes of purple and white.

"Is there such a thing?" Bruce Dalton asked.

No! It's perfect! And beautiful! Marissa, Natalie, and Ava confirmed. Each girl held a dripping paintbrush, which would have been even more alarming if the room hadn't already been emptied and the old carpet and pad removed. The only casualties were the girls' play clothes, hair, faces, and each and every scrap of exposed skin.

If fun could be counted in paint spills, the girls were having a blast. Both Natalie and Ava had chosen the colors and fabrics that would be used in their rooms, but Zachary had shuddered in horror when Brooke had suggested that they do the work together and had instead insisted on hiring a slew of expensive painters, fabricators, and cabinetmakers.

Brooke looked at Bruce Dalton, who had purple streaks in his hair and down one cheek. Purple spatters from an unfortunate run-in with Ava's paintbrush covered the back of his shorts. Brooke hadn't fared much better.

"I think we're going to have to hose everyone down when we're done," Bruce said.

"And then you said we could have pizza," Marissa reminded her father. Her eyes glowed with excitement. "With extra cheese and pepperonis on it."

Bruce and Marissa had made another surprise recipe for dessert. Afterward Brooke would show Marissa the curtains she'd made from a bold polka-dot print they'd chosen together. Brooke had thoroughly enjoyed the hours she'd spent cutting out the fabric and sewing the panels. It had been so long since she'd had the opportunity to work with her hands. She laughed when Bruce ran a hand through his hair, leaving a purple stripe in its wake.

He shook his head in mock dismay when he realized what he'd done. "It's going to take more than a hose to get all of us clean."

"Maybe we can jog through a car wash?" Brooke suggested.

The girls squealed with laughter. Bruce shot Brooke a wink. She couldn't remember the last time she'd felt this comfortable in her own skin—even if it was doused in purple paint.

"I like purple way better than blue," Natalie said.

"Me, too," said Marissa.

"Only boys like blue," Natalie said.

Ava nodded in agreement. Her frizzy red curls were squashed together with clumps of purple paint. "Daddy hired-ed a painter and that's what color they painted the nursery."

Ava scratched her nose, leaving a telltale blob of purple, but Brooke barely noticed. Her brain was stuck on what Ava had just said. "A nursery?" she asked.

"Yeah," Natalie answered importantly. "For the new baby boy that Sarah's going to bring home."

Time slowed down and may in fact have stopped while the words sank in. The paintbrush fell out of her hand and landed on her tennis shoe in a puddle of purple paint as their meaning sank in. She bent to pick it up, taking her time as she tried to process this new development and all its ramifications.

"All right, girls, you keep up the good work," Bruce said. His hand found and cupped Brooke's elbow, offering support as she straightened. "Brooke and I are going to go place the pizza order and get cold drinks for everybody. We'll be right back."

Gently he led her out of Marissa's bedroom. He stopped at the hall bathroom but didn't let go of her. "Are you all right?"

"I don't know. I guess I just kind of got the wind knocked out of me."

"I can imagine," he said. "It's hard to believe he didn't think to let you know."

"Not really." The admission was painful but it was true. Zachary had stopped thinking about her feelings long before he left her. "But thanks for giving me a minute to regroup."

"I can do better than a minute," he said as gently as he'd led her into the hall. "Go ahead and wash up and then help yourself to a cold drink or a glass of wine. I'll go back into the purple palace of princessdom and supervise that last wall."

"Thank you." She smiled but even she could feel how tremulous it was.

"No thanks required," he said. Then he turned and left to do exactly what he'd promised.

IT WAS LATE OCTOBER AND THE BREEZE HAD STIFF-ened, gathering the strength it would need to pluck the rest of the faded and curling leaves from the trees. Claire had killed several hours strolling through the Atlanta Botanical Gardens and all over her favorite parts of Piedmont Park. Now she was seated at a picnic table with the now dog-eared journal open in front of her. For the last twenty minutes she had poured out every random observation, thought, and feeling from Edward Parker's impeccable manners and possible taste in women to Samantha Davis's solemn looks and guarded comments.

She nibbled on the end of the pen then began to describe Brooke Mackenzie's careful tiptoe through the lobby or parking garage; her sometimes Lucy-like attempts to avoid seeing her pompous ex-husband and his girlfriend, who not to be uncharitable, Claire thought was getting kind of chunky.

Claire reread what she'd just written and smiled grimly. *Now* was so easy to write. A romance set in seventeenth-century Scotland, not so much.

The pen slowed and she thought about the rush of relief she'd felt after she'd admitted her inability to write to Samantha and Brooke. But that relief had been short-lived and hadn't come close to squashing her terror of running out of time and money before the book was complete.

Please, God, let me figure out this book. It was her heartfelt prayer at bedtime and her first thought each morning. Claire ran a finger over the lined paper that she'd covered with her scribblings. If it were possible to make a living writing journal entries, she'd be a multimillionaire by now.

Her cell phone rang and she glanced down at the screen. It was the second call from her agent in as many days. Twice as many calls as she'd received from her in the previous year.

Claire listened to the ring, and only began to breathe normally when the ringing stopped. No doubt Stephanie was even now leaving another voicemail that Claire wouldn't be able to bring herself to delete. But also couldn't imagine listening to.

She felt like a thirst-crazed woman who'd crawled through hot desert sands from heartbreaking mirage to mirage, only to lack the strength to swallow a sip of water when she finally reached the oasis. The phone rang again. Hailey's number jarred her back from the disturbing desert images. The fact that she considered not answering shocked her to the core.

"Hi, Mom." In the face of her own misery, the happiness in her daughter's voice was equally shocking.

"Where are you headed?" Claire asked, hearing the sounds of wind and movement.

"Brit Lit. How about you?"

"I'm at the park. Writing in the journal my lovely daughter gave me."

"Cool," Hailey said. "I've been writing in mine, too. I might need a new one for Christmas."

"Ditto."

They covered Hailey's classes, which were great, the library job, which remained lame, and Will, the boy from her writing class, who had apparently just attained "boyfriend" status.

"So how about you, Mom? How's the book coming?"

Claire looked out over the bare-branched trees and remembered the hours they'd spent discussing Claire's glorious year of writing. Hailey had won scholarships and insisted on a work-study program so that she could help Claire have her year. Claire would cut out her tongue before she told her daughter that the opportunity of opportunities had knocked and she didn't even have the strength to open the door.

"Everything's going great," Claire lied. "I'm still roughing things out, trying to get my characters squared away."

"That's so cool. My friends up here can't believe that my mother is a full-time *published* writer."

"Yeah, it's . . . unbelievable all right. So, when do you get out in November?" Claire asked eager to change the subject. "We'll need to make arrangements for your plane ticket."

Claire breathed a small sigh of relief when Hailey pulled up her phone calendar and began to scroll through the next month. And an even larger one when Hailey reached the English building and had to hang up.

Claire gathered up her journal and tucked it into her backpack. As she walked down Peachtree toward the Alexander, she cursed herself for her weakness. It had left her stranded in no-man's-land teetering between truth and lies, fact and fiction.

In all the years it had been just the two of them, she'd only ever lied to Hailey in order to protect her. If Claire didn't figure out how to take advantage of her opportunities and get to work soon, she'd find herself sliding down that slippery slope where lies would be necessary. And the only thing those lies would protect Hailey from would be finding out that her mother was a chickenhearted fraud.

Chapter Twenty-Eight

Late Wednesday afternoon Brooke paused just inside the front door of the Alexander. She'd looped Darcy's leash around her wrist so that she could hold Ava and Natalie's hands on the way back from the park. Now, in the shadow of the enormous potted palm that anchored the space between the entrance and the concierge desk, she peered out from behind the tree trunk to determine if the coast was clear just as she'd done each day since the Barbie and Ken pregnancy bombshell had been dropped. She breathed a little easier when she noted that it was James at the desk. Unlike Isabella, with whom they'd have to stop and chat while the actress practiced her British accent, James only smiled at Brooke and the girls and tipped two fingers to his forehead in a friendly salute as they passed.

Like a Secret Service agent on the alert for danger, Brooke did a continuous scan of the lobby as they moved. A couple sat near the fountain. An elderly gentleman she didn't know read a newspaper in a distant club chair. Relieved to see no sign of Zachary or Sarah, she proceeded at a quick but steady pace. Careful not to give the impression of scurrying, Brooke stayed close to the potted palms that lined the lobby much as small animals in a forest might keep close to potential camouflage just in case a larger predator, and his pregnant girlfriend, appeared.

They were only two potted palms away from the elevators when footsteps came up behind them. Brooke kept walking, the girls' hands tight in hers, but just as they passed the next to last palm of potential refuge Darcy stopped suddenly. Her tail began to wag.

"No, Darcy," Brooke hissed. The carpeted hallway that led to the elevators beckoned just ahead. The old man looked up from his newspaper. She tugged lightly on the leash, but Darcy had gone stiff-legged and didn't budge.

"Wait!" Zachary's voice and the sound of two sets of footsteps came up behind them.

Brooke froze. She would have paid large sums of money for an invisibility cloak. Even more for the ability to time travel; a solid fifteen minutes from now would work.

"It's me!" Zach shouted as if this would be an inducement to turn around rather than race for the elevator with her hands over her ears.

The old man was watching her with interest as if he suspected she might make a break for it and didn't want to miss it if she did. But the girls had already dropped her hands, shouted, "Daddy!" and whirled around. Darcy gave a euphoric woof. Her tail went into overdrive. In her frantic effort to reach Zachary, she wrapped the leash around Brooke's legs.

Trapped, Brooke teetered precariously. Desperate to remain upright, she dropped the leash temporarily so that it could unravel. Somehow she managed to turn without wiping out. Having to face Ken and Barbie was bad enough. She could not do it from the marble floor.

Zach was dressed in gray slacks and an open-necked dress shirt. He accepted the whimpering adoration of his daughters and his former dog as his due. Sarah was perfectly groomed as always in a pair of simple black slacks and a tunic top. Aside from the pooch of a stomach she remained lithe and trim, unlike Brooke who had simply swelled to two or three times her normal size with each of her pregnancies. Even four or five months pregnant Sarah Grant was glowingly beautiful and knew it.

Zach's expression made it clear he saw nothing remotely awkward about this encounter. Like Jennifer Aniston had said of Brad Pitt, the man seemed to be missing a sensitivity chip. Sarah knew exactly how uncomfortable it was for Brooke and delighted in it.

"I wanted to talk to you about Thanksgiving," Zach said. "I need to take the girls a few days earlier than I'd planned."

Sarah slipped her hand into his. Zach gave it a gentle squeeze.

Brooke looked away from their hands and tightened her own on Darcy's leash. "Why?"

"Because I'm taking the girls up to Boston to have Thanksgiving with my parents."

Sarah squeezed his hand back. Her eyes remained on Brooke.

"I want them to meet Sarah." He raised Sarah's hand to his lips. The diamond ring that glittered on her finger was so bright that if Brooke hadn't looked away she might have been blinded. Once Sarah was certain Brooke had seen the trophy that proclaimed her the winner she turned her eyes up to Zach's. He looked down at her with what could only be love shining in his eyes. Brooke couldn't remember the last time he'd looked at her that way. Or if he ever had.

Zach looked down at his watch, not letting go of Sarah's hand. "We're ordering pizza tonight, munchkins," he said to the girls as if he might actually be looking forward to it. Instead of sniffing in disapproval as he had when Brooke had opted to order in or pick up takeout instead of cooking. "I'll be down to pick you up in twenty minutes."

Bile rose in Brooke's throat. She'd begun to believe Zachary no longer had the capacity to hurt her, but she'd been wrong.

She swallowed. A hand fluttered up to clutch her throat in an attempt to hold back her gorge as Zachary and Sarah rounded the corner that led to the elevators. Struggling for control, Brooke looked up in panic and saw Claire Walker headed toward them with purposeful strides. Claire quickly unwrapped Darcy's leash, handed it to Natalie and escorted Brooke over to the nearby potted palm. There she blocked Brooke from view as Brooke bent and emptied the contents of her stomach into the hard-packed dirt.

"Oh, God," Brooke moaned. "Please tell me I didn't just throw up on a poor defenseless palm tree."

"Don't worry. I'm sure it's biodegradable," Claire said.

"Do you think we need to let James know so someone can clean it up?" Brooke cut a look toward the old man and was relieved to see the club chair empty. She flushed with embarrassment and hoped he'd left before she heaved all over communal property.

"Don't worry about it," Claire said. "I'll walk you all upstairs. Then I can escort the girls up to their father's so he doesn't have to come down to get them."

Brooke closed her eyes on the tears that threatened; a wave of gratitude washed through her. She took Darcy's leash back and brought the dog to heel.

"Come on, chicks," Claire said brightly to Natalie and Ava. "Let's take your mommy upstairs and get her some ginger ale for her tummy. Then I can walk you up to your dad." She turned them all around and got them headed for the elevators. "Do you know what sound a baby chick makes?" she asked gaily.

"Cheep! cheep!" Natalie and Ava tucked their fists into their armpits to make wings then flapped their elbows up and down. "They go cheep, cheep!"

By the time they got to the apartment Brooke's stomach had settled though the embarrassment remained. The girls' overnight bags were already out and Claire waited while Natalie and Ava raced around their rooms stuffing them with their pajamas and clothes for school tomorrow.

"Are you okay, Mommy?" Natalie asked as Brooke kissed each of the girls good-bye.

"I am, sweetie," she said in her most reassuring tone. "I'm going to have some ginger ale right now and I'll be good as new when I pick you up from school tomorrow."

"I'll expect you up at my place in fifteen minutes," Claire whispered in Brooke's ear as she leaned in to hug her good-bye. "I'll call Samantha to see if she's around. We can order something in ourselves. If you have a bottle of anything, bring it."

"Oh, no, I don't think that's a good idea," Brooke said, wanting nothing more than to forget the whole humiliating encounter had taken place.

"You're not going to sit here rerunning that little scene in your head," Claire said.

"I can't believe I threw up in the lobby!"

"Stop worrying about the potted palm," Claire said. "It was looking a little droopy. I'm pretty sure it needed fertilizing."

Brooke's laugh was shaky.

"Come on, chickadees," Claire said gaily as she led the girls out the door. "Let me hear those cheeps." In the doorway she turned and looked at Brooke then motioned upstairs with her thumb. "If I don't see you in fifteen minutes, I'm coming back down for you. If you come under your own steam, you'll save me the extra trip."

BY THE TIME SAMANTHA REACHED CLAIRE'S APARTment, Claire and Brooke were settled on the sofa, an open bottle of wine on the cocktail table between them. Three wineglasses stood ready.

Samantha had offered to have them up at her place, where she'd done little but pace and think and think and pace, but she was actually glad to be in Claire's studio apartment. The small space was warm and cozy. Maybe this was why people downsized—to create a space too small to leave room for doubts? "Are you okay?" she asked Brooke as she settled on the chair opposite the couch.

"Yes," Brooke replied. "I guess I just wasn't ready for the sight of Sarah's stomach. Or the diamond ring on her finger." She shook her head, still struggling with the reality.

"Sometimes no amount of forewarning prepares you for the really awful things," Samantha said. "No matter how carefully you tiptoe or how gingerly you tread. Sometimes shit just happens."

Brooke looked up with damp eyes. Her nod was weary. "Zachary never looked at me like he looks at her. That's what made me sick."

"Do you think he looks at her that way because she's pregnant?" Samantha was embarrassed by the wistful note in her voice. How long had she told herself things would have been different/clearer/better if only she'd been able to have a baby?

Brooke shook her head. "*Especially* not when I was pregnant. For one thing I looked like the Goodyear blimp both times. For another he always blamed me for getting pregnant when he was in the middle of his residency and we couldn't afford it."

"As if you got that way all by yourself," Claire huffed. "What an asshole!" She winced. "Oops. Sorry. Should I have asked permission to call him that?" She filled Brooke's wineglass.

Brooke snorted. "Thanks for asking. But I'm guessing his assholiness is pretty obvious to almost everyone?" She looked between them.

Samantha wasn't entirely certain what Brooke wanted to hear.

"Sorry," Brooke said quickly. "I didn't mean to put you on the spot like that." She raised her glass. "To his royal assholiness!" She forced a jovial tone, but tears had begun to squeeze out of the corners of her eyes. They slipped down her cheeks. "It's just that . . . I can't bear that he never looked at me that way. And now I know for sure he never will." Brooke sniffed and finished her glass in one long gulp. "I mean, I knew that when he left me. And I knew it even more when he divorced me. But I don't know." She swiped at her cheeks and eyes with the back of one hand. "I guess there was just some part of me that refused to believe I was that unlovable."

Claire slid an arm around Brooke's shoulders. "You are not unlovable. And you've already got Bruce Dalton wanting to take you out. Which is more than I can say after sixteen years of being single."

"Bruce Dalton is looking for someone to mother his daughter. I happen to be Private Butler's mother in residence, that's all."

"You're underrating yourself," Samantha said. "Just because Zachary, I mean, His Assholiness, didn't understand your value, that doesn't mean you're not worth a great deal."

"That's right," Claire said pouring them each another drink. "You're great. And you throw up more neatly than anyone I've ever met."

The tension in Brooke's shoulders loosened. Samantha laughed as Claire filled her in.

"Seriously, it's a talent," Claire said. "When you live in a space this size you appreciate someone who can be economical with their movements."

There was more laughter, but Brooke didn't join in. "It's easy for both of you to joke. You're the one who chose to end her marriage," Brooke said to Claire. She turned to Samantha, her brown eyes still filled with hurt and pain. "And you've been married to Mr. Gorgeous and Wonderful practically forever. And he apparently still worships the ground you walk on."

The observation hung in the air between them. Instinct, and years of practice, told Samantha to simply acknowledge her good fortune, knock on wood so as not to jinx that good fortune, and then turn the subject. No one felt sorry for poor little rich girls.

Except that she'd now spent close to two weeks without anything more than the most basic of communication from her husband—impersonal texts like *Heading for Phoenix. If you need anything, call Margaret at the office.* And finally, yesterday, *En route to Chicago for meetings with Andrew Martin. Not sure how long.* She'd been forcing herself to keep her regular appointments, attend her regular committee meetings, and act as if all were well. But alone in the condo she'd done little but pace and worry, neither of which had warded off the fear that her marriage was as over as Claire's and Brooke's.

She thought about her mother-in-law's warning. What if her insecurity drove Jonathan into the arms of a Sarah, who would know that Jonathan loved her and chose her and who might have no trouble at all getting pregnant? This thought made her sick to her stomach and in possible need of a potted palm of her own.

"Well, that just goes to prove that how things look and how things are can be entirely different." Samantha hadn't fully realized she intended to speak until the words were out. But she was so tired of carrying the toxic mix of guilt, doubt, and fear everywhere with her. There wasn't a part of her life that wasn't colored by it.

"My husband married me out of pity," she said. "He was only twenty-seven and although our families had known each other forever, we'd never even been on a date when he proposed. Oh, and this was just after my father had embezzled a fortune from his family law firm before he and my mother died. But he married me anyway and helped me raise my brother and sister."

They stared at her, saying nothing. Their mouths gaped open in surprise.

"And he's stayed married to me all these years because that's the kind of man he is."

The phone buzzed from downstairs undoubtedly to announce the arrival of their pizza. Nobody moved.

Now she was the one with tears oozing out of her eyes and scalding their way down her cheeks as she laid it all out for them. How she'd been rescued by the prince and lived with him in a succession of castles. And how the prince had recently galloped off with barely a backward glance.

Brooke looked as if she might cry again as she listened to Samantha's story. Claire's expression was harder to read. "What?" Samantha asked finally as the relief at sharing her fears ran smack up against the fear that she'd made herself vulnerable by sharing too much. "Why are you looking at me that way?"

"I don't know," Claire said. "I mean, I'm sorry that you and Jonathan are going through this. I know Brooke and I are here for you."

Brooke nodded and reached out a hand to squeeze Samantha's.

"I hope everything gets resolved soon. My writing career, such as it is, has been all about happily-ever-afters and I'd love to see you and Jonathan have one."

"But?" Samantha asked Claire, needing to hear the rest.

Claire smiled somewhat sheepishly. "But I guess in a completely selfish and extremely weird way it's a little bit reassuring to know that even fairy-tale princesses have problems just like the rest of us."

BY THE TIME THEY'D EATEN AND DRUNK THEIR FILL it was one thirty a.m. Nothing had been solved but whether it was due to her confession, the way it had been received, or the amount of wine she'd consumed, Samantha felt considerably lighter when she and Brooke left Claire's apartment. The two of them stood in the eighth-floor hallway in front of the elevators, giggling about how they'd each have one whole elevator to themselves. As if this were some decadent use of space that they were about to get away with.

Samantha poked her head out the elevator doors. "If we press the door close buttons at exactly the same time we can see which elevator is faster."

"I doan thin so," Brooke said sounding oddly like Ricky Ricardo. "Doan you live on a different floor from me?"

"Oh, yeah." Samantha swayed a little. Which was really weird since the elevator door was still open and she was fairly certain they couldn't go anywhere that way. "Is your elevator moving?"

"Only a little," Brooke said. "But it's mostly"—there was a loud hiccup and a giggle from the other elevator—"just the button."

Samantha stepped inside her elevator and mashed her finger onto the button with the outward pointing triangles although she wasn't sure why. She swayed slightly listening for Brooke in the silence. "Are you still there?"

"Yeah." There was another loud hiccup. "I'm thinkin' 'bout callin' Zach and tellin' him I doan 'ppreshiate the way he doesn't look at me. An that we think he's a ash hole." A brief silence then, "What do you think?"

"No," Samantha said. She closed her eyes but it didn't stop the swaying. "It's not a good idea to drunk dial your ex-husband. I read an article about it in *Cosmo*." She hiccupped. "At the beauty salon."

"Shure?" Brooke asked.

"Think so."

"Okay." Brooke's elevator doors closed and the elevator took off.

Samantha swayed for a few long moments. Then some instinct must have penetrated her mental fog, because her finger zeroed in on and pushed the top number. She made it to her apartment and even managed to insert the key in the lock and push the heavy door open. But the idea of husband calling had taken hold. The warning bells that might have stopped her had been muted. Or at least wrapped up in cotton wool. Without any internal debate at all—or at least none that she would remember later—Samantha pressed Jonathan's number on her phone then stood swaying in the foyer while it rang. Never once did she try to recall whether the article that had advised against calling your ex had said anything about drunk dialing a man you were still married to.

CHAPTER TWENTY-NINE

CLAIRE STOOD ON HER BALCONY AND LEANED over the railing so that she could stare down at Peachtree. It was the beginning of November and the temperatures and humidity levels had obligingly dropped along with the last of the leaves. Although Thanksgiving was still almost three weeks away, holiday decorations had begun to go up. Claire knew this for a fact because she'd spent a lot of the last week writing in her journal and watching this happen from this very spot. And from her favorite bench in the park as well as from "her" table at the corner Starbucks.

Her laptop, which remained closed on her dining room table/desk and had begun to collect dust, had not joined her in any of these places. She rarely opened it because she was afraid to see her agent's response to her intentionally vague and misleadingly confident promises to send chapters when she had them and could no longer handle Karen and Susie's cheerful enthusiasm and motivational quotes. These she suspected would soon turn into threats of much-needed butt kicking, which both of them lived too far away to make good on.

The highlight of each week had become the Sunday-night screenings, twice-weekly power walks with Brooke, and Wednesday night dinners with Brooke and Samantha. Her only other human contact occurred during the ringing up of a purchase or the placing of an order.

Claire's cell phone rang. When she saw Hailey's number she answered happily hoping that her vocal cords would remember what they were designed to do.

"Hi, Mom."

Claire cradled the phone against her ear and shoulder, which was no easy task given how small her phone had become. In just a few weeks she'd have Hailey back for ten whole days. "Hi, sweetie," she said, pleased to hear how normal her voice sounded. Apparently talking, unlike dating, *was* like riding a bicycle and did not require regular practice. "What's up?"

"Oh, nothing special," Hailey said. "But, well, there's something I wanted to talk to you about."

Claire's heart cartwheeled in her chest at the discrepancy between Hailey's tone and her words. Could she be ill? Injured? Pregnant? Claire's brain clicked through every conceivable worst-case scenario in no particular order—all of them chilling and life altering in their own way. "What's wrong, Hailey? What's happened?" The words came out in a rush, thick with worry and coated in fear. "Are you all right?"

"I'm fine, Mom," Hailey said. "It's just. It's just that I don't know quite how to say this."

Oh, God, she *was* pregnant. Or had an STD. Or maybe she'd been so preoccupied with her boyfriend that she'd lost her library job. Or failed a course. No, Claire quickly rejected this last one. Hailey had been a driven 4.0-plus student since her first day of preschool.

"You're killing me here, Hail. Just tell me straight out. Because I'm a writer, remember." Or at least she had been when she could make herself face her computer. "I've already imagined at least eight fates worse than death—and I didn't even know there were that many." She paused, trying to calm herself. She'd often panicked in the years of single motherhood, but she'd usually done a far better job of hiding it. Children didn't confide in parents who freaked out too easily. "You didn't accidentally switch identities with an international terrorist or anything did you?" There, that was better. "Or join the CIA's office of clandestine affairs without telling me? They've been advertising on the radio pretty heavily down here."

"God, Mom. It's kind of scary in that brain of yours. In an odd, funny, twisted sort of way."

"Tell me about it," Claire said. An imagination came with positives and negatives attached. Like when you were in an airplane at twenty thousand feet and a spot of turbulence became the beginning of a death spiral. Or a dorsal fin off in the distance when you were swimming in the ocean cued the opening music for *Jaws* in your head. "But you can't tease me like this. We've always been a rip-the-Band-Aid-off kind of family. Not a wussy easing-it-off kind. Just tell me what it is right now. And I promise I'll try not to stroke out."

Hailey laughed. "I have a feeling my news is going to sound really tame compared to everything that brain of yours has come up with."

Claire sincerely hoped so, but she would be the judge of that. She kept her mouth shut and waited.

"The thing is . . ." Hailey hesitated again. "I'm . . . I'm wondering if you'd be okay if I didn't come home for Thanksgiving."

There was silence as Claire tried to process this.

"It's just that Will asked me if I could go home with him. And, well, I don't like the idea of leaving you alone on a holiday." Hailey swallowed; Claire could actually hear the sound. "But . . . I'd really like to go, Mom."

Claire's heart stuttered. Between its earlier cartwheeling

and pounding over her worst-case imaginings, it didn't seem to have a whole lot of beat left in it.

Since Claire's parents had become infirm and then died ten years ago it had just been the two of them. Thanksgiving had been a cobbled-together affair—cooking a turkey, inviting other "strays" to join them. Then Hailey would leave to be at her father's while Claire confronted how alone in the world she was. The next morning they'd get up at dark-thirty to hit the day-after-Thanksgiving sales.

Hailey was all she had. And this year she wouldn't even have her.

But as exhausted as it might be, her heart knew that it didn't really matter what Claire thought or how she felt. Despite Hailey's attempt to tamp down her excitement in order not to hurt Claire, it was clear just how much Hailey wanted to go home with her boyfriend.

"Of course you'll go," Claire finally said. "I can't think of a single reason why you shouldn't."

"I don't know, Mom," Hailey said. "We've never spent a Thanksgiving apart."

"I know. But we've never lived in different places before, either, and that seems to be going okay." She noticed that she'd been pacing the tiny balcony and forced herself to stop. "It's all part of it, Hailey. I want you to go. And I'll expect to hear a full report."

"But what will you do?" her daughter asked.

"I'll have turkey and then I'll have the whole day and holiday weekend to work." Claire clamped down on panicked images of the starkness of a holiday weekend completely alone with a computer she couldn't even bring herself to open. "You know, now that I think about it Brooke will be on her own too—her kids are going to be in Boston. I'll bet she'd be glad to share a turkey or go out for a holiday meal or something." She cast about for anything else that might reassure Hailey. "Plus I've told Edward Parker I can be available to do some occasional jobs if he needs someone. I'm working a party next Saturday that Samantha's brother has planned." She stood and leaned against the railing. "Seriously, Hailey. Don't worry about me. Go with Will and have a great time. I'll miss you, but I'll be perfectly fine."

"Are you sure?"

"Positive."

"I'll pay for the cancellation fee, Mom," Hailey promised. "I think for a hundred dollars I can just change the ticket to fly home at the end of the semester."

"Sounds good, Hail. Honestly." Claire smiled at the excitement now evident in her daughter's voice. "And I'm really glad you didn't join the CIA without discussing it with me first."

"You've got such a warped sense of humor." Hailey laughed. "Maybe you should be writing comedy instead of historical romance."

Claire's laughter joined Hailey's. "I'm not sure there's a huge audience for my brand of neurosis."

"I don't know," Hailey said. "Woody Allen's had a pretty solid career."

That was true. "Maybe I can find a way to do both. What do you think of neurotic Highlanders in kilts?" Claire teased. If she could find a way to work in some former Navy SEALs transported back to seventeenth-century Scotland, she'd be golden.

"Sounds good, Mom. Way better than naked neurotic Highlanders without them."

"I'll talk to you later, sweetie," Claire said. "And when my Twisted Kilt series hits the *New York Times* bestseller list, I'll be sure to let everyone know that you were the one who came up with the idea."

SAMANTHA AND THE OTHERS WATCHED IN SILENCE that Sunday night as Downton Abbey was turned into a convalescence home and Thomas, who still plotted with

O'Brien, was put in charge. Captain Matthew Crawley and William, the footman, were still missing in action, prompting Mrs. Crawley to head for France to find her son. Ethel, the fired housemaid, showed up pregnant. No one moved for several long moments after the episode ended.

"Gosh, that was intense," Brooke said finally. "I'm exhausted just from watching it."

"I know what you mean," Samantha said, though the truth was she was exhausted from worrying about what she might have said to Jonathan while she was drunk and from pretending that she wasn't scared to death that life as she'd known it was over forever.

At that Wednesday's lunch, which Cynthia had refused to let her wiggle out of, Samantha discovered that Jonathan was still in Chicago and would then go on to Boston.

"Thank goodness he'll be back for Thanksgiving! But I do think he should have flown in the night before rather than the morning of," Cynthia had said while watching Samantha's face for a reaction. "Don't you?"

"It's wonderful that he'll be able to get back," Samantha had said doing her best to hide her hurt and surprise. But the whole time Cynthia nattered on about which pies Doris would make and which silver Zora would be asked to polish, Samantha had fumed. Had he been planning to text her this information from the plane? Or had he thought he'd just show up at Bellewood as if he hadn't abandoned her for a whole month? And when had he decided to make Cynthia his messenger?

With the exception of their one drunken conversation, Samantha hadn't heard her husband's voice for a full four weeks. And she was fairly certain that the only reason he'd answered that night was because he'd assumed that no one—including his wife—would call at two a.m. for anything less than an emergency.

Once again she flushed with embarrassment as she remembered the change in Jonathan's voice when he'd realized she wasn't in an ambulance on the way to a hospital. No matter how hard she'd tried to recall their conversation, her only remaining memory was of the blinding headache and vague sense of wrongdoing she'd woken with the next morning.

"Are you up for a brandy and a strawberry tart?" Claire asked as they left their sofa for "afters."

"Sure," Samantha said, though she wasn't certain whether she'd be able to swallow either. Her appetite had pretty much disappeared; even favorite dishes from Atlanta's finest restaurants seemed unable to revive it.

They were lingering in their usual spot just outside the clubroom near the elevators when Edward Parker came out to join them. "Are both of you ready for next Saturday?" he asked Claire and Brooke.

"Aye, aye, captain." Claire saluted.

"I seem to be the only person in Atlanta who's not going to attend or work Alicia Culp's birthday party," Samantha said.

"I'm going to be checking guests in when they arrive and Claire's going to be assisting Hunter with the family, but I think we still need a coat-check person," Brooke said with a smile.

"The planning has been very impressive," Edward said. "Hunter's brought the whole Culp family in as if they're just here for the party. But after she's given the weeklong private Mediterranean cruise as her gift, she'll find out that the whole family is going. They'll leave for the airport in a procession of limousines just before the party ends."

"Goodness," Samantha said. She'd grown up with money and married more, but even she couldn't imagine spending so much on a single birthday. Leave it to her little brother to spare no expense with someone else's money.

"Hunter said that with the economic disaster in Greece, everyone is hurting and yachts and captains can be had for a song," Brooke said.

Samantha felt a small frisson of pride; not something she was used to feeling with either of her siblings. It seemed that tough love had been the right thing after all. Perhaps if she'd cut him off sooner . . . no, there was no point in going there. She'd been carrying around far too much regret already.

"I must say when he puts his mind to it, Hunter is a veritable force of nature," Edward Parker said.

"I'm so glad to hear it," Samantha said, relieved. Like a hurricane, her brother could be unpredictable and destructive.

"He's different than I thought," Claire said. "He explained the whole European Union crisis and the devaluation of the euro to us. He knows a lot about investments and corporate structure. And the importance of diversification," she added.

"When did you discuss all this?" Edward asked. Which was what Samantha was wondering.

"We had that meeting last week at the aquarium, where the party's being held, to go over the logistics and timing," Brooke said. "This event has a lot of moving parts."

"I'll say," Claire agreed.

Samantha tried to absorb the fact that Claire and Brooke now saw her brother in a far better light than they had on that Sunday night outside the clubroom. But then Hunter had always been able to make a good impression when he wanted to. She wondered if he had really changed under Edward's tutelage. Or had simply figured out how to camouflage his spots.

"When is Mr. Davis due back?" Edward asked.

Samantha flushed. "He's flying in Thanksgiving morning."

"Oh, that's good," Brooke said. "Do you cook the Thanksgiving dinner?"

Edward Parker, who'd sent runners for replacement dinners on numerous occasions, remained mercifully silent. The man really was the soul of discretion.

"Um, no," Samantha replied. "Thanksgiving is always at Bellewood." She'd learned early in her marriage that there was little point in suggesting otherwise.

"What's Bellewood?" Brooke asked.

"My mother-in-law's home in Buckhead. It's where Jonathan grew up," Samantha explained.

"Ooh-la-la," Claire joked. "It has a name and everything. It must be fancy."

"Oh, it is," Samantha said a little more forcefully than she should have. "And their cook, Doris, does a wonderful traditional southern Thanksgiving spread." She still couldn't believe her first time seeing Jonathan would take place with Cynthia's eyes pinned on them, dissecting their every word to each other—assuming there were any.

"Do you celebrate Thanksgiving, Edward?" she asked, eager to banish the image.

"Well, it's not a holiday I grew up with, but I have been to some lovely Thanksgiving meals. Only one or two since I came to Atlanta. And my hosts were transplants, so the meals weren't particularly southern."

"What are you doing for the holiday?" Samantha asked Brooke and Claire, realizing she hadn't heard either of them mention it.

"Oh, you know," Claire said. "Eat a little turkey. Watch *Miracle on 34th Street* and *White Christmas* on cable."

"When will Hailey be home for the Thanksgiving break?" Edward asked.

"She won't," Claire said. "She's going home to Pittsburgh with her boyfriend."

"You mean you'll be on your own?" Samantha asked, ashamed that she'd never even thought to ask. She'd been so consumed with her absent husband and forcing herself out of bed every morning that she'd barely thought about the women who'd so unexpectedly become her friends.

Claire and Brooke exchanged looks. "Not exactly. You know Zach is taking the girls up to Boston, so we're going to do Thanksgiving together."

Samantha had an image of Brooke and Claire sitting in Claire's tiny apartment, eating frozen turkey dinners and watching ancient movies on television; what should have seemed pitiful seemed more attractive than the elaborate meal in the sterile environs of Bellewood.

With a warm good night, Edward boarded an elevator. Claire gave them each a hug and headed down the hall to her apartment.

Brooke and Samantha waited for an elevator. When two arrived Brooke shot her a wink. "Shall we race?"

Samantha smiled back. But she was far too sober and preoccupied to sway or giggle about it.

As she entered the too-silent penthouse, Samantha vowed to call Cynthia and see if there would be room at the Thanksgiving table for Brooke, Claire, and Edward. It would be nice to have some sort of buffer to help smooth over what was bound to be an awkward "reunion" with Jonathan. Assuming it was a reunion at all and she hadn't said or agreed to anything on the phone that night that she'd have cause to regret.

ALICIA CULP'S SIXTIETH BIRTHDAY PARTY WAS HELD in the Georgia Aquarium's Ocean Ballroom. Beneath a blue-lit wavelike ceiling and surrounded by mood lighting, the one hundred and fifty family members and guests must have felt as if they were deep beneath the ocean's surface. The occupants of the two massive aquarium tanks that pierced two of the ballroom's walls swam and swirled in the water watching the guests almost as eagerly as the guests watched them.

Brooke greeted each guest and made sure they had their table assignments while Claire spent much of the night following in Hunter's wake, receiving and communicating last-minute changes and instructions.

After drinks, passed hors d'oeuvres, and a sumptuous Mediterranean-themed dinner, the crowd watched a television-worthy video of Alicia Culp's life to date. This was followed by ribald toasts and poignant testimonials from the people who were closest to her. But the pièce de résistance was the small fleet of limousines that pulled up at midnight to whisk Alicia and her family to the Learjet that would fly them to Greece for their weeklong private cruise.

Edward watched Alicia Culp's face as Hunter Jackson assured her that this was no joke, that her family was coming with her, and that her suitcases were already packed. By any standard the party and the cruise that was about to follow were a resounding success.

"Thank you so much. I can't get over how spectacular an evening it's been," a tear-streaked but smiling Alicia Culp said to Edward as her husband handed her into the lead limo.

"That boy of yours certainly knows how to deliver the goods," Jim Culp said. "And he knows how to sell a concept. I'm thrilled to be in on the ground floor of a company as impressive as Private Butler. And I wouldn't be a bit surprised if most of our guests feel the same."

"Thank you." Edward watched Hunter Jackson as he orchestrated the group farewell with lots of personal smiles and politician-worthy handshakes to some of Atlanta's wealthiest and most influential citizens. Despite the amount of work he'd done, he still looked—and acted—far more like one of Alicia and James Culp's guests than one of the employees. "He does have a decided flair," Edward said.

"And he knows how to spend money," Culp said. "Lots of it. Had to talk me into some of the expenditures. But every one of them was worth it." Culp slid into the backseat next to his wife. With impeccable timing Jackson stepped up, leaned into the backseat to offer the couple a personal farewell. The moment he closed their door the limousine driver and the string of perfectly matched Lincolns drove off.

"Well, you certainly made an impression on James and Alicia Culp," Edward said to Hunter as the last taillight disappeared from view.

"Is there something that didn't satisfy you?" Jackson's question seemed both idly curious and slightly taunting.

Edward chastised himself for being stingy with his praise. Jackson had done an impeccable job. He simply had no interest in mastering the demeanor of a concierge whose only true goal was the customer's satisfaction.

"To the contrary," Edward said. "I apologize if I've seemed at all unappreciative of what you've accomplished. I'm hugely impressed. You've managed to exceed both my and the client's expectations."

Jackson smiled what might have been the first real smile Edward had ever seen cross his face. Edward was struck with how many potent personal weapons Mother Nature had put in Hunter Jackson's arsenal. But he couldn't completely shake the feeling that Jackson might not have the restraint required to avoid a total nuclear meltdown.

Chapter Thirty

LIKE A FOOTBALL PLAYER PREPARING FOR A BIG bowl game, Samantha spent the days before Thanksgiving "suiting up" for her first encounter with Jonathan in thirty days.

The fact that this encounter would play out in front of Cynthia, Hunter, Meredith and the unexpected New York boyfriend, as well as Claire, Brooke, and Edward both comforted and terrified her.

She'd been threaded, waxed, shaped, plucked, manicured, pedicured, Botoxed, massaged, colored, and cut. All she needed now was a coach to give her a pep talk and tell her which "play" had the best chance of success though she was no longer certain whether a clear victory was even possible.

She was so nervous the night before that she barely slept and awoke at six a.m. on Thanksgiving to once again debate her clothing options. The red Kamali suit would say "confident but attractive" while the Stella McCartney dress whispered "soft and sexy." She liked the navy-and-white St. John knit but was afraid it would make her look like his mother.

She alternated closet dithering with apartment pacing and coffee drinking until she was a jangling, caffeinated mess. No matter how many times she told herself, "This is Jonathan, you'll know what to say when you see him," she felt like an unprepared rookie about to go into a title-clinching game.

What if her mind went blank? What if she'd studied the wrong playbook? Deep down she was afraid that she'd already lost the most important contest of her life without even knowing she'd entered it. Jonathan had told her that attempting to be the "perfect wife" wasn't enough, but she still didn't know what was.

With trembling fingers she showered, put on makeup, and blow-dried her hair. After retrying all three outfits, she finally decided on a ruched black matte jersey dress. Its square neck and three-quarter sleeves made it casually stylish, and she was counting on its wide leather belt to keep it from hanging like a sack and disguise the shrinking of her curves.

She spent the drive to Bellewood in her own pregame pep talk so that by the time she got there all she wanted to do was tackle Jonathan, pin him to the ground, and demand to know what it was he wanted to hear. Only Jonathan hadn't arrived yet. Nor had he seen fit to text her his arrival time. She'd slit her own wrists before she asked Cynthia what time he was expected.

At the drinks cart in the living room she found Hunter, Meredith, and Meredith's friend from New York. "I've missed you two," she said, hugging her brother and sister. "How've you been?"

"Good," Meredith said as she reached toward the stranger. "Samantha, this is Kyle Bromley." A small smile played on her lips; her usual air of dissatisfaction was noticeably absent. "Kyle, my sister Samantha Davis."

"Hello, Mrs. Davis." Bromley put a hand out to shake hers. "It was so nice of you and your mother-in-law to extend the invitation for Thanksgiving. I didn't know until the last minute whether I'd be able to get down to visit Merry."

Hunter coughed into his palm. Samantha started at the nickname she hadn't heard, let alone thought, since Meredith had hit puberty. "It's a pleasure to meet you. How long will you be in town?"

She smiled and nodded in what she hoped were the right places as he answered, but her attention was focused on listening for any hint of Jonathan's arrival. "And you, Hunter, I heard how fabulous the Culp birthday was. Congratulations."

"Thanks." He smiled and shrugged as if it were no big deal.

"I can't wait to hear more about the party. Edward Parker and my friends Claire and Brooke should be here soon."

Hunter's face registered surprise and something else she didn't take the time to try to analyze. Clearly her siblings were doing far better without her intervention and supervision. She felt a tiny loosening of the band around her chest. But she couldn't stop listening for the sound of a car. Or worrying about why Jonathan had chosen not to fly in until this morning.

Samantha wandered into the kitchen, which was redolent with warm and wonderful smells. "There you are!" Doris wiped her brow with a handkerchief and enveloped Samantha in a big puffy hug. "I'm gonna make sure you get extra today; you look like you've started wasting away."

"You know I'll never be able to pass up your oyster stuffing," Samantha said.

"No, ma'am, you better not. I'm gonna have to give Mr. Jonathan a piece of my mind for letting you get this skinny."

"I've always heard a woman can never be too thin," Samantha said, running a nervous finger under the belt at her waist.

"Humpf." Doris went back to basting her turkey as Samantha greeted Zora, who was dressed in a crisp white uniform.

Reluctantly she went in search of her mother-in-law and found her in the foyer examining herself in the large gilt mirror. "Hello, Cynthia," she said, offering a dutiful hug and accepting air kisses to both cheeks.

"Hello, Samantha. Jonathan's due any minute," she said happily. "He texted just after he landed."

Samantha tried not to blanch at the fact that his mother had flight information while she'd been left in the dark.

Cynthia looked Samantha directly in the eye. "I'm glad he's finally come home," she said. "I wouldn't want to see anything or anyone drive him away again."

They stared at each other. Samantha refused to be the first to look away. "Then we have the same goal."

Cynthia's lips thinned, but for once Samantha didn't care. She'd come here determined to straighten things out with Jonathan; she could not allow Cynthia to deter or distract her.

"So maybe we should try playing on the same team for a change," Samantha said, apparently unable to let go of the football metaphor. "Because frankly I think that if you stopped rooting for our marriage to fall apart, all of us—including your son—would be a lot better off."

One of Cynthia's eyebrows shot upward. "You have no idea how painful it is for a mother to see her child's unhappiness and be powerless to stop it." The comment was more observation than put-down.

"No." Samantha had no idea whether the fierce protectiveness she'd always felt for Meredith and Hunter differed from what she might have felt for a child of her own. She would never know. She'd been without her own mother for so long that she'd become little more than a comforting memory. "Jonathan's lucky to have a mother who cares so much about him. But whatever's wrong between Jonathan and me is up to us to work out. If we can."

The doorbell rang. Samantha's heart hammered in her chest until she reminded herself that no matter how long Jonathan had been gone he would not be ringing the doorbell of the home he'd grown up in. Samantha spotted Edward, Brooke, and Claire through the sidelights and stepped out of the way so that Cynthia could open the door.

"Welcome." Despite the conversation that had been interrupted, Cynthia did a fair impression of a hostess glad to see her guests. Samantha hugged all three of them, even the proper concierge, and introduced them to her mother-in-law.

"Thank you so much for the invitation," Edward said with a slight bow that only he could pull off. He handed Cynthia a gift bag from the three of them, which she placed on the foyer table. "It's lovely to be included and I so look forward to experiencing a traditional southern Thanksgiving." He gave her a dazzling smile. "I can't tell you how much I've appreciated your referrals to Private Butler."

Cynthia smiled and laced her hands through the concierge's bent elbow and escorted him into the living room her head tilted at a coquettish angle.

"Did you see that?" Samantha asked.

"The man has some serious skills," Claire said.

"I'll say," Brooke agreed.

The two of them stared at her. "What?" she asked. She knew she didn't have anything between her teeth because she'd been unable to even swallow toast that morning.

"Are you all right?" Claire asked.

"Of course," Samantha said brightly.

Claire and Brooke looked at her.

"Or I will be as soon as I have a chance to talk to Jonathan. You don't have any tranquilizers with you do you?"

They laughed, though Samantha wasn't sure she'd been joking. If ever a person could use rapid tranquilization, it was she.

That laughter died as footsteps sounded on the marble floor.

"Ladies." Jonathan's voice directly behind her made her stiffen. Her breathing grew shallow and rapid. Though she'd been waiting impatiently for this moment, now that it was here she didn't feel remotely ready. "Samantha."

"We'll just go join the others," Claire said. She and Brooke greeted Jonathan and disappeared.

"Jonathan." Her voice wasn't the only thing that shook as she turned and searched his face for some sign of how to proceed. She clasped her hands together to keep them from fluttering about, but wasn't as successful controlling her inner southern belle, which surfaced without warning. "I swear, you've been gone so long I almost forgot what you looked like," she said with a ridiculously saucy lilt. She barely managed to close her mouth before a "fiddle-dee-dee" escaped.

Jonathan continued to study her and once again she found herself worrying about what she might have said to him during their drunken phone call. A vee of concern formed between his eyebrows. "Mother assured me that you were fine. But you've lost weight. And you don't look good. Have you been sick?" He sounded surprised.

Had he really imagined a month without him would have no impact? The fear and panic twisted inside her and began to grow into something strong and unfamiliar. He'd made it clear he didn't want her gratitude. At the moment that was fine with her. Because she was beginning to realize just how ungrateful she was that he'd left her without any real explanation and then refused to speak to her for an entire month.

"I've been on a diet. And Michael stepped up my workout program," she lied. He of course looked practically bursting with good health. His sleeves were rolled up to reveal lightly tanned forearms. His blond hair was sun streaked and a fresh smattering of freckles spanned the bridge of his nose. Whatever he'd been doing for the last month it didn't include pining away over her. "What have you been up to?" She held his blue eyes with her own trying to read his thoughts, still looking for a clue, but he gave nothing away.

"Oh, just business. And the occasional golf game." He shrugged. "I spent time in Chicago going over expansion plans with Andrew Martin. And then I took care of some things for him in Boston. He and his wife both asked about you."

He was so calm, so casual. Clearly he hadn't spent this morning with sweating palms and a racing heart. Had she really considered throwing herself into his arms and begging him to just give her another chance? Had she actually imagined it could be that simple?

She pulled herself up and raised her chin. The emotions bubbling inside her separated like an unbound braid and she recognized the steeliest of them as anger. She'd spent four weeks agonizing over how she might fix whatever was wrong between them. But had he really left to let her figure it out? Or had he left to punish her?

"Oh? And what did you tell the Martins?" she asked. "That you'd decided to take a break from your marriage? That you'd told me you weren't happy and left me sitting alone trying to figure out what I'd done wrong like some child given a time-out by her parents?"

The dinner bell rang. Voices in the living room signaled a move toward the dining room.

"Did you tell them that instead of returning any of my messages you hid behind texts and relied on your mother *who barely tolerates me* for information about my well-being?" She saw his eyes widen in surprise at her tone and how close she'd come to shouting.

Her chest rose and fell as she tried to regain control. She'd never lost her temper or even raised her voice to him, not once in twenty-five years. But then he'd never abandoned her before. Or refused to communicate. Short circuits of emotion spiked through her.

There were tentative footsteps and the clearing of a throat. "Miz Davis asked me to let you know that supper is being served."

"Thank you, Zora," Jonathan said. He crooked his elbow. "If you're finished, I expect we should go in?" he said to Samantha in the same polite tone he might have used to inquire if she'd like an iced tea or suggested the pecan rather than the praline pie. She might have turned and left if it weren't for her guests.

They entered the dining room together, but she'd never felt so alone.

* * *

EDWARD AND THE OTHERS HAD JUST TAKEN THEIR
seats when Jonathan Davis escorted his wife into the dining
room, seated her between Edward and Kyle Bromley, then
took his place at the head of the table. His mother, who sat at
the opposite end, offered a carefully worded prayer of thanks,
welcomed them all, and urged everyone to begin. "Zora will
serve the turkey and ham," Cynthia said. "But please help
yourself to the dishes you see on the table. We're treating this
as a family dinner. I hope you won't mind the informality."

Davis maintained a pleasant smile as a tall black woman
in a white starched uniform carried in a gigantic oval platter.
Dishes and serving platters covered the diamond-cut table-
cloth. Baskets of warm corn bread and dinner rolls as well as
an assortment of gravy boats anchored each corner while pats
of butter imprinted with the letter "D" sat on each bread plate.

"You'll want to try both the corn bread and the oyster
stuffings," Samantha told him. "And the sweet potato souf-
flé as well as the green bean casserole. And I guess I should
warn you that the ham has a Coca-Cola glaze. This is Atlanta
after all. And we do love our Coke products." She smiled but
her eyes were guarded. "In fact Asa Candler was a close
personal friend of Jonathan's grandfather."

"Interesting," Edward said as a basket of still-warm corn
bread and biscuits reached him. He felt Hunter's eyes on him
and wondered if the boy was uncomfortable having his
employer there.

Samantha nodded to the basket. "Doris's corn bread and
biscuits are completely worth the calories. And you'll want
to leave at least a little room for the desserts." Samantha kept
up a running commentary on the food and its origins, turning occasionally to make sure Meredith's young man was
included, but Edward noticed she put little on her plate and
ate even less. Her cheeks remained flushed and though she
interacted with Claire and Brooke, who sat on either side of

her husband, she never actually addressed or looked directly at him. Davis looked at his wife often but only when her attention seemed placed elsewhere.

Meredith laughed and Samantha smiled. "It's nice to see Meredith happy."

Edward nodded and looked more closely at the middle Jackson sibling, whom he'd always considered of average looks. Without her usual expression of pursed-lip disappointment the resemblance to her sister and brother was more apparent.

"Kyle's the first person beside Jonathan who's ever thought to call her Merry." Samantha's eyes flickered to her husband then skittered back to her plate.

"My grandfather used to say that 'every pot has its lid,'" Edward replied.

"I like that," she said wistfully. "It's so hopeful." She reached for her glass of wine, her look pensive. "But what happens when the fit isn't as tight as it's supposed to be?"

"That I don't know," Edward said. "I thought I'd found the right lid once. But it turned out that I was mistaken."

"I can hardly believe someone who cooks as badly as I do is discussing pots as a metaphor for love," Samantha said as laughter erupted on the other side of the table.

"But you've never stopped trying to cook," Edward pointed out reflecting on the number of times in the six months since he'd arrived at the Alexander that he'd arranged to have food picked up after a failed attempt. "I think that says something about you."

"Oh, I'm sure it does," she replied. "But I'm a little afraid to find out what."

There was more laughter. More looks aimed their way.

"What's so funny?" Samantha finally asked.

"Your sister was just telling us a story about the year you cooked the Thanksgiving turkey," Claire said.

Samantha groaned. Her face flushed with what could only be embarrassment.

"It was the year we were married." Jonathan looked straight at Samantha for the first time since he'd seated her. "We were coming to Bellewood, but she wanted to contribute something meaningful to the meal."

"Yes, we were microwaving bits and pieces of that poor bird until almost midnight." Cynthia's tone was droll.

"I didn't find out until after Thanksgiving, when I went in to complain, that a turkey can be labeled 'fresh' if it hasn't been frozen more than once. I thought that fresh meant unfrozen so I didn't even attempt to defrost it," Samantha explained. She rolled her eyes at their laughter. "That's the thing about cooking. The directions often seem unfairly unclear." Her voice trailed off. Edward followed her gaze and saw Jonathan regarding her with an odd smile on his lips.

"We were afraid none of us would survive when Sam first started trying to cook," Hunter said.

"Why?" Brooke asked. "What did she make?"

"It didn't matter," Meredith said.

"Why not?" Claire asked.

"Because it all looked like hockey pucks in sauce."

Even Samantha joined in the laughter this time.

"Fortunately, Jonathan was there to save us from starvation," Meredith said.

"How did he do that?" Edward asked, trying to envision Jonathan and Samantha without the elegant patina of their current life surrounding them.

"Wait a minute," Jonathan said to Hunter and Meredith. "We made a pact. I believe there was even a vow of secrecy."

"Right," Samantha said. "Like I never saw those McDonald's bags in the trash outside. Or smelled the French fries on all of you when you'd come back from those ridiculous after-dinner errands."

The conversation moved on, the mood lighter as the table was cleared and the desserts and coffee served. Edward wondered at the furtive looks Samantha and her husband stole at each other. And the careful looks Hunter, who'd begun to regale the table with stories about his first assignments for Private Butler, began to aim at Edward.

"Here, you have to try this chocolate pecan pie and Doris's praline pumpkin pie with maple rum sauce." Samantha put a piece of each on a plate and placed it in front of Edward, then prepared similar plates for Brooke, Claire, and Kyle Bromley.

"You should have seen me driving Mimi Davenport to Nashville in her ancient pink Cadillac. Which she refuses to allow to be driven over forty-five miles per hour." Hunter shook his head with amusement. "'Young man,'" he drawled with a slight quiver to his voice in a dead-on imitation of the elderly woman. "'There is no need for undue speed. I would like to survive this trip and return home in one piece.'" He laughed. "And when we stopped for lunch at this broken-down roadside diner outside Chattanooga she put the silverware in her purse."

Edward's lips tightened. One didn't share a client's behavior with others and certainly not for laughs. "I believe that's privileged information," Edward said tightly.

"Did you hear that, Jonathan?" Hunter called down the table. "Apparently what a concierge sees is as privileged as information that passes between client and attorney. What do you think of that?"

"I think that if your boss tells you that, you need to listen," Jonathan replied evenly.

Brooke and Claire shifted uncomfortably in their chairs. Meredith's forehead wrinkled in consternation. Her boyfriend looked over his shoulder as if scoping out potential escape routes.

"You did such a fabulous job on Alicia Culp's party," Samantha said to her brother even as she laid a hand on Edward's arm. "You have a genius for organization that we never realized. But I can understand how important discretion is in this type of service business." Her tone grew more adamant, as if she might still convince him of the merits of good behavior. "You can't just pick and choose which parts of your employer's instructions you want to pay attention to."

"Maybe, maybe not," Hunter said. "I'll tell you what I have learned from the estimable Mr. Parker." He fixed his green-eyed stare on Edward once more. "I have learned that I can take almost any crap job and make it into lemonade." His smile conveyed no humor. "But it would take a lot more than I've been paid and a sight more respect for my abilities to feel the need to keep my lips sealed."

Cynthia frowned. "Hunter," she admonished. "It's Thanksgiving. And there are guests."

"I'm sorry," Hunter said without an ounce of sincerity. "I didn't mean to spoil dessert."

An uncomfortable silence fell. Edward could feel Samantha's distress and Cynthia's disapproval on either side of him. Jonathan Davis's eyes were pinned on his brother-in-law as if he'd seen this before and wasn't looking forward to what was coming.

"What I'm best at is seeing the potential in a business," Hunter went on as if someone had asked. "Even when its creator doesn't get it. And I am truly gifted at explaining that potential to investors."

"Yes," Claire said, breaking the uncomfortable silence that had settled around the table. "That's why I invested in Private Butler when Hunter explained the opportunity."

"Me, too," Brooke said. "He showed me how to take the equity in my condo and put it to work. Even Isabella and James put money in after Hunter told us he'd signed Mr. Fitson and Mrs. Davenport and James Culp. Everybody wants to put money behind you, Edward."

Edward felt a brief moment of confusion. It evaporated as Hunter Jackson's lips curved up in a derisive smile. At the end of the table Jonathan Davis's eyes closed briefly.

"Well, that money isn't actually going into Private Butler," Hunter said, staring directly at Edward. "Because Edward made it clear he didn't want investors. Or expansion. Or, to put it bluntly, progress of any kind."

"I don't understand then," Samantha asked on a quick intake of breath.

Edward thought back to James Culp's comment at his wife's party and understood all too well.

"The money, almost half a million dollars of it, is going into a private concierge company that I've fashioned after Private Butler," Hunter said. "A company that I'm going to build and then franchise." Hunter's green eyes grew even more brittle. "I wish you would have agreed to succeed, Edward," he said. "I could have raised this money for you and helped you grow your business."

No one moved or spoke, least of all Edward, as the horror of what had taken place—what Hunter Jackson had done—sank in.

"It was amazing how many of your satisfied clients and employees begged to give me their money when I explained how much could be made building a company like Private Butler. Almost as amazing as how few of them read the fine print on their investment documents." He shook his head and shrugged as if it was all beyond his control. "I'm not sure if they fully understood that we're parting ways. They could hardly hand over their money fast enough."

Edward heard Brooke and Claire's gasps as they were forced to confront the truth. He felt pretty short of breath himself.

"Well." Hunter stood, dropped his napkin on the table, and bowed slightly to Edward—a perfect and mocking imitation. "I guess we can consider this my resignation. I appreciate the training and the concept." He bowed to Brooke and Claire, who were still processing the fact that they'd invested in Hunter and not in Private Butler. "I appreciate your confidence in me and will be sure to keep you posted."

With a final nod and thanks to Cynthia, Hunter swept out of the dining room. They were still sitting in shocked silence when the front door slammed shut behind him.

CHAPTER THIRTY-ONE

MINUTES AFTER HUNTER'S EXIT, THANKSGIVING at Bellewood came to an end.

"I'm so sorry," Samantha said repeatedly as she walked Edward, Brooke, and Claire out to their car. "I had no idea. I . . . I'm so sorry!"

They looked at her numbly. Equally numb, she stood on the brick drive and watched them drive away. When she came back inside Zora and Doris were clearing the table. Cynthia had retired to her room with a headache. Only Jonathan remained.

"I can't believe this," Samantha said. "Edward barely looked at me. Claire and Brooke didn't say a word."

"Everyone's in shock right now," Jonathan said. "I'm sure this can be sorted out."

"But how?" She was practically wringing her hands. "I told Hunter we wouldn't bail him out anymore. But reimbursing the investors wouldn't be bailing him out, would it? It would be protecting them from him."

"It's not your place to fix this," Jonathan said. "Hunter's

an adult. And so are the people who gave him money. You're not responsible for his every move."

"But you know he misled them. Oh, God, I asked Edward to take him on." The words rushed out in a torrent of guilt. "I put him in Brooke and Claire's path. That makes me responsible. But I don't know what to do."

"Normally, I'd say we could simply buy out anyone who thought they were investing in Private Butler and doesn't want to leave their money with Hunter," Jonathan said. "But . . ." He hesitated. "We don't actually have the cash to do that right now."

She looked up at him so quickly she was lucky she didn't give herself whiplash. These were words she'd never heard cross his lips. "What? What did you say?"

He hesitated again but finally spoke. "A lot of our and the firm's money is tied up in real estate. Real estate values here are still in the toilet. A lot of people, including a lot of our clients, have been wiped out." He offered it as a simple statement of fact, but she saw the tick in his cheek. The tension in his body.

"But you never said anything." She could hear the shock in her voice. And what sounded a lot like fear. "Why didn't you tell me?"

"I didn't want to worry you. After what happened with your parents . . . well, I've always known how important financial security is to you." He didn't add that he knew that was why she'd married him, but then he didn't have to. "It's not that we don't have money," he said. "It's just that we aren't liquid at the moment."

The comment and the burst of remembered panic that followed it brought her up sharp. What was she doing? Before the meal she'd been hurt and furious at how he'd thrown her gratitude in her face and then left her to stew like some badly behaved child. Now, at the first hint of trouble she'd turned to him just like that child. Just like she always did.

She forced herself to meet his eyes. He was watching her carefully, his blue eyes intent, looking for something from her that he once again refused to name. She dropped her eyes under his regard, trying to still the panic. She was no longer the twenty-one-year-old girl who'd found herself suddenly parentless, saddled with her parents' debt and responsible for her brother and sister, but those same feelings coursed through her. When she raised her eyes again his were shuttered.

Was it something she'd said? Or something she hadn't?

She'd arrived at Bellewood praying for some sort of resolution between them but things had only grown more complicated. Her mind swam with uncertainty, robbing her of the ability to think. How could she right things with Jonathan when he wouldn't even tell her what was wrong? How could she think about her marriage while she was frantically trying to grapple with how to save her friends from her brother?

"I need to go home." She held her breath wondering—hoping—if he would ask her to wait while he went to get his things.

"I guess I'll stay here," he said, his tone making it clear that she had, in fact, failed some sort of test. "I'll be tied up in meetings for most of the next couple of weeks, coming and going at odd hours. If I stay in the guest wing I won't bother anybody." He said this as if it were a logical reason to stay at Bellewood rather than in their home with her.

She wanted to argue but her heart was too heavy, her panic too real. Weak-kneed, she retrieved her purse, went into the kitchen to thank Doris and Zora, then returned to where he stood at the door. "Please give your mother my thanks for the meal and for inviting my . . . friends." She would not utter the word "former" though she was afraid that's what they were.

With her marriage in tatters and lacking the funds to make things up to Edward and the others, she drove home, pulled on her most comfortable pajamas, and crawled into bed. Where she spent a sleepless night trying to understand how she'd lost her husband, tallying the number of people Hunter had wounded, and shivering from guilt for introducing her brother, the financial terrorist, into an unsuspecting crowd.

SAMANTHA GAVE HERSELF THE HOLIDAY WEEKEND to wallow. But on Monday when Michael buzzed to be let up for their morning workout she couldn't seem to stop. Feigning illness, she lay there for most of the week ignoring the phone and the doorbell until she was no longer pretending but felt sick in every sense of the word. Sick with disappointment in her brother and in herself for doing such a pitifully poor job of raising him. Sick with remorse for letting him loose on people she'd come to think of as friends. Sick with fear and regret that her husband was finally in town and yet she felt farther from him than when they'd been on opposite ends of the country.

When the phone and doorbell finally stopped ringing, Samantha lay on her bed in the silent apartment staring at the ceiling, the wall, the carpet. Even getting to the kitchen felt like wading through quicksand.

On the rare occasions when she got hungry she ordered pizza or Italian food delivered.

With no outside stimuli her brain consumed itself with questions it could not answer. How could she force Hunter to fix the mess he'd made? How might she make things up to Claire, Brooke, and Edward? And what in the world was she supposed to do about Jonathan?

Her brain shut down completely on this last question, unsure whether her marriage was repairable and unable to even imagine trying until she'd fixed the damage that Hunter had done.

On Sunday evening the front door opened and footsteps sounded in the foyer. Jonathan came into the bedroom. He settled his large frame on the chaise. She could see the firm-jawed resolve on his face. His eyes were flat and dark as if someone had drained both color and emotion out of them. "It's been ten days, Samantha. You can't just lie there indefinitely."

She stared at him mutely. Waiting to see if he might try to snap his fingers and command her to feel better. And if so, whether it might work.

"I just came to pick up another suit. I have to fly up to Boston for a few days."

She looked more closely at him, trying to tell if this was more than it sounded.

"I'll be back on Thursday." He answered her unspoken question. "Don't you think you should at least go to the screening tonight?"

She might have laughed but for the energy required. She could just imagine the looks on Edward, Brooke, and Claire's faces if she showed hers in the clubroom. And what about Mimi Davenport? She winced at the memory of Hunter's nasty imitation of the older woman. Which hadn't prevented him from taking her money. Isabella would be unlikely to waste a syllable of her accent on the sister of the man who'd conned her out of what little she'd had. She simply couldn't face them until she at least had a plan for getting them their money back.

"I spoke to Edward," Jonathan said. "I've offered to look at the contracts Hunter's investors signed. But I'm not hopeful. One of the few details Hunter paid attention to over the years is the importance of tying up loopholes."

He considered her and she had a horrible vision of what she must look like. Not that her excessive grooming efforts before Thanksgiving had made one whit of difference.

"If we could get Hunter and Edward to talk, there might be room for some sort of compromise." His voice was that of an attorney laying out a possible scenario. His face was composed. His eyes were . . . she wasn't sure since she was having such a hard time meeting them.

"It's not up to you to swoop in and fix this," Samantha said. Her voice sounded rusty with disuse. "I'm the one who has to make this right."

"It's kind of hard to do that from bed." It was a simple statement of fact. "If you do manage to get up, maybe you can locate the woman I married."

But wasn't that the problem? Hadn't he said he didn't want that woman or her gratitude?

She turned her head to the wall and squeezed her eyes shut. This was not the time to respond to that question or to dissect their marriage. She couldn't even let herself think about it until she figured out how to make things right. If only she knew how.

They didn't speak again while he pulled the suit from the closet and filled a small suitcase. She lay there in silence as he walked out of the room and let himself out.

EDWARD STOOD AT THE CLUBROOM DOOR JUST after ten p.m. that Sunday night saying good night to the last of that week's *Downton Abbey* audience.

"Are we all set then, sir?" Isabella's accent had become so flawless that Edward sometimes had to remind himself that her last name was Morales and that she'd never left the continental United States. "Yes, Isabella. Thank you. You and James may clean up and go."

"I can't hardly believe there's only one more program of the second season left," she replied as she deposited the plastic glassware in the trash can.

"I know," Edward said. "Plus a Christmas show."

"Will there be a holiday party around it like you said, sir?" she asked.

"I don't know," he replied, watching James shrug out of the livery jacket. Edward's holiday spirit was sorely lacking. He simply couldn't come to terms with how completely everything tied to Private Butler, including Edward's own reputation, had been tarnished by Jackson's machinations. Nor could Edward believe how completely he'd underestimated the younger man's destructive streak.

As if movement might help him dodge his thoughts, he moved about the clubroom, picking up bits of garbage and checking that no personal possessions had been left behind. Edward had called all of his customers to apologize and to explain what had happened. Those who'd invested with Jackson—and he'd been horrified to discover how many of them there were—were shocked and angry. Even Mrs. Davenport had shaken an arthritic finger at him after last week's screening and asked him what he intended to do about it.

Legally, it appeared, the answer was "nothing." Which was, of course, completely unsatisfactory.

Out in the hallway he found Claire Walker and Brooke Mackenzie talking near the elevator. It seemed almost strange to see them without Samantha Davis, whom he'd seen no sign of since Thanksgiving.

"Ladies." He nodded and smiled, though he suspected his was no more convincing than theirs. He bit back yet another apology.

"We were wondering, Edward, whether there was any way that our money could end up invested in Private Butler like we wanted it to be," Claire Walker said.

He met both women's eyes and then wished that he hadn't. It was bad enough that wealthy people like Jim Culp and Mr. Fitson had been conned; even Mrs. Davenport would not be bankrupted by the loss. But these two women and Isabella and James . . . He couldn't believe Hunter Jackson had gone after such tiny fish.

"I really don't see how," he said. He no longer knew whether Jackson would have ever turned investor money over to fund Private Butler's growth under Edward's direction. Or if it had been a scam from the beginning. "I have consulted with Jonathan Davis, but it doesn't look encouraging."

"But what if . . ." Claire began.

"I'm truly sorry," he said, meaning it. "As far as I know, Jackson intends to use that money to build a competing concierge business." He still couldn't believe the man thought he could compete after six weeks in the business. But then there was a lot about Hunter Jackson he didn't understand. "Maybe his sister has some idea of his plans," he said. "Perhaps you should speak to Samantha about it."

Claire snorted.

"We would," Brooke said. "If she'd return any of our calls."

"Yeah," Claire added. "I guess the whole friendship thing was a joint figment of our imaginations."

Edward reached out to push the elevator call button. "I never had that sense," he said. "I've always liked Samantha; I think there's quite a lot of warmth beneath the polish." The elevator arrived and he prepared to step on. "But then I've good reason to question my powers of perception. My ability to size up people and their intentions has certainly fallen far short of the mark."

Claire resettled her purse strap on her shoulder. "It seems pretty clear that our investments aren't going to double and triple like Hunter promised. I just hope the money won't be completely lost."

The reminder of Jackson's potshot promises was one more fist to the gut. The whole thing was a bloody nightmare. He stepped onto the elevator and held down the "door open" button. "I'll do whatever I can to work you both into the schedule," he said. "But I'm not at all sure how many hours I'll have to offer." He didn't yet know how many clients he'd ultimately lose over the whole investment scam. Or how badly Jackson's company, if in fact he actually formed one, would impact Private Butler's bottom line.

Late that night or more accurately, early the next morning, when he was still unable to sleep, Edward dialed England and caught his great-uncle Mason over morning tea.

"Aren't you the early bird?" his great-uncle asked.

Edward caught a glimpse of himself in a nearby mirror,

unshaved face, bleary eyes and all. "I look a bit more like the boogeyman at the moment. Or Frankenstein's monster come to life."

"Still broodin' on the whole financial fiasco, are you?" Mason asked.

"I think brooding might be an understatement. I'm so angry I can hardly see straight. And I keep thinking there must be something I can do."

Edward heard the sound of a spoon against china and the creak of a chair. He could picture his great-uncle in the cozy cottage kitchen that opened onto his tiny garden. Julia Bardmoor surfaced briefly in this vision and he allowed himself to wonder why he'd turned being a concierge into the goddamned Holy Grail. Just like *Downton Abbey*'s Carson and even Mrs. Hughes, he'd given everything up in the service of others. How could he let all those sacrifices be for naught?

"You know, lad," Mason said breaking into Edward's thoughts. "I've been thinking. The boy's methods are reprehensible. Completely beyond the pale. But perhaps it's time to open your mind as I've been urging. Allowing others to invest in Private Butler—especially satisfied clients—might not be so far off the mark."

Edward pondered this as he stared out his bedroom window into an inky patch of night sky. He wasn't sure why he'd been so adamant about refusing money to grow his business, but it was becoming clear that if he stuck to the course he'd charted, he could end up with far less than he'd hoped for and on a path only wide enough for one.

But no matter what he'd once thought, he couldn't simply stand by and allow his clients to be hurt because he couldn't set aside his pride.

IN THE END IT WAS CYNTHIA DAVIS WHO FORCED Samantha out of the apartment. She did so with an unexpected and well-placed kick to the butt.

Samantha was standing in the kitchen eating cold spaghetti and meatballs out of a plastic foam container for breakfast and replaying Claire and Brooke's final agonizing messages for what might have been the fifth time, when she heard a key turn in the lock.

She froze. Stopped chewing. Looked down. She was wearing her oldest, most stretched-out pajamas and a mismatched pair of Jonathan's wool hunting socks. Her hair had been pulled up into a scrunchie two or three days ago. Which was the last time she'd washed—or even looked at—her face. She considered and rejected several escape plans. It was Thursday, the day Jonathan had said he'd be back from Boston. But it was only ten a.m. Her heart skidded in her chest. What if he'd come back early to have things out? Or to tell her he was leaving for good? She wasn't anywhere close to ready for that conversation. But if it were going to happen, she couldn't let it happen while she looked like this.

Turning, she hunched forward and began to tiptoe through the kitchen toward the family room. From there she might be able to make it to one of the back bedrooms or bathrooms without being seen.

"There you are." The voice caught her mid-tiptoe. It wasn't the voice she'd been expecting. "Trying to scurry back into your little mouse hole I see."

Samantha straightened and turned. She held the container of spaghetti and meatballs in one hand, and a sauce-smeared fork in the other as she faced her mother-in-law.

Cynthia held the key that Jonathan had given her years ago in case of emergency. "I've never used it," she said, dangling the key from its gold fob. "But I think this"—she looked Samantha up and down—"qualifies as an emergency, don't you?"

When Samantha didn't answer Cynthia dropped the key and her purse on the counter. She stepped right up to Samantha and removed the fork and the container from Samantha's hands, then laid them in the sink. "You look like hell." It was a simple statement of fact. "Sit down." She pointed to the kitchen table, then added, "There are a few things I want to say to you."

The pajamas somehow made resistance seem futile. Unsure what else to do, Samantha sat.

"As you know, I've never really understood why Jonathan insisted on marrying you," Cynthia said. "But then I was very angry with your parents at the time."

Samantha stilled. Her mother-in-law had not mentioned either of Samantha's parents except as an oath or as a warning from the day Jonathan had proposed to her.

"Your mother was . . . I considered her a close friend. We'd been in and out of each other's houses for years." A carefully penciled eyebrow went up. "But she never could control your father any more than you've been able to control your brother.

"When your father embezzled the firm's funds and almost destroyed it, and your mother stayed with him, our friendship ended. They . . . she . . . died in that accident before anyone could even attempt to make amends."

Samantha could not have moved if either of their lives depended on it.

"I could not understand why Jonathan chose to marry you. Why he would take on the burden of your family's debts, parenting Hunter and Meredith. I hated that he took on all of that baggage when he didn't have to."

She looked at her mother-in-law. Wondered if she knew that she was preaching to the choir.

"The thing is," Cynthia continued. "You don't always understand your children. You may love them more than anything, but understanding is not an automatic part of that love."

Samantha drew a deep breath and let it out. An irreverent "Amen, sister" flitted through her mind. She settled for a small nod, wondering where Cynthia was going with all this.

"You did your best with Hunter and Meredith. You were

far too young—both of you were—but you put everything else on hold to try to give them a stable environment. Sometimes, even without all the trauma and loss that was a part of your parents' legacy, even the most vigilant parenting produces mixed results. Sometimes children turn out poorly despite your sincere best efforts." Cynthia smiled wryly. "Sometimes—as in Jonathan's case—they exceed your expectations and turn out far better than you deserve." Cynthia paused before continuing. "Whatever his reasons, my son chose you and I should have honored that choice. For his sake."

This time Cynthia's smile was fleeting. Her tone turned brusque. "As much as I always thought he could do better, I dislike what I see happening now," she said. "I've watched him these last ten days and I no longer think ending this marriage would make Jonathan happy. Nor do I enjoy seeing you laid so low."

Speechless, Samantha continued to listen.

"You have a lot of your mother's best qualities. You have her warmth and her wit. And her loyalty. And frankly, though we have rarely seen eye to eye, I never took you for a coward."

"But now you do." Samantha looked down, knowing that that was exactly what she looked like. In fact, it was what she was.

"I think you need to get a life; something more than just trying to make everyone else happy. You already have a lot worth fighting for," Cynthia said, more earnestly than Samantha had ever heard her speak. "But I think that in order to mount an effective campaign you're going to have to shower. And while you're at it I'd burn those pajamas. I've seen your wardrobe. I suggest you put a few of those designers on your side."

CHAPTER THIRTY-TWO

THE SKY WAS CLEAR AND THE AIR CRISP EARLY the next morning when Samantha left the Alexander armored in Donna Karan and Stuart Weitzman. She walked the three short blocks to Hunter's building in the midst of early commuters and office workers, intent on catching her brother before he'd had a chance to don armor of his own.

In imitation of Cynthia's surprisingly effective surprise attack, she let herself into the lobby, went up unannounced, and let herself into Hunter's apartment. Her brother was still in bed and she stood in the bedroom doorway for several long moments watching him sleep. In repose, Hunter's face was slack and sweet, reminding her of the boy he'd once been before their parents' disgrace and deaths. He breathed gently, a small smile on his lips. If he'd been wrestling with the error of his ways or felt even a shred of guilt for taking money from people under false pretenses, she could see no sign of it.

Ripping the covers off him was incredibly satisfying. Watching him scramble out of bed stuttering with indignation was even more so.

"Shit! What's . . ." The stuttering stopped as his eyes flew open. "What the hell??"

"My question exactly!" She waited for him to pull a robe on over pajamas, which looked far more elegant than any she owned, and watched him slip his bare feet into a pair of cashmere-lined slippers identical to the insanely expensive ones he'd bought for Jonathan last Christmas.

She allowed him to use the bathroom in private but banged on the door and shouted for him to hurry up; not wanting to give him time to strategize.

His face was shaved and he smelled of toothpaste and aftershave when he joined her in the kitchen, but his eyes were speculative. "I'd offer to make you coffee, but I see you've already helped yourself."

She sipped her coffee, not answering while he made a cup for himself. She could almost hear his brain clicking through all the available data to determine whether an offense or defense would be more effective. She gestured him into a seat, but she remained standing, letting the Weitzmans give her an edge.

"I'll save you the trouble," she said. "You don't need to figure out how to handle me. I'm going to do the talking today. You're going to do the listening."

A look of surprise passed over his face. He glanced at the clock on the wall.

"I don't think it will take too long."

"Sam," he said. "There's no need to get worked up here." He took a sip of his coffee, sat back, crossed one leg over the other as if there was nothing unusual about being dragged out of bed by an angry sister. Then he threw in the wounded little boy look that had always been her personal kryptonite. Images of him as a child, at their parents' funeral, his high school and college graduations, which she and Jonathan had attended in lieu of their parents, bombarded her.

"On the contrary," she said, determined to resist the look and him, knowing she couldn't continue to let her love for him cloud her judgment. "I have every reason to get 'worked up.' You've hurt a lot of people I care about. And you've done it for no apparent reason."

She noted his surprise when "the look" failed. Watched him attempt to regroup. She walked over to the table in the high heels so that she could tower over him. "Bottom line," Samantha said. "You've gone too far this time. What you've done may be technically legal. But it's morally reprehensible and completely unacceptable."

They stared at each other.

"You're going to have to give the money back to every investor who thought they were investing in Edward." Which she assumed would be all of them.

He continued to look at her, as if waiting for her to tell him she was only joking. Finally, he said, "Sorry, sis. No can do. I've already spent a good bit of it on attorneys—after all these years of Jonathan handling things I didn't realize how expensive they are. And since I've been cut off I've needed a salary so that I can pay rent and living expenses. And of course a guy's got to eat. And entertaining clients can be really expensive."

"You had a salary at Private Butler," she pointed out grimly. "And an opportunity to be part of something real."

"That salary was an insult," Hunter said, his voice ringing with righteous indignation. "Edward Parker had no idea what I could have done for him. Hell of the thing is Private Butler has huge upside. Even while Parker was rubbing my nose in all the crap jobs, I knew I'd finally found something I could grow and make my mark with." His smile turned self-deprecating. "I'll admit I've made some bad choices along the way. But all I've ever wanted was a chance to prove myself."

He studied her closely, his green eyes pinned on her face. "But with all his talk about reputation and personal service, Parker couldn't even see the gold mine he was sitting on. There was way too much potential to walk away from."

Samantha studied him back. He always had an excuse. Always came up with a reason that made whatever he did okay. *Just like their father.* "That didn't give you the right to do what you did."

He shrugged not at all repentant. "It's done, Sam." He watched her, but she could tell from his tone that he assumed she'd already done her worst. Had she?

She'd stopped the money flow and forced him to take a job and what had she accomplished? Put him in a position that gave him access to other people's money, which he had for all intents and purposes stolen.

She'd made sure her father's debts were settled, her siblings had had an expensive roof over their heads and everything that money could buy. But she'd clearly failed to teach Hunter the most important lessons. Somehow she'd allowed him to believe that he could trample all over her and Jonathan and anyone else he chose, with impunity.

"You're going to have to give the money back. Or strike some kind of deal with Edward. I don't really care how you manage to do it. You're a smart guy. I'm convinced you can find a way to make this right."

"And if I don't?" His tone was taunting, but she heard the bravado beneath it. He got up to pour a fresh cup of coffee just to demonstrate how completely he'd dismissed her, but she waited him out.

"That's not an option," she said, not certain whether the only thing she had left to withdraw was something he would miss. "I expect you to take care of this, Hunter." She swallowed. "Or I will no longer consider you a member of my family. And I will make it my business to spread the word to any potential investor in Atlanta and the entire eastern seaboard that you're not to be trusted."

The flare of surprise in his eyes was quickly masked. She didn't linger but turned as sharply as the Weitzmans allowed and left him staring after her, unsure whether her butt-kicking abilities were anywhere close to Cynthia's. Whether she'd won this final battle. Whether in the end Hunter even cared whether he belonged to them or not.

CLAIRE SAT CURLED IN HER CLUB CHAIR. THE HEAT was turned up to fight the chill December evening and the apartment was warm and toasty. Her pen moved over the lined page of her journal, the tightly packed words illuminated in a spill of lamplight. She'd found that writing by hand soothed her. The fact that no one but her would ever see what she wrote freed up her thoughts and feelings. There was no room on these cramped pages for uncertainty, no blinking cursor demanding she write faster, no delete key that would allow her to give in to her doubts. No room for her internal editor, but plenty of room for everything good, bad, and ugly—that she'd observed and that had happened to her.

It was a relief to construct sentences even if those sentences revealed that she, who had squeezed every penny within an inch of its life for so long, had lost five thousand dollars—three months of rent—in one stupid move. She'd also lost a friend in the process; and those weren't the only losses.

Four months were gone and wouldn't be regained. And neither would the opportunity at Scarsdale. Just yesterday her agent had left a message informing Claire that due to her lack of response they'd slotted another author into November. Scarsdale would expect *Highland Fling* the following September as originally planned. But her tone made it clear that Claire's inability to meet the stepped-up deadline had hurt her. Her career was in tatters, her grand year of writing not grand at all.

Worst of all, in just a few weeks Hailey would be home for the winter break. And all of Claire's failures would be obvious. Her pen stilled and her gaze wandered over the space that had been so alien but had somehow become home. Much as she'd come to love it, this space was far too small to hide her lack of focus and page production. Even more than the lost time and money she dreaded Hailey finding out that her mother's dreams were not majestic mountains to be scaled but only great big piles of wishful thinking.

A knock sounded on the door and Claire set the journal aside to answer it.

"Ready?" Brooke stood on the threshold, her red hair wild around her face, an olive green sweater belted over a multi-hued skirt.

"Yeah," she said, trying to shrug off her ill humor. "That outfit looks great on you. Hold on a sec while I grab my key."

In the clubroom they received a friendly yet respectful nod and dark British ales from James. Isabella gave a half curtsy and offered sausage rolls and miniature cheese and onion tarts. "A lovely evenin' to ye both," the young woman said, but her perkiness seemed forced.

Claire and Brooke mingled near the food and drink tables while they watched Edward work the room as always, drawing everyone into the fold. "Do you get the impression he's lost a bit of his sparkle?"

"And a whole lot more," Claire observed.

Brooke kept an eye on the door.

"She's not coming, you know," Claire finally said, neither of them needing to clarify who "she" was.

"I just can't believe she's written us off."

Claire thought of how she'd dodged the calls from her agent. "We don't know that's what's happened. But I am surprised she's disappeared the way she has."

"I don't understand why she's avoiding *us*," Brooke said, the hurt evident in her voice. "I mean we're not the ones whose brother took money under false pretenses. What did we do to her?"

"I don't know." Claire shrugged. "Maybe we're a reminder of her brother's bad behavior. Or maybe no one ever told her that friends don't pull up stakes as soon as a little shit hits the fan. Sometimes it seems like rich people have a different set of rules."

"Well, I thought Samantha was different," Brooke said.

"Me, too," Claire said. "But then I've kind of lost count of the number of things I've been wrong about lately."

Edward called for their attention. He headed to the screen and DVD player. Everyone moved toward their seats. When they reached their sofa Brooke and Claire settled into the opposite ends and set their food and drink on the cocktail table. Claire saw Brooke look at the empty spot in the middle, but only because she'd been looking at it herself.

The lights went down and the theme music filled the room. More than ready for a time-out from her real life, Claire turned and fixed her attention on the screen.

SAMANTHA HESITATED IN THE HALLWAY OUTSIDE THE clubroom, not completely sure she had the nerve to enter. Her gaze skimmed over the sea of heads, none of which were moving, to the big-screen TV where Lady Cora lay sick in bed while an obviously guilt-ridden O'Brien tended her. Samantha knew exactly what that kind of guilt felt like.

Samantha's eyes moved to the sofa and she felt a small rush of relief when she saw that her spot between Brooke and Claire remained open. Her hand closed over the doorknob.

"Samantha." Edward Parker's voice was low but near. Startled, her hand fell to her side. "I wondered if you'd be back."

She turned to face the concierge. Who had every right to tell her just what he thought of her.

"Yes," she said. "I came to tell you how sorry I am that Hunter trampled all over you and your business. I should never have talked you into taking him on. I never imagined anything of this magnitude." Horrified by the way she was rattling on, the words she'd practiced in her head on the way down completely forgotten, she dropped her eyes, then forced herself to meet his again. "I just hope that one day you'll be able to forgive me."

"There's nothing to forgive in your actions," he said. "I'm glad you're here."

She stared at him. There were new grooves etched on either side of his mouth and a furrow carved across his forehead; no doubt a result of Hunter's recent assault. A woman would have felt compelled to hide or fill in those lines, but they only made Edward Parker more distinguished.

"I'm glad you're speaking to me," she said, still trying to understand why.

"Of course I'm speaking to you. I would have been speaking to you sooner if you hadn't disappeared," he said. His smile was both sincere and sad.

"Thank you. But I . . . I *am* sorry."

"Thank *you*," he said quite formally. "But Hunter's a grown man. And I believe we're all responsible for our own actions. Or for our lack of them." His lips twisted. "Sometimes what we don't do or choose can be even more telling."

Samantha felt a piece of the load she'd been carrying lift from her shoulders. A tiny piece perhaps, but still she felt lighter for it. She turned her attention back to the clubroom. "What do you think will happen if I go sit in my seat?" she asked, her eyes on the sofa. "Do you think they'll throw me out?" She was surprised at how much it mattered. Most of her adult life the women she'd met, served on committees with, even Sylvie and Lucy whom she'd seen regularly for decades, had been kept at arm's length. She was no longer sure what she'd been afraid of.

"Only one way to find out." Edward opened the door and held it wide for her to enter.

"I guess that makes it time to pull up my big-girl panties." Thanks to her mother-in-law's advice those panties were La Perla. She stepped inside. "Wish me luck. I'm counting on you to retrieve my body and prepare it for burial if things don't go the way I hope."

She walked toward the front of the room bent double so as not to block anyone's view. There were murmurs but she stayed focused on her final destination. Squeezing past Claire's legs, she sidestepped to the right, then sat in the middle.

For a few long moments, which she spent staring straight ahead and trying to regulate her breathing, nothing happened. Just when she'd decided they intended to ignore her completely Brooke and then Claire turned from the screen to look at her. She met each of their eyes even as she attempted to brace for whatever might come. She was still working on this when Brooke and Claire turned their attention back to the screen without uttering a word.

Samantha had no idea what this meant, but it did nothing to slow her breathing or the too-rapid beat of her heart. They hadn't exactly thrown their arms around her and welcomed her. But so far no one had tried to toss her out.

CHAPTER THIRTY-THREE

WHEN THE LIGHTS CAME BACK UP EVERYONE else streamed to the back for "afters," chattering away about the season's ending and the *Downton Abbey* holiday party that Edward Parker had announced. Claire, Brooke, and Samantha stayed where they were, watching each other warily, the air a shroud of discomfort around them. Still nobody spoke.

Samantha was ready to turn and flee when Edward arrived. He carried a tray that held an open bottle of brandy, three glasses, and a plate of assorted tarts.

He gave Samantha a steadying look as he set the tray on the coffee table, then pulled a high-backed chair over next to the sofa. Placing a gentle hand beneath Samantha's elbow he helped her up off the couch and into the chair.

"There," he said, as if that took care of everything. "Now you can look at each other while you talk."

They watched him pour the brandy and position the plate of tarts where they could all reach it. "Just so you know, none of you are leaving this room until you've talked. It's not really any of my business what you say." He didn't look happy about this. "But you need to get past this ridiculous, childish silence. I'm sure we all agree that Hunter has a lot to answer for, but as far as I'm concerned it has nothing to do with my relationship with Samantha." He looked meaningfully at the three of them then walked back to the rest of the group, many of whom were eyeing them surreptitiously.

Samantha clasped her hands in her lap to keep them still, but she felt like the accused on the witness stand waiting for cross-examination. The silence spooled out between them. "All right," she said finally. "I get it. If you're not going to speak to me, I guess I'll just get going."

"Were you planning to apologize first?" Claire asked.

Even though this was exactly what she'd come to do, the question hurt. Edward had told her she had nothing to apologize for. But then Edward had not shared the kinds of confidences these women had before her brother ripped them off.

She felt the pinprick of tears against her eyelids as she realized how much Claire and Brooke had come to mean to her and how much she would miss them. Their friendship, her marriage, everything she cared about had collapsed around her, and she had no idea how to put any of it back together. She looked both Claire and Brooke in the eye and began. "I am extremely sorry that Hunter took your money under false pretenses." She swallowed, her mouth dry and cottony as if all of her despair had settled there. "I hate that he abused Edward's trust and that he stole from you."

They watched her carefully but neither of them said a word.

"I've told him he has to pay back any investor who wants their money." She paused, waited for some sort of reaction, got nothing. "But, of course, I have no control over him. I don't know what made me think I ever did."

Still they didn't speak. At the back of the room the crowd

had thinned. Isabella and James had begun to pack up the food and drink. Edward stood near the door carefully not watching them.

Claire and Brooke exchanged a look.

Claire said, "That's not good enough."

"I agree," Brooke said. "That's really not going to cut it."

"Is that right?" Samantha swallowed back the lump of hurt that rose in her throat. She unclenched her hands, which were slick with sweat. She'd known an apology wouldn't solve everything but she'd never imagined they'd throw it back in her face. "And that's because . . ." she asked tersely, ready to get the hell out of there.

"Because we thought we were friends," Claire said.

"Yeah," Brooke added. "Good friends."

"We are. I mean, we were," Samantha said not following. "At least as far as I was concerned anyway."

"Well you have a weird way of showing it," Claire said. "Because friends don't blow each other off as soon as something goes wrong."

Samantha didn't understand where this conversation was going. Or what it was they wanted from her.

"Which means that when your friends ring your doorbell or call you on the phone—and especially when they do this repeatedly—you have to answer," Claire said.

"Yes," Brooke agreed. "I'm fairly certain that's a key requirement. I mean you don't hurl on a potted palm or cry on an elliptical machine in front of just everyone." Her lips twitched up at the corners.

"No," Samantha said as she drew her first easy breath. "You don't."

"And not everyone will tell your assholiness of an ex-husband off for you," Brooke added.

"No," Samantha said. "Everyone won't."

"Which is why when you find people who will do those things you don't shove them away when things get difficult," Claire said quietly. "Friendship can't be one-sided. You can't only give. You have to accept comfort and support when it's offered."

Brooke nodded. She placed one of the brandy glasses in Samantha's hand. "Are we freaked out about what Hunter did?" she asked. "You betcha. Are we royally pissed off at him and dying to see him punished? Absolutely." She poured brandy into Samantha's glass and then into her own and Claire's. "But it's not your fault. No matter what you think, your brother is a grown man and no one—but you—is holding you responsible for what he's done."

Tears threatened again, but this time they were tears of relief. Claire picked up her glass. No one bothered to make a toast. They simply raised them to their lips and drank.

"We're mad because you didn't even give us a chance to tell you that," Brooke said. "I'd still be wearing beige and scurrying through the lobby afraid of running into Barbie and Ken if it weren't for the two of you. I haven't lost it in a potted palm in weeks."

Samantha swiped at her eyes. This time Claire refilled their glasses. "I guess I'm just used to keeping my thoughts and concerns to myself," Samantha said. "I've never had friends that I could be completely myself with before—without any kind of pretense. I never even really let myself think about who I was or what I wanted to be." Her vision blurred with tears. "I became responsible for Hunter and Meredith when I was twenty-one and taking care of them was always my focus." She fingered the stem of her glass staring down into the burgundy liquid. "That and keeping Jonathan happy." She felt the prick of tears yet again and willed them away. "Because I guess I've always seen him as the key to that."

"All you have to do to keep Jonathan happy is walk in the room," Brooke said. "I've seen the way he looks at you."

"No," Samantha said, wishing it were true. "You're wrong. He stepped in and saved us when we were desperate and he's stayed because that's the kind of stand-up person he is." She lifted her glass, swirled the brandy. "I thought we'd carved out a comfortable life together. But he's never pretended to anything more than that." She raised the glass to her lips, not waiting for anyone else.

"That's ridiculous," Claire said dismissively. "I've written two romance novels and I'd give a lot to be able to capture the way you look at each other when you think no one's looking."

"I wish you were right. But . . . he's moved out. He's been at Bellewood since Thanksgiving."

"Well, I don't believe he's written off twenty-five years of marriage just like that." Brooke snapped her fingers.

"He's got this white-knight complex," Samantha argued. "I don't know where he got it from—definitely not his parents—but he's a caretaker. It's really not about me."

Edward appeared with another half a bottle of brandy and the leftover tarts. "Much better. I'm glad to see you three regaining your senses." He placed a key on the table. "Stay as long as you like. Just lock up when you leave."

They murmured their good nights and watched him go.

"So what's supposed to happen now with Jonathan?" Claire asked when they had the room to themselves.

"I don't know." Samantha lifted her glass and took a sip, wanting to add to the warmth she'd begun to feel inside. Hoping it would eliminate the chill she felt even thinking about Jonathan's absence and what it really meant. "I've been so overwhelmed with what Hunter did that I've barely been able to think. I'm afraid it's too late."

"Well, if he's staying at his mother's house and hasn't taken an apartment or a condo or anything, that's a sign that he hasn't really moved on," Brooke said. "At least he didn't move into another unit in the building with his girlfriend." She took a drink of her brandy and reached for a lemon tart.

"He must be waiting for something," Claire said. She lasered a look at Samantha. "What is it he's waiting for?"

"I wish I knew."

"He must have given you some kind of clue," Claire prodded.

Samantha hesitated, ran a finger around the rim of her glass. "He said he's tired of me feeling like I have to please him all the time."

"That would make him the anti-Zachary," Brooke observed. "But then I guess we already knew that."

"He said he wants to know what I think and feel," Samantha went on. "He wants to know what he is to me."

"Don't you love him?" Brooke asked quietly. "Is that the problem?"

"No. I . . ." The denial sprang to her lips almost as quickly as it sprang into her mind. She'd been denying it for so long. Out of fear that her feelings were unreciprocated. Out of worry that she might rock the precarious boat that she'd been sailing. Out of a certainty that fairy tales were peopled not only with princes and glass slippers but big, bad wolves and houses made of straw.

"I really . . ." She thought back to their wedding and how strongly he'd said his vows when she could barely stammer hers. His sense of adventure. His generosity and warmth. How he made sex feel like making love even though . . . She tried to halt the thoughts, afraid of where they were going. He almost never said the words, but somehow made her feel treasured.

The memory of Jonathan pulling on his tuxedo on his thirtieth birthday to escort a thirteen-year-old Meredith to her first father-daughter dance at the club smote her. She was such a fool.

"I do," Samantha said. "I do love him." She quaked inside as the words left her lips. A tear slid down her cheek and she didn't bother to wipe it away. She'd been in denial for so long.

"Then there is no problem," Claire said. "Just tell him. I bet he'll be back home in a New York minute."

"It's not that simple," Samantha said, though she wished it were.

"Why not?" Claire asked.

"Because I don't know how he feels. How can I tell him I love him when there's every chance he doesn't love me?" Samantha asked, her eyes not quite meeting theirs. "He's only ever said it a handful of times and, well, let's just say we were always naked when he did."

Brooke reached out and squeezed her hand. "I think the man's crazy about you. But if by some weird chance he's not, wouldn't it be better to know for sure?"

Even imagining a life that didn't include Jonathan made Samantha's heart ache. "Am I allowed to say no?"

"No." Claire topped off their glasses. "You're not. He wants to know how you feel and you need to tell him." She took a sip of her brandy and took a moment to swallow it. "And if I were you, I wouldn't go about it in some wussy half-assed way."

"Completely right," Brooke said. "No mumbling, no trying to trick him into saying it first." She raised her glass and tilted it toward Samantha.

"This is definitely the time for a clear statement of your feelings accompanied by some kind of grand gesture." Claire raised her glass in accord.

Samantha's fingers closed around the stem of her snifter. She raised it, grateful that neither of them commented on the way the burgundy liquid sloshed in the glass. Her hand wasn't the only thing trembling. "I guess I'm drinking to that," she said. "But I'd feel a lot better if someone gave me a clue how to say it. Or had some idea about how grand that grand gesture needs to be."

AFTERWARD IN HER APARTMENT, CLAIRE SAT IN BED her back against her pillows, the journal propped against her knees. Warmed by the brandy and comforted by their repaired friendship, she wrote her impressions of the evening in full detail until with a final yawn, she closed the notebook and set it on the nightstand. Sleep came quickly and so did her dreams—a vivid mishmash of color and movement that floated on the mournful keen of distant bagpipes.

At three a.m. she jerked awake, her heart racing. She lay in the dark for a time while her breathing slowed, turning over pieces of her dreams in her mind. Highland lords and their ladies; Rory Douglas and the other members of his clan. All of them were characters she'd created in *Highland Kiss* and *Highland Hellion*. She recognized the tartans and even gowns she'd once clothed her heroines Brianna and Heather in. But their faces—Claire strained to see them more clearly—had all been pulled not from her novels but from her current life.

Claire studied the soft wash of moonlight on the wood floor and wondered at a subconscious that would take Samantha and Jonathan Davis, Brooke and Zachary Mackenzie, even Hunter Jackson and Edward Parker, dress them in kilts and gunnas and drop them among the craggy peaks of the Scottish Highlands.

"Go back to sleep," she said aloud as she plumped her pillow purposefully and pulled the covers back up to her chin. But she'd barely closed her eyes when new images assailed her. Hunter Jackson sneering nastily. Edward Parker standing in front of the clubroom's big-screen TV introducing that week's episode of *Downton Abbey* not in his clipped British accent but in a soft Scottish burr. Brooke Mackenzie ushering her girls through the lobby. The looming presence of Pregnant Barbie and Plastic Ken.

At four she gave up and turned on the lights, trying to separate distant past from present day, truth from fiction. Something niggled at the back of her mind. Some message she was supposed to receive; a task she was meant to complete.

Her gaze settled on her laptop, skittered away, returned.

An unseen hand propelled her to her "desk" where she lifted the lid of her Mac and waited impatiently for it to awaken. The screen roused. Unsure why, she clicked on Word and opened a new page but did not pause to set margins or tabs or anything else that might require conscious thought or decision.

Her friends' faces swam before her. Her story and theirs. In present day and present tense. Intertwined.

She saw herself selling the house in River Run. Carting her things into the Alexander ready to start her new life even as Hailey began hers. It was a tiny life; one that expanded to include Brooke and Samantha and Edward Parker. Brought together by Sunday nights, held together by mutual need.

Her fingertips settled lightly on the keyboard as she at last understood the months of failure and frustration.

She had spent years writing stories of romantic love set against a historic backdrop in order to escape the unromantic realities of single motherhood. But that life was over; she'd created a new reality. From which she had no desire—or need—to escape.

She wanted to write about real people, with real issues. About imperfect love whether it be mistaken love like hers, unreciprocated love like Brooke's, or even sublimated love like Samantha's. Her fingers began to move across the keyboard, tentatively at first and then with growing certainty.

The words came more quickly. They poured out onto her screen in a torrent. She didn't know where they came from and for the first time in a long time she didn't care.

When the sun rose at seven fifteen she was still typing. When she stopped to use the bathroom and forage for something to eat it was late afternoon, but within thirty minutes she was seated again her fingers already curling over the keys, a smile tugging at her lips, her "well" unexpectedly full to overflowing with an almost but not quite forgotten joy.

BROOKE STOOD IN THE CENTER OF HER CLOSET SUR-rounded by a pile of rejected clothing—most of it beige and unexpectedly large. A smaller pile of things she thought might be altered sat folded neatly on her dresser.

She wasn't sure how many pounds she'd lost or even how, but she'd begun to use the time she used to spend catering to Zachary doing odd jobs for Edward and had learned to subdue the panic over the money she'd lost to Hunter Jackson on long, rambling walks with Darcy that they'd both grown to love.

Right now she was thinking a brief after-dinner walk. She dialed Claire's cell phone to see if she wanted to join them.

"It's me," she said when Claire answered. "I'm headed out with Darcy and the girls—we're going to walk down to the park and back. Want to come?"

"Can't," Claire said quite happily. "I'm working." Her statement was followed by what might have been a chortle of glee.

"Okay," Brooke said, slipping on her shoes and moving to the family room to round up the girls. "Have you heard anything from Samantha?"

"No," Claire said. Brooke could hear the sound of fingers clattering on a keyboard in the background. "But I think tonight's the night."

Brooke smiled and hung up, hoping to hell she hadn't been mistaken about Jonathan Davis's feelings for his wife.

"Come on, girls." She hooked Darcy's leash to her collar and waited for Ava and Natalie to put on their coats. "When we get back we can make some hot chocolate."

"With mush mellows?" Ava asked.

"Absolutely. And when you're done with your homework we can work on our Christmas cards." She'd decided that given the need to economize she and the girls would make their own this year and had convinced Bruce Dalton and his daughter to do the same.

They went down in the elevator in a whirlwind of pulling on mittens and arguing over who got to push which button. Brooke was calling after them not to run in the lobby when they sprinted right into Zachary and Sarah's path.

"Crap." She shortened Darcy's leash and hurried toward

the girls. Zachary greeted her arrival with a disapproving stare. Sarah was beautifully made-up and her hair looked freshly styled but her over-plumped lips turned downward and she looked a bit like a sausage trying to break out of its casing. The area under her eyes looked dark from lack of sleep.

Brooke thought back to both of her pregnancies when she'd worked full-time while Zachary did his residency. Even then he'd been more like a demanding child than a helpful partner. She looked at the pair of them and for the first time felt not even a sliver of envy.

"Good evening," Brooke said. The girls had given and received hugs and now were eager to get outside. They skipped over to the concierge desk to say hello to Isabella. It seemed that since they'd begun to see their father more regularly his allure had diminished.

Darcy sniffed around Sarah's swollen ankles and sneezed before retreating to sit on the floor next to Brooke.

"I hear you invested in Hunter Jackson, thinking you'd invested in Private Butler," Zach said aggrieved. "I saw Brett Adams at the bank and he told me you borrowed against the apartment."

Brooke shrugged and looked beyond him to make sure the girls were still at the concierge desk.

"How could you jeopardize the apartment like that when you don't know anything about making money?" His words and tone proclaimed her a moron. How had she ever allowed him to believe he had that right?

"What happens to the apartment isn't really your concern anymore," she said curtly. "And I knew enough about making money to put you through medical school and into practice." She let the words sink in and had the satisfaction of seeing his face flush with anger. "And I knew enough to raise two pretty great daughters." She turned a look on Sarah. "And not to let you turn me into a mannequin."

It hit her then how fortunate she was to be free of him. Whatever came she'd be equal to it. "I've never been afraid of hard work," she said as much to herself as she did to him. "And at least now I won't have to deal with someone belittling me the whole time."

She didn't wait for either of them to comment. There was nothing they might say that she wanted—or needed—to hear. She nodded and tightened the leash around her hand, unable to remember why she ever felt the need to scurry from potted palm to potted palm to avoid Pouty Barbie and Nasty Ken. "He's probably already bought a supply of earplugs so the baby won't disturb him," she said to Sarah in parting. "And he won't be changing any diapers, either. But I'm sure he'll do that tummy tuck and breast lift for you even before you think to ask for it."

The front door opened as Brooke and the girls approached and was held open by Jonathan Davis. They greeted each other in passing and she noted the bottle of wine he carried and the smell of his expensive cologne. Brooke smiled and crossed her fingers on Samantha's behalf as she ushered her happy brood down the sidewalk past the Alexander's elegant façade.

Chapter Thirty-Four

FROM THE MOMENT THE IDEA OF A "GRAND GESture" was raised, Samantha had debated whether to gird herself in designer clothing or greet Jonathan dressed in nothing but Saran Wrap, but she'd known that whatever she decided to wear—or not wear—her grand gesture would include food. And that food would be prepared by her own hands.

It had taken all of her nerve to call him. She'd hung on the line practicing what she would say, each ring like a death knell afraid he wouldn't pick up; afraid that he would. When he finally answered she'd blurted out her invitation to come for dinner so that they could "talk," then held her breath until she was practically light-headed waiting for his answer. She'd been so afraid he'd tell her that there was nothing to talk about that she'd been weak-kneed with relief when he'd agreed.

Intellectually Samantha knew that the way to a man's heart was not through his stomach, but in her own heart she clung to the hope that the right meal, served in the right way, might somehow save her marriage. And so she'd spent two days planning her menu and another shopping for the ingredients with which to make Ina Garten's boeuf Bourguignon with French string beans and herbed new potatoes, determined to create a meal whose sheer wonderfulness would demonstrate to Jonathan exactly how she felt about him and say the things she wasn't sure she could.

For most of her marriage she'd told herself that cooking was a simple matter of purchasing the right ingredients and then accurately following directions. She had been certain that if only she had the time and inclination to focus completely, even she could produce a perfect meal. She had never put this theory to the test before for fear all hope would be lost. Now, after a full day in the kitchen with Ina's *Barefoot in Paris: Easy French Food You Can Make at Home*—a title she felt was sorely misleading—Samantha knew she had been deluding herself. She did not possess the cooking gene and it was clear she never would.

Dully, Samantha looked at her kitchen's flour- and oil-splattered walls. At the high ceiling that was apparently not high enough to avoid the spray of beef stock. At the wadded-up paper towels and dishtowels and every other kind of towel she'd used to try to mop up her accidents, miscalculations, and spills. At Ina Garten's smiling face on the cover of the now-soiled and food-stained cookbook.

She tried to blow a bang out of her eyes but it was sticky with, well, she didn't actually know what it was sticky with, and didn't move. Her back, her feet, her arms, and her neck hurt from standing, chopping, dicing, stirring, and peeling. Her head throbbed from her efforts to carry out Ina's "simple" instructions. Despite all this, her clumpy Bourguignon, half-mashed new potatoes, and limp green beans bore no resemblance to the cookbook's mouthwatering photographs.

"Oh, God." Samantha slumped onto the bar stool fervently wishing she'd ordered from Giancarlo's and gone with the Saran Wrap. Her eyes strayed to the clock and then to the phone. Two calls: one to Giancarlo, the second to Edward Parker or even Claire or Brooke to arrange for pickup. That was all it would take. Samantha reached for the phone.

No.

Her hand dropped. There would be no pretending tonight. She'd feed her husband what she'd prepared for him. And pray that he didn't choke trying to get it down. Or find himself in need of a potted palm once he did.

WITH ONLY AN HOUR LEFT BEFORE JONATHAN'S arrival, Samantha showered and dressed in record time, but her hands shook so badly when she tried to blow-dry her hair that she pulled it back off her face and twisted it into a simple chignon. She kept her makeup minimal, afraid her spastic fingers might leave her looking more like a clown than the domestic goddess she'd spent three days attempting to be.

When the doorbell rang she drew a deep and, she hoped, calming breath, then walked to the foyer where she wiped sweaty palms down the sides of the black cocktail dress she'd chosen. *It's just Jonathan,* she reminded herself yet again. The man she'd known since childhood and been married to for more than half her life. But she could not shrug off the importance of this meal or this evening. The word "just" didn't belong anywhere near his name.

"Hi." Her smile faltered when she opened the door. She'd almost forgotten how attractive her husband was, how easily he handled himself, how relentlessly he could batter defenses to get to what was hidden inside; a skill that made him an outstanding lawyer but could be difficult to live with. How had she managed to hide her true feelings from him and, until recently, from herself?

"Come in." She didn't understand how a person's voice could break on only two one-syllable words, but hers did. She stepped back to allow him entry and felt his presence fill the empty space. He handed her the bottle of wine he'd brought. As if he'd given up claim to the wine closet in the home that they'd shared.

"Thanks." She took the wine and led him into the kitchen where the Bourguignon still simmered. The Caesar salads were already on the table along with a basket of the grilled bread she'd singed several fingers to produce.

She set the bottle he'd brought on the counter and poured each of them a glass from the bottle she'd opened earlier.

"Smells good," he said. "What are we having?"

"Beef Bourguignon. I've always wanted to try it." No amount of room spray had completely eradicated the burnt meat smell—a result of accidentally allowing the liquid to boil off several times. Nor had her frantic additions of wine and water ever brought the stew back to the right consistency.

He helped himself to a cheese straw, which were a little irregular-looking and slightly black around the edges. Realizing she was watching him far too closely, Samantha held up her glass and tilted it toward his. "Thank you for coming tonight."

"Thank you for inviting me," he said.

They sounded like perfect strangers. Or two unfortunates out on a first—and possibly last—blind date. She drank more of her wine than she'd intended and cautioned herself to slow down. She still had no idea what she'd said the night she'd drunk dialed him and only hoped it wasn't something he'd have reason to hold against her. She had to keep her wits about her.

"How's your mother?" she asked.

"Fine," he said. Then, "Meredith seemed in good spirits at Thanksgiving."

"Yes," she said quickly, relieved that they were talking even if it was stiffly. "I think she really likes her job. And Kyle seemed nice. If she's found fault with him, she hasn't mentioned it to me." In fact she'd barely heard from her sister since the eruption at Bellewood. She had no idea if that was good or bad.

"And Hunter?" Jonathan asked, looking steadily at her.

"A major disaster of course. I . . ." She dropped her gaze to her wineglass, which had somehow become empty. "I told him if he didn't give the money back to any investor who wanted it or work something out with Edward, that he wouldn't be a member of our family anymore. And that we'd warn everyone we knew that he couldn't be trusted."

She hesitated, realizing she'd committed him to a course of action without consulting him, but all he said was, "And?"

"And I don't know. That was almost a week ago and I haven't heard a word from him. Edward and the others insist I'm not responsible but . . ."

"You still feel like you are," he said. "Just like you always have."

She tried but couldn't gauge his tone.

"Some things that you've held on to for so long can be hard to let go of." He looked her directly in the eye as he said this and her heart thudded heavily in her chest. Was this a warning? Was he saying that he'd let go of his feelings, whatever they were, for her?

"Shall we go to the table?" Her voice was Minnie Mouse on helium. Embarrassed, she busied herself scooping up the bottle of wine and carrying it to the table. As she refilled their glasses she braced herself for what lay ahead. If only she'd gone with the Saran wrap, they could have skipped dinner and all this awkwardness.

The salad was good, but then the most complex step had been separating the egg for the dressing, which she'd managed in just three tries.

Her hands shook slightly as she ladled the beef Bourguignon over a slice of the grilled bread as Ina had suggested and placed spoonfuls of misshapen new potatoes and overly limp green beans on their plates. Determined not to apologize *before* he tasted anything, she placed their plates on the table and slid back into her seat across from him.

He looked at his plate, then up at her surprised. "You really made this, didn't you?"

"Yes." Ignoring her own plate, she watched Jonathan slip a forkful of stew and bread into his mouth. She didn't speak as he chewed, even though he did this carefully and for a really long time. She barely blinked as he took a long drink of water, which he swallowed even more carefully before retrieving his fork from his plate. He gave her a small smile, then eyed the mounds of food with the kind of steely determination a mountain climber might reserve for his first sight of Kilimanjaro.

Alarmed, Samantha scooped up a large bite of stew and slid it into her mouth. The meat wasn't bad if you chewed it long enough, but a second bite revealed that a lot of the clumps weren't meat; they were glutinous globs of onion skin hot glued around clumps of uncooked flour.

"Don't!" Samantha grabbed his plate to keep him from soldiering on. "I knew it was a little lumpy. It's just that I couldn't decide if the onion skins were supposed to be left on. Then after I singed my eyebrows trying to burn off the cognac I . . . Oh, hell, I can't even remember what happened after that."

Humiliated, she carried their plates to the sink and deposited them with a clatter. She'd wasted almost three whole days attempting to cook one decent meal; time she could have spent thinking out the best way to say what needed to be said. She could barely bring herself to turn and face him. She walked back to the table on legs that had turned to Jell-O. "I don't know why I thought this would work. It seemed so important to serve you a genuine home-cooked meal." She sat and faced him across the table even as she tried to beat back the fear and panic. "I was going to call Giancarlo, but you wanted to see the real me. And I guess this is it. Lumps and all."

He watched her even more carefully than he'd chewed, but she couldn't read his thoughts or his mood. It had been ridiculous to think she could hide behind a meal no matter who had cooked it. But then hadn't she been hiding behind one thing or another since her parents had died? And not only from Jonathan but from herself.

"No matter how much you dislike hearing it, I can't pretend I'm not grateful to you," she said. "Gratitude and the desire to please you *have* been my primary motivators."

His lips tightened and his eyes cooled. Samantha resisted the urge to bolt.

"How else was I supposed to feel?" she whispered. "I was way too overwhelmed when we got married to feel much of anything but relief. I never would have managed my parents' deaths, or their ridiculous load of debt, or my father's criminal acts—not to mention Meredith and Hunter—if it weren't for you."

His mouth opened as if to speak. She shook her head, needing to finish.

"But I couldn't think of any reason you would have for marrying me except for pity. And I guess I was afraid to look too closely." She swallowed again, but the fear and regret refused to be dislodged. "I figured it was kind of like a business deal. You gave us a home and financial security and, well, basically I was yours to do whatever you wanted with. Your mother wasn't the only one who knew I got the best end of the bargain."

He continued to watch her, his eyes deep pools of unfathomable blue.

Despite his lack of response she forced herself to continue. She knew if she stopped now, she'd never say what needed to be said.

"I love you." She said the words quickly, awkwardly, before she could chicken out. "I never meant to," she said, her tone turning wry. "I mean it's kind of stupid to love someone who doesn't love you back, isn't it? Especially someone who's married you out of kindness and rarely utters a word of complaint." She paused, steeling herself. "But I couldn't help it. And then when I realized what I'd done I was afraid to admit it. I just couldn't tell you I loved you and then have you not say it back. I'm kind of a coward that way."

"But, Samantha, I did tell you. I told you more than once." His tone was calm and rational, the antithesis of hers.

"Oh, Jonathan." She looked away embarrassed. "Only when we were in bed. It only counts when you're clothed and sober. And you're thinking with your brain and not your . . ." Her voice trailed off, once again hostage to her embarrassment.

"Samantha," he said more firmly. "You can't be serious. That's . . ."

"No." She leaned across the table and pressed a finger to his lips to shush him. "Just let me finish." She brought her eyes back to his. "So, I convinced myself that we were fine the way we were. Why fix it if it's not broke, right?" She attempted a laugh that fell short and dropped her hands into her lap. "And now all the sudden you're interested in my feelings. After I've spent so much time and energy trying not to have any."

She knotted her hands and blew out a breath of air while she waited for him to speak.

But he said nothing. Good God. She couldn't read his expression. Was that shock? Dismay? Her worst fears rose up to taunt her. She'd finally confessed her love for him and now he sat silent, searching for the words to not hurt her feelings any further when he told her that he didn't love her back.

"Are you completely horrified?" she finally asked. "Because if you are, I can . . ."

"What?" he asked sharply. "Do you think you can take it back?" His eyes plumbed hers, so serious that she went completely still. As if a total lack of movement would better brace her for impact. "I just wasn't sure I was allowed to speak yet."

His lips twitched and she allowed herself to breathe.

"I would have been more surprised if you hadn't already told me that night on the phone."

Her gaze narrowed. "What are you talking about? Which night was that?"

"You know, the night you called me when you were drunk and"—he cleared his throat—"and apparently naked."

She blinked in confusion.

"You told me that you loved me more than Doris's cheese grits. And then you told me you wished I were there so that you could . . ." He paused, then said quite matter of factly, "Well, I think you offered to 'screw my brains out.' "

"Oh." She slumped in her chair, barely resisting the urge to cover her face with her hands.

"If I hadn't had an early meeting, I would have been on the next flight out of Boston. Just to see if that were anatomically possible." He flashed her a wicked smile and she couldn't stop the blush that heated her cheeks.

In the midst of her embarrassment-tinged relief, irritation raised its hand. "So why force me to tell you something I'd already told you?" Samantha thought of the lost weeks and the awful meal her fear had pushed her to produce.

"Well, you were pretty quick to dismiss my confessions when I was either drunk or naked. I thought it might be smarter and more binding if you said it while you were dressed and of sound mind." He smiled almost apologetically. "But I guess that's the lawyer in me."

Samantha tried to process this, but she could barely think let alone sort through the emotions surging through her.

"Before we go any further," he said. "I think I should make one thing clear. I would have never married you if I didn't want to."

"But . . ."

"No." It was his turn to shush her with a finger to the lips. "I could have loaned you the money to pay off your father's debts—half of them were owed to the firm anyway.

It wouldn't have been difficult to work out. I could have even helped with Meredith and Hunter as a friend. Or a sort of big brother." He looked at her and his eyes were clear and forthright. Something deep and promising shone out of them. "Except my feelings for you were never remotely brotherly."

"But I was the one with the crush on you," she said softly. "You barely looked at me."

"I'm not sure your perception was any better then than it has been for the last twenty-five years," Jonathan said. "But I wasn't any braver than you were. I knew why you married me, and given all the gratitude and determination to please me—I was afraid that might be all you felt for me. Especially after the way you reacted at Bellewood when I told you our assets weren't liquid."

"But it wasn't that. It was . . . Oh, God," she breathed as he leaned forward to kiss her. "You love me. You really love me." It occurred to her that she sounded like Sally Field giving her overly emotional Oscar speech for *Places in the Heart*, but she didn't care. She could hardly grasp the wonder of it.

"Always have," he said as his lips settled on hers. "Even when I was afraid I'd never be more to you than financial security, I couldn't stop. Looks like I always will."

He stood and leaned down to scoop her up into his arms. Holding her easily against his chest, he kissed her again, then started toward the bedroom. Samantha looped her arms around her husband's neck and held on.

"You could have told me this before I spent three days cooking that lumpy beef Bourguignon," she said.

"Samantha, I don't care if you ever cook another thing," he said. "I'll hire Doris away from Bellewood if you like. Or we can put Giancarlo on retainer." He traced her lips with his, then kissed her so deeply she thought she might pass out. "Right now I'm planning to take you to bed and let you have your way with me," he murmured. "I'm kind of curious to see if my brains survive." His laughter was soft and husky, his breath warm against her ear.

"Your wish is my command," she teased as his lips found the sensitive spot behind her ear then brushed down to her collarbone. He laid her on their bed and began to undress her.

"What's so funny?" he asked when her lips twisted up in a smile.

"Nothing," she said on a gasp when he'd shed his clothes and joined her. "I was just thinking that the next time we have something to straighten out between us, I'm definitely going to listen to my instincts and cut right to the Saran Wrap."

EPILOGUE

S NOW IN ATLANTA WAS ALWAYS RECEIVED WITH
an odd blend of excitement and panic. With little snow-
clearing equipment and even less experience, the city and its
ring of surrounding suburbs shut down. Its sprawling car-
clogged highways emptied as quickly and completely as the
grocery store shelves on the day that snow was forecast.

It was just ten days before Christmas and the white pow-
der that covered Peachtree Street looked uncomfortable
beneath the streetlights as if it knew it didn't really belong
there. Hunter Jackson looked equally uncomfortable though
he was doing his best to hide it. Edward turned from the
clubroom window to contemplate the younger man. "You've
surprised me again," he said, clapping a hand on the younger
man's shoulder. "But in a favorable way."

"Is that right?" Jackson maintained a gruff demeanor, but
he didn't shrug off the hand or the compliment. Edward
thought he detected a relief similar to his own.

"You could have saved everybody a lot of trouble if you'd
agreed to let me raise money for your company in the first

place," Jackson said. "It's kind of weird that somebody as old as your uncle and half a world away would be the one to figure out how to settle things."

"No doubt," Edward said, though he was certain Jonathan Davis's suggestions hadn't hurt. "But I think this feels right, don't you?"

"It's okay." Jackson's admission was grudging. "I didn't really want to have to be involved in a start-up anyway." This had been the younger man's rationale for starting the conversation with Edward that had led to their agreement; those who had given money to Jackson would, in fact, receive shares in Private Butler while Jackson turned over the two hundred fifty thousand dollars he had left and worked for the firm until Edward had been paid the rest. After that, well, then they'd see.

EDWARD PATTED HIS JACKET POCKET IN WHICH HE'D placed envelopes containing the newly minted Private Butler shares for Isabella, James, Brooke, Claire, and Mimi Davenport. Investors had already been notified of the arrangement, but these certificates would make it official; a little extra marzipan on tonight's Christmas cake.

With a final smile and nod Jackson turned to leave. Edward watched his progress, then heard a small gasp when Hunter and his sister came face-to-face in the doorway. Jackson pulled back stiffly, but Samantha managed to hug him anyway. "I heard what you did," she said. "And I'm proud of you."

Hunter glanced around as he stepped back but Samantha seemed unconcerned with their audience. "We're having Christmas at our place this year," she said. "Now that things are settled, I hope you'll come."

The young man left as Samantha, Brooke, Claire, and Claire's daughter, Hailey, swept into the clubroom. Isabella and James, who had just finished setting up the drinks and food tables, greeted them. A small Christmas tree twinkled in the corner.

"Please tell me those are not shandies," Claire said as Edward joined them.

"They're not shandies," Edward said, though of course they were. "We had quite a few requests I'm afraid. But we'll be having mulled wine and Christmas cake and pudding for 'afters.'" He smiled. "In the meantime I'm certain your wing-men and your daughter will protect you from temptation."

"Mother!" Hailey laughed. "I should have known you'd be in trouble as soon as I turned my back," she teased.

"Ha! It's all grist for the creative mill," Claire said, match-ing her daughter's tone. "Now that I have the go-ahead to write the contemporary novel I have in mind, even drinking with friends qualifies as research."

"No more seventeenth-century Scotland?" Edward asked.

"Only if one of my characters goes there on vacation," Claire replied. "Or I figure out a way to incorporate some of LeaAnn Larsen's time-traveling Navy SEALs." She grinned. "I just turned in my first three chapters and a full synopsis. I'll be published by a different imprint at Scarsdale, but my editor seems to love what I've sent so far."

"Congratulations," he said as the room began to fill. He handed the envelopes to Claire and Brooke. "I'll do my best to see that your shares in Private Butler increase in value."

"Me, too," Brooke said. "Now that I've been named head of the Family Division." She, too, laughed. It was hard not to with so many positive developments. "Who knew being a full-time mother would make me so valuable in the work-place?"

"Congratulations," Claire said. "I might have to drink a shandy or two to celebrate your new position along with having Hailey home, and a book that seems to be practically writing itself."

The noise level grew as the growing crowd helped themselves to food and drink. "You haven't said much," Claire said to Samantha.

"It's probably hard to talk when you're smiling like that," Brooke said. "My God, it's practically obscene."

Samantha blushed but kept on smiling. "I refuse to apologize for being happy," she said. "And I saw a few smiles on *your* face, Miz Mackenzie, after that date with Bruce Dalton. Does your boss know you've already started going out with the customers?"

Brooke laughed. "It was one date. And I don't think either of us is in a hurry. Honestly, I'm just enjoying doing things any way that I choose and in my own time. And watching Pregnant Barbie blow up like a balloon."

Edward clapped his hands for attention and they all headed for their seats.

"Boy, you all have the best seat in the house," Hailey said as she dropped down into the sofa between her mother and Samantha. Claire slipped an arm across her daughter's shoulders as Edward moved in front of the television. Samantha reached out to the others so that all of them were linked. "The first one who starts singing 'Kumbaya' is out of here," one of them stage-whispered. There were giggles from the sofa.

"Well, ladies," Edward said, taking in all of their smiling faces. "It's been a grand adventure getting to know you all better and sharing my addiction to *Downton Abbey* with you. I hope you'll come back in January for season three. I hear Shirley MacLaine is a hoot as Lady Cora's mother and, honestly, *Downton Abbey* wouldn't be the same without you."

There were murmurs of agreement and he felt the smile stretch across his lips. "Ladies," he said. "I'm pleased to present Christmas at Downton Abbey, which will be followed by mulled wine and a choice of Christmas pudding and Christmas cake shipped over here by my dear old mum."

There was applause. At Edward's signal, James lowered the lights. Edward pressed play. They leaned forward as one, eager to suspend disbelief, more than ready to lose themselves in the English countryside, within the walls of a grand estate, in the midst of a family that had come to feel almost as familiar as their own.

As they watched the show unfold, Edward watched them and knew as he hadn't before, that even an ordinary life could rival the comedy and tragedy of a really great period drama. That fairy tales could come true if only they were allowed to. And that friendship was the most potent magic of all, able to form without warning or explanation and in the most unexpected of ways and places. Just as it had while they were watching *Downton Abbey*.

WHILE WE WERE WATCHING
DOWNTON ABBEY

WENDY WAX

DISCUSSION QUESTIONS

1. How does watching *Downton Abbey* draw these characters together? Do you think this is part of the value of a hit television show? How has watching *Downton Abbey* or any other favorite show added to your life? Could you imagine yourself making a new friend through a shared interest in *Downton Abbey*?

2. *Downton Abbey* chronicles the lives of the very wealthy and the people who serve them. How is this paralleled in the interactions we view between the characters in the book? How do these relationships evolve?

3. Samantha, Claire, and Brooke come from very diverse backgrounds and are each at a different stage in life. How do these differences help them bond and foster their friendship? How would their ultimate outcomes be altered if they had never become friends?

4. The relationship between mothers and daughters is a prevalent theme in this book. Readers witness Samantha's interactions with her mother-in-law, Cynthia Davis, as well as Samantha's motherly bond with Meredith; Claire's connection with Hailey; and Brooke's relationship with Ava and Natalie. Discuss the effects of each of these mother-daughter relationships on Samantha, Claire, and Brooke.

5. In a way, *Downton Abbey* is also a main character in this book. How would you define its role in the lives of those living in the Alexander? How is the show a catalyst for change?

6. Edward Parker's great-uncle Mason says discretion, persistence, and valor "always win the day" (page 100). Do you think this belief is upheld in the book? Give examples from the story to support your answer.

7. Food is often described in the book. What role do you think it plays in different settings, such as during the *Downton Abbey* gatherings, the family dinners with Samantha and Jonathan, and the meetings between Samantha and her mother-in-law? Can you think of other scenes where food is highlighted?

8. If you were to write a sequel to this book, how would it go? What do you think the future holds for these characters?

Turn the page for a special excerpt from
Wendy Wax's novel

TEN BEACH ROAD

Available now from Jove Books

CHAPTER ONE

THOUGH SHE WAS CAREFUL NOT TO SHOW IT, Madeline Singer did not fall apart when her youngest child left for college. In the Atlanta suburb where she lived, women wilted all around her. Tears fell. Antidepressants were prescribed.

Her friends, lost and adrift, no longer recognized themselves without children to care for. A collective amnesia descended, wiping out all the memories of teenaged angst and acts of hostility that had preceded their children's departures, much as the remembered pain of childbirth had been washed away once the newborn was placed in their arms.

Madeline kept waiting for the emptiness of her nest to smite her. She loved her children and had loved being a stay-at-home mother, but while she waited for the crushing blow, she took care of all the things that she'd never found time for while Kyra and Andrew were still at home. Throughout that fall while her friends went for therapy, shared long liquid lunches, and did furtive drive-bys and drop-ins to the high school where they'd logged so many volunteer hours,

Madeline happily responded to her children's phone calls and texts, but she also put twenty years' worth of pictures into photo albums. Then she cleaned out the basement storage unit and each successive floor of their house, purging and sorting until the clutter that had always threatened to consume them was finally and completely vanquished.

After that she threw herself into the holidays and the mad rush of shopping and cooking and entertaining, trying her best not to let the free-falling economy dampen the family festivities. Andrew came home from Vanderbilt and Kyra, fresh out of Berkeley's film school and two months into her first feature film shoot, arrived in the first flush of adulthood and once again became the center of the known universe.

Pushing aside daydreams of the projects she'd undertake once they were gone again, Madeline fed her children and their friends, made herself available when their friends weren't, and didn't even react to the fact that she was barely an appendage to their lives. Steve, who loved the trappings of a family Christmas with the ferocity of an only child, seemed worried and distracted, but when she raised the subject he found a way to change or avoid it.

While basting the turkey on Christmas Day, Madeline realized that she was more than ready for her husband to go back to the office and for her children to go back to their new lives so that she could finally begin her own.

On this first day of March, the house was once again blissfully quiet. There was no television. No music. No video game gunfire or crack of a bat. No texts coming in or going out with a ding. No refrigerator opening or closing. No one—not one person—asking what was for dinner, when their laundry would be done, or whether she had a spare twenty.

Standing in the center of Kyra's vacant bedroom, Madeline inhaled the quiet, held it in her lungs, and let it soak into her skin. Her nest was not only empty, it was totally and completely organized. It was time for her "new" life to begin.

Not for the first time, she admitted something might be

wrong with her. Because the silence that so alarmed her friends sent a tingle of anticipation up her spine. It made her want to dance with joy. Go hang gliding. Cure cancer. Learn how to knit. Write the Great American Novel. Or do absolutely nothing for a really long time.

Her life could be whatever she decided to make of it.

Throwing open the windows to allow the scents of an early spring to fill the room, Madeline mentally converted the space into the study/craft room she'd always dreamed of. She'd put a wall of shelves for her books and knickknacks here. A combination desk and worktable there. Maybe a club chair and ottoman for reading in the corner near the window.

Madeline entertained herself for a time measuring the windows for a cornice that she might just make herself. This afternoon she could go to the fabric store and see what looked interesting. Maybe she'd hit some of her favorite antique stores and see about a worktable and a club chair that she could re-cover.

For lunch she made a quick sandwich and then sat down at the kitchen table to read through the *Atlanta Journal-Constitution*, Steve's *Wall Street Journal*, and the local weekly.

She was in the middle of a story about yet another financial advisor who'd absconded with his unsuspecting clients' money when the phone rang—an especially shrill sound in the cocoon of silence in which she was wrapped.

"Mrs. Singer?" The voice was female, clipped, but not unfriendly. "This is St. Joseph's calling."

Madeline's grip on the phone tightened; she braced for a full-body blow. "A Mrs. Clyde Singer was brought in about thirty minutes ago. She was suffering from smoke inhalation and a gash on her forehead. We found this number listed as emergency contact on the file from her last visit."

"Smoke inhalation?" Madeline hovered near her chair, trying to get her thoughts in order. "Is she all right?"

"She's resting now, but she's been through quite a lot, poor thing. There was a kitchen fire."

"Oh, my God." Madeline turned and raced upstairs, carrying the phone with her. Last month her mother-in-law had fallen in the bathroom and been lucky not to break anything. At eighty-seven, living alone had become increasingly difficult and dangerous, but Edna Singer had refused to consider giving up her home and Steve had been unwilling to push his mother on it. Madeline got the room number and a last assurance that the patient looked a bit beat-up but would be fine. "It'll probably take me about twenty-five minutes to get there."

Exchanging her shorts for a pair of slacks and slipping her feet into loafers, she called Steve's cell phone as she clattered down the front stairs. After leaving a voice mail with the pertinent details, Madeline headed for the garage, stopping only long enough to look up Steve's office number, which she so rarely called she hadn't even programmed it into her cell phone. Adrienne Byrne, who'd sat in front of Steve's corner office at the investment firm for the last fifteen years, answered. "Adrienne?" Madeline said as the garage door rumbled open. "It's Madeline. Can you put me through to Steve?"

There was a silence on the other end as Madeline yanked open the car door.

"Hello?" Madeline said. "I hate to be short, but it's an emergency. Edna is at St. Joseph's again and I need Steve to meet me there."

Madeline slid behind the steering wheel, wedged the phone between her ear and shoulder, and put the minivan in reverse.

"Did you try his cell phone?" Adrienne's tone was uncharacteristically tentative.

"Yes." Maddie began to back down the driveway, her mind swirling with details. How badly damaged was Edna's kitchen? Should she have Steve go to the hospital while she checked the house? "It went right to voice mail. Isn't he in the office? Do you know how to reach him?"

There was another odd pause and then Adrienne said, "Steve doesn't work here anymore."

Madeline's foot found the brake of its own accord. The car jerked to a stop. "I'm sorry? Where did you say he was?"

"I don't know where he is, Madeline," the secretary said slowly. "Steve doesn't work here anymore."

Madeline sat in the cul-de-sac, trying to absorb the words she'd just heard.

"I haven't seen Steve since he was laid off. That was at the beginning of September. About six months ago."

MADELINE DROVE TO THE HOSPITAL AND THEN HAD no idea how she got there. Nothing registered, not the street signs or the lights or the bazillion other cars that must have flown by on Highway 400 or the artery off it that led to the hospital parking lot. The entire way she grappled with what Adrienne had told her and Steve had not. Laid off six months ago? Not working? Unemployed?

At the information desk, she signed in and made her way down the hall to Edna's room. There were people there and noise. A gurney rolled by. A maintenance worker mopped up a distant corner of the hallway. She sensed movement and activity, but the images and sounds were fleeting. Nothing could compete with the dialogue going on in her head. If Steve didn't have a job, where did he go every day after he put on his suit and strolled out the door with his briefcase? More important, why hadn't he told her?

In the doorway to her mother-in-law's room, Madeline paused to gather herself. Edna looked like she'd been in a fight. A bandage covered more than half of her forehead. Her lip was split and her cheekbone was bruised. The eye above it looked puffy.

"Gee," Madeline said, "I'd like to see the other guy."

"The other guy is the kitchen table and the tile floor." Edna jutted out her chin. "Where's Steve?"

Good question. "I don't know. But I left him a message that you were here."

Edna's chin quivered. They both knew Madeline was a poor substitute for Edna's only child. "What happened?" Madeline asked. "How did the fire start?"

Edna dropped her gaze. Her fingers, which had become as knobby and spare as the rest of her, clutched the sheet tighter.

"I don't know. I was cooking . . . something. And then I . . . something must have gone wrong with the stove. Where's Steve?"

"I'm here, Mama." Steve swept into the room and moved swiftly to the bed, where he took one of his mother's hands in his. "Lord, you gave me a scare. Are you all right?"

"Yes, of course," Edna said, her trembling lips turning up into a brave smile. Edna Singer tolerated her daughter-in-law, and seemed to enjoy her grandchildren, but she worshipped the son who, at the age of twelve, had become all she had left when his father died.

Madeline watched her husband soothe his mother and tell her that everything would be all right, but it was like watching a stranger. They'd known each other for thirty years and been married for twenty-five of them. They had two children, a home, a life. And he had failed to mention that he wasn't working?

She looked up and realized that they were waiting for her to say something.

"I just told Mama that when I leave here I'll check her house and make sure it's secure. And that tomorrow when she's released, she needs to come stay with us so we can keep an eye out for her and fuss over her for a while."

Madeline nodded. Really, she couldn't think of any words besides, "Where have you been going every day? How could you not tell me you lost your job?" and the all-encompassing, "What in the world is going on?"

Madeline stepped closer, appalled at how natural Steve

sounded. She wanted to reach up and grab him by the shoulders and give him a good shake. "Will you be able to get away from the office?" she asked. "If it's a problem, I could pick your mama up."

"Nope," he said, all casual, as if he weren't lying once again. "There's nothing pressing on the calendar."

Madeline grasped the bed rail to steady herself as Steve fussed over his mother. She felt brittle, like Edna's bones; one wrong move and she might snap. As she studied her husband, she tried to understand how the person she thought she knew best could be so unfathomable. He had lied to her. Every day when he got up with his alarm, showered and dressed, went through the same old morning routine, and left the house as if he were going to the job he didn't have had been one more lie.

The question, of course, was, why? Why not just tell her, why not share the loss of this job like she'd assumed they'd shared everything else for the last quarter of a century?

Her hand shook. Dropping it to her side, she told herself not to panic and definitely not to assume the worst, though she couldn't actually think of a good or positive explanation for Steve having kept this little bombshell to himself.

Once again she noticed a silence and felt Steve's gaze on her. She looked into the wide-set gray eyes that she'd always considered so warm and open, the full lips that were bent upward and stretched so easily into a smile. For the first time she noticed a web of fine lines radiating out from those eyes and grooves, like parentheses, bracketing the lips. A deep furrow ran the width of his forehead. When had all these signs of worry appeared, and how had she missed them?

"So, I'll stay with Mama for a while," Steve said, dismissing her. "Then I'll run by her house to make sure it's locked up and maybe pick up some things she'll want at our house."

Madeline wanted to drag him out into the hall and demand the truth, but the image of hissing out her hurt and anger in the hospital hallway held the words in check.

"Okay." Madeline stepped forward to drop a dutiful kiss on her mother-in-law's paper-thin cheek, keeping the bed between herself and Steve, certain that if he touched her she would, in fact, snap. "You get some rest now and feel better."

On the way out of the hospital she focused on her breathing. "Just stay calm," she instructed herself. "When he gets home you'll tell him that you know he lost his job and ask for an explanation. He must have a good reason for not telling you. And surely he has some kind of plan. Just ask for the truth. That's all. Everything will be okay as long as you know what's going on and you're in it together."

This sounded eminently reasonable. For the time being she needed to push the hurt and sense of betrayal aside. They were not paupers—Steve was an investment advisor and had built a large cushion over the years for just such an eventuality. They could survive this. And Steve was highly qualified and well respected. Maybe he'd just needed some time off and now he could start looking for a new position. Trafalgar Partners wasn't the only investment firm in Atlanta.

She'd agreed to "for better or for worse." She was no hothouse flower who couldn't deal with reality. Once again, her hurt and anger rose up in her throat, nearly choking her, and once again she shoved it back.

As she drove the minivan through the crush of afternoon traffic, Madeline contemplated the best way to handle the situation; she even thought about what wine might complement this sort of conversation and what she might serve for dinner. She'd just tell him that she loved him and that she would stand by him no matter what. As long as he respected her enough to tell her the complete and unvarnished truth.

It was only later that she would remember that the truth did not always set you free. And that you had to be careful what you wished for, because you might actually get it.

CHAPTER TWO

STEVE DIDN'T GET HOME UNTIL SIX P.M. MADELINE was in the kitchen adding strips of grilled chicken to a large Caesar salad and had already opened and sampled a bottle of red Zinfandel when she heard the automatic garage door open.

She'd decided not to blurt out what she knew, had vowed to act normal and work her way calmly up to the subject.

But now that Steve was here, Madeline could actually feel drops of sweat popping out on her forehead and an unwelcome burst of heat flushing her skin. For once this was not a result of her whacked-out hormones. How in the world had Steve managed to do this for a half a year?

"How did Edna's house look?" she asked carefully.

Steve sighed and took a long swallow of his wine. "The kitchen's a nightmare. Between the fire and the water from the fire hoses, the inside is practically gutted." He looked up at her. "It's a miracle she came out as unscathed as she did. You don't mind if she moves in with us?"

"No, of course not." For once, Edna's antipathy felt insignificant.

"She can stay as long as she needs to or until we can get her kitchen put back together." After all these years, Madeline could wait another month or so to start her "new life." Steve had worked construction summers through high school and college and would know what had to be done at his mother's. Madeline could help supervise the renovation of the kitchen herself if necessary, and maybe Steve would have a new job by the time Edna moved back into her own home.

"I don't mean temporarily," Steve said, though he kind of mumbled it into his wineglass. "She can't live on her own anymore. I've been putting off the inevitable, but now that you don't have the kids to deal with I thought . . ."

"You want your mother to move in with us . . . forever?"

The cheese grater slipped out of her hand and clattered on the granite countertop. The square of Parmesan landed at her feet, but she made no move to pick it up.

"She's eighty-seven, Madeline. Unfortunately, I don't think forever is going to be all that long."

But it would feel like it. "Your mother doesn't like me, Steve. She never has."

"That's not true."

"We've been married for twenty-five years, I see her at least twice a week, we eat dinner with her most Sundays, and she still calls me Melinda half the time." This was no slip of the tongue or mental gaffe. Melinda had been Steve's high school girlfriend.

"She just likes to yank your chain a little bit. She doesn't mean anything by it."

"Do you know what she gave me for Christmas this year?"

Steve pinched a crouton from the salad. "It was a book, wasn't it?"

"It was called *Extreme Makeover, Personal Edition: How to Reface Your 'Cabinets' and Shore Up Your Sagging Structure.*"

"It was not."

"Yes," Madeline said. "It was."

Steve frowned as always, unable to accept that the mother who loved him so fiercely had so little affection for his wife.

But how could she worry about this now when Steve's lies and lack of job loomed over them? She bent to retrieve the Parmesan, which had been left there far too long to invoke the three-second rule. She carried it to the trash while she struggled to tamp down her emotions so that she could broach the subject of his unemployment with some semblance of calm.

Steve was refilling their glasses when she returned to the counter with her shoulders squared. It was clear he wasn't planning to let her in on his not-so-little secret. She wondered if he'd told his mother.

"I spoke to Adrienne today," Madeline said.

He went still much like an animal scenting danger might.

"I called your office trying to reach you after I heard from the hospital. She told me you don't work there anymore. That you haven't worked there for six months." She swallowed and tears pricked her eyelids even though she'd promised herself she wouldn't cry. "Is that true?" she asked. "Could that possibly be true?"

The air went out of him. Not slowly like a punctured tire, but fast like a balloon spurting out its helium. His shoulders stooped as he shrank in front of her, practically folding in on himself. Any hope that he might deny it or laugh at Adrienne's poor attempt at humor disappeared.

"Yes."

She waited for the explanation, but he just sat on the bar stool with all the air knocked out of him, staring helplessly at her.

"But what happened? Why were you let go? Why didn't you tell me?" The pain and hurt thickened her voice and it was hard to see through the blur of tears. Steve actually looked like he might cry himself, which did nothing to reduce the soft swell of panic. Why was he just looking at her like that; why didn't he just tell her? "I need to know,

Steve. I don't understand how you could keep a secret like this from me. It's my life, too."

He took a deep breath, let it out. "The institutional accounts I was handling were actually being funneled to Synergy Investments. Malcolm Dyer's firm."

It was Madeline's turn to go still. She was not a financial person, but even she had heard of the now-notorious Malcolm Dyer, whom the press had labeled a "mini-Madoff."

"I should have known there was something off," Steve said. "But the fund was performing so well. The returns were so . . . high, and they stayed that way for over five years." He swallowed. "It's hard to walk away from that kind of profit. I missed all the signs." His voice was etched with a grim disbelief. "It was a classic Ponzi scheme. And I had no idea."

He swallowed again. She watched his Adam's apple move up and down.

"They closed down our whole division in September, but by cooperating with the government investigators, Trafalgar managed to keep it out of the papers while they regrouped. There was some hope that if the feds could get their hands on the stolen funds that they might be able to return at least a portion to our clients. A lot of them are nonprofits and charities."

A part of her wanted to reach out and offer comfort, but the anger coursing through her wouldn't allow it. For twenty-five years they'd told each other everything—or so she'd thought. "I can't believe you think so little of me that you'd dress and go through that kind of pretense every day rather than tell me the truth." She drained her wineglass, hoping to slow the thoughts tumbling through her head, maybe sop up the sense of betrayal. "How could you do that?"

Steve shook his head. "I don't know, Mad. I just felt so guilty and so stupid. And I didn't want to worry you or the kids. I figured I'd find something else and once I did—when there was no cause for panic—I'd tell you."

Steve looked her in the eye then. His were filled with

defeat. "Only I couldn't find another job. Half the investment firms in the country have folded and the rest have cut back. Nobody's hiring. Especially not at my salary level. Or my age." His tone turned grim. "I've spent every single day of the last six months looking for a job. I've followed up every lead, worked every contact I have. But, of course, my reputation's shot to hell. And I don't seem to be employable."

They contemplated each other for what seemed like an eternity. Madeline felt as if their life had been turned at an angle that rendered it completely unrecognizable.

"And that's not the worst of it." Steve dropped his gaze.

He ran a hand through his hair and scrubbed at his face. As body language went it was the equivalent of the pilot of your plane running through the aisle shouting, "Tighten your seat belts. We're going down!"

For the briefest of moments, Madeline wanted to beg him not to tell her. She wanted to stand up, run out of the room and out the front door, where whatever he was about to say couldn't reach her.

"I, um . . ." He paused, then slowly met her gaze. "Our money's gone, too." He said it so quietly that at first she thought she might have misheard.

"What?"

"I said, our money's gone."

"Which money are you talking about?" she asked just as quietly. As if softening the volume might somehow soften the blow.

"All of it."

There was a silence so thick that Madeline imagined any words she was able to form would come out swaddled in cotton.

Gary Coleman's trademark response, "What you talkin' 'bout, Willis?" streaked through her mind, comic intonation and all, and she wished she could utter it. So that Steve might throw back his head and laugh. Which would be far superior to the way he was hanging his head and staring at his hands.

"How is that possible?" Her voice was a whisper now, coated in disbelief.

He met her gaze. "We were getting such a great return from the fund, that I put our money in." He paused. "Every penny we didn't need to live on went to Synergy."

"But I thought most of our money was in bank CDs," Madeline said. "Aren't they practically risk free?"

"Yes, real bank CDs are secured by the bank. Nonexistent CDs backed by a nonexistent offshore bank? Not so much."

Madeline felt as if she'd ended up in a train wreck despite the fact that she'd never set foot on a train or even gone to the station. The twisted metal of their future lay strewn across the tracks.

"I invested my mother's money in the same fund."

"Is there anything left?" Madeline thought her heart might actually stop beating. She could hear herself gasping for breath, but no air seemed to be entering her lungs.

"Just this." He pulled a crumpled piece of paper from his pocket, smoothed it out, and laid it on the cocktail table in front of her. "The feds are looking for Dyer. In the meantime, he's been judged guilty in a civil suit; apparently if you don't show up, you're found guilty. I filed a claim against Dyer's seized assets." He shoved the paper toward her. "This came yesterday. In addition to our house and what's left of my mother's house we now have a third ownership in a beach-front 'mansion' in Florida. In some booming metropolis called Pass-a-Grille."

MADELINE DIDN'T KNOW WHERE STEVE SLEPT OR even if he did, and she was too numb to get up and find out. She spent most of the night tossing and turning on her side of their bed, realigning her pillow every few minutes as if simply finding the optimal position would grant her admission to oblivion.

Several times she heard Steve moving around downstairs. At one point the family room TV snapped on.

Sometime after three a.m. she finally managed to drift off but slept fitfully, bombarded by disturbing dreams. One involved her mother-in-law in a pointy black hat pedaling a bicycle across a tornado-tossed sky. The *Wizard of Oz* theme played out all night. Steve appeared as the Scarecrow, and then as both the Cowardly Lion and a heavily rusted Tin Man. The worst scene featured Malcolm Dyer as the unscrupulous Wizard caught behind his curtain with Glinda the apparently not-so-good witch giggling in his lap.

Not surprisingly, Madeline awoke groggy and out of sorts. Steve's revelations stole back into her consciousness to command center stage, and she buried her face in her pillow and cried. When the bedroom door opened and Steve padded into the room, Madeline squeezed her eyes shut and feigned sleep.

While he showered and dressed in the bathroom she lay staring up into the ceiling. Although she felt him hesitate beside the bed, she kept her eyes shut and her breathing regular. She didn't get up until she was certain Steve was gone.

By the time he returned with his mother, Madeline had put away the sheet and pillow Steve had left on the couch, tidied up the guest room and bath, and put on a pot of soup.

Determined to make things look as normal as possible in front of her mother-in-law, she kept a smile on her face and her conversation casual. But pretending her world had not been shaken to its core required an Oscar-worthy performance.

"You seem a bit quiet, Melinda," Edna said as Madeline tucked her into the guest room bed and aimed the remote at the television. Madeline willed herself to ignore the insult; it hardly rated in comparison to Steve's revelations. "I'm sorry to be imposing on you. I wouldn't have come if Steven hadn't insisted."

"We're happy to have you," Madeline said, straightening as the hosts of HGTV's *Hammer and Nail* appeared on-screen and wishing this were true. She handed the remote to her mother-in-law, who was already focusing on the remodeling show. "But it would make me even happier if you stopped calling me Melinda."

Edna's gaze left the TV. Shock that Madeline had commented on the dig flared briefly in Edna's eyes.

"I hate to think your mind has really slipped so much that you can't remember your daughter-in-law's name," Madeline said. "Maybe we should do some cognitive testing. We never did go for that follow-up with the neurologist."

Edna snorted. "They're all just looking for any excuse to take away a person's rights. First it's the car. Then they don't think you can live by yourself." She strove for her usual belligerence but Madeline heard the note of fear underneath and chastised herself for putting it there. Her own fear was like a living, breathing thing. "There's nothing golden about the golden years from what I can tell so far."

"No," Madeline agreed, reminding herself that her mother-in-law's jabs were a very minor thing. "Getting older is definitely not for sissies." But then neither, it seemed, was marriage.